# Dead Letters

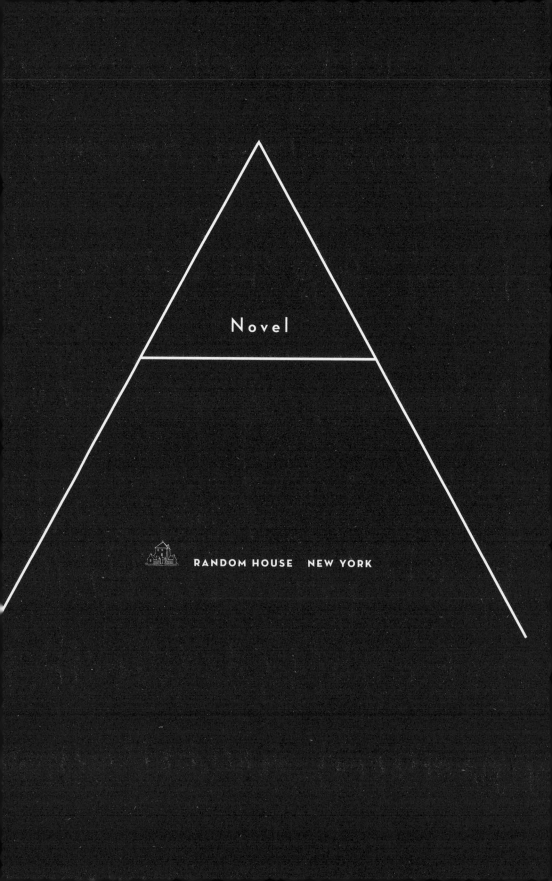

Novel

RANDOM HOUSE  NEW YORK

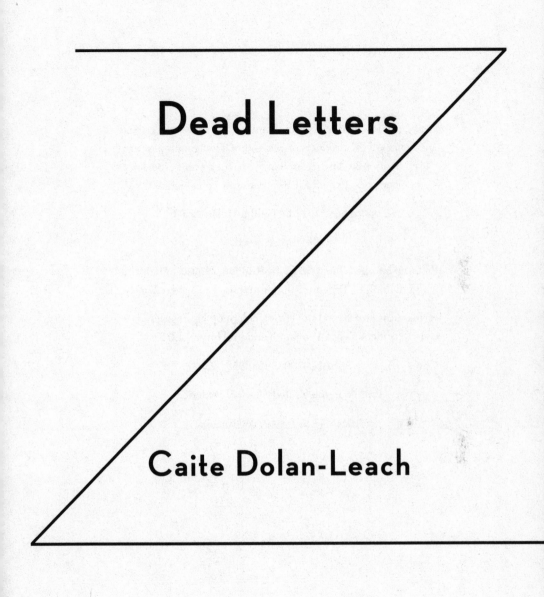

# Dead Letters

## Caite Dolan-Leach

Published in the United States by Random House, an imprint and division of Penguin Random House LLC, New York.

RANDOM HOUSE and the HOUSE colophon are registered trademarks of Penguin Random House LLC.

ISBN 9780399588853

Printed in the United States of America

*Book design by Dana Leigh Blanchette*

From this, one can make a deduction which is quite certainly the ultimate truth of jigsaw puzzles: despite appearances, puzzling is not a solitary game: every move the puzzler makes, the puzzlemaker has made before; every piece the puzzler picks up, and picks up again, and studies and strokes, every combination he tries, and tries a second time, every blunder and every insight, each hope and each discouragement have all been designed, calculated, and decided by the other.

—Georges Perec, *Life: A User's Manual*

*Un dessein si funeste, s'il n'est digne d'Atrée, est digne de Thyeste.*

Atreus might not stoop to such a gruesome plot, but Thyestes sure would.

—Crébillon, *Atrée et Thyeste*, quoted by
Edgar Allan Poe in "The Purloined Letter"

# Dead Letters

# 1

A born creator of myths, my sister always liked to tell the story of how we were misnamed. She was proud of it, as though she, as a tiny blue infant, had bent kismet to her will and appropriated the name that was supposed to be mine. My parents were trying to be clever (before they lost the ability to be anything other than utterly miserable), and our names were meant to be part of our self-constructed, quirky family mythology. *A* to *Z*, Ava and Zelda. The first-born would be *A* for Ava, and the second-born would be *Z* for Zelda, and together we would be the whole alphabet for my deluded and briefly optimistic parents, both of whom were located unimpressively in the middle: *M* for Marlon and *N* for Nadine. My father was himself named for a film star, and with his usual shortsighted narcissism he sought to create some sort of large-looming legacy for his burgeoning small family. Burgeon we would not.

Born second, I was destined for the end of the alphabet. But my sister was Zelda from her first screaming breath, wild and indomitable until her final immolation. A careless nurse handed my father the babies in the wrong order, so that his second-born was indelicately plopped into his arms first, and I was christened Ava. I say "christened" purely as a casual description; my mother would have thoroughly lost her shit had any question of formal baptism been raised. My parents were good pagans, even if they weren't much good at anything else.

Clearly delighted with this strange twist, my father insisted that we keep our misnomers; he said that the family Antipova would turn even the alphabet on its head. My mother, predictably, lay surly and despairing in her bed, counting down the seconds until her first gin and tonic in eight months. Even now, I can't really blame her.

The seatbelt light dings, and I unbuckle in order to root around in my bag for my iPad. I've read the email so many times I have it memorized, but I still feel a compulsion to stare at the words on the shimmering screen.

To: littlea@gmail.com
From: noconnor@gmail.com
June 21, 2016 at 3:04 AM

Ava, honestly the whole point of you having a cellphone is so that I can call you in an emergency. Whicf this is. If you'd pick up your goddamn phone, I wouldnt have to tell you by EMAIL that your sister is dead. There was some type of fire following one your sisters drunken binges, and apparently, she didnt make it out. If you leave paris tomorrow, you might make it time for the service.

I can't really tell whether the misspellings are because a) Mom is drunk, b) she never really learned to type ("I'm not a fucking secretary. I didn't become a feminist so I could end up tapping out correspondence"), or c) the dementia is affecting her orthography. My money is on all three. I've never seen Nadine Antipova, née O'Connor, greet any kind of news, either good or bad, without a quart of gin in the wings. The death of a daughter, especially that of her preferred daughter, has probably rattled even her. My guess is that she was already three sheets to the wind when they told her, and she wasn't able to get through to me on my cell because she either couldn't remember the number or misdialed it. She would have had to toddle upstairs to the decrepit old MacBook gathering dust on what used to be my father's desk. She would have lowered herself into the rickety office chair and squinted at the glare of the screen. After several frustrating minutes and false starts (and probably another slug of gin), she would have located Firefox and found her way to Gmail, if she didn't try her old and defunct Hotmail account first. She probably would have sworn viciously at the screen when asked for her password. Nadine would consider the computer's request for her to remember a specific detail as personally malicious, a couched taunt regarding her slipping faculties.

She would have tried to type something in, and the password would have been pre-populated, because Zelda had, in her own inconsistent and careless way, tried to make our mother's grim life a little easier. And then, drunk, aggravated, angry, and frightened, my mother wrote me a bitchy email to tell me that my twin sister had burned to death. And if that's how she told *me*, I can only imagine how my father found out.

My first thought on reading the letter was that Zelda would have appreciated that death: This was exactly how she would have chosen it. It was a fitting end for someone named after Mrs. Fitzgerald, who died, raving, when a fire destroyed the sanatorium where she had been locked away for a good chunk of her life. How Bertha Rochester dies, in rather similar circumstances. As children, we played Joan of Arc, and Zelda built elaborate pyres for straw dolls decorated as the teenage martyr (Zelda was Joan; I was always cast as the nefarious English inquisitors). Death by fire was the right death for visionaries and madwomen, and Zelda was both. My dark double.

But then, because I know my sister, I read between the lines.

The whole thing was so very Zelda. Too Zelda. When I finally reached my mother on the phone, she slurrily told me that the barn had caught fire with Zelda trapped inside. The barn out back that Zelda had transformed into her escape hatch when she could no longer stomach being in the house with our ailing, flailing mother. I knew she liked to retreat to the apartment on the second floor, to stare out the window and chain-smoke and drink and write me emails. The fire investigators seemed to believe that she passed out with a cigarette (*Classic, Zelda!*) and the wood of the barn and all the books she kept up there caught fire in the dry heat of the June day. Burned alive on the summer solstice. With the charred remnants in plain sight of half the windows in the house, where my mother can't help being reminded of Zelda, even with her brain half rotted and her liver more than half pickled. My sister couldn't have contrived a more appropriate death if she had planned it herself. Indeed.

The drinks trolley rolls by, blithely smashing into the knees of the long-limbed. Compact and travel-sized, I have plenty of space, even in the cramped and ever-diminishing airline seats. I secure myself a bland Bloody Mary in a plastic cup, wondering for the dozenth time about the name of this precious, life-giving elixir—related to the gory bride we conjured in mirrors as girls?

I swirl the viscous tomato juice among too many ice cubes and not nearly enough vodka, sipping through the tiny red straw. I love these thin mixing straws. I love their parsimony. I'm trying very hard not to think about what I'm leaving and where I'm heading. Traveling this way across the Atlantic has always seemed cruel; you leave Europe at breakfast and arrive in the United States in time for brunch, exhausted and ready for happy hour and dinner. The sun moves backward in the sky. You face your bushy-tailed friends and relatives having been awake for fifteen strenuous hours, having spent those hours exiled in the no-place of airports and airplanes. Forever returning to Ithaca. Or Ithaka. I will be collected from the tiny airport and brought to my childhood home, fifty yards from where my twin sister is supposed to have crackled and sizzled just a few days earlier—all before dinner. I wonder if the wreckage is still smoldering. Does wreckage ever do anything else? We have been twenty-five for nearly one month.

I will walk into the house, instantly accosted by the smell, the smell of childhood, my home. I will walk upstairs, to my mother's room. If it's even one minute after five (and it likely will be, by the time I make it all the way upstate), she will be drunk or headed that way, and I will sit with her and pour each of us a hefty glass of wine. We will not discuss Zelda; we never do. Eventually (and this will not take as long as "eventually") she will say something devastating, cruel, something I can't really brush off, and I will leave her. If I'm feeling vindictive, I will take the wine with me, so that she will have to carefully make her way downstairs for another bottle, risking cracked hips and the possible humiliation of failure.

I'll walk outside with that bottle of wine, and I will look at blackened timbers of that barn. I will scrutinize that dark heap of ashes. And then I will start trying to unravel my sister's mystery, and I will find her, wherever she is hiding. *Come out, come out, wherever you are. What game are you playing, Zelda?* She has always been so bad with rules.

To: littlea@gmail.com
From: zazazelda@gmail.com
September 5, 2014 at 8:36 PM

Darling Sister, Monozygotic Co-leaser of the Womb,

Well, is Paris all and everything? Does it glimmer the incandescent sparkle of mythology and overrepresentation? I'm betting yes to both, at least as far as you're concerned. Let me guess what you've been up to: You landed, disposed of your baggage, and went immediately for a triumphant stroll along the Seine— you know how you always must be near water in moments of jubilation, a genetic gift from our maternal forebears, beach striders all—you strode, nay, frolicked along those hallowed banks until your blisters popped, and then, because you are our mother's daughter, you promptly sought out some sort of cold alcoholic beverage. And, because it is very important to you to blend in with the locals but also to feel historically rooted in "authenticity," I bet that drink was . . . Lillet! Or, very possibly, Champagne,

but I would put money on the chance that both shame and fru-
gality prevented you from slapping down sixty or seventy euros
for an entire bottle of the bubbly. I'm betting you sipped your
Lillet, tried out your perfectly acceptable French, basked in your
escape, pretended you didn't want anything else to drink, and
bought that Champagne from some charming "authentic" wine
store on your way home to the tiny shoe box you will be living in
until you get this Francophilia out of your system (or until you
squander Dad's hush money and must retreat home). All the while
resolutely not thinking of what happened before you left us. Why
you left us. I'm right, Ava, *n'est-ce pas?*

Well, I'm very happy that you're fulfilling your dreams and
whatnot, even if it did mean forsaking your beloved twin sister,
whom you left languishing in the hammock with a touch of the
vapors at the thought of bearing sole responsibility for our matriarch. I know you always say that she prefers me, but GOOD GOD,
you should see how she's moping around without you. I really
think she thought that you were bluffing, that you weren't serious about this whole graduate degree thing and were all along
planning to settle in with her out at the homestead, to mop her
brow and hold her hand as she trembles through the daily DTs,
slowly losing all sense of self. Oh, but her bug-eyes when your
suitcase came down the stairs! She can't remember much, but
she remembers THAT betrayal. Jilted, she kept waiting for weeks
in quivering, agonized suspense, disbelieving that she could be
abandoned with such a flimsy explanation!

I'm not trying to guilt you (I would never! Not. Ever. Not after
everything that happened . . . ) but am instead attempting to
sketch a portrait of how life will proceed hereabouts in your absence. I'm going to stay in the trailer (I will! No one can force me
out! Not even that damned bat) rather than move back to the
house on the vineyard. Mom's in iffy shape, true, but I'm planning
to be there every day, as you know, and she's still lucid enough to

manage in the nights. I think. The Airstream is less than a mile away, in any case—I should be able to see the plumes of smoke rising if she burns down the house, ha ha! I've considered hiring someone to stay with her a bit and take care of the more unsavory activities (diapers are just around the corner, really), but I'm reluctant to dip into the dwindling Antipova/O'Connor pot o' gold. Barring some sort of harvest miracle with the grapevines, I think the years of a profit-yielding Silenus Vineyard might be behind us, Ava. Seriously. But at least the failing entrepreneurial venture gives me the illusion of a profession, which is very useful at the few grown-up cocktail parties I attend, and almost nowhere else. And it ostensibly gives me somewhere to be. And obviously keeps me in wine. No wonder the proto-satyr Our Debauched Father was so enthused by the prospect of running a vineyard. He was not entirely foolish, that man.

Well, I've been rambling—I'm sitting and typing on this antique laptop, here on Dad's old desk. I've been trying to teach Mom, but she can barely remember to pull up her undies after she pisses (better than the other way round, I suppose!), so I imagine I'm mostly trying to entertain myself. When I finish, I will have to go collect Mother from her sun throne and tempt her with just enough booze to get her inside without a battle. Time to rip off the Band-Aid. I'm sure you have some Brie and baguette to feast on—but remember, not too much! Never! If she were (t)here, our mother would remind you that she recently noticed a slight wobble in your upper arm, and at your age, you can't afford to overindulge. The irony.

In all seriousness, I miss you madly. Surely you WERE joking about this whole graduate degree thing?! And surely we can start talking again?

Eternal love from your adoring twin,
Z is for Zelda

——

Several hours, another flight, and another tinny Bloody Mary later, I stare through the tiny airplane window at the swath of lakes stretched out below. The engines are so loud that my jaw and temples ache. When the plane tilts for its final approach into the Ithaca airport, I can see all the Finger Lakes in a row, a glistening, outstretched claw catching at the late-afternoon sun. I am, of course, late; the immigration lines in Philly took hours, my bag was the last on the carousel, and I missed my connecting flight. And the next flight to Ithaca was canceled, which happens fifty percent of the time. More often in winter. The airport broke me, spiritually; microwaved Sysco food and eight-dollar beers make it impossible to relax, everything else aside. Food and drink are my only sources of true and deep (if conflicted) pleasure. In that I resemble my father. I am actually grateful to be in this noisy plane, circling above the lakes like toothpaste circling the drain. Spiraling down.

I wonder again whether it was a mistake to come alone. Nico offered, in his tender Gallic way, in bed last night. Tentative and generous, as always. This place would rip him to shreds. He would be baffled and caught off guard by such wanton cruelty. He would politely try to drink the wine, but his glass would stay half full all night. He's not a snob, but he is French. And above all else, Nico is well-mannered; he would be completely out to sea amid my friends and family, who would be too busy chewing one another to pieces to bother with Continental pleasantries. I'd love to have him with me, to know that at the end of each brutal day he would be waiting upstairs in my fluffy, too-white bedroom, waiting to comfort and console me after the most recent onslaught. At that thought, my stomach does a little flip, doubting my decision to leave him behind. I told him that if I have to stay longer than a couple of weeks, he can come visit then. More incentive for me to get the hell off Silenus Vineyard, and away from Seneca Lake. As if I needed the additional encouragement.

The wheels touch down, and I look grimly toward the airport windows. I wonder if my father will actually show up to fetch me, as he has promised to do. I can already taste the sharp, acidic local Pinot Grigio that my mother keeps in the fridge, and I realize how badly I want it.

My father, Marlon, is entrenched outside the airport, napping on one of the benches. His straw fedora is pulled down over his eyes, and I have a feeling that he's been here like this for a while. I nudge his feet to wake him, and his eyes open sloppily beneath the hat.

"Little A!" he coos, sitting upright. He's wearing all linen, his shirt and pants elegantly rumpled. His sharp green eyes are not so sharp right now. I haven't seen my father in more than two years, but he looks more or less the same. His dark hair is maybe lighter, the lines around his eyes a bit deeper, but he's still the effortlessly debonair rake he has always been. And, as always, at the sight of his smile, I feel incredibly tempted to forgive him for his shortcomings, his abandonment. My mother spent a decade and a half forgiving this man, and she is not a forgiving person. I marvel at his magnetism and wish I had inherited that, instead of his green eyes and fondness for comestibles.

He leaps up as soon as his eyes focus on me, surprisingly buoyant for someone who has lost a child. But I know he will be chipper and all smiles, performing for me. Wanting to be liked. He's about to scoop me up in a big hug when he seems to recollect himself, remembers how things are between us. He is still slender, though I can detect the beginnings of a paunch beneath the creamy linen shirt when I give him a slight, distant hug, encumbered by my carry-on. He squeezes me, tightly.

"Hi, Daddy. Glad you could make it." I really do try not to inflect this with sarcasm, but it can't be helped. He pretends not to notice. My father loathes conflict. Probably why he prefers his second family to his first.

"A, I'm so, so sorry. God, I can't imagine . . ." He grabs my shoulders and peers intently at my face. I realize that I might cry, in spite of myself, and I gently shuck him off. His face is lined: the tragic patriarch, kingdom in ruins, daughter dead.

"I know, Dad. It's . . . okay. Let's head over the hill." Old family joke. As in: "We're all over the hill out in Hector." Less funny now to be sure, and doubtless only to degrade with the years. Much like our family. "I'm sure Mom is . . ." I'm not quite sure how to finish the sentence. I'm sure Mom is a mess, I'm sure she's already had at least one bottle of Pinot Grigio, given how late I am, I'm sure that there is going to be a scene of remarkable nastiness when Marlon turns up at the house. He makes a show of gallantly taking my suitcase from me and heads toward the parking lot. Effortlessly, he hoists the bag over his shoulder, an easy demonstration of masculinity.

"You didn't bring much with you, A."

"I packed in a hurry. Besides, I still have a bunch of stuff at the house. And I can always wear Zelda's."

He flinches visibly and refuses to meet my eyes. Nico balked, too, when I said this last night as I was flinging random clothes into my suitcase, while he perched in nervous concern on the edge of my bed, clearly worried for my sanity. I can see why it might be something of a faux pas to don my sister's outlandish clothes and flit through the house looking just like her mere days after her death, an alarming corporeal poltergeist. But I always wear Zelda's things. It would be a concession to her scheme if now I didn't.

"Have you spoken to your mother?" Marlon asks.

"Briefly, on the phone last night. She was pretty disoriented, so I didn't get much out of her."

"Has she been doing . . . okay?"

"What, haven't you called her?"

"I tried, Little A. She hung straight up on me." He pauses. "Can't say I blame her. Must be hell."

"I don't really know how she is, Dad. I don't talk to her all that often. She's been very . . . angry since I left for France, and Zelda said she has fewer and fewer good days."

"Listen, kiddo, I'm . . . sorry that you have to deal with this. Her. It's not fair. On top of everything . . ." Marlon seems unsure how to continue. This is as close as I will get to an apology from him. He's

very good at apologies. You realize only later that he has accepted responsibility for exactly nothing.

"Let's not talk about it, Dad. I'd like to . . . just enjoy the sunshine."
We've reached the car, which he optimistically parked in the pickup
and drop-off area. He has a ticket, which I'm sure he will not pay. This
part of the world has yet to adopt the post-9/11 attitude typical to
transit areas in the rest of the country, and airport security rather
lackadaisically enforces its modest anti-terror protocol. In New York
City, Marlon's car would have been towed and he'd be in police cus-
tody by now. But here in Ithaca, just a ticket.

He has rented a flashy convertible, of course. My dad likes to travel
in style, regardless of finances, seemliness, tact. He tends to think of
any economic restriction as a dead-letter issue, a rule that does not
apply to him.

"Nice ride," I say. He grins mischievously as we load my bags and
ourselves into the car and speed off. I hope he's okay to drive. I haven't
driven in two years and don't even have a driver's license, but I might
still be the better choice if he's drunk. He seems reasonably coordi-
nated, though, and once we're on the other side of the city, we'll coast
along traffic-free dirt roads, kicking up dust and free to veer across the
graded surface as much as we like. I relax as we speed down Route 13,
Cayuga Lake on our right.

"So so so. Paris! How the hell is it, squirt?"

"About what you'd expect, Dad." I shrug.

"C'mon, it's one of the greatest cities in the world! That's all you
have to say about it?"

"It's far away from Silenus. Even farther than California."

He ignores the frosty tone in my voice. He is buoyant, but I can
hear the strain in his throat as he tries to be cheerful for me. "Always
so lighthearted, Little A," he teases. "Levity, oy vey." He whistles a
tune as we drive through the city, the breeze ruffling his thick black
hair, which isn't curly like ours but, rather, wavy. When we learned
that curly hair was a recessive gene, Zelda and I started speculating
about our heritage. But there are too many other stamps of Marlon's

paternity on our genes, and we abandoned the possibility of filial mystery as an exercise in wishful thinking. The letters of our DNA signify our origins, even if they can't inscribe our futures.

"What did you do while you were waiting for me?" I ask, though I know the answer. I'm wondering if he'll lie.

"I stopped in to see some old friends, and we went out for a bite to eat."

"Oh? Where did you go?"

"Uh, what's that place downtown called? With the cheap margaritas?"

"Viva."

"Yeah, very average Mexican food." He grins. "But it's the only place open between two P.M. and dinner in this one-horse town."

"The only place with a bar, you mean," I say, half-teasing.

He smiles again. "I'd forgotten how charmingly . . . sedate it is 'round these parts." He signals with his blinker, and we ride silently for a moment or two.

"How *is* your 'old friend,' Dad?" I ask. He blinks. He's a very good liar, and I can tell he's considering whether to lie now. But I'm betting he'll come clean. Because I'm older now. Because my twin sister just died. My twin sister, who, incidentally, inherited this particular talent for deception.

"Sharon, you mean?" he says.

"Who else?"

"She's okay," he says uncertainly. We've never had a real conversation about the woman he was fucking during my middle school years. I've wondered more than once whether he knows that Zelda and I knew. Our mother certainly did.

"That's good. Do you still see her often?"

"No," he says softly. "It's been years."

"And how is the third wife? Maria?"

"She's well. The girls are well too. Six and eight, if you can believe that! Scrappy little things. I'll show you the pictures on my phone, later." He pauses. "Blaze is a bit of a terror, and Bianca sometimes reminds me of you, when you were little. She's so . . . neat."

"Napa is treating you well, then?"

"Yeah, yeah. It's pretty great! The vineyard's doing really well—we were in *Wine Spectator* last month." I know. We own a vineyard, too, and have had a subscription to *Wine Spectator* since 1995. Which he knows; he insisted on the subscription, and left us with the bill. "You should come out and visit, while you're back in the States. I know Maria wants to see you girls." We both flinch at his use of the present tense, the plural.

"Maybe. I need to get back to Paris kind of soon, though."

"It's summer, Little A! Live a bit! You never relax. Your studies can wait until fall, surely." He nudges me with his elbow, annoyingly.

I nod. "Sort of, I guess. I'm working on my dissertation now, though, so I'm busy. I'm interested in the intersection of Edgar Allan Poe and the OuLiPo movement, their shared emphasis on formal constraint—"

"Poe never struck me as particularly restrained," Marlon interrupts, presumably thinking himself to be clever.

"Not restraint. *Con*straint. Specifically, I'm interested in lipograms and pangrams. I've got a theory that while both are obviously important for OuLiPo texts, they might appear unconsciously in Poe's works. So far I've focused mainly on alliteration and repetition, and because Poe's work is explicitly invested in the unconscious—"

"A pangram—that's like 'the quick brown fox jumps over the lazy dog'?" Marlon interjects. I expect he's trying to impress me.

"That's the idea. So far I've been working on this one essay he wrote on poetry—"

"It sounds really erudite, Little A, and I can't wait to talk about it more. But can't you take a break? It's summer, and, well, your sister . . ."

I capitulate. Marlon is not remotely interested in what I spend my days thinking about.

"Yeah, well, Zelda was the relaxed one. I was the responsible one."

"You still are, sweetie," he says, trying to be comforting.

"No, I'm the only one now." I suddenly feel like my mother, nastily baiting this man into feeling like shit. "I'm sorry, Dad. I'm just not . . . sure . . ." I trail off, watching in the mirror as Ithaca disappears behind us and we head up the highway on the other side of the lake.

"It's okay, kiddo. You say whatever you have to." He pats my knee. I realize that since greeting me, my father hasn't looked at me once. As if he can't. I root in my oversized bag for my sunglasses and put them on, in case I start to cry. But as I gaze out at the dazzling spray of too-green leaves and the shimmering water, I suspect that I'm not going to.

# 2

Brutally jet-lagged and insufficiently buoyed by Bloody Marys, I can't keep my eyes open and doze off somewhere on the dirt roads that will take us across the narrow, rugged span between the lakes, and I wake up just as we hit the top of the hill overlooking Seneca. The view is spectacular, with the sun about to set on the west side, and my breath catches a little, as it does every single time I make this drive. This is the longest I've been away from home: twenty-one months. I glance over at Marlon, and though he has his sunglasses on, I think he's been crying. Weeping, even. I'm startled and distressed by this—his charming, fun-loving façade so rarely cracks, and when it does, I feel as though my world is being unmade. Maybe Marlon knows this, because as he sees me waking up, he instantly transforms, flashing me one of his brilliant, toothy smiles. I know that he loved living here, loved our subpar vineyard. Even loved my mother and us girls. But his love for us is tempered by years of discord and cruelty, whereas the love he feels for this modest patch of ground is unadulterated. I smile back at him, because in spite of myself, I've missed it too.

The car skates over the dirt roads as we descend lower and lower, closer to the lakefront. There are fields of grapes all around us, and the pleasant hum of billions of insects thrums in whirring cadence.

The temperature drops suddenly in mysterious swaths of air, and goosebumps ripple on my forearms and thighs as we whip through them, warm cold warm. I can smell cold water.

Silenus Vineyard is up on the hill, with acres of vines stretching out below the tasting room, which is fronted by a rustic deck looking out at the water, scattered with a few picturesque barrels for ambience. It doesn't have much of a yield, and the wine is barely mediocre, even for the Finger Lakes.

I peer as closely as I can at the grapes as we drive by to see what Zelda has been up to in the last twenty-one months. It's hard for me to imagine my unpredictable and self-indulgent sister tilling the land like a good farmer, but she's managed to keep the place from total destitution, basically on her own. I wonder if *he* has been here, if *he* has been living in the Airstream trailer with her, if *he* is the one who organizes the spring trellising and the autumn harvest. I have to assume so; Zelda has never cared much for schedules, and I can easily picture her frittering away all of May and June drinking Pimm's cocktails on the deck and swearing that she'll move the catch wires tomorrow. Unless she really commits to doing something, and then she is an unholy terror. A terrier. I know I will have to see him soon, maybe today, and I squirm, thinking of what I'll say.

My father clears his throat awkwardly.

"You know, it's the weirdest thing," he begins. "I think I must be losing it." He pauses. "It's just that while I was at the bar . . ." He shakes his head, his waves of hair bouncing fetchingly. He doesn't go on.

"What?" I prompt.

"It's silly."

"What is?"

"I thought I saw your sister." I keep my face as blank as possible. "Or you, of course. But she walked like Zelda. I don't know, all loose." Marlon chuckles at himself. "Ridiculous, right?"

"Grief does funny things to your head," I answer, trying to betray nothing. Did Zelda intend for him to see her? Is she in Ithaca? Or California? I lean back in the seat, thinking about my sister. Thinking about whether she would even bother to toy with Marlon. After he left, it was almost like he stopped existing for her. Whereas I pined.

Dad pulls into the long, steep driveway that leads to the tasting room and the house snuggled next door. Nadine and Marlon built the house after they built the tasting room and the new cellar, solidifying what the real priorities were going to be. A place to drink, *then* a place to live. My mother, with her exacting, nitpicky taste, designed the house with an architect friend from the city, and each window, molding, and corner mirrors her love of right angles, modernism, abstraction. It is not a warm, cozy house. And next to the house is the barn.

The blackened shell of that barn appears as Dad crunches into the gravel parking area. The view is partly obscured by the house, but I can see charred timber poking up from the ground. I catch a glimpse of yellow tape cordoning off a large chunk of our lawn. A police car is parked near the rubble, and someone official is rootling around the periphery, looking fiercely intent and professional. My hands suddenly start to tremble and I don't want to get out of the car. *Zelda, what the fuck did you do?*

Dad wordlessly takes both of our suitcases from the trunk, and I realize in a vague panic that he's planning to stay here, under the same roof as Mom. He seems shaken, and I'm actually relieved to see his equanimity at least a little disrupted. His first-born child is, after all, presumably smoking in the wreckage of the barn he built himself, that one achingly long summer when my mother couldn't bear his presence in the house. Her house. Dad is resolutely not looking at the barn as we go inside. Or at me.

"Mom?" I call uncertainly, trying to guess where she'll be. The sun is setting, and I wonder whether she will have gone ahead and eaten without us. I don't know if Betsy, our lumpy, matronly neighbor, will still be here; I called her after I got off the phone with my mother and asked if she could go over to the house, make sure Mom had some food and didn't stumble down the stairs. Betsy was all comforting murmurs and practical country clearheadedness on the phone; she knew of course, had seen the fire from her house, just a mile away. She'd already been over and had just come home to pick up a frozen casserole when I called. She wanted to tell me the whole story, but I had been desperate to get off the phone, to slink into bed with Nico and let him mumble to me in his accented English.

"Betsy?" I call.

"Upstairs!" someone, presumably Betsy, answers. Dad sets the suitcases down by the door and looks around skittishly. I can see him summing up what has changed in this house. The medical-looking banister railing. The locks on certain cabinets in the kitchen. My mother's favorite print, a Barnett Newman reproduction that used to hang in the hallway, gone. Zelda, in a blind fury, tore it down and threw it into the lake during a particularly violent argument, before the dementia was diagnosed, while Mom's moods were still inexplicably abrupt. I can tell that Marlon does not want to go upstairs.

"I'm, uh, gonna look around for a minute, use the bathroom. I'll bring us up a bottle and some glasses in a minute," he says uncomfortably, scuttling away from the staircase and my mother's silent, spider-like presence upstairs. "Maybe it would be a good idea to warn her that I'm here, kiddo. She, uh, might not be all that happy to see me."

I nod. I know he'll go straight to the liquor cabinet once I'm out of sight, but he'll be disappointed to find a combination lock barring his entry. Zelda informed me in one of her chatty emails, with a gleefully vindictive tone, that she installed it after my mother nearly OD'd on Scotch last year. Apparently, Nadine forgot that she had already been drinking wine and popping sedatives all day and almost boxed her liver with a bottle of Glenmorangie. Marlon will just have to rustle up something with a lower alcohol content from the fridge.

I skip upstairs, feeling the familiar grooves of the wooden stairs beneath my feet. I have instinctively taken off my shoes; my mother loathes the presence of footwear in her once-pristine Zen paradise.

She could be driven to apoplectic rage by someone sitting in the living room with boots on their feet. The house is definitely dirtier than it was during my childhood; I suspect Zelda fired the housekeeper I'd hired from Craigslist before leaving for Paris. I feel grit and dust accumulating on the soles of my bare feet, and as I touch the banister, a layer of grime coats my fingertips in a seamless transfer. But the stairs are the same beneath me and I feel each creak in my body with intense recognition.

Mom and Betsy are outside, on the balcony that opens from the library. Betsy has her back turned to the barn, but my mother is facing it full-on, glaring belligerently at the scar in our lawn, zigzagged with crime-scene tape.

"Hi, Betsy, thanks so much for this," I say, preparing myself for the inevitable hug as Betsy lurches out of her chair to greet me. "Really, you're a lifesaver." I wonder at my choice of words, but Betsy smooshes me to her breasts with a squeeze.

"Oh, Ava, I'm so sorry about—about your sister!" She instantly begins to cry, her substantial chest heaving up and down, her brown doe eyes watering. I pat her shoulder, trying to create a crevasse of space between our bodies. Her sweat moistens my shirt.

"Thanks. I'm so grateful you were here." I pause. "Hi, Mom." I lean in to kiss her cheek, interrupting her stare toward the barn. "How are you?"

"Goddamnit, Zelda, what the fuck did you do to the barn? How many fucking times do I have to tell you not to smoke up there?"

I flinch, knowing I should have expected to be confused with my sister. "Mom, it's me, Ava," I say patiently. "I just got here, I flew from Paris?"

"Very cute, Zelda. God, you're exactly the same as when you were four, always trying to hide behind your sister whenever you screwed something up. I'm not an idiot, nor am I insane. I expect you to deal with that"—she gestures imperiously toward the barn—"immediately. And with none of your usual dramatic *bull*shit, please."

I glance at Betsy, who is unable to tear her eyes from this scene. The rapt rubbernecking of good neighbors. I turn to her.

"Betsy, thanks again for everything. I know she can't have been easy the last day or two. And thank you for calling the fire department. Who knows . . . what could have happened."

"Oh, Ava!" Betsy carries on huffing and puffing without skipping a beat. "It was so terrifying, the whole barn just lit up like that! I rushed over as quickly as I could but—your sister!"

"Zelda, I need more wine," Nadine says sharply, interrupting Betsy's whimpers. I ignore her.

"How are your kids, Betsy?" I ask.

"Kids? Mine? Oh, they're okay, I guess," she titters. "Rebecca just started working as a dental assistant, actually. And you remember Cody?" she says, fishing. Yes, I do. Cody was one of the irredeemable assholes who graduated with me. I'd love to tell Betsy how he used to follow the one openly gay kid in our school around, whispering "Faggot" and smacking his ass.

"Yup. How is he?"

"He lives in San Francisco now. With one of his college roommates," she announces proudly. I suppress a giggle. That's perfect.

"Zelda, for Christ's sake," Nadine interjects.

"I'll deal with her now, Betsy," I say. A gentle dismissal. She seems grateful.

"No, no, of course, Ava. It was no problem. Anything I can do, really. I'll stop by tomorrow with more food."

"You don't have to do that," I say quickly. "Really, you don't."

"No, no trouble. I'll check up on you then. Nadine's already eaten, and there's more casserole in the fridge." That should make it easy not to eat. She dabs at her tears with the collar of her oversized batik-print muumuu. "At least I got her to eat this time. Last time I was here, she wouldn't touch a thing."

"Thanks, Betsy. Oh, and Marlon's downstairs—you can say hello on your way out."

Betsy's face tightens perceptibly—she's one of the few people who isn't taken in by my father's charm; she has a long memory and can't forgive Marlon for the way he left. It makes me want to like her more.

"I will, of course. And, Ava? My sincere condolences," she says earnestly and hugs me again. She bobs her head and waddles through the glass doors, trundling her way downstairs. I flop into the Adirondack chair she has vacated, glad that it faces the tasting room, though it is unpleasantly warm from her body.

"You look pretty good, Mom. All considered."

"Don't take that tone with me, Ava," she says.

I smile widely. "So you did know."

"As I said, doll, I'm not insane. Not entirely. I just despise that woman, with all her clucking and sanctimonious . . . good-naturedness." Mom has to pause for the right word, but I can tell she's lucid-ish. "She's thick as a plank and doesn't have the good grace to realize it. I've been listening to her prattle for the last twenty-four hours about how it's going to be fine, you'll be here soon, et cetera." She rolls her eyes in exasperation. "I came out here and parked in front of the barn, hoping that it would scare her off. But she's *got to do the right thing*. God, and that casserole . . ." She shudders theatrically.

"What happened, Momma?" I ask.

"How the hell should I know? I slept through the whole thing. Goddamn drugs your sister gave me." Mom takes a slug from the wineglass in her hand, which trembles as she clutches the stem. Reflexively, I look around for the bottle, to gauge how much she's had. She catches me looking.

"Jesus, you're worse than your sister. At least she has the manners not to make me drink alone. You haven't ended up in AA, have you, Little AA?" She's sneering, making fun of my father's nickname for me, and goading me into drinking with her. I know it, and it doesn't change the fact that I want to.

"Dad's on his way up with glasses and a bottle," I say casually, and enjoy watching her flinch.

"Marlon is here? The big fish that got away?" She tries for a light-hearted tone, but I can hear the anxiety in her warbling voice. She touches her face in instinctive, irrepressible self-consciousness, the gesture of a woman who knows she doesn't look good.

"Got in this morning. Surely you must have known he would come home for his daughter's funeral."

"Yes, I gathered he would. Surprised he didn't bring that new ball and chain of his."

"Maria is hardly new, Mom. They've been married almost eight years."

"Maria? I thought her name was Lorette."

"That was my girlfriend when we met, Nadine," my father says from the doorway. He's studying her with a strange expression on his face; I can't remember the last time they saw each other, but I know she has to look shocking. She is so thin.

"Oh, of course, I remember," Mom says automatically. I know she doesn't, but she will work very hard to convince us otherwise.

"You could be forgiven for forgetting. The relationship was very brief," I snipe. Nadine snorts. Dad holds up a bottle of sparkling wine and three Champagne flutes with a slightly sheepish look on his face. The glasses hang suspended between his fingers, clinking magically. I love that sound.

"There's only sparkling in the fridge," he apologizes. I nod, giving him permission. He puts the glasses down on the deck railing and deftly divests the bottle of its wire cap and cork with a practiced series of movements. All three of us cringe at the jubilant sound, and Mom and Dad both flick their eyes toward the barn, as though that Pavlovian signal will summon Zelda, perhaps even from beyond the grave. Champagne is her favorite drink, of course. Though this is obviously a sparkling wine, made in our own cellar. Dad pours our delicately burbling wine into flutes and distributes them, my mother first, then me. I lift my glass defiantly.

"Well, family. Cheers." They both look at me blankly, and I turn my head toward the lake, draining my glass in a hearty gulp.

To: littlea@gmail.com
From: zazazelda@gmail.com
Subject: Mademoiselle Pout
October 1, 2014 at 12:45 AM

Dearest Begrudgeful, Silent Sister,

Don't you think this a little silly, Ava? You really are milking the whole thing quite atrociously, as though we were still in high school. I mean, yes, it all goes back to high school, so perhaps you get SOME leeway for behaving like a hormonal hot mess, but surely with our blossoming maturity you can LET IT GO? If it makes any difference, I'll get rid of him; just say the word.

In other (frankly more interesting) news, our mother is a psycho. And a lush. Last night I had to scrape her out of the field, raving and half clothed, drinking a bottle of that atrocious Fauxjolais Nouveau that Dad insisted we try to manufacture, in spite of the fact that it always tastes like grapy horse piss. And yet, out of some dark-seated nostalgia, Nadine insists on reproducing it every year, as though *this* vintage will be drinkable. It's like she thinks if she could just produce a bottle that was even a little palatable, Marlon would reappear, and she could sit on the deck and watch him work the fields, as ever. Her very own *contadino*.

Anyway, last night she was yelping and sobbing, insisting that she wanted to return to the earth or somesuch. I think she was trying to make it down to the lake, quite possibly to throw herself in. One of these days I may just let her. But as it was, I gave her some of her "medicine" (what a useful euphemism for heavy-duty sedatives!) and dragged her back to bed, the whole while listening to her screech like a demented banshee. You can bet I poured myself a substantial tumbler of the good stuff. I'm not just being selfish: Her wee pills give her a respite, as well as me!

Autumn has really dug in its heels; the leaves are leached of their chlorophyll and are whirligigging their way to the ground at an alarming rate. And Paris? I Googled photos of Les Tuileries to see what it looks like (that's where we wanted to live when we were little, right? Though I can only assume you live *near* the garden, rather than in a fairy fortress within it, as previously planned), and it does seem very picturesque. Still, hard to beat the view from Silenus. The harvest was brutal; another year or two of this and I'll be dribbling into my Riesling like Momma. We'll see what we get out of it. I'm guessing it will be more of the same.

But really, are you planning to not talk to me for the rest of forever? Or just until you wind up in bed with a chain-smoking, shrugging Parisian? Really, Ava, it's not that big a deal, what happened. I'm over it. He's over it. Weirdly, I find myself washing and changing your sheets on a regular basis. I barely even wash my own. What do you think that's about?

Your repentant, embryonic other half,
Z is for Zelda

I bundle Nadine into bed, though I don't lock the door behind her—Zelda wrote that she has started sleepwalking lately, but I can't bring myself to lock her in. What if there's another fire? After setting Marlon up in the guest room, I creep outside with a flashlight. Everything still smells of smoke, and I head toward the barn's remains. It's still warm; summers have been getting hotter and hotter here, though many of our die-hard Republican neighbors still refuse to comment on why this might be. Zelda speculated about what it would do for the grapes ("Did you know French Champagne growers are buying up real estate in the south of England? They're predicting that the growing conditions will be more Champagne-esque than Champagne in twenty years! Do you think we'll be, like, the next Chianti?"). I'm barefoot, so I make my way gingerly across the lawn, avoiding bits of burnt wood and other debris. I scan the flashlight over the area and finally squat down a few yards from where the barn doors would have been. There's a small yellow flag poked into the burnt wood and ash.

Shutting my eyes, I can see the structure perfectly; I imagine sliding open the heavy doors, padding my way across the cement floor where we kept all sorts of menacing farm equipment, and climbing up the steep ladder rungs to the loft.

Marlon built the barn with some rustic fantasy of cramming the loft full of hay, keeping a few goats and sheep downstairs in the quaint mangers he constructed. But he left before we ever acquired either hay or critters to feed with it, and the barn became ad hoc storage for the ancient tractor and backup steel wine drums and random bits of equipment that weren't used often. Zelda colonized the upstairs as her own stately pleasure den, insisting on loading books and furniture up through the hay chute in her teenage stubbornness. She had a few cast-off futons up there, a big worktable, some chairs, lots of ironic art (mainly featuring baby farm animals) that she had picked up at the Salvation Army in Ithaca. Even in her teens, she'd felt trapped in the house with our mother and had hidden out here whenever they fought. Used to watching her abandon projects, I observed her rehabilitation of the barn with surprise. It seemed terrifically unlike her.

As high school ended, she began to invite people over to what she had started calling the Bacchus Barn (Zelda names everything). My mother would grit her teeth in passive-aggressive fury, staring out the window at the lights in the barn, the sound of music keeping us awake well into the night. Nadine never knew what to do with Zelda. Or this property.

We had a collective story about how Silenus came to be, cobbled together from four different people with radically different narrative designs. The gist of it, the median account of that particular yarn, is this: My mother's money paid for Silenus, though it was my father's vision. Marlon was not the sort of man my mother usually went for; she liked very Waspy men, men who had been to law school and golfed on the weekends. Men who knew how to tie a variety of knots and always specified "Tanqueray" when they ordered a martini. Marlon Antipova, perennially relaxed and pathologically easygoing, all sun-weathered and full of vim, was the antithesis of what she always thought she had wanted in a partner. But when Nadine's mother died after a lengthy, debilitating illness (Parkinson's), leaving her an orphan, she pulled up stakes and moved to New York. At thirty-two, she had to decide what to do with herself and her money. When Marlon sauntered into that bar in the Village where she sat slurping gin and tonics and avoiding the silent, carpeted apartment she had rented on the Upper West Side, she saw escape, from herself and her past. She launched herself without blinking into a haphazard life with the adventurous Florida-born wanderer.

My father was never a practical person, but he had aspirations: a dangerous combination. He gave an impressive impersonation of a vagabond bohemian, all the while zealously keeping his quiet ambitions just behind that convincing veneer of exceptional recklessness. I've spent quite a bit of time imagining that scene, so pivotal in our family story. A time when they wanted each other, when the future hadn't barreled disastrously into their plans. Zelda and I used to tell the story to each other, handing off the narrative like a *cadavre exquis*.

I would always start: Marlon's pickup pulled onto the graveled shoulder that would someday be the bottom of our driveway. The lake spread out below him and my mother, and Marlon crunched the truck to a halt as they neared the dusty For Sale sign drummed into the ground. A telephone number was written out in Sharpie ink, with no area code in front of the seven digits. Locals only, the sign was subtly suggesting.

"Is this your grand surprise, then?" Nadine asked him, trying not to sound either disappointed or eager. She sought to remain impassive, to never betray what went on behind those cool blue eyes of hers. To neither lose her temper (as she was prone to do) nor reveal her excitement, her happiness, which was a new experience for her. Having spent the last few years watching her parents' unsightly decline, she was free now, for the first time since early childhood. Still young(ish), with some money and self-determination, she could do whatever she pleased. And what pleased her most was this sly, smooth man with a ponytail and an easy smile. How strange that he would choose her, with her stiff manners and the tight kernel of anger she carried with her. That he would go rapping, rapping on her apartment door at all hours of the night, and saunter into her bedroom with a bottle of bourbon and the southern drawl that he revealed, seemingly only for her, for moments of intense intimacy beneath her expensive down comforter. She had never allowed anyone so fully into her life, her inner world, and sometimes she would stare at Marlon in disbelief that he wanted her.

Zelda would take over then, to explain our father: Marlon always pretended not to notice these guardedly fond moments but felt more confident in her attachment to him whenever he caught that intense, shrewd gaze. This woman was everything he wasn't, everything he aspired to. She ordered drinks without looking at the menu—she knew what she wanted and was not particularly worried about price. There was never any question of whether she could afford it, whether the bill would arrive and she would come up short. Marlon had left behind a number of threatening business partners and outstanding debts (monetary and otherwise) in the swampy town of his childhood and had disappeared into the anonymous horde of penniless musicians here in New York out of necessity. He imagined a future where he would sit and look out at his own land. He had learned a word, years ago, *pedigree*, that he would sometimes, after five or six drinks, slosh around on his tongue. Nadine, who kept herself aloof and separate, and so rarely allowed him to know what went on in that inscrutable head of hers, was classy in a way that Marlon found hopelessly erotic. Her pale Irish skin reminded him of marble, and her ramrod posture of a statue. So different from the bronze, wiry girls he had tussled with as a young man, in smoky dive bars and tropical rainstorms.

"It *is* grand, isn't it?" He allowed a strand of black hair to fall across his face as he leaned across the cab toward her. "C'mon, you. Hop on out. I'll give you the tour." Nadine obliged, and Marlon snatched a picnic basket from the bed of the borrowed truck. With his other hand, he led her down into the field, tall with alfalfa and wildflowers. "They're selling the whole property," he finally said, watching Nadine's face carefully as she assessed everything. He had learned not to push her too quickly or too hard; when she felt cornered, she balked, like some trapped wild animal. Nadine simply nodded her head, her eyes measuring each blade of grass with that sharpness he had come to expect. He spread out the picnic blanket and sprawled on it, popping the cork on the bottle of Champagne he had brought. It fizzed warmly, and they both leaned in to lap up the bubbly spill as it ran down the edge of the bottle.

"Just thought you might want to take a look. You've been talking about leaving the city so much lately," Marlon said with a shrug. "A nice getaway, anyway."

"It's beautiful. It's so nice to breathe the fresh air," Nadine agreed. "So this place is what, a farm?" She was careful not to appear too interested, but she couldn't help feeling nervous excitement at the sense of possibility. Some quiet voice that she hadn't heard for years kept suggesting a new beginning. She didn't examine this prompt too closely; she would inspect it later, when she was away from Marlon and could think properly, without all the noise and hormonal interference his presence created in her.

I would interrupt here, derailing Zelda's artful dialogue. She could perfectly capture our parents' voices, a born impersonator. But I liked the history of the wine, and of the ground that it came from.

"I was thinking a vineyard, actually."

"What, here? In New York?" Nadine arched her eyebrows skeptically.

"I know, I know, it seems weird. But there's this Ukrainian guy who brought some *vinifera* grapes over from Europe, and they've done very well. Some other guys are trying it now, and I don't know, I have this feeling that the region could get pretty valuable." Marlon shrugged, sipping his cup of Champagne. "Just a hunch."

"A hunch, huh?" Nadine smiled slyly. "I'm not a complete ninny, you know. I figure you're the kind of guy who likes to financially re-inforce his hunches."

Marlon glanced at her in surprise. He thought he'd managed to conceal his proclivity for putting his money where his mouth was.

"I like risk," he said lightly. "And I'm about to take another." He drew a deep breath. "The real reason I wanted to bring you here. I've been thinking." He paused to stare at Nadine. "I want to marry you. I want to run away with you and give you babies and spend the rest of our lives naked and drunk." Without breaking eye contact, he unbut-toned the first three buttons of her shirt, then stopped, his hand poised at the open collar, near her throat. Nadine's face registered only still-ness. She waited long enough that Marlon began to wonder if he hadn't drastically overplayed his hand. But finally, she covered his hand with her palm and slid both inside her shirt.

"Fine. But we'll talk about those babies later."

Needless to say, whatever conversations they later had about those babies, nothing stuck. I've never known if Zelda and I were accidents; at least we both knew that whatever our status, desirable or planned, we were on equal footing. Either we were both wanted or neither was. Perhaps Nadine had unconsciously hoped for kids and grown careless with her contraceptives. Or maybe Marlon had worked his insidious magic until she relented. Our father said we were wanted, "beginning to end, *A* to *Z*," always with a playful grin. Nadine had said that it was a moot point.

By the time we were born, the reality of the vineyard's disappoint-ing prospects was becoming clearer, and our parents were just begin-ning to swat nastily at each other, like house cats cooped up too long indoors. We often wondered, as I imagine many children do, whether we were the cause of our parents' eventual rupture. If they had been different people, a better team, things might have gone differently. This was early days for modern Finger Lakes winemaking, and Marlon's selection was actually prescient; property prices went up over the next decade, and plots of land like ours were hotly coveted by ambitious investors and hotheaded fools alike. But Nadine and Marlon fought each other viciously on every petty decision. Soon, Silenus transformed from a prospector's fortune to a time-consuming forfeiture while Zelda and I ran feral and barefoot in the fields, gnawing on unripe grapes and making gowns from the sickly vines as our family and its investments tumbled down around us in molting shudders of decay.

I open my eyes and look at the wreckage. I scan the rubble for any sign of the tractor, which probably would have been in the barn two nights ago. As I suspected, I don't see it anywhere, and no matter how hot the fire, there should still be something left. Zelda loved that tractor; of course she wouldn't let it burn. I get up and walk slowly around the perimeter of the burn, letting the flashlight dance over it. A dull, menacing heat still radiates from the ground. Bats swoop in a leathery rush, hunting. I'm looking for a sign, a message from my sister about what happened here. I don't for a second believe that she's actually dead. *Come out, Zaza. Time to face your sister.*

# 3

Completely irreconcilable with what I've consumed, I wake up the next morning feeling surprisingly un-hungover. My bedroom is dazzling in the high summer sun, still way too white. The walls are white, the bedspread is white, the curtains are gauzy and white, and there's a white sheepskin rug just next to my bed. I chose the color scheme in contradistinction to Zelda's bohemian-gypsy vibe across the hall; her room is all purples, reds, blues, and golds, fringed shawls, dull lighting. I hear raised voices in the kitchen and grab a cream kimono from my closet. I haven't unpacked yet. I'm reluctant to do so; I slept in one of my prim nighties from high school.

As I walk down the stairs, I can hear my mother's shrill voice.

"I don't care who you think you are, who you say you are, I saw you! I saw you in the cabinets, stealing. You've been taking my things while I slept, and I want you out!"

"Calm down, Nadia, it's me, Marlon." I hear my father say her pet name in his very best conciliatory tone, though with a small note of panic. My mother is having none of it. Never did.

"Fuck you and your lies. Get out. I'm calling the police." She sounds scared. I walk into the kitchen, yawning. It is surreal to see both my parents here, surrounded by the walnut cabinets they built together, bickering as though it's still 2003.

"Morning, Dad, Mom," I say, heading straight for the coffeemaker.

"Zelda, get this man out of here. He was stealing my jam from the cupboard!"

"It's Ava, Mom. And that's my dad, Marlon?"

"Like hell it is. My ex-husband is dead."

"Not just yet, Nadine," my dad says with an edge. But his snark is bravado. He looks genuinely harrowed. He glances back and forth between me and Nadine, clearly unsure what to do.

"Zelda, I will count to three!"

"I'm not four years old. And I'm not Zelda. Are you screwing with me again today, Mom?" I study her more closely. She actually looks terrified, and her expression makes me hesitate. I don't think she's faking to get a rise out of us.

"I want Zelda!" she wails, and my stomach clenches.

So do I.

Nadine's going to pieces now, mumbling quietly to herself.

"Zelda . . . is already outside," I lie, starting the coffeepot. "Why don't we just go back upstairs for a bit? I have some medicine for you." I lead her back toward the stairway. Marlon stands there, almost paralyzed. Nadine's hands are shaking, and she seems suddenly frail, flimsy. Her shoulders stick out like wings, and she feels somehow light, as though she's evaporating in front of us. I give her a sedative and put her back in bed. I know this is not a long-term solution; I'll have to work out a system later. This time, I lock the door.

Downstairs, I pause in front of the bathroom. I hear barely controlled sobs behind the door. My father. I hesitate, tempted to knock but unsure what to say. Instead I go to the kitchen and start breakfast.

When he joins me at the table, he is again smiling and light, determined to put me at ease. I don't know what to say to him, so I say nothing. We eat some of Betsy's bread and one of Zelda's bizarre jams from the cupboard. This one seems to be peach curry. It is not a total

failure as a condiment, but it is weird. Marlon doesn't look good; either he stayed up drinking or he couldn't fall asleep. Possibly both. We
barely speak over breakfast. I can tell he is truly rattled by Nadine's
outburst, and I have no desire to discuss it with him. As I'm putting
the dishes in the sink, I clear my throat.

"I think I'm going to drive to the police station in Watkins Glen. I'd
like to learn more about the fire," I say flatly. "See if there's anything
they need from us to investigate the, uh, accident." I really don't want
him to invite himself along, which he seems to sense. "Do you think
you could look after Nadine for a little while? I know that's not ideal,
but . . ." I trail off. Marlon nods cooperatively, though I imagine he
can't be excited about this. "We'll have to do something about the funeral. I know you called some people already, and I'll try to find some
of Zelda's friends. I don't know if we need to worry about the announcement."

Marlon is still nodding along as though he knows all this, but I'm
sure he hasn't thought of it. I'm pretty sure he thinks that birthdays
and funerals and dishes and housework are all magically arranged by
some sort of domestic deity who oversees life's practical consider-
ations. He always looked confused when there weren't clean towels in
the bathroom or when the kitchen counters grew sticky and fly-infested
after someone had spilled honey on the wood. As though he thought
something had suddenly begun malfunctioning, rather than just continuing along its natural entropic path, unimpeded by the feminine
forces that typically stood in its way.

"Listen, I'll text you a list of what all needs to be done. And Nadine
should be quiet for a few hours. Just feed her some of Betsy's casserole." I can't help wrinkling my nose in snobby reluctance at the suggestion. If she weren't half out of her mind, my mother would never
contemplate a tuna casserole, regardless of circumstances. "And give
her the meds in her pill dispenser once she's eaten. And don't let her
start drinking until at least four. Though I should be back by then."
Marlon nods mechanically. "Thanks, Dad. It's good to see you,
even . . ." I turn to leave the room, scooping the car keys up as I go.

"Ava?" he asks gently. I stop. "Do you think there's something a little . . . off about this?" He looks reluctant to even be suggesting it.

"I don't know. Zelda was in a weird place. I . . . don't know what to think," I concede. I'm not about to say that I think Zelda might be holed up somewhere with one of her crazy friends, laughing at all of us and cooing over her escape. I know that would sound crazy to him, like denial. Yet the combination of Zelda's letters the last few months and the bizarre neatness of all this feels too much like one of my sister's elaborate plots. But if she *is* up to something, she wouldn't want Marlon to know. After he left us cold, she'd want him in the dark. Strange, that I should still be attentive to her wants, that I should give a flying fuck after everything that's happened, but . . . what can I say. I'm loyal to my twin, even if I haven't spoken to her for nearly two years.

I bob my head at Marlon and walk out the door, carrying one of Zelda's bags. There are two vehicles in the drive, and I reflect that maybe I should have asked Marlon to borrow his fancy rental, rather than drive my mother's (now my sister's) unreliable pickup. Zelda's bedraggled, antique jalopy, which sits decaying in torpid disrepair, slowly oxidizing in the upstate moisture, was a point of acquisitive pride for my jackdaw sibling. Having long coveted the truck, she had finally prized it from my mother following an eye-exam coup that left Nadine humiliated and without a license; she had no choice but to transfer the title to the gloating Zelda, who made a point of inappropriately revving the engine and briskly ramming the body into the deep culverts that ran alongside the fields, battering the suspension and brutalizing the alignment.

Watkins Glen is only seven or eight miles from here, though, and Zelda drove the goddamn thing all over the vineyard every day. Besides, I'm home now. I can't be cruising around in a flashy convertible. That would just be asking to get pulled over. Zelda's the driver. As an afterthought, I dig around in the glove compartment and pull out her driver's license. Can't hurt.

The drive is relaxing, and I feel better the farther I get from my own nest of crazies. I try very hard not to think about how I'm going to keep it together for the next few weeks. I'm good at repression (as Zelda loves to point out), and this task is surprisingly easy. I find a pack of Zelda's cigarettes on the tattered seat of the truck and light an American Spirit, the smell of Zelda filling up the small cab. Frankly, there's no way she can be dead. I would feel it, would know with the cells of my body, which are so entwined with hers.

Watkins Glen is sleepy, and the truck putters along until I pull up in front of the police station. American flags billow from every storefront and porch, in a show of patriotism that is almost shocking after my time in France. I wonder vaguely if I should have called ahead to the station—I don't know what the protocol for this is. I'm already regretting the cigarette, which makes me feel nauseous and light-headed. I find gum in the glove compartment ("Because you never know when you'll have to talk to a cop shit-faced, Little A!") and get out of the truck. I half-expect to see people I know on the streets; even though I've been in town for only twelve hours, it feels weird that I haven't seen anyone.

The air-conditioning in the police station is turned up unjustifiably high (very upstate New York), and no one is at the reception desk. I wander around the reception area, exploring before anyone shows up. I like to find the corners of rooms, see what brochures are moldering in the rack on a cluttered side table, peer down empty hallways, locate the bathroom. I'm a snoop. I'm just leafing through a pile of crisis-hotline fliers when a cop wanders in. He seems surprised to see me. I can't imagine that the Watkins Glen police have much to do: Make sure people are staying on the trails on the gorge hikes, check boat permits, rescue kittens, wait for NASCAR weekend. I wouldn't think that many citizens are burned alive in their homes in this backwoods municipality.

"My name's Ava Antipova," I say, jauntily sticking out my hand. The cop flinches.

"I know. You . . . look like your sister."

"Oh, you know—knew Zelda?"

"Yeah, I, uh, wrote up the report. I was the responding officer, after the fire department. Officer Roberts."

"Good. Then you're the man I need," I say, smiling brightly. "You may have noticed that my mother is not exactly . . . with it. I'd really like a more reliable account of what happened, what the report says."

"Um, yeah, of course. I'm sorry I have to ask, but do you have ID? I'm only allowed to release details to the family and, well . . ."

I nod sympathetically, hunting in my bag. I'm ninety percent sure I don't have my passport with me, which is my only government-issued ID.

"Um, I don't have a driver's license"—shit, hope he doesn't ask how I got here—"and I seem to have left my passport . . . but I do have a Metro card with my photo and birthday? I live in France," I explain. He looks uncomfortable. Is he kidding? "I'm obviously Zelda's twin," I point out. "If you have a picture, you could compare . . ."

"Of course, ma'am. I mean, that won't be necessary. Of course." He fumbles awkwardly through a heap of papers. "Would you like to hear what I wrote up in the report?"

"That'd be super." He clears his throat and prepares to read aloud to me. I barely suppress a snort. Really?

"I responded to a phone call from the Antipova residence at just before one A.M. on the night of June 20. Watkins Glen Fire Department had already arrived on the scene, and they were putting out the flames. A Mrs. Betsy Kline had alerted them to the fire from her own residence and then rushed immediately to the Antipova residence, where she discovered that Mrs. Antipova—"

"O'Connor. *Ms.* O'Connor," I correct.

"Uh, okay, Mrs. O'Connor was found to be sedated, in her bed, sleeping. Apparently she has some, uh, health issues?" He looks up at me.

"Quite."

"Well, the FD was eventually successful in putting out the flames, but it came to light that Miss Zelda Antipova was suspected to be in the structure when the fire began, according to Mrs.—O'Connor's statement."

"You got Nadine awake? With all those sedatives?" I say, surprised. Zelda always joked that she gave Mom horse tranquilizers and Nadine would barely breathe for ten hours.

"Yes, after some effort. She was, uh . . . uncooperative at first."

"I'll bet. But she said Zelda was in the barn?"

"Yes, but her statements seemed a little, well, unreliable." He looks embarrassed to be telling me that my mother can't be trusted, as though it's news. "Mrs. Kline told us that Miss Antipova typically spent the night in an Airstream trailer about half a mile away, so I went to investigate. No one was there, but I did find a cellphone belonging to the deceased. I mean, Zelda. Miss Antipova." The cop turns a pretty shade of pink. I can't believe how young he seems. "The last text messages on June 20 were with someone named Jason. They made plans to meet at the barn at eleven that night. It appears the fire started just before midnight, leading us to believe . . ."

"That Zelda was there. Jason who?" I ask. I don't recognize the name.

"It didn't say on her phone—he was just Jason. We called the number back but got no response, no voicemail activated. We've requested registration info from the phone company, but it will take a few days."

"So is Zelda . . . officially dead?"

The cop squirms. "No, ma'am, not officially. But I'm not gonna lie—it seems very possible. Right now we're running her cards, license, and plates, to see if she turns up anywhere. We've called in some specialists, and we share a coroner with Montour Falls, so we'll get him out here. We're obviously looking for, um . . ."

"Bones or something," I finish. Good luck, Sparky. "Anyway, I don't want to have a funeral without a death certificate. It would be unseemly," I say, and the poor kid looks stricken. "Thank you, Officer, for answering my questions. You'll keep me posted?"

He bobs his head at me, clearly relieved that the conversation is over, and I turn to leave.

"Ma'am?" he says tentatively as my hands reach for the door. I face him, one eyebrow raised. "There's just one other thing that, uh—well, we're still looking into one more thing." He swallows. "It's just that the barn doors were—well, they were chained shut. From the outside."

April 30, 2016 at 3:12 PM

Dear Pouty, Crabby, Puerile Twin,

And so we finish year two of your stubborn radio silence. Okay, Ava. I get it. I'll do my time, keep on writing you, wait for you to shake off your huff. Let you have your temper tantrum so that you can save face. It's fine, I don't mind; I've always been less proud than you. I don't mind admitting that I MISS YOU and that I'M GOING CRAZY WITHOUT YOU. Do you think that will soften your brittle crustacean shell? Will it weaken your resolve to maintain this transatlantic muteness? I don't know. You were a soft touch when we were girls, but maybe you've toughened up, ensconced yourself in some sort of emotional fortress. I remember you crying pitifully when we saw a homeless man begging in Watkins Glen. He was a raggedy-ass specimen, too tan and wilted, with his cardboard sign entreating us to HELP because HE WAS A VETERAN. As though his life was inherently more valuable because he had the bad luck (or, even worse, the misguided desire) to end up in the military. Oh, but you were moved! You tugged our father's hand, pleaded with your very best Tender Ava eyes, and he gave you ten dollars to hand to the man. A testament to both our father's complete inability to deny you anything and his endless profligacy in all things financial. The man chews through cash the same way he devours imported cheese (the two behavior patterns may be related). You gave the old vet the ten bucks along with your tattered spare change. And later, when we went for ice cream and you had no money, I bought you one.

But now you've seen something of the world, and perhaps you're less fragile, more cynical. Maybe. I'd put money on not, though. Bet you're still dropping euro coins into the hats of amputee hucksters who will unfold their hidden limbs at the end of the day and traipse off to the nearest bottle shop, living proof that the performance of suffering is worth money. A lesson our mother learned young. These days, however, it is a woefully unprofitable adventure, for her at least. I imagine the begging industry is still going strong. But Nadine seems to have run up against some empty coffers, and she's not taking it all that well.

I fear that Silenus may be going under, dearest Ava. I know it won't be too surprising to you, but perversely, I hope it keeps you up at night. I certainly toss and turn a bit these long dark evenings, before giving in to temptation and chasing some of Nadine's fancy tranqs (tranks? How would you spell it?) with a glass of Scotch. Then I sleep like the dead; I wouldn't wake up if I caught on fire, lolz! Bad for my hepatic well-being, but it's the only way I can get spreadsheets of collapsing finances out of my brain. I'm getting ready for the spring bloom (mind that moisture!), but I know that this year might be the last, that if this season doesn't go well, we're fucked. Not what you want to hear. Or maybe you don't care.

Your increasingly desperate twin,
Z is for Zelda

I leave the cop station with a feeling that resembles vindication. I knew something was going on, knew there had to be. *But what, Zaza? What could this possibly achieve?* I drive too fast, which is obviously a terrible decision, since getting pulled over will mean more than a speeding ticket for me. But I'm racing, and before I realize I have made the decision to go there, I'm pulling down the driveway where Zelda keeps her battered Airstream. She has so many places to run to, when she's running from our mother. But all within the confines of the family estate. Zelda holds her ground—I'm the one who flees.

The trailer rests on a cobbled-together deck that Zelda built herself the summer we graduated high school. I could see her jaw growing tighter and tighter as that summer waned, and I, naïvely, thought she was nervous about starting college. We were both going to live at home, but I had gotten into Cornell and Zelda was headed to a community college in Ithaca; her grades the past two years had been appalling, and she hadn't even bothered to apply to Cornell. I thought she was scared of growing up, that she wouldn't be at home outside her circle of wild high school friends. But she was really afraid of losing her sway over me.

That whole summer she toiled away on the elevated plywood deck, eyeing me warily as I sat in a ragged lawn chair doing my summer reading. She circled me like a predatory cat, and I was blissfully unaware of her prowling, happily absorbed as I was in my stack of books (and the carafe filled with spiked lemonade that we replenished lavishly throughout the day, growing more heavy-handed with the vodka as the sun drew lower in the sky). I was happy, elated, caught up in my academic fantasies, while Zelda was growing increasingly anxious to devise a scheme that would keep me caught up in her drama. And boy, did she achieve that, though I wouldn't know it for several years.

The door to the Airstream is ominously ajar. I slam the truck's door and hop up the semi-sanded steps, an image flashing before me of Zelda with her orbital sander, cursing these steps. "Our fucking paterfamilias had to go and destroy the belt sander while he was wasted, and now I'm trying to sand the steps with this rinky-dink piece of shit." She furiously lit a cigarette and stared malevolently at the off-kilter stairs. I looked up from *Lolita* and laughed at her, standing there in her cutoff shorts, engineer boots, and bikini top. Gypsy hair, wild corkscrews shooting off from her head, and her dark tan made her eyes look terrifying. I had slathered on coats of SPF 50 all summer long, and Zelda's newly tawny skin successfully marked the two of us as distinct beings. That summer, we looked different. I washed my hair religiously, combing and straightening it so that it looked tame and silky, while Zelda's raven hair was just short of dreadlocked glory. Her eyeliner was dark and messy, while I wore just a smidge of sedately hued eye shadow. All our lives, we had embraced our spooky similarity, opting for the same haircut, same makeup. Different clothes, always, but clothes can be swapped, inducing all kinds of Shakespearean identity mishaps. Not that summer, though. She had giggled right back at me and flopped onto the deck chair next to mine.

"Fuck this foolishness," she declared. "We'll all just have to deal with the splinters and drag them around as reminders of benevolent neglect. Mine and Marlon's both. How does it go, something something beam in the eye?"

"You're proposing that we all suffer through beams in our feet?"

"If that's what it takes!"

"You're drunk," I point out.

"Judge not lest . . ."

"And you're mixing your biblical references."

"Yes, but they all address hypocrisy. So there. Take that. Come swimming with me, please. You're sweaty."

"Always telling me what I am," I mock-complain.

"No, I usually leave that to you, boss lady." I let her tug me away from my book and we ran down to the dock, close in step, our feet moving in pace. I imagine that if you saw us from the side we would have looked like one body moving together. Fillies in dressage. Running with her, I felt whole, as though I was what I was meant to be. In the water, we splashed happily until Wyatt showed up with beverage reinforcements and joined us, to romp in a cozy haze of vodka. And happiness.

I enter the Airstream and my breath is nearly sucked out of me. It smells so much like Zelda that it physically slams into me. *I don't think you're dead, Zaza. But God, I've missed you.* I've been pretending for the past two years that I can live without her, that I don't miss her with a visceral, embodied ache, all the time. Pretending that what happened severs the phantom umbilical cord that has tethered us together for more than two decades. As I look around the trailer, every cranny of it steeped in Zelda, I realize that I've been fucking kidding myself. I want my sister so bad it hurts. And I realize, suddenly, that that's what she's been trying to do. This entire scheme—the fire, her supposed death—is a little show, a spectacle for my benefit. She'd had enough of my punishment, and this is her saying: *You can't ignore me, Ava, you can't live without me. You can't get away from Silenus, you can never leave ME.*

Scarves, fabric, textiles, prints cover all the walls. I can see at least three of Zelda's colorful kimonos draped on various surfaces. The bed is rumpled, unmade, and I sit down on it, holding a pillow to my face, breathing in her scent. There's a lump in my throat that I'm working very hard to dislodge. Maybe I've overreacted, these past two years. Could I have been blowing it out of proportion? It was a betrayal, yes. And what happened afterward doesn't even bear dwelling on. But maybe . . . Then I realize that Zelda is manipulating me without having to say a single word, and I toss her pillow across the room in frustration.

The pillow takes out a lamp on its way, and I lean my head back, annoyed, unsure why I've come to the trailer after all. Just to feel close to Zelda? No, to figure out what game she's playing. We're playing. Who on earth is Jason? And the locked barn doors? I suspect her of staging everything, but why let the police think it's murder? If she was going to fake her own death, she'd only be making everything more complicated by leaving clues suggesting that it was not accidental. Why risk alerting the cops that all is not as it seems? My recent fixation on Poe immediately makes me think: locked-room mystery. As though she knows how this would tantalize me.

I get up and pad around the trailer, looking at Zelda's artifacts. A bizarre ceramic sculpture here, a spent candle toppled onto its side next to a pile of sketch notebooks carelessly scattered on the table. Good way to start a fire. The trailer is cluttered with years of Zelda's accumulated disarray. I pick up a dish full of sad-looking apples and chuck them into the garbage. I'm straightening stacks of books and moving glasses to the kitchen sink before I even realize what I'm doing. Tidying up after Zelda, like always. I stop in exasperation and almost storm out of the Airstream, fed up with myself and with my sister, filled with that itchy combination of fatigue and anxiety that my entire family produces in me. An allergic reaction for which antihistamines can do nothing. I want a drink.

But as I prepare to walk out the door, I pause and look in Zelda's favorite "secret place." Our whole lives, she's been obsessed with secrets, and as a girl, she liked to squirrel away notes, money, tiny treasures in hiding places all over the vineyard. I double back to the bed and lean down along the side. The carpet is loose in this corner, and I peel it back, revealing a small hole. Zelda systematically used these secret places after the first time our mother called the cops on her and she got busted, at fifteen, with a dime bag in her pocket and a quarter ounce in her bedroom (one hundred hours of community service, probation). I remember her fishing a baggie of pills out of this corner during my first semester of college. She always told me that I knew where all her secret places were, that I was the only one who knew all of them. I believed her for years.

My fingers curve around something cold and rectangular, and I pull an iPhone out of the hole. Zelda's real phone. I wonder briefly what phone the cops found. What she intended them to find. The battery is low—it's probably been in there for at least two days—but I can still turn it on. Password protected. I try her old PIN for her bank cards; she used to have only one PIN for everything, because she claimed she couldn't be bothered to buy into some paranoid fantasy that there were people out to thieve her identity or scoop the twenty-three dollars from her savings account. It doesn't work.

I'm busy frowning at the screen, thinking, when I hear someone pull up outside. I stand up and peer out from the mismatched curtains. I know that truck. My mouth dries up and my heart is suddenly clamoring to get out of my chest. I can't tear myself away as the door swings open and a familiar body stretches out from the driver's seat, unfurling long legs. I walk numbly to the Airstream's door, realizing that it's here, the conversation I have resolutely avoided for two years. It's going to happen. I'm tempted to hide, to evade, but I'm in a fucking trailer with exactly three feet of room to maneuver, and I know it's time. I slide the phone into my pocket, and I swing the door open, trying desperately to look composed.

"Hey there, Wyatt." His face freezes, and his whole body tenses at the sight of me in the doorway. "You look like you've seen a ghost."

# 4

May 20, 2016 at 11:38 PM

Dear Disapproving, Uptight Twat of a Sister,

Fine. You want me to talk about it, confess? I can do that. It seems my self-flagellation is a prerequisite to your speaking to me, so here goes. I have our mother's blood. I am ready to be a martyr.

Wyatt loved *you.* Since tenth grade, at least. I think he started doodling your combined names in his notebooks around then, embarking on his wholesome fantasy of your blissed-out heterosexual future. Ava Antipova no longer, now Ava Darling. Literally. Wyatt's last name has always been too good to be true; first name, too, for that matter. I know he lusted after your pristine purity, your clean button-downs and tailored jeans, your fitted-waist striped gowns that are crying out (still) for a clambake in Cape Cod. That's the sort of thing they do in Cape Cod, right? I've never been, as you know; I only have the apocryphal tidbits you regaled me with after the vacation you took with that unbelievably white girl after sophomore year, to the beaches that spawned our mother. Wyatt always admired your clean, restrained prettiness, how your hair was always tidy, how you always wear that delicate smirk on your face, like you're busy cleverly narrating everything. All the things other people find infuriating about you, Wyatt loved. But you can keep a man at arm's length for only so long, Ava dear, before you run the risk of him straying. Sounds like something Grandma Opal would say, right?

Let me sketch out a narrative for you, since I know how you love them, crave them, cook them up. I'm the one with a useless (half) degree in The Arts, but you, with your practical, analytical brain, always need to know how we got where we are. So how does this sound?

Boy and Girl go to the same hick high school. Boy is tall and strapping, bright for these parts. Not much money, but from a sweet, wholesome family who all LOVE EACH OTHER. Girl is pretty, smart as a whip, and desperate to erase her own family's insanity, to transition to more sedate familial pastures. Boy is fairly smitten with Girl; strangely, Boy can sense the intense vulnerability that lurks behind all that careful togetherness. He sees the fragile underself that Girl tries desperately to mask with her control. Girl clearly likes Boy, BUT: Girl has gigantic stick up her ass, and Girl (due to a number of actually very reasonable justifications resulting from a traumatic upbringing with an emotionally withholding psychopath—I mean Mom, not me or Dad, ha ha) is unable to tolerate any sort of emotional vulnerability at all. So, she keeps Boy close for years, permitting certain liberties, *ahem*, but maintaining a strict emotional distance. A psychological moat. She strings Boy along in this infuriating fashion for some time. Years, like, seven of them. Boy is a good sport, but Boy is a boy, and Boy eventually weakens when Girl disappears for a few months without alerting anyone where she has gone. Girl is generally presumed to have absconded with Another Man.

Which is when Boy, primed by years of loving someone who is

unable to love, turns to Other Girl, who happens to resemble Girl quite a bit. They could almost be copies of each other. Boy sees in Other Girl some of the same vulnerability, mirrored in Other Girl through a startling level of recklessness and disregard. Boy starts drinking a bit more than usual (he is finally over twenty-one now, after all, legally allowed to indulge) and spends time with Other Girl. Other Girl knows this is dangerous, but Other Girl is also lonely, and feels abandoned and slightly pissed off and/or vengeful. She knows Girl will come home eventually, but in the meantime, out of lonely desperation, she entertains a fantasy that Boy likes her for herself, and that she, Other Girl, might have an actual CONNECTION WITH A PERSON, a person who is not her identical twin. In short, she kids herself. Tells herself lies. Cooks up a story of her own.

Boy pines for Girl, as he has since the tenth grade, and then, one night, there is wine and equinoctial skinny-dipping and human nature, and Boy and Other Girl find themselves in an . . . uncomfortable situation. They can't take it back, though, and both are beginning to doubt that Girl cares for either of them one whit. It has been a long, sexually tense winter of uncertainty. So Boy spends the rest of the spring in Other Girl's trailer. And Girl finds this out in the worst way possible when she returns home unannounced. A confrontation occurs, and shit goes even more horribly wrong, if that's possible, and a few things happen that might be considered irreversible, but which are really just the result of a lot of pent-up libidinous energy and the immoderation of youth. Everyone regrets what happened immediately, deeply, but Girl wigs out (rather disproportionately, in Other Girl's humble opinion). Girl then impulsively storms off to Paris to get a PhD, something she was only vaguely threatening to do before the whole fiasco, and she skips town in a huff, without a word to Boy or to Other Girl, with whom she shares, like, one hundred percent of her DNA. Wanting to preserve the air of tortured mystery, like all wounded young people.

That sound right, Ava? I'm not trying to deflect blame or imply that you forced us into it. I'm pretty sure I could make that case, but I know that would infuriate you, so I won't bother. You loved him, in your way, but your way was so damned cold. You let him pretend, played along just enough, but you never thought it was real. I remember how you used to talk about him, how undecided you were: "He's sweet, and just *right* in so many ways, but sometimes I look at him and think I wouldn't mind if he disappeared forever." Remember saying that? You said he was paper-thin, and you projected a story onto him, to make the whole thing palatable. It was a game for you. Once, cruelly, you said: "If he had been born to different parents, he would probably be a Republican." Absolute condemnation.

So you twiddled your thumbs and kept yourself at arm's length and just waited for something to happen so you could throw up your hands and say, "Ha! I knew it was doomed, I knew I was right to emotionally protect myself! Shove off, you cad!" Just like our fucking mother, who loved Marlon more than anything but literally drove him off the farm because she was so certain everything would eventually go to shit anyway. Maybe I'm finessing *that* narrative a little; another email and we'll do the whole Nadine and Marlon saga. It is useful for our purposes here merely to point out that you were doing the only thing that made sense to you, as a product of *that* particular shitshow, and I see why you did what you did. But I thought I was maybe helping you (stop scoffing). I thought if you were forced to acknowledge how upset you were that Wyatt was with someone else, you would maybe have to acknowledge Wyatt himself. To acknowledge that whatever was between you wasn't paper-thin, not anymore, that you'd played along with the game too long and now it meant something. I wanted that for him too. I may not harbor the same repressed sexual longing for him that you have all these years, but I grew up with the boy, too, and he was around quite a bit. I care for the kid, and I really wanted him to stop moping, to either go for it (you) or move on. Not that I'm claiming altruism. I would never. Not ever. And then That Night happened and everything was moot after that, wasn't it.

Our birthday is in 10 days. Come home, would you? Or I'll end up doing something crazy.

Your Ever-Apologetic, Well-Intentioned, but Deeply
Fucked-Up Sister,
Z is for Zelda

I glare at Wyatt from the doorway of the trailer, my heart skipping in harrowed beats. I haven't seen him in nearly two years, and he looks *good*. Dark hair cropped close, pretty brown eyes wide and warm. His biceps certainly haven't gone anywhere in the last year or two. He's wearing jeans and a frayed T-shirt; no one dresses well in this part of the world, and Wyatt has always been negligent of anything fashion-conscious. I feel a flash of guilt, thinking of Nico, who always wears trim button-down shirts and pressed trousers. Nico wears *scarves*, for chrissakes. He owns not just one but multiple scarves, scarves for different occasions, different types of Parisian precipitation. He is nothing like Wyatt, whose substantial arms are already brown and threaded with muscle, even this early in the summer. I swallow hard.

"Jeez, Ava," Wyatt says, his hands raised in surprise. "You scared the shit out of me."

"Didn't expect anyone to catch you over here?" I'd like to be less nasty, but I'm still so pissed. I thought the hurt had faded in Paris, only here it is, raw and weeping pus.

"No, not really. I thought I'd just come and . . . look around. See if everything was okay over here. I know Zelda always leaves the doors unlocked, and she'd been hanging out with some unsavory characters." Wyatt loves noir films. Unironically. He uses terms like "unsavory characters" and "in a tight spot." I suspect he's drawn to the notion of integrity, a serious man doing his job without compromising.

"The cops didn't even have to break in. Helpful, our Zelda was."

He flinches. "She wasn't, and you know it," he says shortly, and I can't help but chuckle.

"No. The whole thing is rather suspicious. But fuck. It's . . . Zelda." I sit down suddenly, on the steps, unable to stand for another second. Looking at Wyatt, seeing his face lined with grief and alarm, I believe for the first time that Zelda might actually be dead. He looks like he believes it, and he's seen a bit more of her in the last two years than I have. Wyatt moves toward me, but I glare at him and he stops, awkwardly cramming his hands into his pockets. His shoulders are huge.

"Will there be a funeral, Ava?" he asks softly, like he doesn't want to rile me.

"We have to wait for the death certificate, or the coroner's report, I guess. She hasn't been officially ruled dead. I think they're sifting through the ashes for her teeth, or something. But yeah, as soon as that happens, there will be. My dad won't want to stay forever and I . . ." I don't want to talk about Paris. "And I think it would be better to just get it over with. Not drag this out."

"I'd like to help, if I can. With all the details, the food."

"Wyatt Darling, always the good guy."

"No. Not always."

"Maybe not."

"Ava . . . it's really good to see you. Even like this." I nod. I glance at him, scanning his face and body for subtext.

I think we became friends because I never could tell what Wyatt was thinking, I never actually knew. I lived in a house with someone who threw every item of clothing you owned onto the lawn if you spilled iced tea in the dining room. I had been so attracted to someone who just looked at me sleepily and made me *wonder* what was going on.

Now the mystery feels old. I look up at him, elbows propped on my knees, trying to think of something to say. The quiet stretches uncomfortably. Wyatt scuffs the dirt with his farm-boy boots, grubby, worn-in, and practical.

"I've really missed you," he says after a minute. He pauses uncertainly. "Zelda and I . . . that's what we mostly talked about, you know, missing you."

"How nice that you were able to bond. You know Zelda was fucking with you, right? Or, rather, fucking with me by fucking you?"

"I thought so at first, yeah." Wyatt nods agreeably, slowly, not taking the bait. "But the last few months, I started to think maybe not. She was really lonely, your sister." He's achingly earnest, and I can't help feeling a twist of guilt.

"Zelda didn't experience emotions like 'loneliness.' Jealousy maybe, and certainly revenge."

"Revenge isn't an emotion. Vengefulness?" Wyatt says playfully. I roll my eyes. Wyatt is still standing, with his hands in his pockets, looking like he wants to sit down on the step next to me. I don't offer.

"Did you want to get anything in particular?" I ask, waving at the trailer behind me. "Did you leave behind a pair of boxers or something? Boxers, right? You used to wear boxers."

"Ava, we hadn't—"

"I really don't want details. I don't care how many times you fucked. How *vulnerable* you both felt because I left, or how *comforted* you were by each other. That is your business, and hers. Get whatever you came for and go," I snap, my patience gone. Wyatt looks at me, waiting for me to soften. Before everything happened between him and Zelda, this outburst would have shocked him; he would have blushed, ducked his shoulders, and mumbled an apology. Clearly, my sister has had a toughening influence on him. When I say nothing and refuse to meet his eyes, he shrugs and snakes by me to enter the trailer. As his leg brushes my shoulder, I smell his familiar aroma: clean denim, lemon soap, evaporated sweat, grapevines, dirt. I shut my eyes. How have we gotten here?

I hear Wyatt rustling in the trailer for a few moments, and he re-emerges with a big sweatshirt in his arms that I recognize as his, and a puzzled expression on his face.

"Where's Zelda's phone?" he asks. I crane my head to squint back at him.

"Cops took it."

"Both of them?"

I look up at him sharply. "What do you mean, both of them?"

"For the past month or so she'd been dragging around a burner phone, you know, one of those cheap TracFones? She mostly texted with it, but she was all secretive whenever she took it out. Refused to answer questions, made coy little comments. I just figured she was baiting me." Wyatt shrugs again. The boy is too laid-back for his own good: the perfect toy for Zelda. And me.

"Well, the cops said they took the phone. I don't know which phone they meant. I didn't ask. Too busy imagining her skin crisping up as the barn caved in on her."

Wyatt just raises his eyebrows, scanning my face. He seems uncharacteristically watchful, as though he's inspecting me for the first time and finds me strange. Zelda's iPhone feels gigantic in my pocket, and it's hard to believe that he can't see its distinctive shape from where he's standing behind me.

"If you find it, can you let me know?" He peers at my face. "I'd like to check her call history. She was cagey that night. Canceled plans with me. I was supposed to come over to the big house, but she called it off, and sounded all sketchy on the phone. I'm worried she might have been using again."

"Again?" I ask, startled. Eyebrow raised, he looks at me with that same scrutiny, so un-Wyatt-like. He's wary of me, no longer worshipful. I realize in the space of a breath that I have hurt him, that he is looking at me that way because I caused him damage. Zelda's the destructive one, not me, I feel like protesting. But that's not true anymore, is it? Wyatt's face is proof of that.

"Ava, you've been gone a long time. Zelda was getting desperate.

Things on Silenus have been, well, rough and she . . ." He trails off, but I can hear the blame in his voice.

"She was alone," I finish. "I wasn't here with her."

"She's had a weird few months. She needed . . . someone."

"She had you."

"I've helped a bit with the vineyard side of things, but she needed something else. She knew that I—" He pauses, considering his words. "She knew that I wanted you, always have and always will. And having me around sometimes made it worse for her, that you weren't here," he finishes simply.

I don't know what to say.

"Anyway," he goes on, "I'm glad I found you here. I was going to stop by your house next, make sure you were okay."

Again, I say nothing.

"Well, Ava? Are you?"

"I'll be fine." I wave my hand dismissively. I can't talk to Wyatt about how I am. Not now. Maybe not ever.

"You've always been tough," he answers. "I just was thinking— well, I can't imagine what it's like for you. To lose her." His throat sounds raw, and as I look at those beautiful brown eyes of his, I realize he's been crying recently, and may resume doing so shortly. He's grieving. I'm suddenly, savagely jealous. He has spent the day weeping over my sister, missing *her*, imagining a life without her. Irrationally, unforgivably, I want him to still think only and always of me.

"Will *you* be okay? You seem rather distraught," I snipe.

"Jesus, of course I'm distraught! I've known that girl most of my life. She was there during—everything. Christ, I thought we'd maybe be family someday." He shakes his head as though he can't really believe me. I don't like being judged by Wyatt. Not having him on my side.

"And of course, you were sleeping with her for a while there."

"For fuck's sake, Ava! How many times do I have to say it? We didn't want each other that way. It was just . . . a mistake," he finishes weakly, as though he physically can't keep trying to convince me. He seems so heavy, so sad. I want to comfort him, but also to punish him. Once upon a time, if I had seen him in this much pain, I would have wrapped my arms around his ribs, kissed his temple, said anything to make him smile. Now I do nothing, unable to go toward him.

"You should leave that here," I manage, pointing at the high school track sweatshirt. Wyatt ran the thousand meters at Watkins Glen High, and I know the back of the shirt will say "Darling" in white letters, and the front will have "Senecas," the name of the team, scrawled across it. There is a racist drawing of a Native American in a headdress beneath the letters. This sweatshirt reminds me, of course, of our first time together.

It was a chilly day in early, early spring. We were in twelfth grade. Wyatt had pulled a muscle at track practice and was staying home from school, sprawled on the couch watching movies. I texted him during the midmorning break to see how he was, and he responded, Lonely. Come visit me? I nearly wrote back with my usual deflection, something sarcastic or insincere, but as Zelda and I milled around the hallway before the third-period bell rang, I paused.

"I'm going to go over to Wyatt's," I said, almost testing the idea out.

"Oh?" Zelda responded archly. "To take his temperature and tend to his wounds?"

"Something like that." I texted him back: Ok, will dodge the rest of my classes. Be there in a bit. Zelda stared at me, trying to determine whether I was joking. "I'm serious. I'm going to go check on him."

"The Ice Princess caves at last!" she cooed. "I sincerely thought Wyatt Darling would expire from blue balls before you ever allowed him to even hope."

I couldn't help smiling. True, I had been keeping Wyatt pretty solidly in the friend zone for years now, redirecting his amorous intentions just enough to prevent him from abandoning all optimism. But suddenly, I was tired of it. Tired of just being wanted. I wanted to want.

"Go, skedaddle, ye wee harlot!" Zelda shrieked.

"What about my classes?" I paused, already talking myself out of it.

"I'll figure it out. Just scram, before you change your mind. God bless, that boy can finally wipe that hungry look off his face and we can all have a minute of peace."

"Are you sure?"

"Completely! Go!" Zelda shoved me toward the parking lot, thrusting her recently acquired truck keys into my hands. "I'll cover for you." I broke into a silly grin and legged it out the front door of the high school.

I let myself in through the front door of the Darlings' and climbed the stairs to his room. We had spent hours in that room, listening to music, talking, watching movies. Sometimes with Zelda, sometimes just the two of us. Wyatt was propped up on pillows in his bed, his bum leg elevated. He wore only his pajama bottoms, and I couldn't help staring at his hard abdomen.

"Hi," I said, lacking inspiration.

"Hi," he answered softly. I went and stood next to the bed. I reached out and put my hand on his chest, and Wyatt closed his eyes and swallowed noticeably. I pulled my T-shirt over my head and unhooked my bra, so that I stood there in just my jeans.

"Oh, God. Ava," Wyatt managed, and reached for me.

"No, you're unwell. You'd better let me do the work," I said, pushing him back and then unbuttoning my jeans.

Afterward, I lay on his chest, absently flicking his nipple with my fingernail.

"Careful, girl, or you'll start something up again," Wyatt said into my snarled hair.

"Maybe that's what I have in mind."

"Lord, you have to give me a minute to recover." He laughed. "I'm a poor, sick man! I need sustenance."

"Very well. I'm here to care for you, after all. Florence Nightingale, that's me." I rolled across his naked torso, slowly, and stood stark naked in his bedroom. I fished his sweatshirt off the floor and pulled it over my head. It came down nearly to my knees.

"You're so beautiful," Wyatt whispered. I twirled around and skipped out of the room to go forage for something downstairs, returning with some sort of homemade cheese (compliments of Dora, Wyatt's mom) and cold beers. We spent the rest of the day in Wyatt's bed, watching from beneath his blanket as the March sleet splattered the windows. Cozy, warm. And whole.

"I'll put it back," I say, pointing to the sweatshirt. "The cops said they were going to come back and search the trailer again. It might look weird if you remove, you know, evidence."

Wyatt looks surprised. "Do they think there might be foul play?"

"Isn't there always foul play, with Zelda?" I say wearily. He smiles his old lopsided smile, and it hurts me. I need him to leave. He hands me the sweatshirt wordlessly and bounds down the trailer steps. He unthinkingly skips the last step, which is too close to the ground and always makes for an awkward dismount if you don't expect it. He's climbed these stairs a few times before. Zelda fucked up the measurements and never went back to fix it. I'm the perfectionist, not Zelda. I hold the sweatshirt in my arms as Wyatt walks back toward his truck, parked next to Zelda's. The trucks look like twins.

"Ava, you call me, okay? We're not done talking." It sounds almost like an order, chiding. That new note of judgment. I nod. I manage to wait until he has turned the truck around and driven off before I burst into frenzied, racking tears.

I sit on the steps of the trailer, going to pieces in a theatrical display that would make Zelda proud. I cried when I got my mother's email, but in delicate, ladylike shudders, while Nico held me and rubbed my back like I was a sleeping cat. Those first tears were tears of dismay at my family: my demented mother, who chose to get ahold of me that way; my absent father, who should have been there; my lunatic sister, who was fucking with all of us. But now I cried out of guilt. Because I had left, twice now, and with disastrous effect both times. I cried because I had left Zelda stuck here, tethered to the vines and to our mother like some maiden sacrifice, while I had flounced across Paris, happily bumming Gauloises cigarettes all the while. I had left her with a failing vineyard and an ailing parent, and I had refused even to speak to her. Wyatt was right; she had needed me, and I'd been off having a hissy fit because she'd slept with someone I had. And what if I had now lost both of them?

I had always cared about possession; as a girl, I'd hoarded the few dolls and stuffed animals I owned (my mother thought most toys were tacky and amounted to bribery, and she felt that it demeaned her to have to bribe a five-year-old). I was obsessed with their being "mine." I would stack them on my neatly made bed, and anyone who wanted to touch them would have to ask my permission, which I only occasionally granted. Zelda, on the other hand, barely cared. Our grandmother Opal gave us American Girl dolls when we were seven or eight; I chose Josefina, who was a recent addition to the American Girl family (a gesture of racial diversity after the dazzling whiteness of Kirsten, Samantha, and Molly), because she most closely resembled me and Zelda. Amazing how "vaguely Slavic" and "Mexican" looked the same in the American Girl universe. Zelda went for Addy, the escaped slave doll, whose story Zelda immediately replaced with that of "Amazon warrior queen." When Zelda and Addy kidnapped Josefina during a tribal raid, I took every one of Zelda's stuffed animals and brought them outside (I had seen my mother do this with our belongings countless times—leave a sweater on the floor, it ends up in the yard). I dug a hole in our front yard and buried them all in shallow graves under the sparse grass, a plushy cemetery.

Surprisingly, my sister was unruffled. Usually, Zelda was prone to transfigure from quietly scheming force into berserker, whirling like an exuberant dervish in a haze of deranged, violent joy. But after the furry burial, she bided her time. She waited so long that I thought she had forgotten, or forgiven. One day, the skies over the lake darkened and there was a torrential downpour for hours. When the rain stopped, Zelda calmly informed our mother of my misdeed. Nadine told us that now Josefina belonged to Zelda, as she had no other toys. I dug up the stuffed animals, which had been marinating in mud, and even put them in the washing machine in an attempt to get Josefina back, but Zelda wouldn't budge. She didn't want Josefina for herself, but she had learned that I did, and she sacrificed her own menagerie to win the game.

I cry helplessly, remembering this, feeling like the bratty child I was at eight, vindictively punishing Zelda, though punishing only myself in the end. Even now, I can't tell whether I feel remorse because I'd made Zelda suffer alone out here or because now I am suffering, and I don't know how to put it back how it was before. I'd been living on my own in a foreign country for nearly two years, and after just one full day of being back on Seneca Lake I had regressed to feeling like a child.

I clutch Wyatt's sweatshirt, and even though it's a hot day, I pull it on. It smells like him and like Zelda, like the two of them together, which makes me cry even harder, but it feels good, and I breathe in deeply, moaning softly into my knees. My wailing is almost self-indulgent, but it helps.

"What happened, Zelda?" I sob into my legs. "I can't do this without you." I've been rocking on the porch step for a few minutes when the phone in my pocket vibrates. I sniff and fumble to get the phone out of my pants. Faced with the password-protected screen, I try her usual password again, the last four digits of the house phone. No luck. I try our birthday, 0531, which doesn't work either. Then I smile, remembering Zelda's disdain for passwords, and go for 0000. *Z* is for *zero*. The screen disappears, and I'm left with her background image. It's a picture of both of us, age fourteen. I'm rolling my eyes and standing primly next to Zelda, who is jumping in the air, a halo of her insane curls encircling both our heads. She's wearing a strange knee-length caftan and has a forearm full of bangles; I've got on a snug floral sundress and ballerina flats. I smile, remembering that day.

I notice that the mail icon has several new messages, and I tap it open. There are six or seven new emails, and I scroll through them. All but the most recent are ads. The last one, from one minute ago, is from Zelda herself. I freeze and look around nervously, as though I'll see her lurking somewhere nearby. I open the message.

To: zazazelda@gmail.com
From: zazazelda@gmail.com
Subject: A Brief Correspondence from Beyond the Grave
June 23, 2016 @ 11:42 AM

Ahoy, Ava!

Welcome home, my sweet jet-setting twin!

So glad you were able to wrest yourself away from your dazzling life in the City of Light; I hope my "death" hasn't interrupted anything too crucial. I'm sure you've run into Wyatt already, and I doubt that you two just fell into each other's arms, filled with remorse at the squandered years. Bet you made him squirm, Ava. But (and this is a recent development) I bet he made you squirm a bit, too; he's not the gormless, innocent boy you left behind. I hope you don't mind my improvements.

Well, what's the gossip? Am I dead, or am I "just being Zelda"? What does Dad think? I'm sure Mom has been too pickled and loopy to assert an opinion either way. She probably doesn't even think I'm gone, with you there to fill the holes. Just think of how you could permanently damage my relationship with Mother, with her presuming you to be me! Such an opportunity. And you could remain the talented, ambitious sister living a full life away from her clutches, while I (you) torment her with your frustration and indifference back at home. Such fun!

I'm sure you never really thought I was dead. I mean, you maybe considered it, but I doubt you really believed it. That would fuck all your plans up, that would make you the mean twin who let her sister die alone in a fatal blaze, never having forgiven her now-dead twin for a childish mistake, a few evenings of thought-lessness. That would make *you* the sister who ditched her respon-sibilities, her training, and flew the coop, leaving her (woefully underprepared) sister to take care of all the tasks they were sup-posed to share. Of course you couldn't entertain *that* reality; it would portray you in a bad light. So all along you've figured I'm still running around out there, up to my old tricks.

You're going to come look for me, right? Hide-and-seek, Ava, your favorite game. But, for once, you won't be able to just cram yourself into some impossibly tiny space and wait for me to lose my patience and call "Olly olly oxen free!" This time you're look-ing for me.

So: What am I up to? Hint: Your first piece of the puzzle is nearby.

Your ever-playful sister,
Z is for Zelda

Speechless, I stare at the phone for a long time. Tears have dried on my face, leaving it tight and salty. I'm sweating into Wyatt's sweatshirt, my scent mixing with his and Zelda's, but I still don't take it off, even though the temperature is climbing toward ninety. The phone rests in my lap, and I spin through endless possibilities. But only one blinks clearly at me through my hazy thoughts.

Zelda is alive.

I knew it.

Where has she been skulking for the past two and half days? She must have a friend, someone she can hide out with. I'd bet good money that it's not Wyatt. He's never been a good liar; he's got some ex-tremely blatant tells. I frown at that, thinking of the conversation we just had. Evidently, Wyatt has changed. Only I don't think he's changed enough to be able to lie to my face about my ostensibly deceased twin, given everything.

Who has she spent time with in the last few years? Of course I have no idea, having subjected her to a transcontinental silent treatment. Wyatt might be able to help me there. Maybe some of the vineyard people will know, too, having maybe seen friends lolling around with Zelda. She's not a terribly social person, though, and I'm betting it will be a short list. But she's also not the sort to go on an indefinite camping trip in the wilderness, so I think she's probably got some sort of friendly shelter to duck into while she plays her little games. I know I should be annoyed with her, but right now I just feel relieved. And vindicated.

The feeling completely dissipates when a phone starts ringing. For half a second I think it's Zelda's phone again, and my heart beats faster before I realize that it's my own, vibrating from the bag at my feet. I grab it and see that the number on the screen is the house phone at Nadine's. I answer, knowing that whatever this is, it's probably not good.

"Hello?"

"Ava? It's Marlon. Your dad."

"I suspected. Mom's weird about the phone. I'm pretty sure she's barely touched it the last two years. Thinks she's being 'monitored.'"

"I think you should come home, kiddo, your mother's . . . on the loose."

"I won't even begin to guess what that means," I say dispiritedly.

"I, uh, fell asleep for a while and woke up to realize she was . . ."

"What, Dad?"

"Well, gone. She seems to have taken off—thought I should let you know." He sounds a little ashamed. Quite rightly.

"Because you don't really feel like going after her?"

"I would, it just seems . . . unwise." I realize suddenly that he's speaking very slowly, not quite slurring his words but sounding less than entirely sober.

"Are you drunk?" I snap at the phone.

"No. Well, not really. I just took one of your mother's sedatives. Two of them. And I had a glass of wine with lunch."

"Just a glass, huh?" He's mincing his words, chewing on them, gnashing them into easily pronounced pieces so they come out comprehensible, digestible. I recognize the tic—I do it myself. I sigh. "And I assume you unlocked her door?"

"I went in to check on her. I guess . . . I forgot."

"I'll drive back now. I'm at Zelda's trailer. She can't have gotten too far." I smash the disconnect button before he can say anything else, charm me into not being pissed that he only had to babysit Nadine for a few hours and couldn't even manage to keep it together that long. Shaking my head, I swing back into the truck. Part of me is strangely pleased, though—only at home, with my family, am I not the drunken, irresponsible mess. With these people, I'm the one you call in a pinch, the one who shows up to fix a problem. I'm enjoying it.

Mom has not, as it turns out, gotten very far at all. I find her at the top of the drive that leads down to the fields and to Zelda's trailer. She's wearing an expensive-looking silk robe, a bra, and a pair of high-waisted underpants that would look matronly on any other woman her age but that my mother is rocking, even as she sways in the dust of the tractor path, appearing disoriented and scared.

"Zelda, where have you been?" she whimpers to me when I lurch out of the cab of the truck, wobbly with relief. I can tell she wants to sound imperious, but she comes off as upset. She teeters, looking profoundly unstable. I glance at her feet, which strike me as older than any other part of her body. She's barefoot, and one of her toes is bleeding. It seems like she scraped the skin off tripping on the pavement. She's twitching subtly, a bobble to her head. That will be the dementia.

"Momma, what are you doing? You're supposed to be home." I open the door and grab her by the elbow, preparing to hoist her up. She shrieks and pulls her elbow away.

"You're fucking hurting me." She scowls.

"Sorry, Mom. Hop in the truck, though?" I'm wheedling, but I just want to get her inside. God knows how many people have seen her wandering around in her knickers. I imagine this isn't the first time, though. She looks at me suspiciously.

"Only because I'm tired now," she grants haughtily. I roll my eyes and help her into the cab. "Honestly, where were you, Zelda? I missed lunch, and my midday treat." The word sounds childish and tentative.

"Oh?" I glance over at her curiously.

"You didn't come in to do my nails at lunchtime. So I came looking for you."

"Zelda—I—do your nails every day?" I ask, shocked.

"God, Zaza, and they say I'm the one losing my faculties. Yes, dear, don't you see I'm wearing yesterday's color?" She waggles her fingers at me, and I look briefly away from the road to see that they are painted a pale pink. I didn't notice yesterday. "Today is azure," she spells out. It is unfathomable to me that my sister would paint my mother's nails. This is a universe I don't recognize.

"I'm sorry, Mom. I'll take you home, we'll have some lunch, and I'll do your nails after." I stare blankly at the yellow lines on the road.

# 5

Eating a haphazard lunch of vegetables and sandwiches made from ingredients unearthed in the fridge, we sit around the table. I don't eat much, and Nadine seems mainly to push food around on her plate with her shaky hands. I find myself unable to watch her as she trembles her way through the meal.

Marlon is quiet and avoids eye contact with me, and my mother chatters cheerfully about something she's been watching on Netflix. Apparently, Zelda allows Nadine a generous ration of drugs and props her in front of an old laptop that belonged to one of us years ago, and Mom binges on whatever television piques her interest for most of the day, just like your average equally stoned college kid. She spruces up for her evening allotment of wine, which Zelda doles out according to how well she's behaved that day. Peace for Zelda, and unconsciousness for Nadine. I'm fascinated and horrified. It's almost exactly like periods of our childhood, when Nadine administered snacks and TV privileges to whichever girl had been the prettiest, or nicest, or most cooperative, depending on what trait Nadine was feeling preferential toward that day. Predictably, Zelda and I each thought the other received more snacks. I wonder if Mom will start to tally which of her daughters lavishes more alcohol on her.

Marlon looks glazed and sleepy, and I speculate about whether he really took only two of Mom's pills. He doesn't contribute much to the conversation, and I let him nod along without demanding much. When I get up to clear our plates, I cluck at my mother's nearly full one.

"Mom, you have to eat. You've barely touched any of the grilled cheese."

"I'm not hungry, Zelda. Those damn pills."

I frown. "You didn't get your pills today, Mom."

"Oh. Well, I have to stay trim. I just sit in bed all day—I can't be gorging myself on fried cheese." She waves her hand flippantly.

"Mom, you didn't eat any breakfast, and I'll be busy the rest of the afternoon. I won't be able to drop everything and make you a snack whenever you realize you've made a mistake." Marlon jerks his head up to look at me, and I realize in horror that I've repeated verbatim something Nadine used to say to me and Zelda. Marlon's disoriented expression mirrors the way I feel. "Never mind," I add. "It's okay. You should only eat when you're really hungry." This is a toned-down paraphrase of another of her sayings, which she started to crack out more frequently during our high school years, when eating became inextricably linked with dress size and thinness. I clear the table, flustered.

I dismiss Marlon, telling him to go sleep it off. As I help Mom up the stairs, her hands shake and her neck wobbles. I grab her thin arms and steady her as she trudges up the steps. The sound of her footsteps on the stairs used to be a deeply ingrained pattern, one I could recognize anywhere: the fourth step, which creaked more than the others, the solid sound her foot made striking the top landing. But now, with her tentative steps, her gnarled feet encased in terry-cloth ballet slippers, the kind of thing my mother once would never have consented to wear, the sound is distorted, uncanny. I look down at her pink-clad feet and feel a moment of spiteful enjoyment. I wonder what happened to her beautiful soft leather Moroccan slippers that used to whisper up this staircase.

I tuck her into bed and give her an extra sedative, just to ensure peace. I'll end up destroying her liver if I don't get a better way of guaranteeing that she'll stay quiet for a few hours, but that's a long-term concern (I hope), and right now I can only deal with short-term problems. As she's beginning to sink deeper into her pillows, I tug off her department-store slippers and find a drawer filled with nail polish. Azure, she said. Well, I'm not Zelda. I pick a bright magenta and set to work on her toenails. Even though I'm rushing and anxious, my paint job will be significantly better than the one done by Zelda, who never had the patience for this kind of thing. Zelda's makeup always has the same dramatic unkempt swath of black eyeliner; she gets frustrated with neatness. I tidy up the pink streaks that have bled over Nadine's cuticles from Zelda's last attempt and paint two coats of obnoxious purply-pink on top. The result is a bit textured. Nadine's asleep by the time I leave, and I wonder if doing her toes was a wasted gesture. She won't remember it, and I won't get any good-daughter credit. It occurs to me that maybe this was how she thought about parenting us: as an unbalanced checkbook where she never got the sum she had earned.

When Zelda and I were young, maybe eight or nine, we uncovered a fetid nest of mewling baby mice beneath the hood of the old tractor. It was the beginning of summer, and we had been illicitly fooling around on the tractor, in contravention to one of Marlon's very few rules. When the engine heated up, a few rodents scampered frantically from beneath the front end, making a harried beeline for the back field. We flipped open the hood to find the escaped parents' helpless progeny ensconced near the radiator, about to be baked into tiny, unappetizing kebabs. They were hairless, pink, and unpleasant to look at, but we were nevertheless frantic, manically concerned for the little critters' well-being. Certain that their forebears had abandoned them to their toasty end, we resolved to become their ersatz parents, to raise them to healthy, independent mousehood. We scraped the wads of cotton shreds (possibly a masticated remnant of one of my

T-shirts) and straw from the nook within the tractor and transferred the whole bundle, babies and all, to a shoe box. There were four of them, moist and shut-eyed. We hid them beneath Zelda's bed (she insisted) and pilfered one of Marlon's numerous bottles of eyedrops, stashed furtively in his flannel shirt pockets to combat the perpetual red-eye that betrayed his various vices. Nadine was always furiously pulling them out of the dryer, half-melted and frequently having left strange saline stains on shirts, railing against Marlon's carelessness and antipathy.

We emptied the dropper of its salty contents and refilled it with low-fat half-and-half, the richest liquid we could find in the fridge, reheating the makeshift baby bottle in the aging microwave, which Nadine was already beginning to look at suspiciously and accuse of malicious radioactive goings-on. We began a busy feeding schedule for the tiny rodents, and snuck onto the computer to do Internet searches of how to best care for our adopted creatures. Within a day, their wrinkly skin was starting to sag, and they squirmed listlessly, in apparent discomfort, eyelids still sealed shut, unable to see their looming caregivers. Convinced that we weren't feeding them frequently enough, we upped their caloric intake, working our way through nearly all of the container of half-and-half, most of which ended up dribbling pointlessly into the increasingly squalid wad of material on which the babies lay.

On day two, the first one died. We weren't certain enough of its death to discard its body, so we left it with its siblings in the box. It had begun to stink, but the scent of sour dairy concealed the aroma of its miniature dead body and the mouse vomit and excrement that had inevitably accrued inside the box. Only when flies began to gather did we acknowledge its demise. I wanted to dispose of its little corpse, but Zelda grabbed my hand with her own.

"We shouldn't separate it from its brothers and sisters," she whispered, her eyes glimmering with a curiosity I should have questioned. For whatever reason, I listened to her—perhaps unwilling to recognize my own morbidity, I allowed hers to shine through—and we left the shriveled body in the nest. Its remaining siblings were clearly not doing well, but we continued to fondle and nurse them along, in perverse denial of the fact that we were clearly killing them. I remember trying to convince one to suckle at the eyedropper only to realize that it was dead, its body cooling in my hands. I put it back in the box, and we slid the whole arrangement under the bed. Zelda and I went for a sleepover the following night, and in silent, complicit agreement, we made no plans to deal with our feeble, expiring charges. We felt impossibly guilty, and it seemed somehow as though getting rid of their corpses would make our offense real. The trajectory of this ruinous narrative was so fixed as to seem immutable, and any gesture to avert its recognizable conclusion looked hopeless to the point of quixotic bumbling; we were killing them. So we ignored it. Three days later, when Zelda's room smelled distinctly ripe, we took the whole box and flung it into the lake without opening the lid. Early on, we had proved to be disastrous caregivers.

I shut my mother's door softly behind myself and guiltily lock it again. The upstairs of the house is getting hot, even though my mother had it designed to be "energy efficient." Just another deviation from her plans, to have an upstairs that refuses to stay at room temperature, regardless of the weather.

Curled into the rumpled covers of Zelda's bed, I pull out her cellphone, and start flipping through it. No new emails. I open her Facebook app and scroll through her news feed. I recognize a lot of the names. Zelda doesn't have very many friends, and I'm surprised she's on Facebook at all. Curious, I check her home page, and lo and behold, she joined just six months ago and has posted only a few photos. I flip through them quickly, recognizing only Wyatt. There's a picture of the two of them out on a boat somewhere—looks like Seneca Lake, though it could be Cayuga. Neither of them is really smiling, though Wyatt has a slight curl to his mouth. His nose is sunburned. In another photo, Zelda is kissing the cheek of a pretty redhead with a spray of freckles. The girl is tall and skinny, with poky collarbones and a coy smile. She's staring straight at the camera. I have no idea who she is.

The last picture Zelda posted was from the day before the barn burned, June 19. Zelda was photographed in front of Bartoletti Vineyard, the sign looming above her. She stands right in front of the sign, pointing at it with both arms, eyebrows raised meaningfully in an expression I recognize. I read the caption she posted with the photo: "Begin here . . . for a day of wine tasting." I look at Zelda's face again, and I feel a strange certainty that she's posing for me. That the imperative "Begin here" is directed at me. I study her face, reading mischief. I'm suddenly sure she's giving me an order. Bartoletti Vineyard is just a few miles away; the Bartolettis were friends with my dad, while he still lived here. I doubt that they've kept in touch. Marlon isn't great with correspondence; "out of sight, out of mind" is basically his mantra, and he is religiously devoted to not looking backward. I get the impression that Marlon left some business unfinished there.

I cast my eyes over the heaps of clothes lying on Zelda's ragged Turkish rug, scooped up from an estate sale. Zelda loved owning things that belonged to dead people. Half her wardrobe used to belong to someone's deceased grandmother. I snatch a white-and-turquoise caftan from one pile and put it on. Peering into Zelda's jewelry box, I see that all her favorite pieces are still nestled inside. Frowning, I put on her chunky silver bangles. Zelda imbued these things with almost talismanic powers; I can't remember the last time I saw her without those bracelets.

Downstairs, I accidentally wake Marlon, who has been dozing on the couch. He jerks upright with a start and looks at me in revulsion.

"Zelda?" he croaks. I'm tempted to say yes, to play the ghost of Christmas future and warn him that his dissolute ways will only lead him to grief. But looking at his face, I realize he's already there. He looks broken. Worlds worse than he looked yesterday, as though this place has already aged him.

"No, Dad. 'S me. Ava." He slumps in relief, a slightly silly expression on his face. It is unbecomingly lined from the pillow.

"'Course. You, uh, startled me." He straightens up on the couch.

"I'm going out for a bit longer. But you shouldn't have to worry about Mom. She's sleeping, and I locked the door behind her. I'll be back in time for dinner," I reassure him. He nods blankly. I feel sorry for the man. In pity, I almost unlock the liquor cabinet. But then I decide that I really can't afford for him to get into the bourbon; I can look after only one parent at a time.

I clamber into the truck and drive up the lake toward Bartoletti Vineyard, humming softly to myself. An old Russian lullaby our father used to sing.

The Bartolettis have a sprawling, successful operation. Much more so than ours on both counts. Their grapes win awards; people drive across the whole Finger Lakes region to taste their wines. They make a particularly good Riesling, one with a flavor profile I have always coveted and was never able to approximate. They have a slick tasting room with huge antique beams, expensive-looking lighting, an entire wall of temperature-controlled wine storage behind clean glass doors. "Emerging artists" vie for space on the wall to display their uninteresting acrylics. Tourists flock. Affluent locals buy the Bartolettis' sparkling wine for their children's weddings.

As a young, enthusiastic vintner, my father had endeared himself to the Bartoletti patriarch, charmed the matriarch, and gotten himself invited over for bacchanalian feasts where he soaked up as much booze, information, and cannoli as he could from Seneca Lake's wine tycoons. Mr. Bartoletti had always kind of scared the shit out of me. He was a tall, swarthy Italian, now probably in his seventies but still imposing. When we were younger, Zelda convinced me that Mr. Bartoletti was part of the Mafia, that he ruled the underworld of Watkins Glen with an iron fist. This hadn't seemed at all fanciful at the time.

I pull into the drive and park by the tasting room. The vineyard is busy, it seems; the parking lot is mostly full. I bypass the tasting room and head straight for Mr. Bartoletti's office, in front of which is the sign in Zelda's photo. I'm sure that he's in his office, working. My father had desperately wanted there to be some secret to running a wildly successful vineyard, some occult practice that would guarantee a brilliant harvest, like plucking grapes under the full moon or debauching virgins in the fecund fields. But Mr. Bartoletti's secret was much less glamorous. The man worked with a maniacal, dedicated fervor.

I knock on his office door and hear only a grunt. Interpreting that as an invitation to enter, I poke my head into the office. Bartoletti doesn't look up immediately, but when he does, his face turns scarlet.

"Zelda Antipova. You have some gall to show up in this office," he says, visibly seething. "I knew you probably weren't dead. Seemed a tad convenient, given your predicament."

"Sorry, Mr. Bartoletti, it's, um, Ava. Antipova. Zelda's twin." Bartoletti's scowl barely falters.

"Oh. It seemed unlikely your goddamn sister would show her face in here. So, is she dead after all?"

"Looks that way," I say, annoyed. He grunts and makes a show of going back to his paperwork.

"We'll see if it sticks," he grumbles.

"We're hoping for the best," I say ambiguously. He almost smiles but settles for a harrumph. "Can I ask, though, what did you mean, her 'predicament'?"

He looks up at me, assessing. "She managed to keep it a secret?"

"I've been away, overseas. I've just come home to tie up loose ends, and I found a mention of you in some office paperwork—"

"Just a mention?" he spits. "Your goddamn sister owes me a hundred thousand dollars. Or a tractor. An expensive one."

My eyes widen. "What do you mean? She . . . borrowed it from you?"

"She came here desperate last season. A bunch of equipment had crapped out on her, and she was struggling to keep Silenus afloat. I know she got a raw deal, with both your parents out of the picture. How is your father, by the way?" He forces a deeply unpleasant smile.

"Fine," I lie.

"I should have known, after he left the way he did, that your whole family couldn't be trusted. Hucksters. But Zelda just seemed so upset and . . . well, *sincere*, damnit. I went against my judgment and sold her the tractor. To be neighborly. She had only ten grand to give me, on a tractor worth over a hundred." He snorts and shakes his head, clearly disbelieving how easily he had been had. "We worked out a payment plan that we both thought was reasonable. But the first payment was due months ago, and you can guess how much I've received." He leans back in his chair, eyeing me. I focus on not squirming. "You really do look a lot like her."

"Funny thing about identical twins."

He smiles joylessly. "Any chance you're here to settle her debts?" he asks.

I shake my head. "I'm afraid not. I'll go home and look at the books. Like I said, I just got here. And my mother isn't exactly on top of things over at Silenus," I add, hoping to appeal to any shred of compassion he has left. "Looks like you guys are doing well over here."

"Hard work and solid accounting. Not too difficult. Something your father never quite believed," he says.

"Well, Marlon's ambitions sometimes outstrip his resources," I say.

Bartoletti laughs for the first time. "That's the truth. Any chance he'll be stopping by to settle up some outstanding business?"

"Unlikely, but I'm happy to tell him you'd like to see him." I don't even want to know what Marlon left unresolved with this man. I don't ask.

"Listen, dear," he says, softening. "I'm sorry about your family's business. But Silenus is folding. Zelda knew it—she was just too stubborn to face facts. I've let the debt slide a little, hoping she could pull it together with this season, but . . ." He shrugs. "I'm going to have to collect soon."

Something deep in my stomach squeezes. Money. Dealing with it always makes me feel this way. Like my father, I prefer for it just to appear, and keep appearing, without ever having to peek at checking account balances or scribble out a budget. My mother was the only one in the family with an inclination to pinch pennies. Coincidentally, she was the only one with money.

"I understand, Mr. Bartoletti. If you could just give us some more time to get everything in order . . . I have a funeral to organize, and everything in the vineyard is a bit up in the air."

"How long do you think you'll need?"

"As long as you can give us?" I ask, hoping I sound charming and young, rather than pathetic. But I'll settle for pathetic if it gets me what I need.

"I'll give you a month. Then we'll have to treat the whole thing more seriously. This business, it isn't a game or a hobby. Something your family has never seemed to understand." He returns to his paperwork, and just like that, I am dismissed from his presence. As I reach for the doorknob, he calls after me.

"Oh, and I'm sorry for your loss." He doesn't sound sincere. I scuttle back out the door, murmuring a deferential thank-you as I shut it behind myself.

"Zelda, what have you gotten us into?" I whisper, my head reeling. I climb into the truck and sit behind the wheel, wondering where to go next. Then I realize I already know. My father has taught me a few things: Where there's debt, there's almost always more. I turn the ignition and drive down Route 414, back toward Watkins Glen, and the bank.

I don't know the first thing about finance. Thanks to Marlon's more successful second venture, due entirely to his third wife's deep coffers, he's paid for most of our educations. I almost took out a loan to go to Paris, but at the last second Marlon again came through with a good-sized check, and I've been coasting by, supplementing his dollars with French government student subsidies. I'm not good with money.

Zelda and I have had a bank account at the Community Credit Union in town since we were six years old, when Marlon gave us our first "paycheck," for trimming vines with him out in the field. After we'd done an hour or two of work ("an honest day's labor" in Marlon's rather generous assessment) he loaded us into the truck, each of us clutching a twenty-dollar bill. Ten dollars an hour seems like lavish pay for two distracted six-year-olds, but we weren't going to argue. We still have those accounts.

I park the truck in a fifteen-minute loading zone near the bank, hoping to be quick. Before going inside, I retrieve Zelda's driver's license. I'm not sure that what I'm about to try will work, but I can use all the government documentation I can get.

Not many people live in Hector, New York, and I suspect there's a very real possibility that people at the bank will know that Zelda Antipova is presumed dead. I'm certain they will have heard about the fire, but I'm banking (ha ha) on the fact that they won't know who was involved in it. It's probably a crime to impersonate someone in order to gain access to her banking information, but I can live with that.

I look up and down the street: quiet, as ever. Watkins Glen is called "the city" by those of us who live out here, but that is a rather generous description of our Podunk county seat. There are a handful of sadly blinking stoplights and a clothing store that sells Carhartt merchandise, thick woolen socks, and long underwear for the frigid winter. Farmer gear. A gaudy life-sized simulation of a pirate ship sits near the water. This bizarre reproduction houses an ice-cream stand and a miniature golf course; Zelda and I would lobby to be brought into town on hot summer evenings for raucous, giddy fun. Nearby, a stark pier juts out into the lake, and you can meander out to the tip on raw winter days and imagine you are somewhere near the North Pole. In the summer months, a yacht perches by the dock, offering chartered wine cruises. An overpriced hotel and a similarly overpriced fish joint sit next door to the dock, providing tourists simultaneously with a view of the thirty-eight-mile lake and glutinous, flavorless *pasta al mare* swimming in thin cream sauce, despite the fact that there is no *mare* anywhere nearby and seafood is about as appropriate here as it would be in Ohio. A burger joint, a brewery, and an "Italian" joint that serves microwaved calzones and meatball subs sit along the mostly deserted main drag. Highlights include the huge, freezing-cold public pool and the hike along the (admittedly picturesque) waterfall's gorge. For a few unpleasant weeks during the humid month of August, NASCAR enthusiasts flood the town, and the streets are crammed with aspirational muscle cars and mullet haircuts. The place fairly reeks of Budweiser during this period, and locals take care to steer clear of the city, heading to Montour Falls or Ithaca for any supplies not harvested from the garden. I find myself wondering what things will need doing at Silenus in August, how busy I will be (preparing for harvest!), and shake my head when I realize what I have been imagining. I will be safely back in Paris by the time NASCAR rolls into town.

I muss my hair distractedly as I walk into the bank, momentarily not realizing that I'm imitating one of Zelda's gestures. The bangles shake unfamiliarly on my forearms. Inside, the bank is chilly and air-conditioned, and I pad softly across the carpet in my sandals to the customer service area. An employee gestures me toward her stall way too enthusiastically, and I walk over, letting my bag plop into the chair. There are always two chairs in front of bankers, suggesting that a single person will never suffice for the creditors.

The woman in front of me is wearing a thick layer of green eye shadow, and her hair is shellacked with hair spray, making the brownish strands crispy and stiff, almost alien in their brittle anti-gravitational mushroom. She has a gigantic smile on her face, and her nails clack unnervingly on the keyboard in front of her. As we face off, I realize that I'm hugely relieved to be doing this in English; in France, I would have had to submit two forms and enter into a verbal sparring match with whoever was at the front desk just to sit down with another human being, which is when the actual negotiations would begin.

This woman may be a foreign creature to me, but at least we speak the same language.

"Hi," I say. A solid beginning.

"Hi there, sweetie. What can I do for you today?" She clasps her hands together and tilts her head attentively. She has clearly attended her customer service training sessions.

"Well, I have a bank account with you, and I'd like to inquire about the status of some loans. I think I've gotten off track with my repayment, and I wanted to know about the remaining balance, see about maybe restructuring?" I don't know exactly what that means, but I am fairly sure it is what one does with loans that one isn't paying back. Unfortunately, the whole incompetent and clueless act works better with middle-aged men; they immediately get all paternalistic and want to mansplain the contours of the particular pickle in which you've found yourself. But I guess I'll have to settle for the kindly, concerned woman in front of me.

"Of course, sweetheart. Can I just see your proof of identity and your account number?"

"I don't have the account number on me, but here's my license," I say, sliding Zelda's across the desk. She gives it a cursory glance before typing in my name.

"And your Social?"

I panic for a minute and almost give her mine, but then I remember Zelda's and spit it out in a relieved rush.

"Antipova . . . that name sounds familiar," she prompts.

"My family owns a vineyard a few miles up the lake. Silenus?"

"Oh." She nods politely, her eyes going carefully blank, and I can tell she recognizes the name of the vineyard and has tasted our wine. She looks at the screen and then frowns. "Oh, goodness," she says, and glances at me with a new expression.

"What is it?"

"This is quite the loan. I'm very surprised they let a twenty-four-year-old—oops, sorry, twenty-five now!" She beams manically. "Anyway, I'm surprised they let someone your age borrow so much. It's, uh . . ." She's tapping away at her keyboard with frank concern. *Zaza, you idiot. How much did you borrow?* "I see your mother, Nadine O'Connor, cosigned?"

I nod noncommittally. How did Zelda get Mom to stay lucid enough for a trip to the bank? How did she make her cooperate? I thought I had power of attorney.

"Do you think you could print me out some updated information? The new balance, the interest rates?"

"Well, the balance has only increased, I'm afraid. Dear, you haven't made *any* payments on this loan. It's two months overdue. The bank will have to take action real soon," she says. She looks genuinely worried for me. I appreciate it, really; I'm just feeling very impatient to get out of here. It's only a matter of time before someone Zelda and I know wanders into the bank, and I don't want to risk being called on my charade.

"Things have gotten a little overwhelming, but I'm, uh, ready to take responsibility. For my actions. Choices. My decisions. If you could just print out the information . . ." I smile brightly.

"Yes, of course. But I'm afraid I will have to notify one of the managers. I'm surprised they haven't gotten more involved at this stage." Her mouth has tightened into a taut line of disapproval. A few minutes ago, I was a sweet girl. Now I am a disgraceful debtor, in over her head. Few things are more shameful than insolvency in a country where poverty is a moral failing.

"I understand. How about I make a payment of good faith? Right now?" I rifle through my bag before realizing with a jolt that the name on my checkbook is my own. "Or tomorrow? I don't seem to have my checkbook with me at the moment," I finish weakly.

She raises an eyebrow, cynical. "Of course you don't. You could transfer from one of your other accounts. I see you have some small savings in your checking account."

"Yeah, let's do that!" I say in relief. "How about a thousand dollars?"

She looks at me blankly. I'm definitely not going to get called "sweetie" again.

"You don't have a thousand dollars in your account."

"Oh. Let's just move the whole balance, then." I need to leave. Now.

"Great. I'm moving three hundred and forty-three dollars and seventy-nine cents from your checking account to go toward your loan payment. Which is still overdue. If you're unable to make the full payment before July 1, I'm afraid you'll be looking at foreclosure proceedings."

Oh, Jesus. "Great. That printout? Updated with the payment?" I prompt, looking around the bank. She enters some information, and I hear the clack of an old printer discharging a sheet. She collects a few pages from the printer tray and hands them to me. I grab them anxiously, my bangles jangling, and stand up.

"Thanks for your help with this. And I'm . . . sorry," I say. It's not quite the right thing to say, but she does soften.

"Good luck, sweetie. I hope you're able to sort it out."

I smile, and she smiles falsely back. I notice a smudge of bubblegum-pink lipstick on her tooth. I turn to leave, and as I'm walking away, I know she's shaking her head in disbelief and censure. I'm sure she's never been late on a loan payment. I grit my teeth and head for the door. As I'm pushing it open, someone calls out.

"Zelda!" Instinctively, I turn my head. I have always answered to her name, and she to mine. A young man is hurrying from the other side of the bank. He looks angry. In a panic, I race outside. I don't need any more confrontations. I dodge left once I'm back outside in the clammy heat. I immediately duck into the convenience store next to the bank and move to the back of the aisles. I pretend to browse in the fridge, hiding behind a wire stand filled with potato chips. From the corner of my eye, I see the man run by the door without looking in. After puttering around for a few minutes, I buy a pack of cigarettes at the counter, then cautiously poke my head outside. Coast seems clear.

I don't look at the sheets of paper scrunched in my hand until I get back to the truck. I sit in the cab and will myself to look down at the figures. When I do, the breath is knocked out of me.

Following her recent payment of $343.79, Zelda is left with a balance due of $306,000.21.

# 6

Four hundred grand in debt. I sit in the truck, staring out the window at the bank. The bank statement is on the floor, and I'm fairly sure that if I bend over to get it, I won't be able to get back upright. Zelda has really outdone herself this time. Over four hundred thousand dollars in debt, and that's just what I've managed to find so far. For all I know, she could have other unpaid bills all over town. Christ. Almost half a million dollars. I knew from the emails that Silenus wasn't doing well. I know it's an expensive operation, but this . . .

If I were a practical person, I would be problem-solving. Brainstorming about mortgages I could take out, people with money I could go to. But all I can think is that I need a bottle of something, and somewhere quiet to consume it. I'm immediately sucked into the pleasure of planning, anticipating, the ritual of drink. First, I will go through a list, examine my palate. Will today be a gin-and-tonic day? Or cold IPAs in frosty brown bottles? Or wine, the classic, my old favorite? And if wine, will it be a buttery, oaked Chardonnay? Too warm for red, so no velvety Zinfandel or bright young Chianti. Maybe sparkling? A light, easy Prosecco, or some creamy Blanc de Blancs. Or will it just be my go-to bottle, a bone-dry Sauvignon Blanc, filled with flint and hints of flowers?

After I decide, I'll think of where to buy it. The sensible, economical thing would be to take a bottle from the winery's cellar, but I don't really want to drink that shit. I could go to one of the vineyards between here and Silenus, only I would run into people I know, be forced to answer questions. And dressed as I am, like Zelda, I'll probably raise a few eyebrows. At home, in Paris, I have a favorite wine store, a tiny box on my market street where I can duck in and snag a bottle on my way home, before stopping at the *fromagerie* and the *tabac*. I indulge in a moment of fantasy, of meeting Nico at home with a bottle of something just outside my price range, of us sitting by the window in my tiny nook and sipping out of my petite wineglasses, considering where we'll go when the bottle is gone. But those fantasies are too abstract for my purposes here. Today, I will go to a liquor store in Watkins Glen, and I will browse the racks looking for just the right bottle. I tell myself I will buy an eleven- or twelve-dollar bottle, something decent but not extravagant, but I will walk out with a fifteen-dollar bottle if I'm very lucky. Today might be a twenty-dollar-bottle day.

Then I will have to decide where to drink it. Sometimes I want company, people to talk to while I uncork it. When I'm feeling festive or exuberant, I want to chat and burble, marking my journey into tipsiness with my verbal outpourings, measuring my drunkenness in confessions and, eventually, incoherence. But often, I want to just be alone, to tell myself I'm not that drunk, to pour myself another glass without an audience. I want to sit somewhere beautiful, by myself, and drink.

My ritual is interrupted when I notice a meter woman (my politically correct millennial mind refuses to call her a meter maid) writing a ticket and snapping it under my windshield. I lurch out of the truck.

"Hey, I'm right here," I say. "I'm just about to leave." She looks at me dispassionately.

"Too late. Already did the printout."

"Are you fucking kidding me? I'm sitting in my vehicle, ready to pull out of the space. I just got here."

"Rules are rules, miss. You're in a loading zone."

"This is a fucking joke," I say. "I don't have time for mindless rules today. I'm sorry that the only meaning you derive from life comes from sanctimonious little strips of paper. I just don't have the patience to play nice while we pretend you're anything other than a parasite and a miserable fucking human being with a subpar GED." I'm shocked at what I've said. I sound like Zelda. This is Zelda's doing too. She's turning me into her. One of her favorite games used to be for us to swap clothes and try to fool parents and teachers. Of course she would get off on this. She was always better at the game.

I was born face-to-face with my fetch, and we've been competing over our lives ever since.

"Well, miss, I'm sorry to hear that. Feel free to complain at the court." The meter bitch wanders off, and I'm left seething. More bills to pay. Fabulous. I smother a scream that threatens to escape from my clenched and aching throat, then drive directly to the liquor store without taking the ticket off the windshield. It's in Zelda's name anyway.

After buying the wine (twist-offs, fuck it), I get back into the truck, feeling calmer. Before turning the key in the ignition, I look at Zelda's phone again. There's a new message.

To: zazazelda@gmail.com
From: zazazelda@gmail.com
Subject: Dun dun dun
June 23, 2016 @ 5:04 PM

Dearest Twinlet,

Debt, debt, debt! I'm up to my eyeballs in debt. Which you've doubtless disconcertedly discovered. Does my disappearance make more sense now? You're surely putting together the pieces, Ava darling.

Silenus has been on a downward spiral for the last little while— since before you left, really; it was starting to slip under your watch, dear professionalized twin! But it has gotten really quite bad of late, and I've had to take certain measures I'm not entirely proud of. We needed new equipment, had to pay everyone who works at the vineyard. (Honestly, this living-wage shit is a thorn in my side. Gasp away, my socialist sister. My politics have gotten distinctly rural since the family farm started going under. If there were illegal Mexicans to employ in this neck of the woods, I'd be scooping them up by the truckload.) The bills are due, and we have no more money. Bankruptcy is inevitable, I think, but it will destroy what's left of our mother's shriveled heart. Marlon's, too, I reckon, in some small way, though he has done his best to emotionally divest himself from this place, from us. I hope it hurts him, I really do.

You know, it's interesting. They didn't falter when I sauntered into the bank asking for money. There I was, twenty-four years old, no assets, no college degree, in possession of just a failing business and a failed parent. I was not a good financial risk. But they just signed that check right over with barely a blink and a background check. I was relieved, but I have to say, more than a tad concerned about our national finances. Here we are, post– global financial collapse, and our local bank seems blithely uninterested in vetting its future debtors. Don't we learn through repetition? How many times does shit have to go wrong before we change our fucking behavior? I say this on a macro as well as a micro level, dear sister.

I'm not sure I'm cut out to slum it, though. Penny-pinching is not in our bloodline. I'm afraid I find myself very resentful when confronted with the necessity of "cutting back." The prospects are grim. I was holding out for this particular vintage, one you presided over, Little A, perhaps you remember: a tasty Gewürztraminer, one of the classic Finger Lakes grapes. It was from 2011—do you remember the season? We took a risk and held off harvesting until October, which was dangerously, riskily late, but we were hoping it would pay off with more intense flavor. We wanted a Gewürztraminer with very low residual sugar, nice and dry, low acid and low pH. It was a mild winter, and a nice damp spring gave way to a hot, lovely summer. You and Wyatt were prowling the fields and fussing over your tomato plants like first-time parents with a colicky child. You were working on an internship for your degree and took obsessive notes. Zephyrs scraped across the whole dilapidated vineyard, gouging deeper those juicy fissures we plowed, burrowing into the maxed-out wrinkles that already produced such poor-quality nectar. We hadn't bothered with cover crop that year, relying on chemistry to do the work. You were pinning it all on the Gewürz but by the time the cloudy autumn rolled around, you were flipping the fuck out over Botrytis bunch rot, which had you quaking in your boots. I swear, I could hear your moaning about it at night.

I was hoping that all this nervous energy, this studious and scientific stewing and fretting, would give us the light, expressive, and crisp wine you were after. How could you bear to leave before you knew if the fruits of your labor were everything you'd hoped? If wine is a story, you left just before the ending! But, spoiler alert. It was not a happy ending. Your tweaked and micromanaged vintage was just another uninteresting, slightly puckery table wine. It tasted heavily of cheap floral perfume. *Quel dommage.*

But moving on from past harvests and all the grapes already plucked and fallen. (Why dwell on the done deal?)

Your Scheming, No-Good, Very Bad, Undead Sister,
Z is for Zelda

I almost throw Zelda's phone across the truck in exasperation. I finally scream, letting out the pent-up, hoarse yelp that has been caught in my throat all day, making me gag. I slam the heel of my hand against the steering wheel and shake my head like some sort of feral animal. A fellow boozehound in the parking lot glances at me in concern before tucking both of his brown paper bags more firmly into his armpits and ambling to his car. He probably thinks I'm drunk. I'm not yet, but boy, do I plan to be.

I throw the truck into gear and drive back to Silenus. I know exactly where I'm going to drink.

My father wanders out into the yard when I'm most of the way through the bottle. He has a worried expression on his face, and he looks like he's sobered up a bit. He can't exactly give me grief about overdoing it, considering the morning he had.

"Little A, are you okay?" he asks delicately, looking around. "I mean . . ." I scooch my sunglasses farther down my nose and look at him.

"Why? Isn't this a perfectly acceptable place to sit and think about Zelda?" I wave my arm grandly, gesturing toward the sooty stumps of the barn, the yellow tape. There were cops swarming around when I returned, but they left somewhere during my second glass of wine; I think my presence made them uncomfortable, especially after I treated them to a raucous chorus of Edward Sharpe's "Home." It's just me now, parked in the lounge chair, looking directly at the barn. The lake is to my back, and I have dragged out an ice bucket that I filled with my recent purchases, which sit sweating beads of moisture into the melting ice cubes. I'm wearing one of Zelda's vintage bathing suits, a polka-dotted monstrosity, and a gardening hat that I found in the hallway. It could be my mother's, but I don't have a single memory of her crouched on hands and knees, laboring in the garden. Not her style. My father is staring at me in concern, not looking at the barn.

"I understand you wanting to be close to where Zelda . . . was. But maybe this is a little . . ."

"Grim?" I finish his sentence, and my glass of wine. I hold the empty glass out to him, shaking it suggestively. "Fill 'er up." He looks doubtful, but he leans down and fishes the open bottle of South African Sauvignon Blanc out of the ice bucket and splashes the last bit of wine into my glass. "Cheers," I say, toasting him. "And cheers to you, Zelda. Quaff that kind Nepenthe!" I drink most of the glass in one swallow.

"Ava, what about your mother?"

"She won't eat anything. She says her pants feel snug and she needs to slim down. Hard to imagine how the drawstring of her silk jammies could feel snug, but . . ." I shrug, shutting my eyes for a moment. I can tell I'm getting sunburned, but it feels fantastic. "I gave her a bottle of Gewürztraminer for being a pretty good girl today. Honestly, her stunt should have cost her all but a medicinal tipple, but her kid did just kick it, so I felt bad for her. If it had been her, she would have made me or Zelda go to bed with nothing at all, but *I* think *I'm* the nice one in the family." I'm only slurring a little. Marlon looks at me once more, then just turns and walks back to the house.

When I wake up, the sun has set and I'm freezing cold. I'm still wearing just a bathing suit, and the sunglasses are crooked on my face. There's a knocked-over wineglass by my hand. The wind smells smoky, and there are fireflies blinking in the grass all around the barn. My mouth tastes god-awful; I cringe, not wanting to fully open my eyes.

When I finally stand up, I'm wobbly, but I can tell I'm more or less sober, which means I've been asleep for a while. I estimate that I drank close to two bottles of wine before I passed out, which I confirm by nearly tripping over the empties. They are slippery and cold, slick with early dew, and I kick them out of my way with the side of my foot. It's dark this far away from the house; the barn light used to illuminate the path. I stumble through the damp grass, leaving everything on the lawn. I nearly trip again, this time on a string of yellow tape that cordons off part of the blackened grass.

Inside, the house is quiet and still. Marlon isn't on the couch when I return inside, and I scan the downstairs rooms, wondering where he's ended up. I head upstairs. In front of my mother's door, I hear a quiet sniffling sound and freeze. It is such a foreign noise to me that I'm momentarily stunned, but I recognize it for what it is. It's the sound of my mother crying. I don't know if I've ever heard that before.

"What do you mean, Marl? She can't be," I hear her whimper.

"I know, I know. I can't believe it either. It's . . . I can't tell you how sorry I am." Marlon's voice is soft and delicate. He hasn't spoken that way to her since my childhood.

"My little girl. It's like it's happening all over. No matter what I do, I can't keep them safe!"

"This is not your fault," my father says firmly. "And neither was what happened before. You need to hear that."

"You think it's just a goddamn coincidence?" Nadine snivels.

"It's just life, Nadine. Accidents happen. People die." His voice cracks on this last sentence. "You've done your best. In spite of everything."

"What does that mean?" Nadine snaps in a tone I know all too well. I know exactly where this is headed, and I nudge open the door.

"You guys okay in here?" I say. Marlon is sitting on a chair next to my mother's bed, stroking her shoulder. She's in a fetal position on the mattress, facing away from him. She flinches at my voice.

"Just get out of here! You're the one who's making me sick," she hisses, her voice choked with tears. "You like to see me this way." She starts to mumble something into her pillow a moment later. It sounds like a name, repeated again and again: Zelda, I assume. I pull the door shut and retreat to my room, fleeing the sound of my mother's pain. An alien noise. She has always worked so hard to conceal any evidence of weakness. Maybe Marlon can say something to help her. I strip down to my underwear and climb under the white covers, grateful that I'm too hungover to feel anything at all. I'm asleep within a minute.

# 7

Grimacing before I'm even conscious, I wake up earlier than usual, no doubt due to my early bedtime. I feel intensely grateful that I passed out before I drank anything else, or found my cigarettes. I feel rough but not too fragile, and I roll out of bed with just a few groans and false starts. My hair smells like the smoke outside, and my eye makeup is probably halfway down my face, but it's not like there will be anyone to criticize my appearance downstairs. I knot my silk kimono around my body and sit on my bed for a minute, looking out the window at the fields. Then I gaze around my pristine bedroom, having woken up in it for the second time. Zelda used to tease me, saying that my room looked like it belonged to a middle-aged housewife, all sedate decor and clean corners. I check Zelda's phone, which has been charging on my nightstand all night. There's nothing new, a fact for which I am grateful.

I walk by my mother's bedroom door, and I suspect she's probably still sleeping. God knows how late she stayed up last night, sobbing into her pillow. I wonder if she does this all the time, or if it's because she has some fleeting awareness of what's going on in the house, with Silenus, with . . . the barn.

Marlon isn't in the guest room downstairs, which is a surprise. No one in our family is an early riser, and I expected him to be snoring away at this hour, regardless of what time he went to bed. We must be absolutely the worst farmers imaginable, with our inability to crack our eyes open before nine in the morning. I open the fridge door and find some orange juice, which I chug in sincere gratitude.

"Ava Antipova, what on earth do you think you're doing?" A familiar voice stops me in my tracks, and I slam the cap back on the orange juice instinctively, hiding my face behind the fridge door. Shit.

"Grandma Opal," I say as I shut the fridge door, leaving me exposed in my thin robe, looking like the mess I am.

"Drinking out of the container, honestly. Your mother . . . Well, never mind. You look appalling. Come, give me a kiss," she says. It is not a suggestion.

I cross the kitchen to lean down and hug her tentatively. She's even smaller than the last time I saw her, and I'm afraid to hug any harder; her bones feel like they're cracking even with my reluctant squeeze. She smells like her favorite Chanel perfume, and she's wearing some elaborate turban on her head, with a fringed sweater draped over her expensive-looking maxi dress.

My father's mother is terrifying, and this provides some insight into why Marlon selected my own mother; they're not dissimilar. But where my mother is aloof and haughty, Opal is invasive and aggressively nurturing. She likes to touch, to be connected through skin and blood. She's a micromanager. Whenever she came to stay at Silenus, she would stand behind us while we did the dishes, checking to make sure the glasses didn't spot. While Marlon was still living with us, we were required to make weekly phone calls to her, during which she would ask us if we'd gotten our periods, how often we brushed our teeth, whether we'd kissed any boys yet. She demanded the recited details of physical intimacy. I tried to hide my shame by mumbling into the phone, avoiding any eavesdroppers. Zelda, on the other hand, never minded our grandmother. When Opal asked Zelda if she had any crushes at school, Zelda told her that she wanted to bone our music teacher, then asked Opal if menopause was affecting her shuffleboard activities. I gawked in disbelief, but Opal laughed uproariously and answered with equal honesty. They had always been kindred spirits, with a fondness for animal-print fabrics and bawdy shock value.

As my grandmother clutches me now, her melted and distorted skin folding off her bejeweled fingers, I imagine that she must be extraordinarily sad. Zelda was her favorite grandchild, unless my father's most recent brood of offspring has magically supplanted my sister. And just from looking at pictures of Blaze and Bianca, I find that possibility unlikely. Their blond hair always falls in curtains in front of their downturned faces, their eyes glued to iPhones bedecked in sparkling Hello Kitty cases. They always look deeply affronted that they would be required to do anything so undignified as pose for a photo they are not taking themselves. (I have Facebook-stalked their mother and have perused the prolific catalogue of duck-pouted preening they have all too happily offered up to the Inter-gods.) I can easily imagine Opal terrorizing them, and clucking her tongue in dismay over their abstraction, their distance. I picture her pinching the skin of their young bronzed arms, demanding their attention with her clever, wrinkled hands.

"How are you, Grandma?"

"How do you think, Ava? I'm exhausted and upset."

"I didn't know you were coming. Marlon didn't mention it." I gesture vaguely toward the couch, where Marlon ought to be napping, instead of out ushering his daunting mother to my corner of the world.

"I got in late from Orlando last night and spent the night in the Radisson in Corning. Had to take a cab there. Your father said I shouldn't fly in until we had made funeral arrangements, but I figured there was a fat chance of that happening without me here to oversee things. I think he didn't want me to come." She waves his preference off like the insignificant detail it is. Then, still holding on to me, she pushes me away until I'm at arm's length, giving me the once-over. "You really don't look good, Ava. Probably the jet lag, though," she explains graciously.

"Or the death of my twin." She flinches, and I feel the day's first flicker of happiness.

"Of course you have your reasons. I was very sorry to hear about Zelda. It really is . . . unbelievable." I narrow my eyes, wondering if she has her own suspicions, but there's no glimmer of double meaning in her face. "She emailed me the day she died, you know. We'd spoken a lot this last year, she was so lonely." Grandma Opal looks at me meaningfully, and I know that she considers this my fault. "She wrote saying that she loved me and had always appreciated me. It was the sweetest thing."

"How unlike Zelda," I say flatly.

Grandma Opal hardens her jaw. "She was tough on the outside, dear, but a real softie when it came down to it. *You're* the one who's like your mother." This is an easy shot, but it still hurts.

"Have you seen Nadine yet?" I ask. "I might need some help looking after her, while you're here. There's a lot I have to do still, and I wouldn't want you to have to deal with it, in your condition." She can needle me all she wants to, but Opal hasn't been able to drive herself anywhere since failed cataract surgery a couple of years ago. And in this part of the world, that means she's pretty well stuck. I know being trapped in the house with Nadine will make her reconsider being nasty to me.

"Old age isn't a condition, Ava. It's something only the lucky few get to experience."

"Grandma, could you just let me be for a second?"

"You're fine when you just unclench and relax, Ava," she says, unable to resist having the final jab.

"A popular opinion." I rifle through the cupboards, looking for coffee. There's only a little left, and I sigh in exasperation. I will have to go grocery shopping for the four of us today, plan a menu beyond Betsy's unappreciated casserole. I've gained another dependent. "Where's Marlon?" I ask. "Probably not out working the fields."

"He's gone to the police station, to talk to someone official over there. He said you were sorting it out yesterday, but I told him that was no job for you. He needs to go and take charge, make sure it's done right." The implication being that I can do neither, presumably. But he's welcome to the job. "He's her father, after all. He's the head of your family." Ha.

"They told me yesterday there was no official ruling yet," I inform her. "Maybe they'll have one this morning."

"How can they not know at this stage? It's been days. Honestly, I may have to hire someone to make sure everything's being done right."

"I'm not sure you can hire someone to bring Zelda back from the dead, Grandma," I say sharply, instantly realizing that this may not be true. I think a decent PI could probably find my sister, wherever she's hiding. But I'm hardly going to suggest that.

"I know that, doll." She comes to stand behind me and strokes the nape of my neck in a way that is supposed to be comforting. I do my best not to flinch at the feel of her papery skin brushing my own. "Ava, it's okay to let go, to let down your façade. Everyone knows what Zelda was to you, even if you two hadn't spoken for a while. I know she would forgive you for that."

"Forgive *me*? For the shit *she* pulled before I left?" I shake my head in disbelief. If Opal knew the whole story, which I'm certain no one does, she'd probably still take Zelda's side—but I'm not the one who needs forgiving. Zelda had our grandmother, and everyone else, wrapped around her finger, figuring that I was off having some temper tantrum in Paris. "You have no idea what was going on here, Grandma."

"I know there were some childish jealousies, some sort of disagreement over a boy, but really, Ava, you can't walk away from your twin sister because of some high school crush."

"He wasn't a crush. It was—Jesus, why am I even arguing with you? Zelda manipulated you into feeling bad for her, and that's fine. I don't have to justify every fucking move I make to everyone in this family!"

They are all toxic. I fling a coffee cup into the sink. It cracks into satisfying shards and the noise is immediately comforting. I reach for another, but my grandmother grabs my arm and looks me in the eye. She has our eyes, Marlon's too-green eyes. "That's enough, Ava. There's no need to be unnecessarily destructive."

I snort and raise my arms in surrender, prepared to flee the room.

"I brought coffee," Marlon says from the doorway, looking back and forth between his mother and daughter with a harrowed expression. He's holding a few bags of groceries and some to-go cups of coffee, and I'm almost weak-kneed in relief at seeing him. This is how my father gets away with his perennial negligence and failure to come through: He shows up at just the right moment, with exactly what you need. And because it's so unexpected, you feel this surge of gratitude toward him, like he's accomplished something superhuman. I know this, deep in the marrow of my bones, which are made of the marrow of his, but it doesn't change the fact that I'm momentarily choked up at the sight of the coffee that I will not have to make myself and the groceries that I will not have to buy and put away. How we've idolized that man, that mythological figure who had bequeathed us his ruinous genes and extricated himself from his paternal role, vaulting off in pursuit of his next jaunty lark.

"Thanks, Dad," I say, crossing the kitchen to relieve him of his gifts. I give him a meaningful look with my back turned to Grandma Opal, and he smiles in acknowledgment.

"Ma, I got one for you too," he says, handing her a cup.

"I don't drink coffee anymore, Marlon. It leads to breast cancer. You know that." She looks over at me pointedly. "And you know it's bad for you too," she adds, clucking at her son.

"Great," I say. "I'll give it to Mom. *She'll* appreciate it."

Marlon sets the bags on the counters and starts opening cupboards, trying to figure out where everything should be put away.

"Well, Marlon, what did you learn from the police?" Opal asks. My dad clears his throat uncomfortably.

"Well, they found some, uh, human remains," he says. I almost drop my coffee.

"What? What do you mean?"

"There are some, I guess, bones? A skeleton? They have to do DNA testing to make sure it's Zelda."

I'm speechless, totally without words. *Sweet Jesus, Zelda, who was in that barn?*

"Ava, did you hear what I said?" Marlon prompts me. "They'd like you to come in. They want to use your DNA to confirm whatever they find. They say it may take a few days before they have any results, but they need a family member to confirm. I offered mine, but they said yours would be better."

"Okay," I say blankly.

"They, uh, also want to ask you some questions."

"What on earth for?" Opal says.

"They say they have reason to believe that there's been some kind of . . . foul play?" Marlon sounds deeply unsure that he should be telling us this. Opal and I are both silent. I wonder if we're thinking the same thing.

"They think she was murdered?" I ask.

"Apparently, there were a few, well, red flags. The doors seem to have been chained shut, and the fire was very intense. If it had been started by natural causes, it should have been slower, they're saying. Something about an accelerant."

I want to sit down. I want to get drunk. I want Zelda to walk into the house this second with a silly grin on her face saying, "Surprise! I just wanted us all in the same room, a family again! LOL!"

"So they're investigating a murder," Opal says slowly. "My granddaughter was murdered." She is settling into the role, writing a script for herself as an entirely different kind of bereaved grandmother. Cooking up her own story.

"They don't know for sure yet. They say the first thing is to confirm that it was her. They say she had a text message, before she died? Saying she was going to be at the barn?" Marlon directs this last part at me.

I nod. "That's what they told me."

"It seems she was also caught up in some, uh, unpleasant stuff. She has a drug dealer friend? Do you know anything about that, Ava?"

"Zelda's always been wrapped up in 'unpleasant stuff.' It wouldn't surprise me in the least," I answer. "Do they think it's related?"

Marlon shrugs. "I don't know."

We all look around the kitchen silently, thinking. I sip my coffee, which is now room temperature, the way I like it. Marlon clears his throat.

"There's something else." Opal and I both turn to look at him. "Did you write this, Ava?" He tugs a newspaper from one of the shopping bags and hands it to me. It's open to the obituary page.

> Zelda Antipova passed away this summer solstice in a fiery blaze that prematurely claimed her young life. She was incomparable. She was a shooting star in a darkened sky. She was a cascading waterfall in a lush hidden glen. She was the full moon and the summer sun, a brilliant flower that faded too soon. Of faults we shall not speak but, rather, forgive all those small shortcomings and missteps and bid her farewell with a desolate heart, void of recrimination and blame and, indeed, anything but bitter anguish that she was taken from us so soon. She will be missed, she will be remembered, she will be mourned. She was very special, very loved, and treasured by everyone she touched with her short, too-short life. Etc. Etc.

"Yep," I finally answer through gritted teeth, after reading the eulogy a few times. I can hardly lay the blame at Zelda's doorstep without revealing what I know. Which she knows, goddamn her. How did she get the thing printed? I will try to remember to research how you go about getting an obituary in the local paper. Though this will no doubt look a bit odd, given that I'm meant to have just done it. "It was a mistake. I'd had a few glasses of wine, was feeling maudlin." I shrug. "I emailed it yesterday. We can print a retraction if you want."

"Why in God's name would we do that? I think it's lovely, Ava." Opal leans over and gives me a wet kiss on the cheek. "It's honest, spoken from your real heart. I think everyone can appreciate that." She rubs my shoulders insistently. Marlon doesn't look convinced, just raises his eyebrows and sips his coffee. I feel one of the phones vibrate in my pocket.

"I have to go give Mom breakfast," I say quickly, trying to beat a fast retreat. "Then I guess I'll head back to the station, answer their questions." Marlon nods.

# 8

Hardly able to convince my mother to choke down the banana I offer her, I throw up my hands in exasperation after five minutes of negotiation. I imagine this is karmic justice for some refusal of mine as a child, but this thought does nothing to assuage my irritation with her. I prop her up in bed and leave her with my laptop, the screen open to Netflix. I think she'll be able to figure it out, but I tell Marlon to check in on her occasionally. Opal is hard at work scrubbing the kitchen and bathrooms, which I appreciate. She may be obnoxious, but at least she's tidy.

I'm still annoyed at the last email Zelda sent. She knew that Marlon likes to escape in the mornings. She knew he would flee the ladies of the house and buy the newspaper.

To: zazazelda@gmail.com
From: zazazelda@gmail.com
Subject: Everybody Loves a Dead Girl, Everybody Loves a Murder Plot (Or, the Most Poetical Topic)
June 24, 2016 @ 10:05 AM

Ever-loving twin,
    Enjoy my eulogy? Truly, no one but you is qualified to deliver such an epic elegy, a timeless remembrance of my early exit, but I

feared you wouldn't get around to it in a timely manner. The fire department should be getting in touch with you very shortly (if they have not already done so) regarding my untimely departure, and you'll be expected to go forward with my funeral very soon, but I thought I would cut to the chase, head things off at the pass, jump the gun. I expect Marlon wants to get back to the Sunshine State (wait, that's Florida, the land of his birth. What is California? Google says: the Golden State. Our sun-kissed golden boy), so you'll have to get cracking on the arrangements. Thankfully, we don't have much family to notify. And the locals were already sharpening their pitchforks and marching on the vineyard; I've saved them the trouble of setting me on fire. They'll be waiting at the top of the drive to say a very unfond farewell. If you please, I would like you to sing something really awful. Like "Danny Boy" or "Wind Beneath My Wings." I'd like Mom to wear something black and matronly, please, and I'd like the whole thing to be as campy as possible. White lilies, somber faces, the works, Ava dear. I know your secretly ironic aesthetic is up to the task. If you need inspiration, just ask Wyatt. He'll unwittingly provide you with all the material you need. In the meantime, enjoy this little audio clip.

Never forget,
Z is for Zelda

I play the file from Arcade Fire's *Funeral* that she has sent along with her email as I head back down 414 to town. We listened to this song, "Crown of Love," in high school, sharing one pair of earbuds branching from our black iPod. I park in the lot behind the station. I refuse to get another ticket; God only knows how many Zelda's racked up. Before hopping out of the truck, I check Zelda's phone again: nothing. I tuck the phone into the glove compartment of the truck. I don't want it to ring while I'm talking to the police; that could make for an awkward explanation.

The same young cop greets me in the reception area and ushers me into a windowless room. He offers me a Coke, which I accept, and I twiddle my thumbs for a few minutes while I wait for the officer in charge of my sister's case. I slurp the cool liquid, reflecting not for the first time that it is some sort of magical elixir that cures hangovers. When someone finally enters the room, I'm close to nodding off, but I snap to attention. I hate cops, but not as much as Zelda did. Does.

"Ava Antipova?" he asks me brusquely. He's a squat, balding man with a substantial potbelly.

"One and the same. My father, Marlon, said you wanted to ask me a few questions? About Zelda."

"That's right. I'm Officer Healy, in charge of your sister's case. We're just trying to get a little information on where she was during her final days—"

"So you're pretty sure she was the one in the barn?" I interrupt.

The officer clears his throat. "Well, yes, ma'am, at the moment that seems the most likely. We've spoken to some people who've established that Ms. Antipova—Zelda—slept in the barn regularly, and the text message she sent shortly before the fire began seems to confirm that she intended to sleep there that night—"

"—but the doors were locked, and the fire burned a touch too quickly to suit y'all," I finish for him.

"Well, in a manner of speaking, yeah. I don't want to leap to con-clusions, or for anybody else to, for that matter, but we think we may be looking at a case of arson, and possibly homicide."

"Lemme guess—your prime suspect is this Jason guy. The one she texted?" I can only imagine what the poor sucker did to Zelda to have her framing him for murder. Maybe he'd been giving her the silent treatment too.

The cop looks at me with a perceptible shred of dislike. I can see he doesn't like me taking the wind out of his sails, deflating his bril-liant deductions, but it's hard for me to feel impressed by a guy who's trotting around the dance floor exactly as my sister has choreographed.

Then again, it's probably not fair to blame him for that; he doesn't have a lifetime of experience with Zelda's games, and he has no reason to suspect that she's playing him now.

"He is a candidate, yes. We'd like to find him, but we don't have much information to work with. No last name, and the contact details your sister had in her phone were linked to a TracFone registered in your name."

I sit up straight at this. "I'm listening," I tell him.

"We understand that you've been living in France for the last twenty-one months? Paris?" He consults a sheet of paper in his file. I suspect this gesture comes from watching cop dramas, rather than from a genuine need to remind himself of one piece of information.

"Grad school," I answer with a nod.

"What do you study?"

"Comparative literature."

"Oh? And what do you compare, exactly?" He grins, pleased with his joke. I don't answer. "But you originally studied viniculture? Here at Cornell?" He consults his sheet again, then looks up at me with a quizzical expression, expecting an explanation.

"Viticulture. I had an identity crisis. Switched gears."

"And they let you do that? Without any, well, background?"

"The school I go to in Paris isn't especially particular about that sort of thing. A college degree and a check for tuition pretty much sealed the deal. One of the reasons I picked it. That, and it was an ocean away from my family. And the wine's better."

The cop smiles at me thinly and scribbles something in his notebook. "And you haven't returned home at all during that time?"

"That's right."

"The TracFone was purchased three months ago, right after your sister came to visit you in Paris—"

"Wait, what?" I shake my head at him. "Zelda never came to Paris," I say, my eyes wide.

Healy frowns at his file and pulls out a printout. "We have records showing that she purchased a plane ticket using your mother's credit card, and that she used the same credit card to pay for a hotel in Paris, just three months ago. She was there for four days." He looks at me suspiciously, and I can tell he suspects I'm lying.

"She didn't tell me," I say. "Seriously." I read the address of the hotel: Hôtel Victoires Opéra, on rue Montorgueil, less than two minutes away from my apartment. *Zelda, what were you doing there? Spying on me?* "The hotel is near where I lived—live—but she never told me she was coming, and I didn't meet her. I haven't spoken to Zelda in twenty-six months. I don't even know how she knew where to find me." I'm rattled, but I don't want Healy to know.

"Two years?" he asks.

"It was a boy thing. Just . . . a sibling rivalry that got out of hand."

"How out of hand?"

Great, I think, I've just added myself to the suspect list. No doubt as Zelda wanted. "I just didn't want to talk to her anymore. I needed space."

Healy nods and makes a note, looking very serious. "Okay. Well. She bought two phones after she returned from France, one in your name and one in hers, and canceled her iPhone contract with Verizon. She had apparently been using the TracFone since then, and we suspect that she gave the one registered in your name to this Jason kid and instructed him to text her only from that phone. Any ideas why she would do that?"

"None at all, Officer. Zelda could be a little eccentric."

"It makes it that much more difficult for us to find this Jason."

"I imagine that has something to do with it," I offer sweetly.

He stares at me down his swollen nose, dislike sneaking back into his expression. "Were you aware that there were some financial problems going on with your family's vineyard?" he asks, his tone somewhat harsh.

"Like I said, I haven't been home, and Zelda and I haven't spoken. I just found out about the loans yesterday."

"Apparently, Zelda Antipova made her first payment on a substantial loan just yesterday at the credit union here in Watkins Glen, which we thought was very strange," he says.

I can't help turning mildly pink. "That was me, obviously. I wanted to know how much she was in for, and I didn't think the bank would be allowed to tell me. So I used Zelda's ID. Evidently, she's been having some money issues," I say. "You know how to make a small fortune from a vineyard in upstate New York?"

"Start with a large one," he answers, not looking up. There isn't a person in this county who hasn't heard or told that joke. "We think she may have gotten rid of the iPhone to cut costs, save some money. We also think she's gotten into some other . . . side businesses." I know this won't be good. "She made several cash deposits in the months before she died, a couple hundred dollars each, and, with the exception of the trip to Paris, she hasn't used a debit or credit card in six months. Any idea what she's been living off?"

"I bet you want me to say 'cash,' " I answer obediently. Increasingly, I feel like I'm here to be informed, rather than to offer up information.

"That is what we're thinking. Does the name Holly Whitaker mean anything to you?" Healy asks suddenly.

I pause.

"Nope," I say.

"Well, she just posted a photo on Facebook a little while ago, tagged your sister in it. In fact, she's one of your sister's most active Facebook friends."

"How did you guys get into her Facebook account? Isn't that illegal?"

"Trent, the kid at the desk, he's apparently Facebook friends with Zelda. He's been looking at her page."

I am actually impressed with this. I bet Zelda wasn't counting on that. Then again, in this neck of the woods, you'd have to be an idiot to forget that everybody knows somebody who knows more about you than you thought. Healy seemed almost bashful as he told me this, though.

"Good sleuthing, Detective. But no, I don't know Holly . . . Whitaker, did you say? We didn't go to high school together, and I'm not friends with my sister on Facebook."

"What did you say that 'sibling rivalry' was all about?"

"I didn't." We stare each other down. I win.

"And you've never heard of anyone named Jason? Anyone around town? From school?"

I've been trying to think of any Jasons living in Hector, but the only one I can think of is probably not going to be useful.

"There's this guy Jason Street? Used to play football for the high school, but I think he's in a wheelchair now," I say innocently. Let the cops ask around town for him. Zelda would be tickled. Healy writes the name dutifully in his notebook, and I suppress a giggle.

"And there's this other guy, I don't know his last name. He's always wearing this yellow fleece coat. He's really into sailing."

The cop squints at me—perhaps I've pushed it too far. "Okay, okay," he says, nodding. "So you'd had no contact with your sister? You wouldn't be able to tell us if she'd been behaving strangely in the last few weeks or months? Or if she'd had any disagreements with anyone?"

"Like I said, we hadn't been speaking. She lived with our mother, who's . . . not doing all that well. You're welcome to come out to the house to question her, but I should warn you, she thinks I'm Zelda and has some difficulty keeping track of reality." Healy looks at me in confusion. "She has dementia," I explain. "You didn't notice?"

"She was heavily sedated the night of the fire. We think she may even have been given extra sleeping aids that night, either accidentally or . . ." He obviously doesn't want me contemplating the possibility that my sister was murdered, but it's very clear that that's exactly what he's thinking. Zelda will have them all tied up in knots by the end of the day, no doubt. I wonder what other trails she's left for them—us—to find.

"I see." I wait silently for a few beats, expecting him to go on, but he just stares at me.

"You really look just like her," he finally says.

"Funny thing about twins. Is there anything else I can do for you?" I ask.

"I think those are most of the questions we needed to clear up with you. Now we just need a DNA sample from you. We're going to be testing the, er, human remains, to confirm that they're Zelda's. . . ."

"Do you have any reason to believe that they're not?" I try to sound hopeful. I know they're not hers.

"At the moment, no, we don't. I'm sorry, ma'am." He pats my hand gently, and I tug my arm away before I can stop myself. He blushes, and I drop my eyes. "I'll just, well, send our forensics guy in." He scooches his chair back, his big belly wobbling, and lumbers to the door. "Thanks for your help. Oh, here's my card," he says, remembering, and hands one over. "Please call me if you think of anything."

I nod, ashamed of my rudeness. I don't quite feel like myself. *That's not how Ava behaves*, I chide myself.

The forensic tech comes in a moment later and swabs my inner cheek wordlessly, not making eye contact. He wears gloves, and our interaction is almost robotic. I like that. I like not having to smile at him or let him touch me anywhere without latex between our two skins.

When I'm finished with the DNA swab, I make my way through the police station. The desk guy—Trent—is typing into the desktop computer, and he looks up as I leave. My hand is on the door when he calls out.

"Ms. Antipova? Ava?"

I pause. "What? Do you need me to answer more questions?"

"No, ma'am, it's not that, it's just . . . well, your sister was a really neat girl, and I just wanted to say, well, to say I'm real sorry for your loss."

"You knew Zelda?" I ask with a smirk. This kid does not really seem like her type.

"We were, uh, friends," he says, turning a violent shade of crimson, and I understand immediately that they were not just friends. Maybe she hadn't fucked him, but he certainly thought she might.

"Oh. Well, thanks for your condolences," I say with a polite nod, turning back to the glass door.

"You really look a lot like her," he calls after me as I step back outside into the sun. I wave goodbye without turning around. I know.

It's already getting warm out here. I shut my eyes briefly, to think. *Oh, Zelda. Fucking a cop. Is that how you were getting away with the drugs? Were you selling or just using? And if you weren't selling, where the hell were you getting enough cash to live on? And Paris? Was it me you came looking for, or was it for some other, darker motive?* I sigh, unable to ponder any of this in the heat.

Back in the truck, my head is pounding, my hangover catching up with me at last. I want to look at Zelda's phone, but I'm afraid to, here in the parking lot. Still, I'm too curious to see if what the cop said is true, and I open the Facebook app on Zelda's phone. The red blip on the world icon indicates that Zelda has indeed been tagged in a new post. An hour ago, someone named Holly Whitaker tagged a photo of Zelda sitting on the deck of Silenus, big sunglasses covering much of her face. My mother is next to her, looking distant and confused, wrapped in her bathrobe and staring out at the lake. The photo is captioned "Fucked-up Family Fun with the Antipovas." I scour the picture for any clues to when it was taken, but it's just a summery photo of my mother and sister sitting on the deck. I look at Holly's page and see a series of photos, all featuring her wearing skimpy get-ups, looking high as a kite. I don't recognize her from high school. I wonder if she doesn't know that Zelda's supposed to be dead or if she's too stoned to realize how weird the post seems if she does.

I want to take a nap, but I desperately don't want to go back to the house with Marlon and Opal and Nadine, all waiting for me there, each of them wanting to devour me with their special brand of neediness. I want my goddamn sister to be there, so we can roll our eyes and laugh at them and snort when they don't understand our mockery. I need to sleep, so I drive to Zelda's trailer. It looks lonely and cozy, perched on the hill amid the rows of grapevines.

I open the door and breathe in Zelda smells. I tug the mismatched curtains over the living-area windows to block out any light. It's hot and stuffy in the trailer, but I don't care. I start poking around, knowing it has to be here somewhere. Checking her usual hidey-holes reveals nothing, so I search the fridge and freezer, the top drawer, the frame of the ugly Pomeranian painting. I turn circles in Zelda's hotbox of a home, annoyed with her and with myself for not being able to figure her out.

But then I see the dolls, Addy and Josefina, tucked away on a bookshelf, staring at me with their blank, baleful eyes. Let's see, would Zelda pin it on the black girl or the Mexican? That, of course, is the wrong question. She would pin it on me. I reach for Josefina, and when I take her from the shelf, a familiar small box falls to the floor. I pick it up, the edges smooth and worn. Zelda has had this box since we were thirteen, one of the last gifts our father gave her before his flight to California. In high school, Zelda called it her "box of false promises."

I open it up and am only mildly surprised to see a needle, spoon, and stretch of elastic nestled in with a slender bag of snowy powder. Zelda was always going to try heroin eventually. This part of the world is having a minor opiate renaissance: Rich white kids get hooked on Oxy, and heroin is a cheaper fix. I wonder if Zelda waited until I was gone or if she was using before. I'd like to write off her whole dalliance with Wyatt by that simple explanation: She was high. But that wouldn't be the whole story. I'm unwilling to think about the whole story. In fact, I never want to think about it again.

Heroin isn't what I'm after, though. Zelda always said that deep down I was conservative, timid, that I would never live wildly, even though I fancied myself a bohemian. I resented it then, but she was right. I'm surprised that my search for Xanax comes up empty. That used to be one of Zaza's favorite come-down drugs. Instead, I settle for a Valium, which is almost as good. She has lots, probably lifted from my mother's supply. There is a zip-lock bag filled with them, clearly labeled with a Sharpie. I swallow two, take off my clothes, and crawl into her bed, waiting to fall asleep. The exquisite prandial sun is beating violently down on the white tin roof of the trailer, and just as I'm drifting off, I imagine I can hear it sizzling, crackling, scorching.

# 9

To: zazazelda@gmail.com
From: zazazelda@gmail.com
Subject: Irritating, right?
June 24, 2016 @ 3:00 PM

Inimitable, Impeccable Ava,

Having fun yet? I bet you are, in your heart of hearts. You always liked to pretend that you were above games, that you couldn't stand manipulation, wheeling, dealing. Sordid political jousts for power. You mocked Wyatt in high school for his fondness for winning, for getting first place. Do you remember when he wanted to run for student council and you virtually forbade it? He was crushed, but he did everything you asked him to, as always. He was such a good, obedient boy. Until you left him and he thought you weren't coming back.

Have you caught on yet? Have you figured out what's happening? You're a sharp, clever girly, so it's not impossible. But if I had to guess (and I have to, since I obviously can't just pop up and ask you), I'd bet you've been too single-mindedly blotting out consciousness to have paid really close attention. But I've given you time to process and mope; from now on, you'll have to focus harder and figure out what I'm up to. You'll stumble across the rules of the game eventually, I'm confident. But here's a nudge, to get you to the next step: What's the thing you've always been the most afraid of?

I know your thoughts have immediately leapt to that old juvenile fear, the titanesque sturgeon ruffling their extra-large gills along the bottom of our lake, and I recognize your yawning, primordial terror, I do. Remember when we went out in the rowboat with Dad? And he began spinning his tall tales? (Ever the fabricator, our pops!) This one involved something about industrial runoff from Cornell creating these marine dinosaurs that had developed a taste for human flesh. You wouldn't even know they were beneath you and—bam! They'd nibble off your feet or maybe swallow you whole. Your face went totally pale, and you begged and begged us to paddle to shore. And then, laughing mischievously, Dad dumped you into the water, just picked you up by the torso and chucked you in. You screamed and screamed, splashing in terror, and Marlon almost relented because it looked like you might drown. You pulled it together, though, and you swam, furious and panicked, back to the rocky banks of safety, storming off to the house without a backward glance, looking like a miserable drowned rat. You refused to speak to us for nearly a week. Silence always was your favorite weapon. You never remembered that I swam after you.

But, no, I don't mean the sturgeon. What is the thing that you've feared and avoided your whole life long, that you've scampered away from at every opportunity? Another hint: I don't think it's coincidental that you're irrationally afraid of a cold fish.

When you figure it out, you'll know where to look.


Your inspired, innovative, indefatigable sister,
Z is for Zelda

———

I roll out of Zelda's bed feeling groggy, as well as deeply annoyed. Zelda's trailer has turned into a sauna. I'm surprised she doesn't have an air conditioner down here, though not entirely: Zelda loves extremes. I've napped for several hours, and my hangover is largely dissipated, though Zelda's most recent communiqué has left me feeling nauseous and irritable. Goddamn her. I don't want to play her fucking game. But it's too late. I'm already all in, and she knows it. She understands that the reason I never played games is because I *have to win*. I am my mother's child, and I can't handle defeat. Zelda is fully aware that she's enticed me to play, and now I can't let it go until I've figured her out, found her, looked her in the eyes and told her that I know her BEST, that I GET HER. Which, of course, is how she will win too. Zelda never plays a game she's not certain of winning.

As kids, we were always wary of playing against each other, of competing; someone else was always on the opposing side. We refused to beat each other. For us, no card games or long rainy days filled with Monopoly or chess. Whenever there was a game of tag or capture the flag at a birthday party, we were always on the same team, and we would win. No matter what. Zelda once chipped a little girl's tooth, refusing to be taken prisoner in capture the flag. During one obsessive summer, she got her hands on an old Nintendo and played *The Legend of Zelda* alone in her room—she was fascinated with the heroine who bore her name, and at some point she wanted all of us to call her Hylia. She wouldn't let me near the game.

Once, disastrously, we played Scrabble. We were in ninth grade. So certain was I of winning, with my clever, bookish brain, that I sat down in front of my sister with nary a qualm. I excelled at school, got fabulous grades and glowing reports from teachers, while Zelda terrorized them and turned in homework on a schedule that could only be described as capricious. Confident of my success, I agreed to a dangerous bet, certain that I wouldn't have to honor it. Zelda played a lackadaisical first few words (*harp, try, gasp*) until I was lulled into complacency. She then swept back into the game with dazzling ease, tossing down big scorers (*gherkins, blowzy,* and, distressingly, *za*). I challenged this last word, which she had slapped on a double letter score, only to meet Zelda's smug expression as she handed me the dictionary.

"There's no way you could have known this is a valid Scrabble word," I pointed out, trying to get a handle on my rage. I was realizing just how effectively she had played me.

"You thought I knew nothing about the game, little sis," she said. "Always assuming I'm all loosey-goosey. But I've recently become a prodigy." She leaned back in her chair and informed me that as the loser, I would have to buy weed from her extremely dodgy older friend and smoke a whole joint in the middle of the dining room while Nadine was upstairs. She wanted me to break the rules, which I always followed to the letter. I did, and was miserable. We never played Scrabble again.

I honestly don't know if Zelda would really have put us on opposing teams now. She's been angry at me, that's clear, but I still feel that we're both working for the same objective, heading toward the same goal. Not knowing what that goal really is makes me nervous.

Reluctantly, I turn my mind to her email, and what she wants me to think. She's right: The first thing that leapt to mind when she asked what I feared most was those god-awful sturgeon. Wyatt told me later that they were a rural legend, that of course there weren't actually any gigantic forty-foot fish slowly slicing their way through the dark waters of the lake, four hundred feet down. That they obviously never swam up to the surface to feed, that they weren't attracted by the sound of human legs churning through the water. He said my dad had just been teasing me, like he always did, like dads do, trying to get a reaction. That he'd succeeded this time but I shouldn't let him win by being terrified of the water. I knew that Wy was speaking good sense, but for a long time after that day, I wouldn't go in over my head in the lake. Zelda's right about another thing: I don't remember her jumping in to rescue me. I remember watching later as she frolicked in the water,

seal-like and almost too far from the shore to see. Unafraid and able to
do something I was now too frightened to.

I've never feared my mother, exactly. I knew from an early age that
she was a formidable foe, and I had no desire to anger her. In fact, I
eventually learned that I didn't want to attract her attention at all. I
was safer when she wasn't watching me, when her notice was fixed on
someone else. If she never noticed me sitting there, just out of sight,
her sharp words would never be directed toward me, and her blind
fury would be aimed elsewhere. Usually toward Zelda, who seemed
rather to thrive on the rage, the cruel taunts, the endless harping.
Zelda used our mother's wrath as fuel; she held it inside her and un-
leashed it when she needed a blitzkrieg of her own. Zelda never
avoided proximity to our mother; she sought it out. When she saw
Nadine getting ratty, Zelda would provoke her, taunt her. As I shrank
away from our mother, Zelda would go on the offensive. I always assumed it was her combative spirit, but maybe Zelda was trying to
protect me, to attract Nadine's rage so that I would be spared. And I
learned to retreat, to avoid engaging anyone, because it always led to
conflict.

And so I know what Zelda wants me to say, to acknowledge: I am
afraid of intimacy. I sit in her trailer, remembering the day I left for
France. My bags were packed, waiting by the door. Nadine was more
lucid back then, but stress made her worse, and for days she had been
lashing out and disoriented. That day, she fumed around the house,
ripe with the awareness that I was abandoning her, leaving her here,
but unable to put her finger on why. She was livid and cranky, and my
skin was crawling with the desperate need to get out, to get away.
Zelda was lurking around the house, uncharacteristically quiet and
docile. Manifesting guilt, or as close to it as she could come without
ever experiencing guilt. Remorse, maybe. She had even offered to
help me pack, a gesture I had greeted with a narrow glare and a
hunching of the shoulders. My stomach had turned over when she
had offered, and I'd wanted to cry, to tell her she just needed to apolo-

gize and repent and I would stay, that this was crazy. All I wanted was for us to look each other in the eyes and acknowledge that that evening after I found them should never have happened, that we couldn't take it back but maybe we could forget it. But I couldn't say the words, and she had said nothing more, just slunk off to the kitchen for a mimosa.

Our mother had started her mimosas somewhat earlier, and I knew from her glassy eyes and gingery steps that Nadine was approaching the danger zone, the state between mildly and mindlessly drunk wherein she could marshal enough sobriety to do real damage but was uninhibited enough to not care how much damage was inflicted. Appearing in her room to say goodbye, I felt like she had scheduled her imbibing precisely so that she would be about four drinks in when I was walking out the door, her arsenal primed. She couldn't always remember what year it was, but she had a warrior's instinct that guided her even as her conscious mind deteriorated.

The scene was unpleasant, and though Zelda tried to stay out of the way, she was drawn upstairs by the sounds of conflict, a moth to the flame. I didn't put up much of a defense; I was too tired and heartsick, and I just wanted to retreat to the taxi that was waiting outside to take me to the airport. Mom raged, called me neglectful, ungrateful, cowardly. She said I was a nasty, spoiled little girl who was throwing her toys because she couldn't have everything she wanted, and I wondered momentarily if Zelda had actually told her about Wyatt, about what had happened between the three of us. Mom said she wouldn't give me a single penny for my foolish, infantile fantasy, that anyone who abandoned her responsibilities to go for a joy ride was shameful and selfish. And then, finally, she looked at me.

"Ava, I've never said this to you, because I didn't want to hurt you. But even as a child, there was something wrong with you. You didn't want to be held, or touched, even when you were nursing. You've spent your whole life flinching away from real connection, and now, instead of dealing with how you feel, you're flinching again. Your whole life, you've been a cold fish, running from intimacy." She waved me away then and went to stand by the window, staring out at the lake and refusing to look back at me.

"Bye, Mom," I managed, and I retreated. In the hall, Zelda was watching me, her eyes shrewd and calculating. I knew she was thinking about whether she could deliver a final blow, if she could find one well-placed word that would break me completely, make me stay. I knew she could find it, if she thought hard enough. "Mercy, Zelda. Just let me go," I said, looking into her eyes for the first time in months, since learning about Wyatt, since that spring night when we destroyed everything. I expected her to pounce, to read my weakness and lack of spirit and go for the kill, true predator that she was. But she didn't. She said nothing, just nodded her head and followed me down the stairs. She picked up my suitcase and took it to the taxi, where the driver was waiting impatiently.

"It costs more if you're running late and I have to sit here," he informed me.

"Then you can't possibly care how long it takes her to say goodbye. You're getting paid," Zelda snapped, manhandling my suitcase into the trunk. She looked at me, and for half a moment I thought we might actually hug. But I had never really hugged my sister; she had never hugged me. She knew I didn't like to be touched. And we couldn't ever touch again, not without that memory resurfacing. We just gazed at each other for a moment, and then I slid into the warm leather of the backseat. I put my earbuds in as the taxi pulled out of the driveway, and without looking back, I knew Zelda had gone into the house, and wasn't watching me leave.


Remembering that scene makes my stomach clench with renewed frustration and helplessness. My mother had been right, of course: I was trying to get away from feelings, from my family. I feared intimacy, deep in my marrow. It was why I had held Wyatt at arm's length all those years. Why my grandmother made me flinch. Why I had been so completely unable to forgive Zelda for calling my bluff: She was the only person I had ever shared true intimacy with, and she had used it against me in one of her games, trying to force my hand.

I sigh, knowing where she wants me to go. I put another caftan on, and it clings to my humid flesh. I wipe the fragile skin under my eyes with a forceful scoop of my index fingers, trying to clean myself up. Outside, I leave the truck parked in front of the trailer, and I walk up the hill, heading to the house and our mother's bedroom, wondering what Zelda has left for me there.

# 10

Just entering the house is a relief after the temperature outdoors, but it's muggy, even downstairs. Marlon is nowhere to be seen, nor is Opal, and I wonder what they're getting up to. I'm briefly annoyed that they've left Mom alone in the house, but I decide that this is probably just a case of introjection. I've internalized her accusations that I've abandoned her, neglected my duties, and the whole time I spent in France I'd been feeling the guilt. It's supposed to be me here, holding down the fort, being responsible, being sensible. Me, with my practical, easily justified B.A. from the Ag school, major in viticulture and enology, conscientiously maintaining the quaint family enterprise while Zelda screwed around, while my father sucked down excellent Pinot Noir in California, while my mother lost her mind. But I took off for Paris, of all the irresponsible places. I broke the rules, and now I'm being punished.

My phone starts vibrating inside the fringed bag I've borrowed from Zelda's trailer, and I claw it open in a panic, hoping, fearing, certain that it's Zelda, that she's somehow been watching me and knows that I'm headed upstairs to my mother's room. But Zelda's phone is black, shiny, and lifeless, just a cool piece of glass and metal in my hand, radiating my sister's presence like an alien doppelgänger.

I realize with a slight lag that it's my own phone ringing, and I set Zelda's down on the counter.

It's Nico. I jump with a guilty start, realizing how thoroughly he's been pushed out of my mind. This man, whom I wake up next to nearly every day, whom I've said I love, has been eclipsed by just a few days with the Antipovas. *And by Wyatt,* a nasty little voice suggests, and I think it sounds like Zelda. I dither with my finger above the answer icon. I don't want to answer the phone, I realize. But that's the old me. Not the Paris me.

"Nico, *salut!*"

"Ava, is that you?" Nico says in his thick French accent. I love that accent. It sounds like a caricature. Even though I'm capable enough in French for us to communicate well, I always prefer to speak English with Nico, to hear his silly Gallic pronunciations. A cruel part of me has occasionally wondered if I like having the upper hand linguistically, if what I enjoy is actually being able to supply tricky vocabulary terms and to correct grammatical slips. Growing up between hyper-verbal Zelda and sharp-tongued Nadine has made me hungry for linguistic supremacy in any arena. But who doesn't like to be on top of the conversation? To win?

"Yes. It's so good to hear your voice."

"I thought you would call when you debarked the plane, but I didn't hear. . . ." There is a tiny hint of recrimination in this, and I realize that I had promised to call on my arrival. It was one of the last things I said after kissing him on the brow, while he lay sleepily on the foldout couch in my tiny apartment.

"Oh, God, I'm so sorry! Things have been a little disorganized here—I've really had my hands full."

"I thought that. Are you all right?"

"I'm . . . yeah, I'm okay. It's all a little crazy at the moment, but I'm trying to get a handle on what needs to be done."

"Your sister . . . she is . . . ?" Nico trails off delicately.

"Well, there's still some official confusion—the cops have to confirm everything," I say vaguely. I can hardly tell him that I think Zelda is alive and well, laughing at all the mayhem she's created from a safe distance. I would sound crazy.

"And your father? He came for you?"

"Yeah, he picked me up. He's . . . the same as ever," I answer with a shake of my head.

"Your mom? How is she?"

"Just okay, I think. She's been really disoriented. Thinks I'm Zelda half the time."

"That . . . must be difficult," Nico says after a pause. I realize I'm making him do all the conversational work; I've clammed up and am now just politely responding to questions. I hate the phone.

"It must be really late there—are you okay?" I ask, trying to redeem myself.

"Oh, not so late. I had a few glasses of wine after work," he says. I can hear a smile in his voice.

"Tell me where you went," I say eagerly. I want to be back in Paris, meeting him at one of our cafés for an Armagnac.

"We went to Le Compas. Your favorite," he says, still smiling. I groan in envy.

"Oh, c'mon! You're forbidden to go without me!" I immediately regret this; I've never given him rules before, never consciously tried to control his comings and goings. I'm not the same Ava there; I've changed. But he doesn't seem to notice. He just chuckles.

"It wasn't the same without you. I kept looking for you in the corner, anytime a girl with black hair walked by. I saw someone I thought to be you. She resembled you."

"I miss you," I gush, comforted and absurdly touched by this recognition of my absence.

"You are missing me," he answers in a favorite play with French grammar. I smile at the old game.

"*Tu me manques.* Is it hot there?"

"Not too much. But I am inside the most of the day." Nico works in finance, at the Bourse, not far from my apartment. He wears stiff, clean suits that always smell very faintly of cigarettes, and he carries a leather bag filled with important papers. I love this about him, how thoroughly sanctioned he is. He has stuck to the guidelines of capitalism, and he's winning at it.

"And what are you going to do now?" I ask.

"I'm going home to your apartment," he answers promptly. "Just around the corner. I want to sleep in a bed that smells of you."

"I miss you," I say again, in English this time.

"I miss you too."

"I'll let you go to bed. I was just about to go check on my mother."

"Good luck, Ava. I think of you."

"Me too."

"Will you call me tomorrow?" he asks with a hint of hesitation.

"Of course I will. *Bonne nuit,*" I say and end the conversation. I stare out the window for a moment before sliding the phone back into my bag. I go into the kitchen and open the fridge. In the right-hand crisper I've hidden some nicer whites: wines we didn't make ourselves. I pull one of them out. I reach up into the too-tall wooden cabinets that my mother insisted on and get down two wineglasses. I hope Mom will see this as a treat or, maybe, a bribe for her cooperation. She's not usually allowed real wineglasses in her room, not since the tremors started intensifying. One of Zelda's emails detailed a harrowing experience wherein Mom managed to slice open her fingers with a broken wineglass, and Zelda was convinced that Nadine had tried to off herself. Though I can't say there wasn't a longish moment, as I stood in the doorway, dear sister, when I thought: Damn, if I'd just come upstairs a little later, Zelda had written. But it had apparently been accidental, and Zelda had patched Nadine up quite nicely.

I rummage in the drawer for a corkscrew but can't seem to find one.

I climb the stairs slowly, wineglasses dangling downward from one hand, clinking together like wind chimes, the cold bottle sweating moisture into my other hand. I'm dwelling on my conversation with

Nico, wondering why it hadn't once crossed my mind to call him to see how he's doing. The conversation has left me with a ripe, too-creamy taste festering away at the back of my tongue, like a wine that's gone through too much malolactic fermentation. Like bad dairy. Hearing Nico's voice was comforting, but it has left me feeling hollow. I wonder if I didn't call him because I liked the idea of him going about his business in Paris, missing me, more than I wanted the reality of hearing him say it. Nico is incredible, and aside from Zelda and Wyatt, I've never been so close with anyone. But. But. Removed from all the magic and distraction and performance of Paris, I feel as though Nico is flattened out somehow, rendered just a cookie cutout of someone I'm supposed to love. I shake my head in frustration. This place is bad for me.

My mother's door is closed, of course, and I pause in front of it, childlike in my sudden timidity. But I'm not eight years old anymore, and Nadine can just try to terrorize me out of the room. I have what she wants in my hand. I tuck the bottle of wine under my armpit and turn the handle of her door.

Mom is sitting in her chair, looking out the window that faces onto the lake. It's a hot, hazy summer evening, a few hours before sunset. Everything is glowing with the filtered light, and the temperature is starting to drop. She doesn't turn around when I come in.

"Hi, Mom." She still doesn't turn. There's an extra chair in the corner of her room, and I set down the glasses to grab it with one arm and carry it awkwardly, pressed painfully against my hip. I set it down next to hers, looking out at the vineyard and the lake. I'm strangely reluctant to let go of the wine bottle; it's a talisman against her viciousness. I want her to see me holding it before she opens her mouth. "Happy hour?" I say cheerfully.

"Among my favorite words in the English language," she answers, and I can't help smiling. I go back to where the glasses are perched on the table and realize that I never managed to find the corkscrew.

"Fuck," I say in irritation.

"There's one in the drawer next to my bed," Mom says uncannily.

"You never did come prepared. Always a little . . . spacey. That's what your first-grade teacher said, at least." I clench my teeth, already on edge. Which of us does she think she's talking to? I find the opener and deftly uncork the wine, slopping it into the expensive, thin wine-glasses. It's a soothing noise. "I'm afraid I don't have an ice bucket," Mom adds. "I'm sure you forgot to bring that up as well."

"Knowing you," I snap, "I assumed the wine would be long gone before we had to worry about it getting warm."

Nadine says nothing, but she looks at me balefully when I hand her the glass.

"My, my, real glass today. I must have been a good girl." Her hands shake as she accepts the delicate stemware, but I don't know if it's a symptom of her illness or if it's the DTs.

"Has Dad brought up dinner yet?" I realize, with a frisson of ac-complishment, how long it's been since I've eaten.

"I haven't seen your father in years," she says airily, with a wave of her hand. "Good riddance. I can go a few more without seeing him too."

"You had wine with him last night and lunch earlier today," I say sharply, unfairly.

"Oh." She looks perplexed, scared. "Other than that, of course," she continues, attempting a casual tone. "I meant, of course, that it's been years since we've had a proper dinner together."

"Right." I drink a healthy swallow of the crisp wine. I'm thirsty after my sweaty nap in Zelda's trailer. I wonder just what Zelda wants to accomplish by suggesting this tête-à-tête, what further information I'm supposed to glean by trying to spend time alone with Nadine. What could Zelda be plotting? And what information could my mother possibly have?

"And how is Paris, Ava? I should hope that you're at least *enjoying* your childish escapade."

"Delightful, Mom." I pause. "How has it been here?" I say tenta-tively.

"How do you think? I'm fucking losing my mind in little bits and pieces every day, and your sister has managed to single-handedly destroy the vineyard."

"I hardly think it was single-handed," I say.

"Well, she's done an appalling job of managing even day-to-day operations. You were the one with any knowledge of how this works. It was supposed to be you taking care of things."

"Well, I'm sorry I didn't drop everything to pursue your half-cocked dream," I snipe in annoyance. "And sorry that Zelda was singularly unprepared for it. We can't all have your resources, Mom. Oh, yeah, what did you eat for breakfast?" I can see her flinch slightly. "What, can't remember?" I know this is unfair. But I sit in silence for a long moment. "I'm sorry. I don't want to be nasty with you."

"You were never much good at it, anyway. Too thin-skinned," Nadine says.

"Listen, this is all sort of rough on me. I'm jet-lagged, hungover, and . . . grieving," I say.

"Grieving?" Nadine snorts. "For Zelda? The sister you abandoned?"

"The sister who died," I say.

She snorts again. "You think so?" she says lightly.

I turn my head to look at her alertly. Does she know?

"What do you mean, Mom?"

"Come now, Ava. I know you're naïve and occasionally blind to reality, but you knew Zelda almost as well as I did."

"Almost as well? *We're twins*," I hiss in annoyance, unsure why this challenge to my ultimate knowledge of Zelda wounds me like it does. Why should I care if Mom knew her better? Is it a bloody competition? But of course it is.

"Yes, but I grew both of you inside me. I gave you life," she explains, draining her glass and imperiously gesturing for more. I fetch the bottle from the table and bring it to sit between us, refilling both of our empty glasses.

"Either way. What did you mean?"

"She's not really dead, Ava. Gullible as you are, you must surely know that."

"What makes you think so?"

"Come, now. It's all a little too neat and perfect, isn't it. Like one of Zelda's games."

I look at her in surprise. "You know, Mom," I say, "for someone slowly falling apart from dementia, you're surprisingly lucid."

She laughs. "I'm not entirely gone yet. I know it comes and goes, but I still have good moments. Good days." I nod, but I remember her reaction just a few minutes ago, her scared, vacant expression. "Anyway, I'll have to be really out of it before I fail to recognize one of your sister's schemes. She's up to something." Mom glances toward the cinders that sit where the barn once did.

"Yeah, I know," I say softly. "Fuck knows what, though."

"It's for you," Mom says simply. "All of her games, all of her plans—it was always about you. Zelda always needed an audience, and she was born with the one she preferred most. This . . . is about you. When you were little, she would make up stories for you, would spin these long tales. You would sit for hours, listening to her."

We both stare out at the lake, silently sucking down Sauvignon Blanc. When my glass is empty, I stand up to go. I don't know why Zelda sent me up here, whether what Nadine just said was the information she wanted me to have. Why would it matter, anyway? I've already suspected that this is somehow about me, about Zelda trying to suck me back in. Why would she need our mother to confirm it? And how could she depend on Nadine to actually be present enough to express it? I shake my head in annoyance. Maybe I've gotten the clue wrong: Intimacy with Nadine is harder than with anyone else, sure, and my mother is the person who called me out on it, but maybe Zelda means something else entirely.

"Ava, would you bring me another bottle?" Mom sounds almost plaintive, and I flinch at the soft, pleading edge in her voice. She's asking nicely, instead of barking orders or intimidating me. I'm a sucker for that, as she must know, and I yield. I go downstairs and fetch another bottle of wine from the fridge. I'm about to snag one from my stash in the crisper, but notice some iffy local Rieslings lined in the door, already cold. I realize belatedly that Marlon must have restocked the fridge. Of course that would be the one domestic duty he would reliably take on. I bring the bottle upstairs and uncork it, using the opener I left on the table. After I refill Nadine's glass, I impulsively plant a kiss on her forehead.

"Night, Mom. There's a sleeping pill next to the bed if you need it."

"In case the bottle doesn't finish me off?" she asks with a sharp tone.

"Just . . . in case," I say with a weary sigh.

"Put the corkscrew back, Ava," she snaps, all the soft wheedling tones gone from her voice. "Your stuff is always all over the house, and I can't live like that. If you'd just put things back where you got them from, you'd have them when you need them. You spend half your life looking for things."

I grit my teeth in fury. How the fuck would she know what I'm like? I'm tempted to just walk out of the room. But I am not, in fact, the messy person my mother maintains I am. I fold my clothes when I take them off; I do the dishes as soon as I've finished using them. I've always done as our mother insisted, out of a sense of rightness. Zelda is the whirlwind who leaves destruction, clutter, mayhem in her wake. I pick up my wineglass from the floor and open the drawer to put the corkscrew back where I found it. I frown as I'm returning it. In the drawer is an envelope addressed to me in my sister's handwriting. I glance over at my mother, unsure whether she knows that this has been here. Is she in cahoots with Zelda? But she doesn't turn around or give any recognition that she knows what I've just found.

"I guess I'll just go to bed, then," I say, wondering if she'll come clean or give any sign that she knows more than she's telling.

"I don't give a shit," she snarls, her mood snapping. I know that it's a symptom of the dementia, but it's hard to remember that. She's been unstable her whole life. I wonder, not for the first time, if the dementia has been a part of our lives all along. Maybe the disease gets diagnosed only after it reaches a certain degree of severity. Maybe she was sick during all of our childhood. Maybe there's an organic, chemical reason why she treated us the way she did. Other than the alcohol, of course.

"You and Zelda both. Just lurking around here, waiting for me to say something stupid. You love this," she screeches, her voice growing shrill. "You couldn't be happier. You want me to look like a damn fool. Well, Ava, are you enjoying your revenge? Are you?" she screams.

"Of course not, Mom. This is hell for all of us."

"What do you know of hell? *You* don't live like *this*! Get out, you miserable, gloating bitch!" Nadine hurls her wineglass at me, but it veers wildly to the left and crashes onto the floor in the hallway, where it shatters most dramatically. Nadine will be remorseful as soon as I've closed the door—not for having screamed at me but for having sacrificed her drinking receptacle as a prop in her tantrum. At the moment, I honestly don't care if she slices off every one of her fingers with the broken glass before moving on to her toes.

"Night, Mom," I say as calmly as I can. I clutch the envelope and walk out of the room, shutting and locking my mother's door behind myself, for once feeling no guilt at all for the twist of the key.

In the hall, I step gingerly around the broken glass. Zelda would probably just leave it there, waiting for someone to come tidy it up, or for the glass to be ground into fine sand between boards and soles. Zelda revels in entropy. But I obviously can't leave the shattered wineglass lying on the ground, so I stoop to pick up the larger shards. I walk them to the upstairs bathroom, where I find a broom and a dustpan. I slice my foot open in a tiny, raw gash as I kneel to sweep up the rest of the remains, but I let the wound bleed onto the cool floor, ignoring it.

Standing in front of my mother's door, I open the envelope, feeling nervous. Even though I've been receiving emails from Zelda, this feels strangely intimate, physical. I can't remember the last time I got a real letter from anyone. Something about a person's writing is immediate and corporeal, present. Could she have been in the house while I was out? Could she have planted the note for me earlier today? Or did she do it before the barn burned?

Inside the envelope, there is no letter, though. Just a scrap of paper with the name *Jason* scrawled across it. I flip the paper over, and on the back is a short P.S.: *Surely there's some photographic evidence somewhere, eh, Ava?*

# 11

Kitchen-bound, I escape downstairs. At the sink, with a cold washcloth fixed to the back of my neck and my wineglass spruced up with a refill, I stare out the window toward the barn, thinking. I'm so distracted that I barely hear Marlon and Opal coming inside, and I jump when Opal touches my shoulder.

"Ava, doll, are you hot?" Her hands reach for the washcloth on my neck, and she takes it away, runs it under the cold tap, wrings it out, and puts it back on my neck, her gnarled and bejeweled fingers rubbing my nape with circular motions. I grit my teeth, trying not to scoot away. I can feel the heat of her body close behind me. She's smaller than I am, and she peers out the window over my shoulder. "Oh, sweetheart. I know." She grabs my hand and gives it a squeeze. I flinch visibly, but Opal doesn't seem to notice or care. I take a big swallow from my glass and glance toward Marlon, who is slumped in one of the chairs in the living room.

"Glass of wine, Pops?" I ask cheerily. He gazes at me blankly for a second before trying for a smile. It's an appalling attempt. He looks haggard, old, the skin beneath his eyes puffed and bruised. My elegant, dapper father, who until recently looked like a man of forty, now hunched and wizened. Deflated.

"When I wanted one earlier, we didn't seem to have any fucking corkscrews," he complains. "Had to go to the Dandy Mart to buy one."

I go to the fridge and fill a glass for him in pity.

"I'll take one, too, Ava—thanks for asking," Opal says testily. I pour her a third of a glass, a little passive-aggressively, and she accepts it with a roll of her eyes, perching on a stool at the kitchen counter. "Come here, sit, dear. I'd like to talk to you." I desperately don't want this, but I sit nonetheless. "Now, Ava. What are you doing with yourself, over there in Paris? No, no," she cuts me off as I open my mouth. "I understand youthful experimentation and the desire to define yourself. Believe me. I spent a semester in Spain when I was your age. It was the best thing for me. Which is why I didn't raise an eyebrow when Marlon asked for the money to send you to do your little degree in France . . ." She smiles indulgently at Marlon, who is looking pointedly out the window.

"I didn't realize you were bankrolling it, Grandma," I say, looking directly at Marlon. He has definitely implied that his successes in California were financing my "youthful experimentation." Opal raises her eyebrows and looks over at Marlon too.

"Oh, well. Not entirely, but yes. And I'm not saying that gives me any right to comment on your choices or to help make those choices but . . ." Yes, it does, I think sourly. You've bought me, Grandma. Let's see what it costs.

"No, no, I'd love to hear your opinion," I say obligingly, and she smiles, patting my hand again. She holds on to it this time.

"Well, dear, I was very impressed when you finished your first degree, studying something that would be truly useful to you and your family. Silenus is such a complicated investment, and it really needs someone with skill and training. But you're very young, and I know you want to go out and sow your wild oats and all. When I was young, only boys were allowed to sow their oats, and I think it's amazing that your generation is able to give women the same privilege," Opal says with a judgy smirk.

"We're making all kinds of headway in gender equity," I agree, with only the barest note of sarcasm. She doesn't really hear me; I've always spoken too quickly, and I suspect Opal catches only half of the words I say.

"But I wonder about this little . . . undertaking. What is it you're doing? French literature?"

"I'm actually looking at a French literary movement, OuLiPo, and the American author Edgar Allan Poe. Particularly in how they think about constraint. Both Poe and the OuLiPo authors place formal restrictions on how they write, believing that these imposed rules actually produce more creative insight. Being limited forces you to become more creative. I'm interested in possible intersections—"

"I mean, I'm sure it's very interesting, but what practical use is it?" Opal interrupts. "I know we all tolerated Zelda's adventures, her experiments in the humanities, but Zelda was . . . artistic and, frankly . . . not all that practical. Without her, it's especially important that you be realistic. I mean, what sort of job are you going to be able to get?"

"Probably none at all. I was hoping to marry some French count."

She frowns. "Well, I'm just not sure that's reasonable. You've been in France for, what, twenty-one months?" She says this casually enough, but I realize that she's been counting quite closely. I wonder if the coffers aren't quite as deep as we've always assumed. But Opal has always been parsimonious with her cash.

"About that long."

"I just think maybe with Zelda . . . gone, it's time to think about the future. Really consider your options." Her fingers are stroking my knuckles. I want to scream.

"I have been, a bit. I'm just . . . not in a good place to make decisions right now. The shock," I say.

Marlon finally speaks: "Ma, let her be for a minute." He sounds tired. "None of us can really make much of a plan right now. I'm sure Ava will be here for a few weeks, taking care of business, and you'll have plenty of time to consider . . ."

I wince. I don't want to be here for a few weeks. I want out.

"Yes, I'm sure after you've gone back to Napa," Opal says, "we'll have lots of girl time to really talk about what's important. And I'm sure Ava has some stories about French men to share when her father's not around." Opal winks at me, giving my hand another squeeze.

"When are you going back to California?" I say, trying to keep the note of panic out of my voice.

Marlon avoids eye contact. "I, uh, well, have to go back for some business stuff. The police are still wrapping up loose ends, and I thought I could fly back for a funeral, once they've, uh . . ."

"I see. Okay." I toss back the rest of my glass. I'm suddenly shattered, utterly spent. These people. Family fatigue, the pervasive companion of my weary, exhausted heart, that organ that I cannot exorcize of its boundless, quaking dejection. I have to get away from here. "Well, I've got plans." I stand up clumsily.

"You're not driving anywhere, are you?" Opal says in concern, peering into my eyes. I'm sure she's practiced in assessing Antipovan inebriation.

"Nope," I answer. I saunter toward the door, realizing vaguely that I haven't eaten all day. But I know I can't. Food would only fill me with despair and a strong sense of failure, and I would just be tempted to go puke it up. And I promised Zelda that I would stop that. Not that the promise always prevents me, but right now, it feels more important. Just as I'm walking out the door, Opal calls after me.

"Your phone, Ava! You've left your phone!"

I frown in confusion; I can feel my phone in the bag slung over my shoulder. I've left Zelda's phone out on the counter, for everyone to see. Idiot.

"Thanks, Grandma," I say, going back to claim it in relief. Jesus, what if someone realized it was Zelda's other, secret phone? I must be losing my mind. I wave good night, and though I'm tempted to snag a bottle of wine from the fridge, I'm reluctant to do it in front of Opal. I feel like I'm sixteen, trying so hard to play by everyone's rules.

Outside, the sun is setting, and the fireflies are blinking along the path to Zelda's trailer. I head there automatically, unsure of what to do. I refresh her email, hoping for another missive that will point me toward this Jason guy, but there's nothing there. I open the Facebook app and flip through all the photos she's posted in the last six months; there's no one who could be a Jason in any of the photos. I stare at the shots of Holly Whitaker, hoping her face or body will jar some memory loose, but I genuinely can't recognize her.

I'm walking along the driveway, barefoot, and I can feel dirt and crud accumulating in the cut on my foot. Normally, I'm the sort of person who goes straight for the disinfectant, followed by antibiotic cream, followed by Band-Aids changed regularly. But not tonight. I realize I haven't showered in a while either. Tonight, I glory in my grime. Or, rather, I wish I did. Which is close enough.

After striking out with the Facebook pictures, I pause. Could there be an actual, physical photo out there? Should I have stayed up at the house to look through the photo albums? That seems all wrong, though; Nadine kept those albums. She had gone through a period of photographic frenzy, obsessively documenting our growth, our activities. She took snapshots of us swimming, eating, playing dress-up. The photos would all be printed, and neatly arranged in clean, black-and-white albums, which she would crack out whenever anyone accused her of being a bad parent; it was her proof, her evidence that she must love us. Otherwise, why would she have bothered taking so many pictures? I reflect that she would have loved Facebook; she could have posted picture after picture of her pretty twin daughters, wearing her most recent costumes, immersed in the most recent, glamorous adventure. People would have liked her photos, and she would have received the affirmation of her superior mothering that she craved, that she felt was her reward for submitting to the indecency of motherhood. I realize that I'm thinking of her in the past tense. Or maybe it's conditional; I don't know. The mother that could have been.

She'd stopped taking pictures when we hit puberty, though, and went through a chubby patch. Or, rather, when I did. My childish, sharp angles softened, my once-spindly arms looked swollen, my breasts grew fleshy and my belly rounded. The camera disappeared into a closet, and suddenly we found ourselves eating kale salads for dinner most nights. Zelda remained angular and fairy-like, but I looked puffy and plump. The phase didn't last very long. I was a quick study, and I soon realized that home life was markedly less tempestuous if I ate my mother's tiny green portions without complaint. Without noting that Zelda was given a small heap of pasta alongside her kale. Zelda, pitying me and my Spartan portions, sometimes secreted away starchy treats, which she would sneak into my room at night. Though this was probably motivated by kindness, my competitive self couldn't help seeing it as sabotage.

For our fourteenth birthday, Zelda was given a beautiful green vintage Chanel dress (size 2) and I was given a two-year subscription to *Health* magazine and a very expensive juicer. By our fifteenth birthday, I was borrowing Zelda's Chanel dress, which she usually left in a heap of dirty clothes, and she barely even noticed when I tugged it on over my newly slimmed hips. My mother didn't comment when I descended the steps in Zelda's party gown. She did, however, pour me a glass of Champagne and congratulate me on a "very good, disciplined year."

The memory of that birthday makes me feel relieved and pleased that I haven't eaten dinner; the dull ache in my belly fills me with warmth, and I smile quietly in the dark. I continue to fiddle with Zelda's phone, flipping through the screens. I look at all the open tabs on Safari and search through the photos on her photo app. Nothing. Finally, I notice that she had installed the Instagram app.

I tap it open and am greeted with a series of pictures glimmering with filtered light. She has photos taken from Silenus's deck at sunset, a few pictures of our mother in unflattering poses, one shot of Wyatt. In the most recent photo, I recognize Holly Whitaker, and I squint at it. It looks like she's in a bar. The next photo is also of her, with her arm draped around a shortish, beefy guy with a crew cut. They're standing in front of a bar that I immediately recognize. Kuma's. Or Kuma Charmers, as it is officially named. It's a strip club located about halfway between Seneca and Cayuga Lakes. I've never been inside, but I've driven by it on many a Saturday night, when rusty pickups cram into the parking lot just off the county highway, on display for everyone to see. I wonder if this is Jason, if this is what Zelda wants me to find. Walking down the hill, I flick through the rest of the photos but find nothing else that raises eyebrows. I flip back to the picture, studying it for any other details. On closer inspection, Holly has glazed eyes, and "Jason" looks like he might be holding her upright. The way she's dressed makes me wonder if she could be an employee of Kuma's.

I stop short in front of Zelda's trailer when I realize there's another truck parked outside. Wyatt. He's sitting on the steps of the trailer, leaning back and looking up at the sky. His jeans are snug, and he's wearing a tight V-neck T-shirt. Zelda's work, I suspect.

"Can't stay away?" I say, wishing I had something wittier to offer.

"I figured you wouldn't want to stay in the house with your momma, especially with Marlon up there. Thought you might want company."

"I've had an awful lot of company today."

"I'll go, if you want. I just thought you might appreciate conversation with someone who doesn't share any genes with you. To remind you that crazy as you are, you're the sane one," he says.

I can't help smiling. It might be flattery, but I believe him, and it's what I need to hear. "Well, it is nice to have some confirmation."

"It must be a madhouse up there."

"Even my grandmother is here."

He makes a face; he doesn't much care for Opal. She's touchy-feely with him, too, and I suspect she may have been too appreciative of his biceps when she visited for our high school graduation. She hadn't stopped fussing at me that whole weekend: "Is that lovely boy your boyfriend? He certainly is good-looking. Don't string him along too long, Ava." I suspected Zelda of oversharing, but in retrospect, Wyatt's and my taut game of sexual tension and emotional withholding had probably been painfully obvious to anyone not caught in the throes of high school hormones.

"Icing on the cake. Your mom drinking?" he asks.

I snort. "What do you think?"

"And you?" He knows he's on thin ice here, so he's keeping his tone very light.

"A bit."

"Did you eat any dinner?" I look at him sullenly, guiltily. "You look thin, Ava." I know it's not meant as a compliment, but I can't help it. I'm pleased. "Let me take you for a bite to eat."

"I'm afraid I have errands to run," I say in irritation. I fumble in my bag for the keys to the truck, but I drop them on the dark ground. Wyatt moves catlike from his perch on the steps and has them between his fingers before I can bend down and scoop them up.

"Ava, don't be stupid. You trying to kill yourself with carelessness?"

"Runs in the family. I always was just a little behind Zelda," I say petulantly.

He squints. "Don't you fucking say stuff like that. You have to take better care of yourself. Hey, you hear me?" he says when I start to turn away from him.

"Thanks for your patronizing suggestions. Noted."

He softens. Wyatt hates to fight. "Hey, I'm just worried, Pea." His casual use of that old nickname makes my breath catch in my throat. Pea, short for "Sweet Pea." Corny as hell, but it hits home, like nicknames are supposed to. Shortcuts to intimacy. "Let me take you for a snack, and then we'll do your errands together. Though I'm afraid to ask what errands you might be doing at this time of night," he adds with a nervous quirk of his mouth.

I look at him, considering. I am a bit tipsy, and even though it's all back roads to Kuma's, given my druthers, I would still prefer not to drive drunk. It also crosses my mind that having him along when I head to the strip club might not be the worst idea. And, if I were to be candid with myself, a glimmer of something else flickers through my mind. I miss him.

"What's for dinner?" I ask.

# 12

Like everyone else in Hector, we get dinner from Stonecat, up the road from Silenus. It's a simple barn-shaped building that appears deceptively hick. Inside, though, there's a rustic bar, a raised back deck that looks out onto the lake, and a shockingly capable kitchen that whips up gourmet country food. I always struggle to describe Hector to anyone not from here; it is slippery in its distillation of bumpkins, rednecks, foodies, right-wingers, and wine snobs. Some of the people I see at the bar tonight work outdoors with their hands all day and have never left the county. I recognize a neighbor who I know for a fact went to Ithaca for the first time two years ago and celebrated the journey as though he'd ventured halfway across the world. At the other end of the bar is someone who, rarely enough, made some money in the wine business and has a second home in Tuscany.

I can tell from the way the bartender looks at me that Zelda must come here often, possibly with Wyatt; I recognize him from high school and wiggle my fingers in greeting. He squints back at me suspiciously, and without greeting me in return he asks if I also want no red onion on my falafel sandwich. I don't want onion, but perversely I tell him I'll have it. I feel like I have to eat it, because Zelda doesn't. Wyatt squints at me strangely.

"You know, she liked red onion," he says when I raise my eyebrow at his expression. "She stopped eating it 'cause of you."

"She did?" I furrow my brows, trying to remember her eating it. "No, she always asked if there was red onion before she ordered tuna salad sandwiches. She said it ruined it."

"That was for you. You guys usually split your food."

He's right. I'm caught off guard, having been so blind to a small generosity. I wonder if there are others I have failed to catch.

As we wait for our sandwiches, we decide to order wine. This, too, is new for Wyatt; in high school he was definitely a beer guy. He orders me a glass of dry Sauvignon Blanc without asking, which both irritates and charms me. Wyatt drinks a red, even though it's still hot out. The bar buzzes with summer and alcohol. His thigh brushes up against my own, hot and solid, and I feel a tremor deep behind my navel that I'm desperate to ignore.

"So, Wyatt, what are you up to these days?" I say, scooting away from him. I'm grateful when the bartender slides my glass of wine across the old cherrywood bar. The twin of this bar, an identical slab of wood, split from the same tree, props up similarly rural barflies in Trumansburg, a scant fourteen miles away.

"I thought Zelda would have told you."

"Zelda detected that it was a sensitive subject. She didn't mention you too much. In the emails."

"Ah. I knew she was writing you. I assumed it was to, uh, explain. I figured I'd better let her handle it." I squint at him, wondering if there's subtext to the comment.

"Nope. I think it was to guilt me into coming home." I shrug. "Finally worked."

"Well, I finished up my degree. Environmental science and sustainability."

"I remember," I say testily.

"I've been at Silenus a lot. Helping out. You know. With the grapes."

"I figured."

"Zelda's done okay, you know. She learned a whole lot, worked her ass off. She can really commit to something when she wants to." I don't answer, just swish the wine in my glass. "And the rest of the time, I'm working on the farm with the 'rents," he continues.

"Soybeans still?"

"And some veggies now. We want to start a CSA, maybe. Eventually."

I nod. Wyatt's parents are old hippie farmers who have been out in Hector for decades. When they're not farming, they run a meditation retreat center that attracts primarily other old hippie farmers. They're nice people, but they never liked me much. They (quite rightly) thought I wasn't very good for their son.

"And you don't mind working with them?" I ask casually.

"It's been . . . a little strange," he admits. "But it feels good too. Knowing they can rely on me as they get older." He blushes suddenly and looks away.

"It's okay, Wy. I've made my peace with abandoning my mother and my responsibilities. I had to do it." He nods, unconvinced. "Have they at least gotten less passive-aggressive with their disapproval?" I ask.

He laughs. "Not entirely, but they've toned it down. Strangely enough, they liked Zelda. Superficially, at least, she was more their kind of girl."

I'm hurt, but not surprised. Wyatt was unapologetically preppy in high school: neat haircut; clean, boring clothes. He played sports, made good grades, and was an all-around Goody Two-shoes. His bedraggled, pot-smoking leftist parents were alarmed and dismayed that their only child turned out to be so straitlaced. They wanted him to rebel, do mushrooms, start a political newspaper, date men, grow his hair. Wyatt was the antithesis of their flower-child fantasy, with his strong chin and lack of imagination. When he brought me home, I could see their internal shudder; I could be wrong, but I think I was even wearing pearls when he introduced me to them. I was another confirmation that Wyatt had been corrupted by the conservatives in the school district, that he would live out a life of commercial conformity and would throw away everything they had fought so hard for.

"I imagine Zelda won over their hearts and minds pretty easily. What, did she bring a joint?" I ask in amusement.

"She told you?" he says, surprised.

"No!" I chortle. "A guess. She *didn't.*"

Wyatt grins sheepishly. "Yep. In her best garb too. Flowers in her hair, some crazy kimono thing."

"I bet they loved her," I say with a rueful shake of my head. I'm sharply jealous but grateful for the lighthearted, casual tone the evening has taken thus far, and I don't want to create drama. Above all, I want to avoid talking about that night.

"And, uh, Paris?" Wyatt asks, looking intently at the smooth red of his Pinot Noir.

"Good. Magical. Expensive," I answer nonchalantly. No one in Hector knows about Nico, and I'd prefer it that way. I'm listening to the banjo jiving in the background, gazing at the dwindling liquid in my glass, and fixating on the possibility of another when the bartender catches Wyatt's eye and hands him a bag filled with our dinner. Wyatt nods and shakes the guy's hand in a hearty gesture that would make anyone else look absurd. He is uncannily likable. I shake my head, smiling privately.

Wyatt leads me out of the bar, which is quickly filling up with locals. A handful of young, dandily dressed twentysomethings, but mainly weathered-looking farmers, wearing dirty shirts and worn jeans, their brown faces wrinkled and furrowed by decades without sunscreen. I nod politely at another neighbor, who doesn't nod back. I can't tell if it's because he's drunk or if there's some sort of angry undertone. I wonder if everyone over here on the lake judges me for leaving. Or maybe he thinks I'm my sister. Ah, country living.

As we walk across the parking lot, I hear someone hollering behind us and instinctively whirl around. Some guy with a thin blond mustache and ropy muscles in his neck is heading toward me, yelling.

"You fucking cunt. Where the fuck is my sister? Where the fuck is she?"

"Whoa, cowboy," Wyatt says, stepping between us. He's a gentle soul, but I've seen him throw a punch or two when he's appropriately riled. His arm curls around me, protecting me. "Kyle, right?"

"Fuck you, asshole. I'm talking to her!" The guy is short and has to sort of leap around Wyatt to point his hand at me in a distinctly menacing way. "She's the goddamn lesbo been fucking my little sister!"

"I think you have me confused with someone else," I say slowly, my eyebrows raised. *Oh, really, Zelda.* "I'm Ava Antipova. Zelda's twin sister."

The angry guy looks barely convinced by this, but he does back off. "Fuck you. I know what she and Kayla been up to. When I find Kayla or Zelda, they're both fucking dead! They better both stay disappeared," he spits out, making that absurd roosterlike gesture that men make when they're trying to be assertive. "Bitch." He strides back toward the bar in a self-satisfied stroll.

"Uh . . ." I say to Wyatt.

"You remember Kyle Richardson? Upperclassman? A real prick. His little sister is Kayla Richardson. She and Zelda were, uh, friends."

I make a note to see if she's the girl on Zelda's Facebook page. "Were they having sex?" I ask tonelessly.

"I don't really know. Zelda could be real secretive. And she and I hadn't. I mean we weren't—" He coughs uncomfortably. I shrug.

As I jump up into the cab of Wyatt's truck, I realize that I am starving. I fish out our falafel and start devouring my own, not minding the *tzatziki* that is leaking into the bag in my lap. Wyatt watches in amusement, silently unwrapping his own sandwich. He neatly, almost daintily, polishes it off in a few bites.

"Well, Ava? Where am I taking you?" he asks, poised in the parking lot.

I hesitate for a moment. He's staring at me with an expression I can't read.

"Kuma's."

"Are we thinking of the same Kuma's?" he asks with a raised eyebrow.

"I only know the one. I'm looking for a guy named Jason," I explain. "I think he has something to do with . . . what happened to Zelda."

"What do you mean?"

"Zelda texted him from her burner phone the night of the fire, asking him to meet her at the barn at eleven. I don't know if Jason met Zelda or not." I pause again, wondering whether to disclose the rest of what the cops told me. "But the cops are looking for him too. I guess there were some chains on the barn doors."

Wyatt goes entirely white, and his hands grip the steering wheel. "Jesus, Zelda," he says quietly. "Does it have to do with the money? Or the drugs?"

"I have no idea. I've never heard of this guy. But . . . I think Zelda wanted me to find him and talk to him."

Wyatt frowns again, and I know he suspects something. I don't know what he's thinking, so I roll down the window and stare out at the trees lining the highway.

We're both lost in thought as we drive toward the strip club, and I keep checking Zelda's phone, expecting a new message or clue to pop up at any second. I wonder how she's keeping track of me—if she's watching me somehow or if she just knows me too well. Is she trying to escape her debt? Is it just some elaborate ploy to keep me sucked into her chaotic life? And why did she come to France?

Wyatt drives exactly at the speed limit, stoically silent. I imagine that he has questions, too, but he'll keep them under wraps until he's swollen and sore with anger. He'll be all calm silence and quiet support until something snaps, and then he'll be blind fury and raging emotion. That's a dangerous trait to have around us Antipovas; we like to wind people up and then release them, like some bored Greek deity with a flair for chaos. And Wyatt is a soft touch. Once, feeling mischievous, I asked Zelda to pretend to be me on the phone—we could never play switcheroo with Wyatt in the flesh; he knew us both too well—and he realized what we were up to after a few minutes of suppressed giggles. He hung up, and I assumed that was the end of it. But the next time I saw him, he was livid. He asked me, "How could you? Why would you make me reveal things to your sister that were meant only for you?" His cheeks were pink and he hollered at me, pacing and upset. Taken aback and suddenly feeling very guilty, I watched him with wide eyes, saying very little. It didn't occur to me how very much he cared. He finally said, "I say things to you I would never say to another person." I melted and let him lift me into his arms.

Some ten miles later, we pull into the parking lot at Kuma's, and my heart starts thumping. I've never been to a strip club, and I feel strangely nervous. I examine this anxiety. I'm not afraid of the female body, no matter how buck-nekkid or bedazzled. I don't think I'm afraid of seediness, or of male desire. Which suggests I'm afraid of what Zelda has left waiting in there. I glance at Wyatt as I slide down from the truck, and he looks deeply uncomfortable.

"You can wait in the truck, you know," I offer gallantly. I'm tough, independent. I can do this alone.

"And let you go in by yourself to confront this guy? You have to be kidding, Ava." He shakes his head as though I'm deranged, and I am relieved in spite of myself. I take a deep breath and stride across the parking lot. There are only a handful of cars here tonight, and I look around to see if I recognize any. It's mostly nondescript pickups. With a deep breath, I open the door.

It's dim inside, and very gritty. There's an elevated stage, with a pole in the middle, and a scatter of seats upon which half a dozen men are slumped, blankly ogling the fake-tanned limbs of a bland-looking dancer. I reflect, not for the first time, that film and television have robbed us of shock, of seeing things for the first time. Kuma's looks like the cheap strip club it is.

The bouncer by the door immediately asks us for seven dollars each, and I hand over a twenty. I'm appalled by how cheap the cover is. The bouncer doesn't even look twice at me, and I suspect I'm not the first woman to have shown up here. Fuck knows why any woman would come here, though. Any man either, for that matter. It can't be for the eroticism.

I can't help suspecting that the other men in the room feel the same ambivalence, though maybe not for the same ludicrous reasons. I marvel again at male sexuality—these men must be somehow getting off on this. Do they go into the parking lot to jack off? Or the bathroom? Do they fuck each other there? Or is it all oneiric, psychic wankery? And then I wonder about the woman dancing. Is she getting off too? Or is this just a marginally better paid job than waitressing, where you exchange physical and emotional labor for pocket change rather than dollar bills tucked into your G-string? I shudder with a wave of both guilt and relief that I will probably never know.

Wyatt is staring at the walls, seemingly trying to take in the decor. The walls are mostly empty, though, and the interior decorator seems to have gone for minimal ambience. We are both trying not to look at the clientele; something instinctive tells me that they would not appreciate our gaze, while theirs is so fully fixed. I glance around and am surprised that there is no bar.

"There's no booze," I whisper to Wyatt, even though the Lady Gaga song is playing so loudly that I wouldn't be overheard even if I shouted.

He nods. "Illegal in New York State. She'll probably, uh, take off that . . ."

I smile as he blushes again.

"Her thong?"

"Uh, yeah. They can't serve alcohol if it's full nudity."

"Oh." This is disappointing. "So they just go and drink in the parking lot?"

Wyatt shrugs. "I don't know. I've never been here, Ava."

"I'm shocked." I glance around, trying subtly to spot the guy who was in the photo with Holly Whitaker. With his tatted beefcake arms, I should be able to pick him out reasonably well, but he's not here.

"What now?" Wyatt looks at me helplessly. I settle down onto a stool, and Wyatt lurks protectively by my shoulder. I'm not quite sure what I was expecting. Wyatt's hand rests on my leg.

Another song comes on, and a new dancer appears on the stage. I immediately recognize Holly Whitaker; her crimpy hair and over-plucked eyebrows are hard to mistake. Why is Zelda's closest friend a stripper?

"Wyatt," I say uneasily, "you don't think Zelda was . . ." I trail off.

His eyebrows lurch toward the ceiling. "Jeez. You think she was . . . dancing?" He sounds physically pained. I don't blame him. I'm suddenly nauseous, the falafel roiling in my pickled stomach.

"I don't know. With the debt . . . She's always been sort of reckless. . . ."

"It is the sort of thing that would appeal to her," Wyatt acknowledges.

"It makes for a good story. She gets into stupid amounts of debt, tries to pay it off by dancing at a strip club for a while, privileged girl learns the ropes of seedy underworld . . . the sort of extreme narrative she would like." I'm convincing myself. *Fuck, Zelda.* It could explain what she'd been living off. All that cash. I fish around in my fringed bag for more money and sidle up toward the stage, waiting for the song to end. Holly is upside down on the pole, her inverted face appearing surreal and almost grotesque. Blue eye shadow. A tough look to rock. She rights herself, and I can hear her thighs squeaking along the pole even through the Katy Perry cacophony. I'm uncannily reminded of playgrounds, of sliding down poles wearing skirts, the slight burn of dry skin against warm metal. A sensation maybe only little girls and pole dancers know. The image of the playground in this place seems both deeply disturbing and fundamentally appropriate, especially since Holly is (well, was) wearing a schoolgirl outfit.

As the song ends, I lean forward with my twenty and try to catch Holly's eye. She sees me immediately, and her stage smile collapses.

"Can you meet me outside? In the back?" I ask in the lull between over-amped pop music tunes.

She regards me suspiciously but nods. "I'll try. I have to get changed, though." My hand stays where it is, holding the twenty extended, but she just looks at it, clearly disgusted, before collecting the other bills that have accumulated on the stage. She saunters off, and as she turns I get another glimpse of her neatly waxed nether regions. I wonder how Zelda felt about that. She was fervently anti-waxing. Predictably. She always liked things messy.

I nod to Wyatt and we walk back outside; I flash a pack of cigarettes at the bouncer by way of explanation.

"You smoke now?" Wyatt says in the parking lot.

"France. You know," I say, lighting up.

Wyatt looks distressed. "I always thought . . . never mind."

"What? Zelda smoked," I say, taking a drag. I smoke occasionally with Nico, because it seems like the right thing to do on a Parisian street while you're flirting outside a café. But I don't like cigarettes. I appreciate them as a prop, but there is something essentially dirty about inhaling them. I don't tell Wyatt this, just watch as he battles disappointment in who I've become. "Want one?" I tease.

"No," he says humorlessly. We walk around the side of the building; I have no idea what's out back, but I figure there has to be somewhere for patrons to sip inconspicuously out of their flasks. Surely. I've driven by this place dozens, maybe hundreds of times, always assuming that it was a bar, imbued with the cozy safety inherent in a public drinking place. Knowing that it's technically dry transforms its architecture into something suddenly strange, unreadable. It no longer makes abstract sense to me.

We loaf around the back, near a door I'm hoping leads to the stage. The cigarette is making me feel light-headed, a replacement high in the absence of booze. I know it will very shortly lead to nausea, but whatever. We mill around uncomfortably, and I check Zelda's phone and Facebook again. Could she be here? I scan the exterior walls, as though I might be able to suss her out with some twinly X-ray vision. I tell myself I'm not a prude, that I wouldn't care, but I really hope she hasn't been working here.

After a few minutes, Holly walks outside, a cheap kimono covering her schoolgirl costume. My addict reptile brain notes almost immediately that she has a bottle of something under her arm.

"You're Ava," she says huskily. The blue eye shadow is even more jarring away from the stage lights.

"You're very sharp," I say, before I can stop myself. I need this girl to like me, answer my questions. But I imagine that if she's friends with Zelda, she has to be used to some emotional abuse. "And this is Wyatt."

"I know," she says with a flirtatious smile, and both Wyatt and I raise our eyebrows in alarm. I shoot him an arch look, but he seems as surprised as I do. "I've seen pictures," she explains. She turns back to me and holds out the bottle. "Drink?"

I take a swallow; it's cheap coconut-flavored rum. It tastes god-awful, like sunscreen, but I'm grateful.

"So," Holly says after she's taken a slug. "Zelda's dead."

"So it would seem."

"Idiot girl. I told her to lay off the smack." I think her expression softens, though I can't really tell. "I assume that's what happened?"

"You were friends?" Wyatt asks, not answering her implied question.

"Yeah. Zelda came here looking for Jason a few months back and ended up in the dressing rooms. She brought nice Scotch with her, and we got talking."

"Jason? You know him?" I say quickly.

"Everyone does. His brother's the manager. Jay takes care of the . . . side business."

"Drugs?" I blurt out. She just smiles back coyly, like I'm a fucking idiot.

"Was she dancing? Here?" I ask, not able to completely conceal the note of anxiety in my tone.

Holly looks surprised, though not offended. "God, no. Zelda just wasn't the type, you know. And her tits were too small." She smirks and regards me sympathetically. My tits are no bigger than Zelda's.

She reaches over and plucks my cigarette away. She takes a long drag, eyes half-closed in pleasure.

"You smoke the same brand," she says, amused. "She said you were every bit as crazy as she was," she continues. "Damn. That girl was something."

"Can I ask you something?" I say, lighting up another cigarette. She nods. "Why did you post that photo on Facebook earlier today? I mean, had you not heard about the fire?" I can't bring myself to say "that Zelda is dead," because I'm worried that it will sound like the lie I know it to be.

"No, I had. But a few days earlier, she asked me to post the photo at ten A.M. on the twenty-fourth. She was really insistent about it, said it was really important and she needed me to do it at exactly that time. Even if it looked weird." Holly shrugs. "Zelda was pretty damn weird, though, so I didn't think too hard about it. I owed her some favors." She smiles that mysterious smile again, sleepy and supremely relaxed.

"And Jason? Is he ever here? I kind of need to talk to him," I say.

"Is this because he went over to the house? Before the fire?" Holly says innocently.

"Yes. I need to know what he was doing there."

"Well, how about you ask me?" a voice behind me says. I whirl around to face the man from Zelda's Instagram photo. He's only a few inches taller than me, but he is wide and muscular. His arms are huge, each one the size and color of a small ham, and his shirt is tight across an inflated chest. *That has to be uncomfortable,* I think. *All that muscle.* It looks unwieldy. The Maori tattoo from the photo curls out from under one taut shirtsleeve. I realize that he's probably been lurking there for a while. Absurdly, I stick out my hand.

"Holly told me you showed up. Wanted to introduce myself," he says, shaking my hand with a slight smile. He has a chin dimple. Of course he does. "And you are?" he asks coolly, rounding on Wyatt. Testosterone is thick in the air.

"Wyatt Darling. Old friend of Zelda's. And Ava's," he adds, and I feel a slight niggle of hurt at being second.

"Huh. Zelda didn't mention you," Jason says casually, and I see Wyatt clench his teeth. He turns back to me. "But she did say *you* were going to pitch up here eventually." He pokes my collarbone to emphasize the "you," and I recoil. He's standing too close. "C'mon back inside, I got something for you." He turns and waves us back toward the strip club. He goes in through the back door, and the three of us follow, Holly confident, Wyatt and me tentative.

The dressing room is brightly lit and smells of perfume, cigarette smoke, and something chemically clean—feminine hygiene spray? I don't quite recognize it. The blonde who was onstage when we came in is reapplying lipstick, and a petite girl with wide-spaced eyes is backcombing her hair, teasing it into a frizzy, voluminous halo. I try not to stare, but it is a wonderfully foreign world. I wonder if Zelda really has been back here. She would love its tawdry disarray. We're led into a hallway, and through a glass door, I glimpse a small room bathed in red light. A completely naked woman is grinding mechanically, a spookily empty expression on her face, and I can see a pair of knees poking out from beneath her. Wyatt coughs behind me, and I know he's noticed.

Another door opens back into the club, and we follow Jason through it. Several customers nod toward him, and he waves back before heading to a DJ station snugged up next to the stage. A song is ending, and a new girl is scooping up bills from the dance floor, letting men slide others into her garters.

"Zelda wanted me to play a song for you when you showed up," Jason explains, fussing with the sound equipment. An old song comes on, incongruous here in the club. As the familiar tune gathers momentum, Zelda saunters onstage.

From the way Wyatt freezes, I can tell he's fallen for the disguise too. For a moment, my heart stops; Holly has donned a black wig that resembles my and Zelda's hair, and she is wearing one of Zelda's kimonos. When I see her, I realize that I've been expecting Zelda to appear all along. Nat King Cole sings cheerily: "*L* is for the way you look at me, *O* is for the only one I see . . ." Holly dances coquettishly, mouthing along with the lyrics and baring various parts of her body in an imitation of old-fashioned burlesque. I find this much more sexy than the spangled-thong-and-pole exhibition, but that's beside the point; I look at Jason in confusion.

"Zelda wanted you to play this? For me?"

"Yup. Don't ask me why. She didn't tell me, just said you'd figure it out."

I frown and look over at Wyatt, who wears a similar expression. "Any ideas?" I ask him. "Did she ever mention this song?"

"I remember her singing it, a few weeks ago, but . . . I can't think what it means," he answers slowly. The trumpets blare, and Holly shucks off the kimono, revealing nipple tassels and nothing else. I watch her dance, wondering if there might be clues in the choreography. But the short song winds down, and Holly does a quick shimmy as she exits the stage.

"Did she give you any other messages for me?" I ask Jason in desperate confusion.

"Nope. She could be one mysterious girl."

"You were sleeping with her, right?" Wyatt growls. He sounds just a bit too protective and pissed off to suit me.

"So what if I was? She wasn't married," Jason says, his dander clearly up. I smell a fistfight.

"Can you tell me why you were at the barn the night it burned down?" I ask shrilly, trying to defuse the pissing contest I can see unfolding.

"She texted me. Said she had a little surprise for me, if I brought some of the new stuff."

"Heroin," I clarify.

He gives me an entertained look. "Yes, sweetheart. But she didn't use it that often. Or if she did, she had another hookup. I barely ever sold it to her. She wanted benzos," he says with a shrug. I frown. "Texted me on the burner phones she bought a few months back. Said if we were going to be *involved*"—he coughs delicately and meets Wyatt's eyes defiantly, double-daring him—"she wanted to be sure there was no record of it on her real phone. I thought it was kind of sexy," he concludes with a fond smile. "Figured there must be a boyfriend or something." Another malicious grin in Wyatt's direction.

"So you went over to the barn that night?" I ask.

But Jason doesn't get a chance to answer. The front door slams open, and two angry-looking cops storm in. I recognize the young one, Trent, from the police station, and he looks furious. The small handful of customers sit up straighter in their seats, and Jason leaps for the dressing room door in a nimble, instinctive movement. But his burly muscles slow him down. Trent manages to grab him and slam him against the wall.

"Are you Jason Reynolds?" he growls.

"Maybe," Jason answers.

"I'm taking you in for questioning for the murder of Zelda Antipova," Trent tells him, not letting go of his shirt. Nat King Cole has begun to sing again, accidentally cued up in the hullabaloo. "*V* is very, very, extra-ordinary . . ." And as I watch Trent manhandle Jason toward the parking lot, I suddenly realize what my sister is up to.

# 13

Mingling with the smallish crowd of gawkers that has gathered in the parking lot of Kuma Charmers, I glance around nervously before yanking Zelda's cellphone out of my bag. I scan through the emails she's sent me, scrutinizing each one. I nod my head as I go, convinced that my theory is right. That clever fucking bitch. I knew it. Knew she was fucking with me. Wyatt looks at my shaking head and tense shoulders questioningly, but I wave off his curiosity and launch myself into the truck's cab.

"Let's go home," I say, realizing it sounds like an order. Wyatt doesn't seem to notice. Still holding Zelda's phone, I go back to the first email she sent me after the fire. Her nudge at the bottom . . . which, combined with the Facebook picture I saw, led me to the Bartolettis', where I found out about Zelda's loan. Then I had gone to the bank, where I found out about Zelda's insane debt. . . . I look at her second email, with its too-cute alliteration, then the next one, where she talks about her eulogy. . . . I scan through most of the communication we've had since the barn, and I start chuckling to myself as I put more and more pieces together. Finally, I open a new pane to compose a message and type out a quick email:

June 24, 2016 @ 10:37 PM

Narcissistic, Nasty, Nuts, Necrotic Sister Mine,

Now, now, now, Zelda. I've figured out your little game. Should have seen it coming, but forgive me, I was too preoccupied dealing with your aftermath to really focus on such diverting distractions. Dial M, right? I applaud your creativity, dear sister. You fucking psycho.

Love,
Not-so-nice, nearsighted, naïve Ava

By the time I'm done writing, we're close to home.

"Did you know she was doing this, Wyatt?" I ask, pocketing the phone.

"What?" he asks, startled. He has been quietly driving while I retraced my steps during the last few days.

"Her little game. Did you know?" I look over at him, but he seems genuinely baffled. "No. Of course not. This is just for me," I muse. "It would have to be."

"What are you talking about, Ava?" Wyatt has slowed the truck down, and he peers at me with concern. "What's going on?"

"Zelda's not dead."

"What do you mean?" He looks at me with genuine alarm. "Ava, I know grief . . . er, one of the stages . . ."

"I'm not in denial. She's not dead. She's been sending me emails since I got home."

"I know how hard this has to be for you—"

"Damnit, Wy, I'm not crazy. She's been toying with me this whole time. Look." I show him the date and time of Zelda's last email. He glances at it, swerves onto the shoulder, and throws the truck into park.

"Jesus." He breathes out in a huff and gets back onto the road. "Jesus Christ."

Soon he pulls into my driveway. I can see that his hands are shaking as he turns the wheel. "I mean, I know Zelda can be twisted. But this . . ." The truck crunches down the hill of the drive. He turns the ignition off and stares blankly through the windshield. I know it's not funny, but I can't help smiling at his distress. I *do* know how he feels.

"Want to come in for a drink?" I ask with a wry expression.

"Yup," he says without hesitation. "And I want you to tell me just what's going on."

"Let's go sit on the upstairs deck," I suggest in a whisper once we're inside. Marlon is asleep on the couch, the fan directed toward him and turned up full blast. The sound muffles our steps. Opal has claimed the guest room, where I assume she is now.

"What about your mom? Won't we wake her?"

"Are you kidding? We could go sit on her bed and she wouldn't notice we're there." I gesture for Wyatt to head upstairs to the library and I head to the liquor cabinet, where we keep the decent but not cellar-worthy wine. It's still shut with the combination lock; I realize I haven't opened it once since getting home. I have to think for a bit before I remember the combo. The lock clicks open, and I take it off the clasp as quietly as I can. I don't want to wake up Marlon and risk him and Wyatt bumping into each other. I can only imagine what fun that would be.

It's too dark to see well, so I use my cellphone to hunt out a bottle of red, since that seems to be what Wyatt prefers—and since I assume my progenitors will have polished off any white wine that's been in the fridge, even the bottles I hid in the crisper. I leave the Silenus labels where they are, untouched, and search behind them, hoping for something French or Italian. Instead, my phone illuminates a slip of paper taped to a bottle. It reads, *For Wyatt, darling,* in Zelda's handwriting. I pull the bottle out, and on the label is a sketch of a tormented-looking man, his arms crossed in front of his chest and shackled to two unseen objects. His feet are in irons, and his face is shrouded by a formidable beard. Underneath the engraved illustration, the wine is labeled "The Prisoner." I pull the note off the bottle; on the back, Zelda has written,

*Caught between the two of us, as ever. Hope you can taste the poetry, and that Ava likes the flavor too.*

I climb the steps with a bottle of wine and two wineglasses for the second time that night, thinking of the repetitive patterns of home. How many times will I climb these steps, bottle in hand? In the library, I slide open the door onto the deck, where Wyatt is standing, staring out at the ruined remains of the barn. His shoulders are broad, his back muscular, and I feel a flicker of unease as I realize what this looks like. I ask myself what Nico would think if he were to witness this scene: starry summer night, lightning bugs winking in the tall grass, a bottle of red wine shared with my first love, my bedroom just a few steps away. The glimmer of guilt makes me swallow thickly, and I tug self-consciously on the low neckline of Zelda's caftan, where I know that the slight curves of my breasts are visible. The wineglasses chink together, and Wyatt turns at the sound.

"Note for you," I say casually, setting the glasses and the bottle down on the rail and handing Wyatt the scrap of paper addressed to him. His face turns white.

"Jesus. Zelda . . ." He trails off helplessly. "You just found this?"

"Yep. But she probably planted it before the fire. I hadn't looked in the cabinet for the good stuff yet, as she could have guessed. She knows my rituals. And she would have had a hard time slinking into the house to leave it during the last few days."

"Unless she pretended to be you," Wyatt points out. True.

"Who knows. I'm not sure what she's really trying to accomplish. I expect she will slowly reveal herself." I've got a corkscrew with me this time. I open the bottle and pour. "Do you know the wine?" I ask. Maybe it's another clue.

"No." He drinks a big gulp. "So. She's been writing you."

"At first I thought she just wanted to fuck with me," I say.

"She doesn't?"

"Oh, she does." I laugh. "But it's not just that. She's playing a game. It's a puzzle. She's laying little clues, for me to figure out where she is."

"What do you mean?"

"Did you ever play any alphabet games when you were a kid?" I ask.

"Like in the car? That game with the license plates? Where you have to point out cars that have licenses that start with each of the letters of the alphabet, in order?"

"Yeah, like that. Our father used to tell me and Zelda, when we were kids, that we were the whole alphabet to him, $A$ to $Z$, and we contained the whole world between the two of us. It was a nice idea. And it spawned a series of alphabet games. Zelda loved them."

"Okay . . ."

"She's playing one now. Look." I hold out Zelda's phone. "She left this for me to find in her trailer, and she's been sending me clues and emails on it. Oh, look. She's just sent another email." I open it.

I'm not where you think I am ☺

"Jesus. You just got this from her?" Wyatt looks alarmed.

"Yep. She's been sending me clues. This was the first one." I show him the photo of her in front of Bartoletti Vineyard.

"But that's for . . . $B$," Wyatt says slowly.

"$A$ is for Ava. It always is," I explain hastily. "$B$ is for Bartoletti. I found out about her loans and went straight to the Community Credit Union, where we opened up bank accounts when we were little. $C$. $D$ is for *debt*, which Zelda has lots of, and $E$ is for . . . *eulogy*." I show him the email beginning with the capitalized E and explain about the newspaper obituary. "$F$ is the photo that Holly posted and captioned on Facebook, 'Fucked-up Family Fun'—I think $F$ is for all those things, including Facebook. Like Holly told us, Zelda asked her to post it ahead of time. Then $G$ . . ." I pause, thinking. "I don't know what $G$ is for," I say with a frown. Wyatt squints.

"Could $G$ be for . . . Grandma? Opal?" he suggests. My eyes open wider.

"It could be. She showed up before I saw the photo, but it could have been a timing issue. Zelda can't control everything, after all. . . ."

"And *H*?"

"For Holly, I think. Holly Whitaker. The police asked me about her because she'd posted the Facebook photo. And she was the one in the photo that sent me to Kuma's, looking for Jason."

"Okay, that's *K* and *J*, obviously," Wyatt says. "What's *I*?" I hand him the phone again, and he reads the email, shaking his head. "I don't get it."

"*I* is for intimacy, I think."

"You . . . got *intimacy* from this?"

"Well, I thought she was referring specifically to intimacy with our mother, which I think she was. The 'cold fish' is the hint."

"The sturgeon?" Wyatt says, puzzled.

"No, not the sturgeon," I explain testily. "Zelda says it isn't the sturgeon. It's something my mother said to me the day I left for France. She was . . . fairly blunt in her analysis of my psychological shortcomings. Fear of intimacy topped the list. So I figured Zelda wanted me to go spend time with her. And I found an envelope in her drawer."

"You went through your mother's drawers?" Wyatt looks scandalized.

I realize this would be unthinkable in his functional home, where privacy is respected and people share willingly with one another. "I needed the corkscrew. Which I suppose Zelda predicted. Actually . . ." I think back. "That clever fucking girl. She filled the fridge with sparkling wine and locked up the liquor cabinet. She knew we would drink the bubbly that first night, because she planted it. Marlon couldn't open the liquor cabinet because he doesn't know the combo. I couldn't find the corkscrew in its usual spot, so she knew I would go to that drawer when I went to see Mom."

"Good thing you rarely drink twist-offs," Wyatt says. I snort. "What did the letter in the envelope say?"

"It was just a note. It had Jason's name doodled on it, and it hinted that I was supposed to look for a picture. So I checked her Facebook page again, and there was nothing. But then I was fussing with her iPhone and saw that she'd opened an Instagram account a few weeks ago. I logged into it, and there was a picture of Jason and Holly standing in front of Kuma's. Come to think of it, *I* is probably for Instagram," I say with a frown. "Either way. I knew she wanted me to go talk to this Jason guy, but I assumed it was because he was supposed to meet her at the barn the night it burned. I thought he might be able to tell me something about the night or the drugs, but instead . . ."

"Instead, he played you a song. That *L-O-V-E* song, by Nat King Cole," Wyatt finished.

"Which got me thinking about the alphabet, just like she knew it would. Then, when the cops showed up, talking about m-m-m-murder . . ." I shrug. "A bit slow, I acknowledge. Should have seen it coming."

"No one can read Zelda's mind," Wyatt says darkly, patting my hand. "Not even you." I get goosebumps where he's touched me, and I realize I am thrumming with a red-wine buzz. Trouble trouble. I swallow some more. We're reaching the end of the bottle.

"She can read mine," I say. "Always has." I stare out at the water, frowning. "Could she have known the cops would come while I was there? How would she have worked out the timing?" I mull this over. "She'd want the letters to go in order. . . ."

"Anonymous tip once you left the house?"

"Do you think—do you think she's watching us?" I ask, voicing an anxiety I've been feeling since Zelda's first communiqué.

"Maybe technological surveillance?" he suggests. The words sound faintly ridiculous, coming from him. "Spying on your phone—or hers, I guess—so that she knows what you're up to?"

"Could be." I go to take another sip of wine, but my glass is empty. So is Wyatt's. So is the bottle.

"Should I go get another?" he says tentatively. I pause. There's a secondary question here. We've both been drinking, and if Wyatt has much more to drink, he'll probably be over the legal limit to drive home. Which wouldn't necessarily prevent him from driving—the roads don't exactly crawl with cops out in Hector, and we know where two of them are—but it would introduce a new element of hesitation into his decision of whether to go home. A decision that would also be rather emotionally impacted by the two bottles of wine we had just consumed. I know all this, and I know what it might lead to. I look at the illustration on the bottle, the man caught between two shackles, and I wonder if we're going to talk about it, review what happened after I found him and Zelda together. I don't know that I can. I also don't know that we can avoid it. I nod yes.

"Sure. Look for any more notes. Maybe Zelda has a tasting course planned out for us. I'm just going to check on Nadine and use the loo. I left the cabinet open. Try not to wake Marlon."

I note that he takes the empty bottle down with him to put in the recycling. Responsible Wyatt. Little things like that endear him to me. Zelda would have left empty bottles on the railing until they fell off, and then she would have let them accumulate in a jagged heap beneath the deck. Our mother would wait for the vanished servants of her childhood to come and collect her detritus and, failing that, would have raised holy hell until we picked them up. And Marlon? Marlon would disappear before anyone would think to accuse him of neglecting the task. I'm the only one who would take it downstairs to the recycling before getting a new bottle, I think bitterly. Me—and Wyatt.

I'm wobbly crossing the room, but I'm not that drunk; I've been going slow tonight, and all the drinks have been spaced out. I'll be okay for a couple more. Should definitely stop after this bottle. Probably. We'll reassess afterward.

I fumble open the door to my mother's room and step inside. It's stuffy in here, and I realize she has closed the window, knocking the fan onto the floor. I reopen it and turn the fan on. I use her bathroom and look at my face briefly in the halogen light. My kohl eyeliner is nearly gone, except for a messy smudge beneath my eyes, and I clean it off with a damp corner of the white washcloth hanging on the towel rack. Zelda always did that, and Nadine and I would fume at the half-moons of mascara that stained nearly all of our towels; it never totally came out in the wash. I reflect that there must be some sort of clever pun there, about our family and all the things that haven't come out in the wash, but my mind is sluggish, and I give it up as a wasted exercise. One of my favorite things about alcohol is that it helps to silence the constant narration, the chatter of my brain. I dampen my neck and try to scrunch my messy curls into a more appealing look.

My mind is swirling with everything that's happened. Zelda has set everything up so neatly. She must have known that I would show up, that I would eventually cotton on—hell, she's been leaving me clues the whole while, waiting for me to catch up. Does she want me to go to the cops, to spring Jason and tell them that she's still alive? I'm reluctant to do that, because we haven't gotten to the end of this game, clearly. I can only guess at what she has scheduled next. I should be angry, furious at her for jerking me, everyone around like this. And I am angry. I am seething with quiet fury at my sister, as I have seethed most of my life. But I realize with a twist of dismay that I've been missing this, missing her. Even though this has been emotionally draining and torturous, I'm happy to be playing a game with her. Because it means we haven't lost each other.

I almost trip on the doorjamb coming out of the bathroom, and I squint at it in the dark. Should fix that. Nadine will fall and break a hip. I'm about to walk out of the room when I turn and look at my sleeping mother. She's perfectly still, breathing heavily, and I assume she has taken her pills. I'm overcome with an impulse I haven't felt in years.

With a glance at the door, I walk over to the bed and climb into it. Nadine doesn't stir. I curl around her, realizing dully that my feet are filthy and might be staining her cream duvet; I scoot in closer anyway. She smells as she has always smelled, of her obscenely expensive La Mer moisturizing cream. I snort at the French homonym; the mother smells of the mother. Underneath the fragrance is a sharp, unfamiliar smell, though, and I wonder if it's the scent of liver failure. We'll clean up a little tomorrow, I swear to myself. Nadine's nightgown is fresh and laundry-scented, and I reflect that Zelda must have done a load just before the barn burning, making sure there were clean nightgowns laid out for our mother. Planning everything carefully. I snuggle in for just another moment, relishing the deliciously foreign feeling of physical proximity with my mom. On an impulse, I kiss her neck before leaving the bed, then tidy the covers where I have rumpled them. I see a stain near the bottom of the comforter, and I realize my foot must be bleeding again. Shit. I have left a trace of my need.

I close the door behind me, then hesitate before locking it. But lock it I do, and return to the deck, where Wyatt has already opened the next bottle of wine. I look at him, wondering if he saw me curled in bed with my mother on his way up the stairs, but he shows no sign of it.

"Any new notes?" I ask. Wyatt shakes his head and hands me a glass. Pinot Noir. I read the label and realize it's one of Marlon's wines, from California. I didn't know we had any of his recent vintages. Once, I had jokingly, obscurely implied that his new Zinfandel was not up to scratch, an insinuation that was met with quick and excessive anger. I take a sip, and it's not bad; he's clearly learned a thing or two. It's certainly better than anything Silenus produces. But of course it is: Marlon upgraded. He snagged a better vineyard, a better location, a better wife. And presumably better daughters. We were the first attempt. Repeat as needed. I look at the wreckage of the barn.

"So what do you think is next?" Wyatt wonders aloud, trying to look away from the burn site.

"Well, *N* usually comes after *M*, right?" I giggle.

He smiles. "What do you think it stands for?"

"Nadine? Necrophilia?" I shrug. "Zelda wouldn't like it if we tried to get ahead of her. It might ruin her momentum." I don't mention the email I sent my sister.

"You're right. She doesn't want anyone to be smarter than her, ever."

"She's always got to be the clever one," I agree. "She would probably sabotage any attempts to shortcut her little game. And we know
where it's going to end up, in any case."

"Z is for Zelda?" Wyatt guesses.

"Starts with me, ends with her. I'm sure she'll lead us on a merry
chase. I say we relax and enjoy it."

"Cheers, Zelda." Wyatt raises his glass in the barn's direction,
openly acknowledging the blackened structure for the first time. I
snort, nearly inhaling my wine. "You having fun yet, Ava?"

"Yeah, a regular vacation from my tedious life in Paris." I wave him
off.

Wyatt thinks for a moment. "You like Paris, right? You're happy
there?"

"Of course! It's Paris—what's not to like?"

"I just . . . I'm glad you're happy, Ava. After . . . everything." He
looks at me so earnestly that I almost burst out laughing. Oh, Wyatt.

"I'm sorry Zelda's dragged you into all this," I tell him. "But then,
she was always trying to push things along with us, even from the very
beginning."

"What do you mean?"

"You remember our first time?" I ask.

"How could I forget." He raises an eyebrow suggestively.

"Well, Zelda's the reason. I would have chickened out if not for her.
But she sort of . . . nudged me. Not that I didn't want it," I add hastily,
seeing his hurt expression. "What I mean is, she took the fall. She pretended to be me and went to the nurse, got sent home sick as me. But
she got reported for cutting third period and had to spend a week in
after-school detention." I snort. "She said it was worth it, though.
That another day of watching us 'pant at each other' would permanently put her off the whole idea of sexual attraction."

"I never knew that," Wyatt says. "She never told me."

"Yeah, well. I guess you were always just caught in the cross fire."

"I like to think it was more than that," he says, sounding wounded.

"You know what I mean," I reassure him, backpedaling.

"You mean that I was just a tool in the mind games you two play with each other. An innocent bystander." His eyebrow lifts, challenging me.

"Well . . ." That is sort of what I meant. I never really thought Zelda cared about him for himself; I always imagined that she saw him as a way to hurt me, exact her revenge, get under my skin.

"Ava, that is bullshit. We had something long before Zelda was part of it. Stop pretending that you and I meant nothing!"

"You were always more to *me*. You were my only ally against . . . these people," I say, gesturing toward my house, indicating my entire family. "Just with Zelda, I don't know."

"I'm not proud of it, Ava, but she and I *did* have a relationship." He sounds strained, uncomfortable. "We got close while you were gone. It was hard for both of us, when you just . . . left."

"I didn't just 'leave,'" I spit out angrily. "I found you two in bed and spent months making a rational plan to get out of here. It was an eye-opener, that's all."

"That's not all. That's not all that happened," he says. A precarious silence follows, and I turn my face away. He sighs. "I meant before, anyway. Before Zelda was even part of it. You just disappeared," he says, and he still sounds hurt and angry, after all this time.

"I . . . had to go. I'd just finished this degree that committed me to staying here in Hector and running Silenus. Then Nadine was diagnosed. I was twenty-two years old, and I was freaking out a little. I . . . panicked."

"So you just took off? Where did you go, Ava?"

I bite my lip and hide my face in my glass.

"Where were you that winter?" he asks again.

When I again don't answer, he turns away. "You ran off with that guy from Cornell. Jordan. I knew it, that whole time, I effing knew it."

"Jordan was gay, Wyatt," I snap. All of my senior year at Cornell, Wyatt had been touchy and aggressive with Jordan, a friend of mine from my soil ecology class. He was a fine, upstanding guy from Oregon, into biking and hiking and surfing and other athletic, outdoorsy activities. He wanted to go home and start a vineyard near his family's house, not far from Willamette. I'd liked him for his frank good-naturedness. And the fact that he knew no one in my family, never once compared me to Zelda or Nadine. He was bouncy and fun and uncomplicated, and his presence had driven Wyatt nuts. Even Zelda had started hinting that we were more than just study buddies.

"You left with him, though. He picked you up, in February, and you drove off with him," Wyatt says, pouting. While I had graduated on time in May, Jordan had had several more credits to complete, and he'd stayed through the winter semester before getting his degree. I'd puttered around Silenus listlessly all that autumn, wondering what I had gotten myself into, realizing that I had merely acquiesced to my mother's plans for me. I knew I was stuck, and I was flailing. Zelda had dropped out of the community college by this stage, and Nadine had been getting more and more unpredictable. When we finally took Mom to a specialist in January, we had all begun to suspect that it wasn't just menopause that was making her moods erratic and her mind leaky. She was forgetting things nearly all the time and had had one or two episodes of hallucinations. At least, that we knew of. Her gait had became strange and off-kilter. You could have a conversation with her that she would be completely unable to remember five min-utes later. Most staggering was her new tendency toward confabula-tion, a rather clinical description for making shit up. Not lying—she genuinely believed the stories she was telling.

Jordan stayed through winter break because I begged him not to leave me, promising hot toddies and long gossip sessions. He stayed until the end of January. But then he announced that he had gotten a winemaking internship in Willamette and he was leaving in ten days. I fretted, and paced, and stared out at the cold water of the lake, the frozen gray slopes, my future; the day before he left, I asked him if I could hitch a ride with him to the West Coast.

"He drove me to Oregon, and I stayed with his family for a couple weeks. They were nice, and I was having a minor identity crisis. Jordan was . . . very kind." He had been; he had barely batted an eye when I'd told him I didn't know what I was going to do next, and he had put clean sheets on the bed in the guest room and told me to settle in. I sip at my glass of Pinot Noir, so similar to the glass of wine Jordan handed me in the guest room of his parents' home while telling me to figure my shit out and take my time. I feel choked up at the memory. "I stayed with them for as long as I felt like I could, and then I realized what I was doing on the West Coast. I took the bus down to California to see my dad."

"Oh," Wyatt says. "You weren't . . ."

"Fucking my gay friend from college all that time? Nope. I was . . ." I take a deep breath, feeling achingly sad. "I was naïvely begging my father to give me a way out. I—fuck, I'm humiliated even now." I worry that I'm going to start crying. The wine is clearly getting to me. I'm not usually a weepy drunk.

"You wanted a job," Wyatt guesses.

"I asked him to let me work on his vineyard for a bit. An internship maybe, or just some entry-level gig. I told him I didn't want to get in his way or affect his new life; I just needed some space from Zelda and Mom. I was qualified. Overqualified. He let me stay for a while, and I didn't work up the courage to come out and ask him for the job until I'd been there a few weeks."

"But he said no."

"Obviously. He seemed embarrassed by the whole thing, remorseful. Like he really wanted to help me out but he just . . . couldn't. I got the impression that his new wife had told him she didn't want me around, and it was her money, her vineyard."

We had awkwardly faced each other across a table at a café in town. I clutched the diner mug filled with coffee I couldn't bring myself to drink and tried to explain.

"It's not like it would be charity, Dad. I'm qualified to do this."

"I know that, Little A! I know you'd be a competitive candidate even if we were doing an open hiring. It's just that we're not really looking for anyone right now—"

"I'm happy to start as an apprentice winemaker. Even a pourer in the tasting room."

"Oh, kiddo, that would be throwing your talents away. You're too good for that!" His phone had rung, and he glanced down at it anxiously. I assumed it was Bianca, who was very precocious with the cellphone. Or his newest wife. "Listen, can we maybe talk about this some other time? If you want to stay out here, I know this great place where you can crash. I'll get you a deal on the rent. . . ."


"You told him about Nadine?" Wyatt asks.

"Of course. I was pathetic. I told him she was sick, that Zelda was crazy, that Hector was claustrophobic and I didn't know if I could live there. I was desperate not to go home, so I humbled myself. I wanted him to take me in, rescue me, but he . . . he rented me an apartment fifteen miles away." I finally crack, a fat tear spilling down my face. "He didn't even want me in the house. It was like I contaminated his picture-perfect family. The New Antipovas. His current wife wasn't a drunk, his new daughters were normal. . . . It's like I was a reminder of his guilt, of the balance he didn't settle here, in Hector." I sniff, crying. I realize I'm monologuing, performing like I do when I'm drunk. But I'm not drunk; I'm fine.

"Oh, Ava. You reached out. And he rejected you," Wyatt says softly, stroking my arm. "You kept yourself so self-contained, for years, and that was the first time . . ." I nod miserably, more tears tumbling from my eyelids. It feels good. "Zelda didn't know?"

"I didn't tell her. I just . . . disappeared. And left her. With Mom."

"You left me too."

"I thought you would always be there. I think I thought I was testing you. Your . . . devotion," I say, not without a trace of embarrassment. "I think in my head, I thought: I'll leave, and not tell him where I am, and if he waits for me, I'll know . . ."

"You expected me to come find you," he says in sudden realization. "You were waiting for me to come and bring you back, to follow you."

I bite my lip. He's right, sadly enough. That winter, alone in my modest apartment near Napa, with nothing to do but drink and wait for spring, I fantasized about him knocking on my door, showing up outside the apartment or Marlon's vineyard one day. Proving that he wanted me, just me. I am ashamed of it now, but I know that's what I hoped for. Only no one came for me, not Wyatt, not Zelda, not my mother. My father stayed stubbornly on the periphery, never explicitly saying he wanted me far away but making it clear we weren't going to be close. I had nothing left, so when winter loosed its grip, I took a plane back to New York. And found that Zelda and Wyatt had done just fine without me.

"I am sorry, Ava. I . . . didn't know," Wyatt says.

"No way you could have. It wasn't like anything . . . really happened, exactly. Small betrayals." That is what a lifetime of this family has amounted to. I swallow more wine, and it calms the lump in my throat. Wyatt leans over and puts his arm around my shoulders, wiping away a tear with his other hand. He pulls me roughly in for a hug, and I let him hold my head against his overdeveloped pectoral muscles, feeling comforted in spite of my old resentment. He strokes my shoulder blades clumsily, and I know he's trying to soothe me. Inevitably, I tilt my head back and his eyes meet mine. Everything else is just instinct.

# 14

Not wanting to acknowledge consciousness in that desperate, dry-mouthed morning-after horror, I'm eventually forced to crack open my eyes. Jolted awake in suddenly sober distress, I blink owlishly and struggle to open my exhausted, quivering eyes, which are agonizingly dry, filched of liquid. Lately, one of my eyelids has begun twitching ominously. The next thing I do is reach for the phone. But there are no new missives from my deranged sister.

Wyatt is still in bed next to me, fast asleep, and my heart starts pounding in an entirely unhealthy fashion. I feel short of breath as the beats thump solidly through my rib cage. I swallow, my mouth dry and cottony from the red wine, and I know that if I look at my tongue in the mirror, it will be a dark purple, the telltale stain of the night before. Though I don't need my tongue to bear evidence; I have one hundred and ninety pounds of moist, male flesh next to me as proof of last night's indiscretions. I roll away from Wyatt, squeezing my eyes shut and wanting to cry, the fragility of an early hangover welling in my eyes. It seems, however, that I did all my crying last night; I remember with another swoop of despair the fat, wet tears spilling down my cheeks as I whined about my neglectful, absent father. I should quit drinking, I reflect. It's not the first time I've had this thought.

My phone is lying on the sheets next to me, and my whole body clenches when it vibrates. I stare in mute dismay at the name displayed on the screen and push the decline icon with a wave of revulsion. At myself, mostly. But I can't talk to Nico right now. Later, after I've marshaled my meager resources, I will call him back and summon the wherewithal to lie to him, tell him I love him, that I miss him. For now, though, I have to focus on getting out of bed.

I work myself up enough to slide out from my white sheets, and I grope around for something to cover myself with. I hate sleeping naked. It's supposed to be sensuous and erotic to sleep with bare skin whispering against pristine sheets, but I have always hated it. I feel unprotected and unlike myself. I need the feeling of a shirt flat against my breasts and belly, of shorts clinging to my thighs and ass, concealing everything and staying close. When I sleep alone, I swaddle myself in the sheets, twining them around my feet and ankles. I have always wanted to be languorous and relaxed, to loll comfortably in a messy bed without a stitch on, but I manage to fall asleep in the buff only when I'm very drunk. Which I was last night, apparently. I slide the kimono over my naked body, but even this is not enough support. I tug on a long Lycra tank top from my suitcase, as well as some boy-shorts underwear, and put the kimono back on over them. The tight fabric makes me feel better, as it smooths out the lines of my body, concealing bulges and ripples beneath its stretchy sheath. With a quick glance to ensure that Wyatt is still sleeping, I scuttle out the door and downstairs, desperate for hydration.

Pausing in the hallway, I spare a thought for something other than my miserable physical state: Zelda's game. She has led me as far as *M* and I have supplied her with the *N*, as was no doubt her intention. I feel some anxiety as I contemplate *O*.

Our grandmother, Opal, mailed us a Ouija board for our tenth birthday. We tore away at the packaging in frenzied anticipation. I immediately wanted to take the board and planchette for a spin, but Zelda gravely proclaimed that we had to wait until dark. Of course she was right. That evening, we crept upstairs, leaving Marlon and

Nadine to snipe at each other below, oblivious and never suspecting that their offspring were about to raise the dead. Like all mediums and hucksters, we understood the importance of setting the scene: Locked in the bathroom, we draped a dark sheet to construct a gloomy tent, lit candles dangerously close to the fabric, and waited until we felt sufficiently steeped in the supernatural.

"Shh, you can feel the air getting colder," Zelda whispered.

"I can't feel it."

"I guess you're not as attuned to the other world as I am."

I rolled my eyes, though secretly, I agreed.

"Give me your hands," my sister whispered, and I complied. Our moist palms hovered over the cardboard plane, and in spite of my strong rationalist streak, my heart thumped a little. What if?

"Who should we call on?" I asked. "Grandpa Chuck?" We had never met our paternal grandfather, but Opal had let drop enough caustic commentary on her late ex-husband for us to be deeply curious about that roguish figure.

"What about . . . Aunt Nina?" Zelda said. I shivered. Nadine never spoke of her sister, and enough mystery and doom surrounded her death for me to instinctively shy away from the thought of summoning her into this house. But that, of course, is why Zelda wanted her. "They say children move more easily between the veils," she uttered, fully in character.

"Isn't it, I don't know, a bad idea? To summon someone who died too early?"

Zelda ignored me.

"I summon thee, Nina, child of my bloodline, ancestor of my bones! In the name of our mother, and her mother before you, I call you to us!" she intoned impressively. Her command was greeted with nothing but silence, and the sound of our breath, weirdly amplified to sound almost like . . . someone else beneath the sheets? My skin crawled.

"Say something!" Zelda hissed. "You have to call her too!"

"Um, I call thee, Nina, my . . aunt. I call you from the otherworld to visit us and . . . speak?" I finished feebly. I could feel rather than see Zelda's eyes rolling, but she continued.

"We are Geminis, the twins, and we live between the worlds, one twin living and one dead. I, Gemini, call thee—show yourself!"

I found this profoundly spooky—I had never heard Zelda describe our sun sign this way. The creeps were amplified when the planchette jerked beneath my fingers, skating across the board on its cheap felt feet.

"Zelda, knock it off! I know that's you!"

"It's not! I'm not doing it!" Zelda answered, eyes wide. In the dark, she looked genuinely surprised. The planchette skittered agilely, coming to rest on the *H*.

"That's not funny!" I protested. Zelda shook her head—she was frightened. The planchette moved, swiftly spelling out a message from the dead. *H-E-L-P-M-E*.

"Zelda, don't! I want to stop!"

"I'm not doing anything! It's Aunt Nina—"

"It's not! I'm not playing anymore!" I tried to stand up, but someone—Zelda, I fervently hoped—gripped my wrist with icy fingers. I stumbled, careening into the sheet and knocking over a candle, which instantly ignited the fabric. In horror I watched as Zelda writhed, struggling to free herself. And in the light of the flame, I convinced myself that there was another body moving beneath that fiery shroud. Panicked, I shrieked and began pawing at the sheet. Zelda emerged with her own yelp. We stampeded to the bathroom door and flung it open to be greeted by Marlon, who had obviously just taken the steps three at a time, and Nadine, close behind him.

Marlon dashed into the bathroom, scooped up the smoldering sheet, tossed it into the bathtub, and switched on the taps in a smooth ballet.

"Girls! What on earth were you doing?" Nadine glared at us, recovered sufficiently from her momentary alarm to look pissed off.

"It was the Ouija board! Zelda wanted to call Nina and she came!" I blubbered, giving up my sister without even batting an eye. I was rattled, and wanted to be comforted.

"Nina?" Marlon sucked in air, looking at Nadine in concern, as though worried the very name would set her off. He wasn't wrong.

"Why? Why would you try to speak to her?" Nadine whispered in a tone that presaged very bad news.

"She's our aunt," Zelda said, stubborn and unrepentant. "*You* never talk about her."

"Girls, I think maybe it's time for bed," Marlon suggested, trying to escape the bathroom.

"She was terrified! She asked us to help her! She begged us—"

Nadine slapped her, suddenly and hard. We were all absolutely silent, watching Zelda. She didn't raise her hand to her face, or start crying, as I might have done. She simply walked out of the bathroom and slammed the door to her room. The three remaining members of the family Antipova stared at one another, each of us feeling guilty and not knowing what to say. Nadine bit her lip, as though wanting to apologize, but I, a follower, as ever, imitated Zelda and left, leaving my parents to clean up the soggy mess.

Zelda hadn't locked her bedroom door, and I slunk into the room, shamefaced and remorseful. She was sitting on the floor, with a book about supernatural sightings open in front of her. I didn't know whether she'd been reading it earlier or had just opened it now.

"Do you think it was really her?" I whispered, curling up next to her and leaning my head tentatively on her shoulder. Stiff at first, Zelda finally took a deep breath and relaxed, giving me permission. And forgiveness.

"I wanted it to be," she said softly. "I wanted to be able to speak to the dead. To talk to someone in our family." I thought she might be crying, and I laid my fingers on her wrist uncertainly.

"What you said about being a Gemini—one of us living, one dead?"

"Don't be silly," she said, sniffing deeply and shaking her head. "I was just playing."

———

Wondering if I've puzzled out the fifteenth letter, I kneel down and look into the bottom shelf of the bookcase in the library, where the games are kept. I tug out the Ouija board and paw through the box, looking for any sign of my sister. There is nothing. To be thorough, I examine the Scrabble set as well, but I'm already losing enthusiasm for the hunt, with my head pounding and light.

I head down the steps, moving slowly. Marlon isn't on the couch, and he (or Opal) has folded up his blankets and pillows.

While I'm in the kitchen, ferreting around in the fridge, the doorbell rings. I'd forgotten we even had a doorbell, and for a few slow-witted beats I don't recognize the sound. I wait, half-hoping someone else will appear to answer it, but of course they don't. Unhappily, I gird my loins for social interaction.

I pull open the door, and sitting on the step is a large envelope. The inscription on the front reads: *Open me, Ava, only one I see!* I scan the driveway and the borders of the yard in frantic frustration; she was just here, in the flesh! She's nearby, possibly yards away from me. But I can't see her. She's lurking offstage, watching me dance. The inscription makes me shiver as I look at the blank, silent pines that must conceal her.

*Dear Obsessive, Obtuse Ava,*

*O is for . . . obvious! Oh, you've figured out the game at last! Of course, I knew you might need some extra clues; close reading was never really one of your strong suits. Ornate as the whole thing may seem, I thought you might appreciate my final efforts to make you think, make you squirm, make you work a little harder than usual. Or maybe just force you to recognize that the whole world usually just bends over for you, that you are never truly challenged, and that it's very good for you when someone puts you through your paces.*

*Oy, enough with the letters! Now that you've cottoned on, we can settle into a less rigorously structured way of communicating, right? Naturally, you're probably tormented with guilt at the notion of poor, maligned Jason, possibly going down for a crime he clearly could not have committed. Are you tempted to saunter on down to the station, clear up all the confusion? I know you are; you have always been worshipful of rules. I trust and hope that you'll be able to suppress your usual instincts, though, until we get to the end of the alphabet. Trust me, Jason has earned some time in the hot seat. Hopefully our underachieving police department will be able to uncover some crimes for which he is legitimately guilty (and, oh, they are legion!) and he'll receive karmic retribution for being the irredeemable scumbag that he truly is. You mustn't worry, Ava dear; I vetted my fall guy meticulously. I considered a sizable fistful of deserving candidates (wouldn't you just love to see the short list?) and contemplated their qualifications very carefully before I settled on Mr. Jason Reynolds. If he goes down for this (and he definitely might; I'm not so terribly confident in the sleuthing capabilities of our uniformed officers), it will be no less than he deserves. Would that I could have framed him for something more heinous than the careless murder of a washed-out, lonely drug addict who had recently begun a downward spiral of recklessness and dissolution. He's earned worse than he'll get. And I don't even know if there's enough to make a murder stick, as they say.*

*Now, back to the mystery at hand. Since you've divined what we're playing at, you're no doubt thinking your way through the rest of the letters. Any guesses for what's up next? Are you preempting, questioning, righteously second-guessing? Thinking ungenerous, vitriolic thoughts, wishing that your damned sister would bugger off and leave you be? Probably, yes. But you're also having the time of your life. I'm pretty sure you'll stumble across P soon enough, sister mine. You're getting closer all the time.*

*Your Opaque, Obstreperous, Oh-so-clever Twin,*
*Z is for Zelda*

*P.S. Did you think I skipped N? Honestly, what do you take me for? N is for nasty. Used in a sentence: Ava and Wyatt did the nasty.*

"Zelda!" I scream into the yard. "I know you're fucking there!" No one answers, naturally. I hope the neighbors can't hear me, far away as they are. I wander back inside to start my day, seething.

Obvious, indeed, I reflect. I have belatedly realized something else: Zelda is competing with me on my own turf. She is upstaging me in my own area of expertise. Like a fool, I haven't thought of it until now, but she is taunting me with my own research. I've been working on OuLiPo and detective fiction, and here she has delivered me a charming locked-room mystery with flavors of Perec. Recycling narratives, playing with the genre—she always liked to say there were no new stories. She has adopted the form of a mystery, cast me as the detective, and set the whole plot in motion, all while forcing us to remain locked in the constrained repetition of the alphabet. I assume she was able to find something about my research project online and has set up this game as a special way to jeer at me. To beat me. To outthink me. To show me she is cleverer.

On the landing in front of my mother's room, I lean my head against the door, the cool wood supporting my forehead. I turn the lock and let myself in. Nadine is groggy and bleary-eyed; no doubt she's hungover, too, from her cocktail of meds and wine.

"No breakfast today, Zaza," she mumbles. "I can't eat. I've gained a pound and a half."

I wonder if Zelda was silly enough to let her have access to a scale, or if this is pure guesswork and paranoia.

"It's okay, Mom. This isn't a beauty pageant. And your nightgowns will accommodate a much more significant weight gain," I answer, leaning over to fluff her pillow.

"I won't eat," she says stubbornly, clenching her teeth and pursing her lips. I glance at the deep wrinkles around her puckered mouth and think that she looks so very *old*. Her vanity seems somehow to have sustained itself even as her body and her looks have decayed. Her beauty has rotted away in this bed, her mind collapsed. This is a terrible way to die.

"You have to eat. You're too thin as it is."

After getting her dressed, we make our feeble way down the stairs, both of us wobbly. I deposit my mother on the downstairs deck and rifle through the fridge. I know I have to drink something, to begin the slow journey out of hangover hell, but I don't want to; the idea of swallowing anything seems preposterous. Finally, I find a coconut water squirreled away in the back of the fridge, and I sip on it delicately while I make my mother a smoothie. I use the full-fat yogurt Marlon has bought with satisfaction, and I add two heaping scoops of high-calorie almond butter. Outside on the deck, I hand over her breakfast without a word and perch on the arm of one of the Adirondack chairs, sipping the coconut water. Not only is Marlon no longer on the couch but the door to the guest room has been left open, the made bed clearly visible. Fuck knows where he and Opal have gone. At the moment, I feel nothing but relief that they are not here while Wyatt sleeps it off upstairs. I fret for a moment, wondering how I will get him out of the house. I don't want to think about any of that. I want to be alone, in a dark room with Internet access, to watch movies all day and not think about myself, my life, my twin.

Feeling unsteady, I slide into the chair next to my mother, clutching my coconut water. I briefly consider getting up to fix myself a Bloody Mary or find a beer in the back of the fridge, just to keep myself going; I know that while it doesn't sound appealing, it will make me feel better. Instead, I grit my teeth with something resembling resolve. I will not drink today. I can't. I have to get myself under control, or this will all spiral quite unpleasantly, even more than it already has. I sip my water and look out at the lake. Its movement makes me nauseous. Closing my eyes unhappily, I let the sun warm my eyelids.

"Ava?" my mother says timidly next to me. I crack my eyelids reluctantly and look over at her sideways.

"What, Mom?"

"Ava, honey, are we in Cape Cod? I don't recognize the beach."

"No, we're at Silenus, Mom. On Seneca Lake? The vineyard you built."

"Oh. Is it . . . a good vineyard?"

"Yes," I lie baldly. "It's great. People come from all over the country to drink your wine."

"Oh." She looks around herself fretfully, as though she doesn't quite believe me. I close my eyes again, and I almost nod off in the sunlight.

"Ava, honey?" Nadine says after a few minutes, jarring me back awake.

"What is it?"

"I'm scared."

"Drink your smoothie, Mom," I say with a resigned sigh, and haul myself out of the chair. Back inside, I flop down on the couch, facing the glass doors so that I can keep track of Nadine. A nap. Maybe if I just take a nap I'll feel better able to get up and deal with Zelda's puzzle and my mother. And Nico. Oh, God. My stomach swoops violently, and I realize what's happening almost a moment too late. I barely make it to the bathroom before releasing a hot jet of coconut water and the dregs of last night's red wine into the toilet bowl. My body is racked with the violence of reverse peristalsis, every corner of my consciousness focused on bringing up the contents of my stomach. Crouched over the bowl, my knees grinding into the cool tile, my arms clinging to the seat, I am the definition of abjection. I feel so thoroughly debased and full of shame that I am actually cleansed. When I finish, I am shaking violently, and tears are running soothingly down my cheeks. My heart is pounding and my hands are trembling, but I feel much, much better. I collapse back and sit against the bathroom wall, letting the worst of the quaking subside.

This old, familiar sensation. How many times have I sat in this bathroom, experiencing this exact feeling? It is one of the most bizarre paths to empowerment, and yet I never feel more in control. I chose this when I chose those last two bottles of wine, just as I have chosen it countless times when I felt that dinner had been too indulgent, or I had eaten too much ice cream, or had fought with my mother. A worried part of me insists that I was not in control of what just happened, no more than I was in control of my choices last night; I am subject to the whims of my chemistry, which says "Drink this" and, a few hours later, "Bring it back up." I have never been less powerful than I am right now. And I wonder if maybe what I really love is being out of control, relinquishing agency and giving free rein to my damaged brain and my warped limbic system. Not being prim, competent, polished Ava. The contents of the toilet bowl are grotesque, and so am I, the person who produced them. Right now, I'm not the kind of girl who wears pearls to meet the future in-laws, or gets perfect grades at Cornell, or seamlessly takes over the family business. Right now, I'm a shattered mess who is leaking bodily fluids and staring at her own shockingly yellow bile. I close my eyes and lay my cheek on the bathroom floor.

The shower mat is a few inches from my face, and I am forcibly reminded of having the flu as a little girl, of dragging myself downstairs to this bathroom so no one would hear me vomiting. I slept on this cold tile floor because I didn't want to creep back up the stairs only to have to throw up again. Spaghetti. We had eaten spaghetti. Zelda snuck downstairs late that night; presumably she noticed that I was gone and sought me out through intuition. She tossed a towel over both of us, and we fell asleep here, the scents of youthful puke and lemon-scented cleaning liquid strong in our noses, our legs twined together. Her small hands holding my shoulder and her cold nose against my clammy neck.

Shivering and remembering that night, I try to stand on wobbly legs, gripping the porcelain seat as I make my way back upright. I flush the toilet and stare at the swirl of my stomach's contents spiraling away. I do feel better, and I know from experience that now I should try to drink something, before the nausea returns. If I hadn't promised that I would try to clean myself up, this would be the moment for a neat swallow of gin, which would effectively halt the next few hours of trying desperately to keep something down.

I peek through the glass doors to the deck to make sure Nadine is where I left her, and sure enough, she's still huddled in her Adirondack chair, sipping her breakfast. Historically, it is the chair of the convalescent and the very ill. I wish my mother had consumption, rather than this other wasting disease. Better to drown in your own blood than sit in a chair while your mind disintegrates. I hear stirrings upstairs, and I close my eyes.

Wyatt makes his way down a few minutes later, holding on to the railing for balance. He looks gray and haggard, deep pouches beneath his eyes and an unhealthy tint to his skin. In just a few short hours, he has transformed from wholesome country boy to debauched lout. Behold my workings.

"Morning," I say as casually as possible, glad that I haven't rootled through the liquor cabinet for the gin. It wouldn't look good.

"Uh, morning." Wyatt remains at the bottom of the staircase, clearly unsure what to do.

"Don't know what your excuse is. You only had about a bottle of wine," I point out cheerily.

"I'm not really used to drinking."

"And you've been spending all this time with Zelda? Unimaginable." He flinches. "Well, you're in luck. Marlon is out, so we'll all be spared that lovely interaction."

"I'm going to run home and, uh, change." He gestures at his rumpled clothes, his stubbly cheeks. I have to admit, he looks very masculine at the moment. I notice that he is in his socks and realize that he must have left his shoes at the door last night, like the good houseguest he always was, indulging my mother's injunction that everyone take off their shoes before treading her hallowed floors. I nod. I have no idea what to say to him. I just want him gone. "Listen, Ava, about last night," he starts, predictably.

"No big deal. We don't have to talk it to death." I wave him off. I'm in no condition to have that discussion right now. Or ever. I know that Zelda is laughing hysterically somewhere.

"Okay, I just—"

"Really," I cut him off. "Seriously."

He looks cowed and shamefaced. I suspect he doesn't do a lot of slinking off the morning after. I suddenly wonder if he's ever slept with anyone who isn't an Antipova. There's a chilling thought. I wonder if Zelda and I are different in bed, if we smell the same. I'm pretty sure that I'm better groomed than my gypsy sister; I religiously go to a very precise Thai woman in Paris who prunes my nether regions, a practice Zelda abhors for the infantilizing gesture that it is, as well as for its concession to order, tidiness, control. I wonder which Wyatt prefers. Maybe I will ask him later, tomorrow, once I've had a drink. Wyatt bobs his head politely and clumsily tries to administer his shoes; when he nearly topples over, I instinctively reach out my arm, and he grabs it with a muffled "Thanks." As he straightens up, his face is red.

"I'll, uh, call you later?"

We both wince at the cliché.

"Suuuure you will," I say with a smile. Just go. Please.

"Okay. Well. You gonna be okay, Ava?"

"I'm perfectly fine," I snap unthinkingly. "I daresay I've had more experience with both hangovers and mornings after than you, darling."

He recoils. *Shut up, Zelda. That's enough.*

"Right. Bye, then." He fumbles with the doorknob and stumbles outside, his usual grace impeded by dehydration and humiliation. I want to call after him, to apologize. *Stay, Wyatt. I'll make us something to eat; we'll spend the day drinking ginger ale and cuddling.* But I can't. He's in his truck and up the drive, while I stand there in my Lycra tank top and kimono in the doorway. What a fucking mess.

I flop back down on the couch and check Zelda's phone again. No new emails, no new posts. I flick through the apps she has downloaded. She doesn't have many; Zelda was always suspicious of technology, uncertain. She shied away from it aesthetically, saying it interrupted her vibe. She was the sort of person who would use a typewriter or buy some vintage leather case for her phone to make everything appear decades older than it was. I'm surprised that she has an iPhone at all.

I frown when I notice an app for the Paris Metro on the screen, and I tap it open. The familiar cobweb of Metro lines appears. *What were you doing in Paris, Zelda? Did you really even come, or did you just book all that on the credit card to throw the cops off? And either way, why?* She knew enough to choose a hotel just around the corner from my flat; she must have extracted my address from Marlon or Opal. What could have motivated her to plan the transcontinental jaunt? I sigh. My head is pounding, and my nausea has returned. I don't want to throw up again. With nothing in my stomach, I know it will be the sour, viscous yellow sauce that lives deep in the belly, and it will come up thick and scorching.

I set Zelda's phone aside and pick my own up. I stare at the missed-call alert from Nico. He has left a voicemail.

"Ava? Good morning. I'm at lunch, I was thinking to you—I wonder what you are doing. I imagined you in your bed and thought to call. Maybe you still sleep, maybe you go out. Call me when you are able, I miss your voice. Okay. Ciao ciao."

I wish I could cry. I stab the delete icon and immediately regret it. Ah, fuck. He's French; maybe my infidelity won't get under his skin too much. He's probably fucking some long-legged Brazilian as we speak. But I know he's not. I know he will care, of course. I can never tell him. And now we begin with the secrets.

I shut my eyes, which makes the world spin. My mind skitters away from last night, from what I might have said and done with Wyatt. It's all a little patchy, and I have only glimmers of images, shreds of conversation. "Does that feel good? I want you. I've always wanted you. Oh, God." And me: "Yes, like that. Yes. Yes." And then: "Fuck me like you fuck Zelda."

I roll over, squeezing my eyes shut, trying to repress the memory. But my brain compulsively returns to it, dredging up more details from the darkness of my bedroom. "Make me come. I've never come with him. Harder." "I love you, Ava." "Call me Zelda. Say my name." "Zelda." "Again." "Zelda!"

Afterward, we lay quiet, drunk, tangled up in my white sheets. I was still coasting on too many chemicals for the guilt to have begun, for the panic to have kicked in. Drunk and happy.

"Was that true, what you said?" he mumbled into my hair.

"Hmm?"

"About never coming with . . . ?"

"With Nico?"

"Is that your boyfriend?"

"Yep."

"And you never . . . ?"

"No, not with him inside me," I admit slowly.

"Oh."

"And with Zelda? Did you like fucking her more?"

"No, Ava. No."

"Right answer."

"I know how competitive you are."

"You really are a prisoner, caught between us," I repeated, tracing his nipple with a fingernail. My nails, usually so neat, have grown ragged in the few days I have been home. I am coming apart, from the edges all the way to my insides.

Now I flip over on the couch, replaying the scene from last night, cringing at other confessions I might have made, tithes I may have exacted from Wyatt. Demands of fealty, declarations of love. I groan quietly to myself. I go still remembering what I said about Wyatt being a prisoner, reminded of the wine Zelda left us. Is *P* for *prisoner*? Seems logical. Wyatt could very easily be the prisoner. Unless the prisoner is Jason, maybe even now moldering in the Watkins Glen jailhouse, being questioned about Zelda's murder? Are there more secrets to be learned from him? Does Zelda want me to go talk to him? Or to Wyatt? What if *P* isn't for *prisoner* at all? What if it's for Paris and Zelda wants me to trace her whereabouts during her crazy trip overseas? I'm exhausted and feel flimsy, miserable, depressed. I don't want to chase after Zelda right now.

A car pulls up outside, and moments later, the front door opens. I struggle to look less dejected. Judging from Marlon's and Opal's expressions, I have not been successful.

"Ava, sweetie, are you okay?" my grandmother coos. "You look a little under the weather." Swooping to my side and pawing at my hair, my forehead. I probably stink of wine, but she doesn't seem to notice as she ministers to me, her wrinkled fingers fondling the contours of my face. "Oh, my goodness, you really should go back to bed. I'm not sure what you're thinking, being up and around!"

"I'm okay, Grandma. Just stayed up kind of late. Might have a touch of the flu or something," I mumble. I can see Marlon's raised eyebrow. He doesn't buy that.

"Well, drinking wine certainly can't help," Opal chides. "Honestly, Ava, I think we should talk some more about your decision making. I know young women today are encouraged to experiment, but you're not getting any younger, and maybe it's time to start acting like the adult you are—or should be."

I sit up, looking for an escape route. Opal is perched on the edge of the couch, hemming me in, her body pressed too close.

"I brought you a Coke," Marlon says, holding up a familiar red can and setting it down with a metallic clink on the counter. Oh, sweet Jesus. He gives me a knowing smile that encompasses an ironic nod to this blatant bribery and an awareness of my pitiful condition.

"Thanks," I manage, scampering off the couch and seizing the chilled can.

"And . . . a straw!" He produces a straw from the bag he's holding and hands it to me. I shoot him an expression of profound gratitude that in this one instant is not even a little jaded.

"Did you guys go for breakfast?" I ask.

"The diner up the road," Opal responds. "A very . . . gritty place. No pun intended. Though the grits are a poor impression of the dish. But it's very . . . inexpensive."

I snort. I know the place, of course: $2.55 for eggs, toast, home fries, and coffee. I don't even want to think about where they get their eggs. My stomach flip-flops portentously as I imagine dappled grease coating the surface of those lemon-colored yolks.

"How's your mother today?" Marlon asks, peering out at the deck.

"Confused but mostly cooperative. I thought it might be nice for her to sit outside for a while." Marlon and Opal both nod. "Actually, would you mind keeping an eye on her? I'd love a shower, and a minute to myself. . . ." I suddenly realize that they must have seen Wyatt's truck in the driveway this morning. Opal's coy, knowing smile confirms that they did.

"I'm sure, dear. It's always nice to have some alone time after . . ." She winks at me, adding in a stage whisper, "You can tell me all about it later."

Inwardly, I despair, but I force a smile to my face. I don't meet my father's eyes. "Thanks. I'll just be upstairs." I scoop up both phones and conceal them with my kimono, hoping they haven't noticed, and dash up the stairs as quickly as my pounding head will allow, clutching my Coke the whole while.

I undress in the upstairs bathroom, stripping off my snug top and turning the water to a scalding temperature. Looking at myself in the mirror, I realize it's been days since I showered. I do my best to scrape off all the makeup that has caked above and below my eyes, then comb my fingers through my tangled hair. Turning sideways, I scrutinize the curve of my belly, patting the small spot beneath my belly button to see if it moves at all. No sign that my teenage chubbiness is returning, thank God. I step beneath the steaming jet and scrub everything. Some fashion magazine I read a long time ago admonished readers against bathing in scorching water—it was supposed to dry out skin and induce premature aging. Another rule broken.

I walk to my room in a towel, everything else bundled beneath my arms. My bed is made; Wyatt has fluffed up the pillows and even replaced the white throw at the base. Of course he did. I reach for a clean tank top and wind my hair in the towel before sliding beneath my sheets. I fondle Zelda's phone, checking to see if she has any music on it. A few albums, some of which I recognize. A playlist or two. I pick out an Iron & Wine album that we used to listen to while driving around the national forest at dusk. I doze off while it plays, tears on my cheeks.

# 15

Ornery and still emotionally hollowed out, I am physically much better when I wake up a few hours later. Zelda's phone shows nothing new. I swing out of bed, almost bouncy. I'm definitely still hungover, but I'm thrilled at the improvement. I head down the stairs, feeling better prepared to face the day, which is now half over.

Marlon is reading the newspaper on the couch, and my grandmother is scrubbing the countertops. She looks vigorous and capable, with a spray container of bleach and some old rags.

"You don't have to do that, Grandma," I say insincerely.

"Nonsense. Just trying to be helpful." She waves me off. I go over and plant a kiss on her soft, wrinkled cheek. She looks pleased with herself.

"Well, thanks."

"Mom still outside?" I ask, hunting through the fridge for something to drink, maybe even something to eat. It's a good sign that I'm hungry.

"She refused to come in," Opal says, annoyed. "She won't budge. I asked Marlon to set up an umbrella for her, so she doesn't burn to a crisp."

I peer through the doors, where I can see a pin-striped umbrella shielding Nadine from the worst of the midday sunlight. It has to be hot out there.

"What are we eating?" Marlon asks from the couch, not looking up from the paper. Opal and I shoot him nearly identical looks of exasperation.

"Don't worry about it, Dad, we womenfolk will take care of the kitchen work," I call. "We'll just serve you, shall we?" Opal's mouth curls in amusement. Marlon looks up, confused, as though he doesn't understand what I'm saying.

"Do you want help?" he offers, several beats too late.

"Oh, no, sweetheart, we've got it," Opal answers quickly. "But maybe if you could just get some plates for us?" She gestures toward the recently rearranged cupboards. We both know from frustrated experience that Marlon is not much help in the kitchen. I blame Opal, for never having inculcated in him the notion that a man should cook, too, and letting him coast through his childhood while she plated up breakfast, lunch, and dinner.

"There's not really much to work with in this kitchen," Opal says. I can't help hearing censure in that comment, even though it was not me who was here to stock the fridge. Zelda seems to have failed to predict Grandma Opal's exacting expectations when it comes to housekeeping. "But I thought sandwiches and potato salad?" she adds.

I find several bags of tuna in the pantry, the fancy, expensive kind that doesn't come in tins. Nadine loathes canned food; it offends her sense of class. Today for lunch we will be having only upper-middle-class tuna. I upend each bag into a bowl and mix it with fancy organic mayonnaise and capers and a handful of chopped celery. I note with amusement that a batch of the pickles I made before I left home is still nestled in the door of the fridge. I'm surprised; Zelda loves my pickles, and I would have thought she would have eaten them immediately. These seem to be untouched. Maybe *P* is for *pickle*. I chuckle as I open the container, which, after some effort, comes unsealed with a satisfying snick. I sniff the vinegar solution laced with dill I grew just outside the house. The pickles smell fine, and I empty the slender slices into a little bowl.

After Opal and I assemble the sandwiches, we bring everything outside. I drink a whole glass of lemonade almost immediately, and it is among the best things I have ever tasted. Nadine looks small and shrunken in her Adirondack chair, which Marlon has rotated to face the table, and we serve everyone a plate. Nadine rumples her nose and refuses to eat anything until I bribe her with a tot of gin in her lemonade. Marlon's eyes light up as I stir her cocktail; rolling my eyes, I splash a dollop into his glass as well. I hover over my own for a second, sorely tempted, but instead I offer the bottle to Opal, who purses her lips censoriously. There is no talk around our table as we all munch mechanically.

"So," I start casually, "did Zelda have fun on her trip to Paris?"

Marlon and Opal look at me like I've lost my mind, and my mother doesn't even acknowledge what I've said, just keeps staring out at the lake and sipping her gin-laced lemonade through one of the straws Marlon bought this morning.

"Zelda's never been to Paris," Opal says gently.

"That's not what her credit card bill says. Or, rather, I suppose it was Mom's credit card. I doubt even a greedy credit card company would give Zelda a chance to dig herself in deeper."

Marlon glances at Nadine. "How did you find out about this, Ava?" he asks.

"The cops. They thought she had come to see me a few months before she died. But if she went to Paris, she certainly didn't visit me."

"But then why—?" Opal asks, her rumpled forehead rumpling even further in confusion.

"I thought you might know, seeing how close you two were," I say, hoping it stings. I want our grandmother to understand that Zelda was unknowable, that any intimacy you thought you shared with her was a fiction she graciously let you maintain. Opal says nothing, though. "Nadine?" I press. "You know anything about Zelda traipsing off to France?"

"That ungrateful girl just took off, left us here to fend for ourselves," she says waspishly. "I haven't spoken to her since."

"Mom, that was me. *I* moved to France. Zelda went to Paris a few months ago. Do you remember that?"

"Nonsense. Zelda has been here the whole time. What would she do in France?" Nadine waves imperiously and sucks down the rest of her drink. "A refill, Ava. Thank you." I pour the lemonade into her glass but keep the gin next to me. Nadine lowers her sunglasses, looking from the pitcher to the bottle with an eloquent arch to her eyebrows.

"We're out of gin," I say, moving the bottle onto the floor next to my foot.

"Don't be childish, Ava. Hand me the bottle."

"Sorry, Mom, doctor's orders. You've got to take it easy." If I'm having an off day, she can afford to slow down on her cirrhosis too. She glares at me, then shoves her half-finished plate of food toward the center of the table in a huff. I am forcibly reminded of Zelda at age six.

"So no one knows a thing about Zelda taking off on a wee vacation?" I look around at my family and scrutinize their faces to see who might be lying. I bite delicately at my tuna sandwich. It smells good, but I definitely don't want to throw it up later. Regurgitated fish. I think of penguins.

"You're sure? That she went?" Marlon asks.

"That's what the cops tell me. Thought I'd poke around and look for the bills here at the house, but God knows why they'd lie about it." I shrug. I wonder if there's any way to prove that Zelda actually went to Paris, and I realize that if she did, there would be a stamp in her passport. *P* for *passport*? I almost leap up from the table to go look for it, grabbing my plate and the bottle of gin as I head inside.

"Are you finished, Ava?" Opal says disapprovingly, as though she's expecting me to ask if I may be excused. As though I'm still a little girl.

"Yes, thanks," I call back. "Very yummy." I leave my food on the counter, putting a paper towel over it—I might finish it later. Then I head upstairs to Zelda's room.

It's nearly impossible to walk across her floor without stepping on anything, so I kick aside old pairs of boots, heaps of clothes, a bottle or two. I tug open the top drawer of an antique dresser and look with alarm at the stacks of papers nestled inside. The contact paper lining the drawer is peeling, and I resist the overwhelming impulse to pick at it. After rifling through the papers for a few minutes, I find what I'm looking for. Zelda titled the contents of this drawer "Important Documents, Official Affidavits, and Papers of Various Interest." Report cards, love notes, parking tickets, business cards from restaurants, receipts of memorable activities—everything went into this drawer, a scrapbook of Zelda's comings and goings.

And her passport, tucked down a few layers, amid a handful of receipts. I recognize a card from a restaurant Nico and I sometimes go to, near my apartment. Flipping open her passport, I quickly locate the stamp from Charles de Gaulle Airport, neat and stark and dated from exactly three months ago. The passport is nearly blank, except for a stamp from a Canadian border crossing years ago. We had both gotten passports with the vague intention of going on a road trip to Mexico; we wanted to drive out and visit our father, then head down to Tijuana, get into trouble, learn the way of the Yaqui, buy drugs, bake like lizards in the sun. The whole thing had been Zelda's idea, of course, and when one of my friends invited me along on a trip to Nantucket instead, I immediately bailed on my sister. The idea of traveling around Mexico with Zelda terrified me. In a huff, Zelda convinced someone to drive her to Toronto for the weekend. She hadn't wanted the passport to go to waste.

I stare at the stamp for a few moments, confirmation that Zelda came looking for me very recently. For a truce? To convince me to come home? Did my sister want forgiveness or a new start? It feels eerie to think of her lurking on my street, steps away, and me not sensing a thing, maybe even passing her in the Metro. Maybe she watched me come and go, waiting for a good moment to intercept me. But if she traveled to Paris just to speak with me, she chickened out. Remained a silent ghost, lingering on the edges. Fucking hell.

I toss the passport back into the mess of documents and start sifting through the papers in hopes of finding some clue about her motivation. God knows she couldn't afford to take a holiday; she must have had a real reason. I find a receipt for the hotel she stayed in and a pile of Metro tickets, but I am still looking when the house phone rings.

I jump, startled. I didn't realize we still had a landline. It's an unfamiliar noise, and my heart is beating quickly as I dash down the hall to answer it. Does the phone still live downstairs? I hear Opal's voice, authoritatively answering questions, and I'm inexplicably annoyed. This isn't her house.

"What is it?" I holler down the stairs.

"Your mother is late for her doctor's appointment, apparently," Opal hollers back. "It started fifteen minutes ago."

"Shit." It's her GP appointment, I'm pretty sure. I noticed it on the calendar in Zelda's phone but promptly forgot. "I'll take her. Just give me a minute to get dressed."

"Are you sure?" Opal calls. "Marlon could do it!" I imagine his expression at her offering his services and grin. I'm almost tempted to make him take her.

"No, no! I'll do it! I want to run some errands!" On impulse, I take another outfit from Zelda's pile: colorful harem pants and a backless tank top. Dashing down the stairs, I pile my hair on top of my head, knotting it loosely, and grab the keys. "Mom, we're late. We've got to take you to the doctor's office."

"What?" Nadine says distantly.

"Get in the car. Dr. Whitcross needs to see you."

"Dr. Whitcross?"

Impatiently, I tug on her arm and help her stand up. "Don't worry about it, just come on." I lead her off the porch and around the side of the house, helping her up into the cab of the truck.

I speed just a bit, turning off 414 onto Rock Cabin Road just as we hit the edge of Watkins Glen, then continuing farther south to Montour Falls.

Fifteen minutes later, I screech into the parking lot of Dr. Whitcross's office. We're late, but hopefully they'll still squeeze us in. I unload Nadine, and inside, a miserable-looking woman ushers us into an exam room. I think I went to high school with her; she strikes me as very familiar, but I can't quite place her face. It's not until she speaks that I realize who she is.

"Sorry about your sister, Ava," Carrie Brown mumbles. She's gained about forty-five pounds since high school, and her once-bony cheeks are rounded and puffy. Under her shapeless pink nurse's garb are a swaying belly and heavy thighs. Her hair is the same bleached shade that it was our senior year, when it was rumored that she got knocked up with Tommy Webster's baby. I can't remember if she ended up graduating or not, or having the baby or not. I can hardly ask now.

"Thanks, uh, Carrie," I say, deeply uncomfortable. I hate running into old classmates. We had nothing in common then, and even less now. "Will Dr. Whitcross be in soon? My mother can get a little temperamental. . . ." Carrie's expression has hardened at my immediate dismissal of her friendly overture.

"Oh, I know," she says. It sounds like she really does. I wonder what Mom did the last time she was in here. "Okay," she says after a long, uncomfortable pause. "See you around. Oh, yeah, he'll be in in a second." She glances at me as she walks out the door with an expression I just can't read, as though she suspects me of being sneaky somehow, that she's on to me. I waggle my fingers in farewell as she shuts the door.

Seated on a stool, I lean back against the wall and flip through the magazines very thoughtfully provided on the table.

"Hey, look, Mom! J. Lo has upper-arm jiggle." I show her the gleefully captioned picture, a big red circle drawn around the purported area of wiggliness.

The door finally opens, but instead of the pink-faced old man who has been our family doctor since I was a girl, a young, somewhat attractive man walks into the room. Slightly built, he's wearing thick-framed glasses and has a very twee haircut. He stops short as he looks up at us and promptly drops the files he was holding. He turns beet-colored and bends down to collect them. I'm tempted to help, but I don't get up. Flustered, the young doctor sets the disordered stack of papers on the exam table.

"You must be Ava," he says, offering his hand with visible discomfort.

"Ava Antipova. I'm sorry, I was expecting Dr. Whitcross. . . ."

"I'm Dr. Whitcross. The second. I mean, not actually with roman numerals after my name. I'm Stu. Stuart Whitcross. My father is the other Dr. Whitcross. This is his practice." The man stumbles over his words as he tries to explain.

"Okay," I say, not especially interested. "So . . . you're my mom's doctor now?"

"I've been seeing her for several months. My father is mostly retired at this point, and I just moved back here from Potsdam."

"That's up in the Adirondacks, right? Basically Canada?"

He nods, some of the fuchsia receding from his face, leaving telltale blotches on his neck and jaw. I have no idea why he is so rattled.

"So, I'm just going to give her a basic checkup. Blood pressure, heart rate. And I'd like to get her weight; she's had some weight loss in the past that we need to keep an eye on. How are we today, Nadine?" he says, shifting over to my mother, who is seated on the exam table. Nadine is still staring vacantly off at the wall, and she doesn't answer.

"She's had some good moments, but it really comes and goes."

"The early-onset form can be tough like that. She's probably been living with the disease much longer than we've been treating it—it's just now getting unmanageable."

"Zelda and I used to speculate about that," I say with a snort. "She was never the most stable person."

The younger Dr. Whitcross twitches at the mention of Zelda as he continues his examination. He guides a reluctant Nadine to the scale, an action that seems to make her skittish. I sympathize—no one likes to be weighed. Unsure what to do with myself, I fiddle with my phone. Nico has sent a text: Hope u r OK, I think about you ;). I stare at it guiltily and don't write back.

"She's been generally disoriented?" Stu says, interrupting my self-flagellation.

"She wanders off, gets confused about who is who. Although when you have twins, that seems fair. I think the whole Zelda thing has her thrown. You've heard . . . ?"

He ignores my question. "You're giving her her meds?"

"Whatever is in the pill dispenser. While I'm here, actually, you should probably give me a schedule of what she's supposed to get. I've just been making her take whatever is set out in that plastic case, but it will only last to Monday."

He nods again, making a note in the chart. "And alcohol?"

"I'd love some." I grin. He doesn't smile back.

"How much has she been drinking." It's not really spoken as a question.

"Too much. She gets uncooperative without it, and I figured these are exceptional circumstances."

"She really shouldn't be drinking at all," he chides.

"Yes, Doctor," I say, nodding along. He looks up, his head cocked to the side. "What?" I ask.

"It's just . . . you're very like your sister," he says slowly, maintaining eye contact for too long.

"You knew Zelda—ooooh." The pieces click into place: the way he's been eyeing me, how strangely he's behaving, the way he cringes whenever Zelda is mentioned. "You were fucking my sister. I should have guessed earlier."

He looks stricken and glances uncomfortably at Nadine, but she seems not to have heard. "We were, uh, seeing each other, yes."

"Isn't that, like, unethical? Dating patients?"

"She wasn't a patient. We did meet here, but she called me on my cell and asked if I wanted to get a drink with her. It was entirely above-board," he sniffs defensively.

This guy does not seem like Zelda's type. That Jason prick made sense to me, because of Zelda's perverse desire for danger and mayhem, but Stu Whitcross is about as far from enticing as a man can be.

"Indeed," I say unsympathetically. "Well, you must be very sad."

"It's been a bit of a shock, yes."

I notice that there's a drop of sweat on his upper lip and a patchy scruff below his chin where he missed a spot shaving. I can't imagine Zelda sitting across from him at a table, sipping a glass of wine and making polite conversation with him. *I didn't really know her,* I think suddenly. *If she wasn't always a stranger, she became one.* The thought makes me unspeakably sad, and I am swamped with sudden despair, the kind that swoops in after a bout of drinking and settles over your neurochemicals like an impermeable sheath.

"Will there be a funeral?" Dr. Whitcross asks.

"I imagine there will be, yeah. But I guess we're waiting on the murder investigation."

He starts. "Yes, I'd heard—I mean, there was some discussion that the police might be—well, I'm just really shocked, is all."

"Aren't we all. But Nadine seems to be holding up pretty well," I say cheerily, patting my mother's knee. It is sharp and bony, and it feels unhealthy. "Of course, she has the benefit of thinking that *I'm* Zelda half the time, so no wonder she's not reeling quite like the rest of us. Have you finished your checkup, Doctor?"

"Yes, and I'll have a nurse print you out the medication schedule. Your mom seems like she's doing fine, considering . . ." He pauses. "You will let me know if there's to be a service?"

"Of course, of course. I'm sure I can find your phone number." I'm pretty sure he'll be in Zelda's phone.

"Well, here's my card, just in case. I'm, uh, really sorry for your loss."

"I'm sorry too, buddy." I stand up and, absurdly, shake his hand. "C'mon, Mom," I say, waving at Nadine. She doesn't stand up or acknowledge me, so I pull on her thin arm. It feels like it could snap between my fingers. Her dismount from the table is ungainly, and I steady her before she falls off the small stool beneath her feet. Dr. Whitcross—Stu—holds the door open for us and ushers us out. He seems like he'll be glad to get us out of the building.

"Just stop at the front desk for the med sheet." He points and turns around. I wave in amusement at his white-coated back. *Really, Zelda? Him?* I pull Nadine along and collect the paperwork. There's a new prescription for me to pick up. Thankfully, I don't bump into Carrie Brown again, and there don't seem to be any other Watkins Glen graduates hard at work. We finally escape back to the truck. Inside the cab, I look through Zelda's contacts. There he is. Stuey. *Very cute, Zelda.* I scroll back through her messages, but she has deleted almost the entire history. There's only one exchange between them.

—Are we all set? All clear on the scenario, dear Dr. Whitcross?
—Yes, my sweet zany Zelda.

I gag. Christ, she must really have been stringing him along. And what could she have meant? I desperately hope this is not some creepy sex game, but with Zelda, one never knows. I look at the time and date of the messages: 8:07 P.M. on the night of the fire. Did they see each other that night? A slight niggling of unease stirs as I remember the locked chains on the barn doors. Was Whitcross there? An image of his shaking hands and his skittering eyes crosses my mind. Suddenly, I want to get away from the whole building.

I feel like an idiot, though, for not having looked for any messages from that night sooner. If I had any sense, it would have been the first thing I checked. But I was too busy worrying about Wyatt and Zelda and getting worked up into some jealous froth.

I pull out and head up the highway, toward Watkins Glen. I wonder if I'll be making it through today without a drink. Glancing over at Nadine, I frown. I'm grateful for her uncharacteristic quiet submission, but it is rather disconcerting.

"You okay, Mom?"

Nadine says nothing, and I reach over for her hand. She jerks her fingers away from mine when I try to give her a squeeze, and she hunches toward the truck door, sliding away from me. I look back and forth between her and the road, concerned. "Momma, what is it? Does something hurt?" I reach for her shoulder, and when I brush it, she yelps.

"Don't touch me," she snarls. "Get back." She swats at my outstretched hand, and I instinctively recoil. Another tantrum. Always the same. What they don't tell you about dementia is how repetitive it is, how that shock of incomprehension and fear returns again and again. And how it hurts all the same, each time.

"Mom, what is it?" I repeat.

"Get away. You don't belong here. You're dead."

"It's me, Ava," I plead, suddenly desperate. "I'm not dead. Zelda—"

"You're dead. You're a dead thing, you're not alive. Don't touch me." She has curled into a tight ball and is looking straight through the windshield, refusing to make eye contact. Swallowing around the lump in my throat, I drive north along the lake, wondering if she's right.

Inside the big house, I call out for Marlon, but there is no answer. Opal's door is shut tight. Nadine immediately flees to her room without my help.

I wander outside through the open deck door. It's a hot, sunny day, and I shut my eyes, feeling the warmth on my skin, the heated wood from the deck reaching up to my toes in splintered fragments. Giving in to a sudden impulse, I dash upstairs and change into a bathing suit and a sarong snatched from Zelda's lair. I grab Nadine's big sun hat and sunglasses, a bottle of water, and head down to the lake in my bare feet.

It's a bit of a walk to the water, all the way along the long tractor trail from the vineyard to our waterfront. We have a dock and a rudimentary pavilion down by the lake, and we used to keep a rowboat and a kayak down there as well. I wonder if they'll still be there. The grass is alive with insects, and my nose fills with the scent of home. Churned dirt, cold water, and, somewhere nearby, a field of alfalfa.

As I approach the dock, I see Marlon, stretched out seal-like. The dock looks rickety and not wholly safe. Marlon has opted for the secure sturdiness of the rocks along the water. This is probably sensible. He appears thin and fit, a California tan bronzing his skin. There's a glass next to him, and a partly empty bottle is bobbing cheerfully in the lapping waves at his feet, glinting in the sun. He sits up when he hears the stones shifting underneath my feet. Used to wearing shoes, my soles hurt as I walk on the tiny rocks, and I pick my way carefully to where he is lying.

"Wine?" he offers pleasantly. I hesitate. I said I would take a day off, that I'd give my liver a chance to regenerate. But I've had a fucking brutal day so far. Just one glass, I decide. Marlon hands me a plastic cup and points to the open bottle cooling in the chilly water of the lake. I help myself to the rest and sit down next to him on the rocks. We stare silently out at the flat blue water. It is perfectly quiet, without even the buglike whine of motorboats or Jet Skis. Far on the other side of the lake, a big sailboat is coasting north, toward Geneva. "I've really missed this," Marlon says softly. "This . . . place." I nod. That will be as close as he'll ever come to saying that he's missed us.

"It's beautiful," I agree. It is, but there is something dark underneath those waters. There is something wrong here; I've always felt it.

"I could never stay, though. Something . . ." he echoes, as though I've spoken aloud.

"We Antipovas have restless feet," I say, trying to let him off the hook. I've been furious with him for so long, have wanted to hear him excuse himself for disappearing and leaving us with Nadine, but suddenly, I don't want the burden of absolving him. Let him seek his own redemption, from someone else in a better mood. I drink down my glass of wine and stand up. "I'm going to go swim," I announce. "Hot day." I shuck off my sarong and stick a toe into the cold, deep water. I glance toward the dock; we used to launch ourselves into the water from its edge, and it is a much easier point of entry to the lake, but I'm reluctant to venture out onto the decayed structure. I imagine that I can see it swaying in concert with the slight stirrings of the lake's surface.

"Have you started swimming again?" he asks.

"No thanks to you," I snap, filled with fury at the amused tone of his voice.

I don't turn around. I plow farther into the water. The bottom is sharp and rocky, and my feet protest, but I move as quickly as I can without tumbling over. Making inelegant progress, I proceed unsteadily. The water is fucking freezing. When I'm waist-deep, I reluctantly lower myself all the way in, submerging my head. I'm instantly sobered by the chill. I kick underwater, stroking along without surfacing as long as I can. I pop up only when I start to panic, when my brain is begging for oxygen and it is all I can think about. I gasp, sucking in air and blinking water out of my eyes. I can no longer touch the bottom, and there is a thick skein of seaweed wrapped around my ankle. I flap around nervously, trying to shake loose from it. A thick barrier of subaquatic foliage separates the shore from the darker blue waters farther out into the lake, even this early in the summer, and I paddle hard to escape the waving tendrils that seek my belly and thighs. Mostly, I try not to think about huge, prehistoric fish sucking through the silt of the lake beneath me. I breaststroke out into the lake, breathing hard and forcing myself to be rational, to let the cold numb me to old terrors. The shore grows smaller behind me, and I stretch out muscles that haven't been used in years. When I finally look back at the shore, I can see my father dozing on the bank, seeming far away and abstract, as ever. I roll onto my back and float and stare up at the pinkening sky and let myself dissolve into the freezing calm of the lake.

# 16

Patiently picking my way through the jagged zebra-mussel minefield of the shallow water, I emerge from the lake as clumsily as I entered it, quivering and exceptionally waterlogged. Marlon is still propped up on the bank, and he looks in my direction only when I stumble across the rough gravel. I flop down next to him, just close enough that I can feel how warm his skin is, and how chilled mine is. I drip-dry on the warmed stones, wringing out my hair like it's a dishrag. Marlon has cracked open a second bottle, and I pour a solid slug into my plastic cup. We are companionably silent. I stretch out on the rocks, replicating the pose of submission to the sun that I had taken in the water, arms over my head, belly stretched, chin upturned. Soon the sun will begin to set in earnest, but now it is still early, just days after the solstice.

I lie back and consider my options. What if I just left? Maybe I could simply go back to Paris, book a flight tomorrow afternoon and leave here. Marlon and Opal could deal with the funeral. Or not. I'm not sure I feel like indulging Zelda with a festive celebration. The morning after next I could be taking a taxi from the airport and sliding into bed next to Nico. The memory of Nico makes me cringe in sudden guilt, and I jettison the feeling immediately, shying away from it.

I can't just leave, though. Zelda has sucked me in, and I want to get to the end of her alphabet. I have to know what she's been up to, and why. I need to know the ending. Have I solved *P* already? *Police, Paris, passport. Promiscuity,* I think with a vaguely contemptuous snort. *Prude.* Are we moving on to *Q?* What on earth will she dredge up for *Q?* Beneath my questions is the sinister reminder of the body; someone died in that fire, and it's only a matter of time before someone else realizes it wasn't Zelda. Why would she risk that? And, perhaps most important: Whose bones are in the ashes of our barn?

I flop over onto my belly and slurp a mouthful of warm white wine, nestling the plastic cup into the rocks. I let my eyes close, feeling the sun on my back. I remember long days on this beach, all four of us. If I squint into the sun, I can almost see me and Zelda there on the dock, tawny-limbed and ten. Our eyes are bloodshot and our shoulders a dangerous russet-pink, our black hair snarled and matted and curled moistly around our necks, plastered to the swath of freckles that erupt like rashes across the bridge of our noses whenever we spend time in the sun.

"Daddy, come play with us!" I watch as my ten-year-old self moans plaintively, fending off a new assault from Zelda as she shoves at my shoulder. "Daddy, please!" I beg—begged—as Marlon cracks open his eyes and sits up in his lounge chair, the muscles of his abdomen neatly folded. He's wearing sunglasses, a panama hat, and his bathing suit. He looks at home in the sunlight, his Florida childhood glistening in the reflection of sweat on his temples. He sets down his drink. Nadine, ever the pale-skinned aristocrat, is shielded by an umbrella and a redundant sun hat.

"Yes, yes, yes!" Zelda chants, chanted, has always chanted, euphorically, affirming everything. We both shriek in hysterical giddiness as Marlon pauses dramatically, then tosses his sunglasses and hat aside and races over to the dock on the balls of his feet, his arms outstretched, lowering his center of gravity in preparation. Zelda and I dance to the end of the dock on excited tiptoes, screeching. Marlon collides with us, each of his arms snatching up a twin while he bellows something wordless and primal. We are both airborne, arcing messily into the water with a splash. I am laughing helplessly, and snort water into my nose as I attempt to resurface. I splutter back up, partly panicked and partly delirious. Marlon, still up on the dock, thumps loudly on his chest and makes King Kong noises of conquest.

"I say foul, sir!" Zelda chastises loudly, already heading back to the dock, making good time with her hybrid paddle that is both doggy and breaststroke. She refuses to practice the official strokes; during our dawn swimming lessons at the Watkins Glen pool, she started cackling when our instructor demonstrated the butterfly, and from that moment she has stolidly eschewed any formal tuition in swimming. I have worked every summer to perfect the choppy speed of the crawl, the self-protecting calmness of the backstroke, the unflagging breaststroke, even the splashy and impractical butterfly. I am the youngest girl (person, in fact) in the advanced swim level, and I have been promised a job as an instructor when I turn thirteen. I cling to this assured future. My dives are picture-perfect, whereas Zelda flings herself recklessly off the diving board, not caring whether her skin smacks painfully into the water as a result of imperfect form. I'm too afraid of the slapping sting to experiment and rigidly repeat my method every time: right hand over left, chin tucked, belly back toward spine, big toes pointed and in contact with each other.

"I feel that's quite enough screeching," Nadine says from her beachfront perch. She doesn't have to raise her voice for us to hear her clearly. The three of us are all perfectly tuned to her frequency, listening for any hints or indications of whether an eruption is imminent. The peak of her umbrella is a glowering, ominous Pompeii, lurking on the periphery of our sun-drenched city.

We quiet down momentarily, and Nadine flips through the glossy pages of her architecture and design magazine, staring at beautiful homes and wondering absently when (whether? No, when) her own home will appear amid these paragons of bourgeois achievement. She

sighs and sips daintily from her oversized gin and tonic, already worrying about what will happen when it is depleted below the halfway
mark. It is early in the day, and she doesn't yet drink the way she will
after Marlon leaves. For now, the pretense of a healthy relationship
with alcohol is still intact.

Our cries of joy are only temporarily stifled, though, and soon
we're squawking again. We are caught up in the frantic joy of play.
The giddy desire to win but also the need to keep the game going in-
definitely, regardless of the winner. To disregard the rules, heaving
them to the side in order to prolong the suspense.

"I say, I say, this is a travesty," Zelda giggles as, back on the dock,
she tries to get leverage against Marlon's hip bone. He deftly skips
away just as she attempts to reinforce her position and lunges at him
with the full weight of her body. Her hands slide off his wet midriff,
her balance is shot, and she collapses into the drink. Her head pops up
immediately. "You are an imitable cad, Mr. Marlon!" she calls out.
She has been obsessed with anything concerning the Civil War for the
last two months. She is entranced by this history of division, a separa-
tion that could have taken place but didn't. She is prefiguring our
parents' divorce, exploring our eternal union. And talking in the most
ridiculous southern belle dialect. It's driving us all insane.

"Yes, ma'am, that's correct," Marlon booms. "But I'm afraid that
I'm"—he picks me up—"the sovereign leader"—he dangles me out
over the water as my feet scrabble for the wood, my fingers grab for his
arms, and I giggle in terror—"of this here territory!" He drops me
summarily into the water. "The Yankees win again!" he crows.

"Jesus, Marlon," Nadine snipes from the shore. "You're the adult.
Someone's going to get hurt." We ignore her.

"But you're not a Yankee, Daddy!" I correct. "You'd be a Confed-
erate! Because you're from Florida."

"Geographically speaking, I would be," Marlon says. "But not in
my heart of hearts." He seats himself on the edge of the dock, his legs
dangling into the water as Zelda and I circle him; we are scheming
little mermaids.

"I'd be a Rebel," Zelda declares.

"Racist," I inform her.

"That has nothing to do with it, idiot," she responds, splashing me. "It's about federal centralization."

"Racist," I repeat.

"Are you going to prevent the second Civil War, darling, or do I need to get involved?" Nadine threatens from beneath the shelter of her pin-striped beach umbrella.

"Let's both try and get Daddy in the water," Zelda says to me. I miss the undertone of her voice, fail to recognize the sound of her plotting.

"Now, I know neither one of you is thinking about pulling on my toes underwater. How absolutely just awful that would be. I know that it hasn't even crossed your minds to try and get me off the dock. . . ." Marlon baits us innocently. I giggle mischievously and paddle down to his toes, pretending that I'm a big fish taking the bait of his white digits. From beneath the water, I can hear him howling in exaggerated horror.

"Oh, God, some fish has my toes!" My knees thrash out and I encounter Zelda's thigh, and she kicks back at me. When I surface for breath, I realize she's trying to tug Marlon off the dock by towing on his calf. Though it's clearly obvious this won't work, I join her and we churn our feet, pulling on our father. "Oh, here I go! Crap, I'm going to fall in!" Marlon protests, subtly heaving himself into the water. We cry out in triumph and swarm around him, starved sharks in a feeding frenzy of parental attention. I cling to his arm joyously, swollen with victory. Now everything is perfect! This is all I wanted. But Zelda has not forgotten the purpose of the game: to win control of the dock. She knew that I would be content with this small conquest, hanging on Marlon's arm and distracted by affection. She has dashed up onto the planking and crows the success of her coup.

"We can't stand for that, can we, Little A?" Marlon asks me conspiratorially. "You ready?"

I nod feverishly, my eyes and nose burning from a day spent largely underwater, and prepare myself to be launched back toward the dock. I put my foot into the clasp of Marlon's hands and he propels me up and through the water. I picture myself landing on the dock fully upright to challenge Zelda, but I've misunderstood the intended trajectory of Marlon's launch; he seems to have imagined me covering a couple feet of water, splashing in, and then hoisting myself up. I realize too late that I am fully unprepared to reenter the water, that my head is angled all wrong, my hands outstretched. Time slows down as I fly toward the dock and collide into it, crashing back beneath the water.

When I come up, I'm wailing. Not just because I'm hurt, though I am, but because my dramatic attempt to retake the lost territory has been so indecorously thwarted. A military disgrace. I've smacked my ribs and swallowed water, and the raw burning sensation makes my eyes leak. It's hard to cry and tread water.

"What did I say?" Nadine asks calmly, not lifting her eyes from her magazine. "Someone always ends up crying in your games, Marlon."

Our father doesn't give any sign of having heard her, though he does collect me sympathetically. "C'mon, let's get out of the water, Little A," he soothes.

"Nooo!" I wail. "I want to keep playing!"

"Maybe in a bit."

"I guess I win," Zelda says, smug, her hands on her hips.

"No, you don't!" I spit out. "The game's not over."

"You lose," she taunts. "I'm Queen of the Dock."

"Zaza, don't tease Ava," Marlon says.

"What? I got hurt too. At least I didn't cry like a ba-by," she chants.

"Ava, c'mon," Marlon says, dragging me toward the beach. I'm thrashing uncooperatively, desperate to stay in the water.

"Look at my splinter, Dad," Zelda says proudly, acrobatically extending her entire leg to show him the sole of her foot. There is indeed an impressive splinter lodged in the ball of her foot, already pulsing red. She displays it to compare our relative toughness, a competition I have also just lost by falling apart in the water. Not only has she won the

dock, she withstands pain better too. I slink back to shore in humiliated defeat. And Zelda, though gleefully victorious, limps back to
where I sit sniffling on the rocks. Marlon and Nadine bicker beneath
the umbrella. ("You're a child." "And you're a shrew.") Zelda sidles up
to me and leans against my shoulder.

"We can rule jointly," she says. "Two rulers are better than one."

I snivel at her, not wanting to accept but knowing I will.

"Okay," I finally say. She tugs me by the hand back toward the
dock, away from our parents and their disagreement. We sit on the
edge, toes dabbling in the lake's surface, and decide on the rules for
our kingdom. Zelda appoints me Lady of the Lake, an honorary position.

Looking at my father now, stretched out on the beach, I wonder if
Marlon is also remembering those games, if he recalls the feel of our
slippery brown torsos as he flung us into the water, shrieking with
pleasure. I wonder if he plays the same games with his other daughters, if he takes them to the pool and launches them by the feet into a
half-airborne dive, over and over again until their eyes are tight with
too much sun and water. If he laughs raucously and romps like a child
himself when he is with them. If he ignores his wife as she sits unhappily nearby, if he lets her fester in her despair and averts his eyes whenever she tries to signal her need for help. Does Maria try to tell him
how miserable she has become, in the only inadequate language she
has at her disposal? Do his daughters pretend it's not happening, putting on a performance of their happiness, hoping to detract from the
desperate gloom that settles over them every time they're together? I
look over at Marlon, trying, not for the first time, to divine what might
be going on behind his relaxed and unconcerned façade, delicately
cracking at the edges but firmly, implacably maintained. Surely he
can't really be so indifferent.

Nearly dry, I stand up and wrap the sarong around my waist. Then
I squat to top up my plastic cup.

"I'm heading back to the house," I tell my father.

He cracks open an eye that might have been sleeping. "Oh? Okay. Do you want to take the tractor? I could stand to walk some of this off," he says, patting his belly good-naturedly.

"You rode the tractor down?" I ask, amused. We loved to take the tractor down to the lake when we were little, perched above the axle, on either side of the driver's seat. Nadine used to roll her eyes, but after Marlon left us, she would sometimes drive down herself. She had taught us how to use it when we were fourteen.

"Thought I'd see if she's still running. You know how to start her up?" he says.

"No, the tractor has just been sitting here waiting for your return. None of us know how to operate it without your masculine expertise."

He doesn't say anything, just shuts his eyes again. I think he might be quite drunk. I wonder if he'll be able to make it back up to the house. The walk will help sober him up, I reason, and he'll be less likely to drive the tractor into the lake or flip it over and kill himself. That would really be Zelda's crowning glory; maybe she could dispose of both of our parents in a single weekend.

# 17

Quietly, I slide open the door to the living room, not wanting anyone to know I'm back. I plan to sneak around silently before hiding in my room for the rest of the night. I've resolved that yesterday's excesses have determined that I can eat only apples for dinner. This is something I feel has been objectively decided, as though it's a mathematical equation: yesterday, falafel AND wine? Today, only apples. I'm thinking this logic through when Opal interrupts me.

"Ava, sweetie, is that you?"

I consider scuttling away but sigh in resignation. There's no help for it. "Yeah, it's me."

Opal reaches for my hand, enclosing it in her own damp palm. "Ava, how are you doing?"

"Just fine," I answer brusquely.

"Because your father and I . . . we're worried about you, sweetie. We're not sure you're processing everything that's happened."

"Everyone grieves in different ways."

"You just seem so distant. And sort of, well, as though you're in denial. We were thinking maybe you wanted to talk. About your feelings, that is," she adds, as though there were some ambiguity, as though maybe she had been suggesting that we talk about the economy or fashion. She wants me to feel that she is available. She is reinforcing the message that her wrinkled fingertips are insisting on as they go to work on my wrist, on the back of my hand: *I'm here, I'm not dead, I'm alive, I'm here.* I can sense her frantic unwillingness to disappear. She squeezes me tightly around my shoulders, kneading my deltoids with her searching, hungry hands. I wonder if her desire for physical proximity has always been so obviously linked to her desire to escape eradication. Zelda and I are her living iterations, her small sip of immortality, and she has covetously massaged and fondled our bodies since our birth, taking tactile comfort in the knowledge that her flesh has been extended. I dislike being deployed this way. I dislike her desperation.

"Listen, Grandma, I'm beat, and I have to get Nadine something to eat, get her ready for dinner, you know," I say, and move away, not waiting for her to release me. Her hands paw at the space where my body was.

"Of course, of course, I'll be fine down here. Don't worry about me. I don't mind being alone." She waves me off.

"I'll be back down in a bit."

Upstairs, Nadine is in her bed, mumbling something. Her palsied hands are shaking, and her head is bobbling more than usual.

"When I was little, I used to go crabbing, you know," she informs me absently, tapping on her knee as though making an important point.

"Oh, yeah?" This conversation seems encouraging. My mother has never talked much about her life.

"With my mother. I used to go crabbing. There was a marsh, near our house. We would go out at low tide."

"What was she like, Grandma Maureen?" I ask. She died before we were born, and I know virtually nothing about her, except that she didn't drink.

"Oh, she was uptight. She could be a real cunty tight-ass." My eyes widen at my mother's language, and I almost burst out laughing. "She grew up poor, outside Boston, and both her parents were drunks. Momma was desperate to get away from all that. She married rich, though maybe stupidly."

"Why is that? Was Grandpa Patrick . . . not a good guy?" I ask hungrily.

She snorts. "He was a controlling, raging drunk, exactly like her father. He sang beautifully, but he was just filled with anger. It didn't take her long to figure out she'd made a mistake, but Irish Catholics don't get divorces." She laughs bitterly, acknowledging her own marital status. "You missed out on the worst years, though. Once you left, they were just miserable."

"What—I never met them, Mom."

"Nonsense. After you died, Daddy just disappeared. He was drunk every night, almost never came home anymore, and Momma just . . . turned off. She did the laundry and cooked meals, but she was just empty." Oh, Christ. Mom thinks I'm her dead sister. Maybe that's what she meant in the car, when she called me dead—she thought I was Nina, not Zelda. Nadine was eight when it happened, and Nina was ten, I think. She almost never spoke of her, but Marlon had explained this to me and Zelda one night when Mom had wept on the couch for close to an hour, drunkenly moaning "Nina" the whole while. He said that she had always felt like her life, and her parents' lives, would never have turned into what they had if Nina had lived. "You were just the light of the family. Precocious, chatty. Fun, above all. Mother and I were always a bit serious. But you. You." She gazes at me fondly. "Everyone loved you."

"And then I died?"

"And then you died. And I knew whenever Momma took me down to the beach in the evenings, she was thinking about you. You'd think they would both have wanted to get away from that spot. . . ." From what I understood, Mom's childhood home had been spacious if not quite opulent, close to the water on the tip of Cape Cod. Grandpa Patrick was a successful real estate broker, Maureen the diligent, red-knuckled housewife. Grandpa was a gambler, not unlike my father. There was a photograph of the house, a sweet bungalow facing the ocean. As a child, it had seemed positively idyllic to me. But Nadine had sold it the second her mother died, clearly desperate to get rid of it.

"Is that why you sold the house?" I ask.

"Of course," she answers. "It was haunted, you know. Once some-one has died, they stay put." I can't help thinking of the barn, of the bones in the wreckage. "There are spiders, all over the walls," Nadine adds conversationally, and I leap up, nearly upsetting the tray of left-overs I brought from downstairs and have set down on the nightstand. I look around in a panic, but of course there is nothing.

"Jesus, Mom." She seems not so much upset by the hallucinated spiders as intrigued, and she waves her hands around as though count-ing them. "Okay," I say, "time for meds and dinner."

"I'm not hungry," she replies, dismissing me. As usual. Has she ever admitted to being hungry, to needing something?

"You still have to eat something. You're not supposed to take the meds on an empty stomach."

"Oh, fuck my meds," she snaps. "I'm not sick. I won't take them."

"Then no wine."

"I don't see any wine," she says with a raised eyebrow.

Puffing in annoyance, I trundle back downstairs and bring her up a bottle.

"Meds first." We go through the tedious process of swallowing the pills from the dispenser that lives by her bed. When she is done, I pour her a measure of Chablis and try to convince her to eat. I'm exhausted with this routine already, with its dull repetition. Again and again, day after day. And I've been home for only a few days—what must Zelda have learned of boredom? When she's done, I help her get undressed for bed, though she changes her mind halfway through and decides she should be getting dressed, and she tries to do her hair and put on makeup. Eventually, the promise of more wine convinces her to sub-mit to her bedtime routine. When I finally get her tucked in, the sun has long since set. I'm planning to leave her to her fussing for the rest of the night, but the way she looks at me as I'm walking toward the door is so full of pure need that I pause.

"Do you want some company, Mom?"

"What? No, I don't need anything," she says casually, even shrugging. "I was just going to watch something on TV." My mother has never really sought out my attention or time, so I'm confused about whether or not this is an overture.

"Um, do you . . . mind if I join you?"

"It's entirely up to you."

I consider, then decide, meh, fuck it. I crawl onto the other side of the bed and reach for the laptop there, which is synced to the big-screen TV across from us. But when I go to open Netflix in the browser, Nadine seems to be logged out of her account.

"Any chance you know the password to this, Mom?" I ask, already pessimistic.

She looks stricken, but to my surprise, she answers me. "Zinfandel three eight one five," she says confidently, and my eyebrows shoot up. All right. Though when I type that password in, it doesn't work.

"Try again, Mom."

She doesn't answer this time, just stares straight ahead. I sigh. The Netflix account is registered to Zelda, so I request a new password and log in to her email from the laptop. Her password has been "ZeeN0tZed" for as long as I can remember, and it still is. My fingers fumble on the unfamiliar keyboard—I've grown so accustomed to AZERTY.

When I log in for the link, there's a fresh email from Zelda waiting in her inbox. I glance at Mom, but I'm really not concerned about her seeing it, even though the computer screen is mirrored on the big screen across the room. I open the email.

To: zazazelda@gmail.com
From: zazazelda@gmail.com
Subject: Quack Quack
June 25, 2016 @ 8:45 PM

https://www.youtube.com/watch?v=f-V1aCjgzlg

That's it. Just the link. With another quick look at my mother, I click on it. It takes me to a YouTube video of *Sesame Street*'s "Letter Q."

I push play and watch as a bunch of cheery, racially diverse kids toss out words that start with *Q.* Ernie plays a joke on Bert. Kermit and Grover draw the letter in orange across the screen. Nadine watches alertly, her eyes wide.

"This mean anything to you, Mom?"

She shakes her head.

I'm not surprised. Even if she wasn't deteriorating from the inside out, it's unlikely that she'd remember an incident from when we were in kindergarten. The letter would mean nothing to her, because she never came to see us there. Our kindergarten class was a pretty laid-back public school experience. A big chunk of the year was to be dedicated to the alphabet and mastering this crucial sequence. We soon learned that our kindergarten teacher had a very special, secret relationship to someone really, really important.

"Okay, everybody," said Ms. Prescott, a pretty young blonde, during the second week of school. "This is a really big secret, and it's super important that you don't tell kids in other classrooms about this, because it would make them feel bad. But. Guess who I know?" A chorus of hushed and reverent "Who?"s greeted this question, and a couple of hands even went up, as though there might actually be a right answer to this ridiculous query. "One of my close friends is someone named . . ." She walked over to a closet in the corner of the classroom, ducked inside, and then bounced back out, exclaiming, "Elmo!"

This piece of information was greeted with near hysteria in our classroom, where it was obvious that everyone watched *Sesame Street.* Elmo was as close to a celebrity as it got for rural five-year-olds, and excited whispers circulated around the oval of squirmy kids when this announcement came. We could not believe our good luck.

In retrospect, I wonder at the injunction to secrecy. It didn't strike us as weird, at the time, but maybe that's because childhood is filled with so many of these strange entreaties against transparency. "Don't tell your mother." "Promise you won't show Mom and Dad." "Becky definitely can't find out, okay?"

We soon learned that Elmo's role in our classroom was to appear every Monday morning with the "weekly letter." Apparently, he would spend all week chasing around the next week's letter, and late on Sunday night, he would finally catch it and trap it in the closet at our classroom, waiting to be liberated by Ms. Prescott on Monday morning.

But. There was a catch. She needed help to bring out the letters, drag them out into the sunny space of our classroom. The implication was that the letters didn't want to be seen, known, unveiled. It took the conjoined efforts of at least three people to midwife them into the class: Elmo, Ms. Prescott, and a classroom parent. This meant that every week, one of our parents would show up to help Ms. Prescott introduce that Monday's letter. Meaning that one of our parents would eventually come to our classroom! Our circle was abuzz with excitement.

Letters were assigned randomly, so that no one became jealous or possessive. For example, it would have made sense to assign me *A*, for Ava. But our class also had an Adam and an Anthony, and they could just as plausibly have laid claim to that primary chunk of our alphabet. Zelda and I were assigned one letter because there were twenty-seven students in the class. Any guesses what letter that was?

Marlon, of course, was the one who brought us to school early one Monday morning in spring, as our kindergarten year was winding down. He wore a wild Hawaiian shirt and mismatched plaid trousers and a bizarre hat with earflaps, exactly the sort of clothes that appeal to five-year-olds. Marlon always knows his audience, and he arrived fully prepared to charm.

"Okay, kids. It's Monday. Everybody know what that means?" Ms. Prescott said.

"Letter day!" we all hollered in frenzied anticipation. There is no explaining why this whole process was so much fun, but it was extremely titillating. The puzzle of that closed door, the jelly-kneed expectation of having some foreign body appear behind it, dragged there against its own volition, even if you knew what came next in that limited queue of letters. We could scarcely contain ourselves.

"That's right!" Ms. Prescott cooed, rabble-rousing. "So, what letters have we done so far?" My hand shot into the air. "Ava?"

"Aybeeceedeeeeeffgeeaitchayejaykayellemenohpeekewaressteeyouveedubbleyouexwyezee!" I expelled in a single breath.

"Almost! You're getting ahead of yourself there a bit, though. That's all the letters. What was the last letter we did?" A few hands poked up, Zelda's included.

"Zelda?" Ms. Prescott pointed. I can only assume that she was giving us both a chance to perform in front of our parent, rather than intentionally fomenting sibling rivalry. But Zelda smiled slyly, with barely a glance at me.

"*P.* And before that *O.* And before that *N.*"

"That's right!" Ms. Prescott congratulated her. Marlon beamed.

"So what's next, guys?"

"*Q!*" someone shouted from the back.

"Hey, what are our rules? We raise our hands, right?" Our teacher sternly arched her eyebrows. "Let's all say it together. What letter are we doing today?"

"Keewww!" we all responded.

"And today, we have a very special visitor." Ms. Prescott looked fondly at my father with an expression that suggested he was indeed very special. "Ava and Zelda's dad. And what's *your* name?" she asked him, in the same tone she used to address us, then immediately blushed because she realized how ridiculous she sounded.

"My name is Marlon!" my father announced, batting not one eyelid. "And I'm here to get the letter *Q* on the hook!" He produced a collapsible fishing pole from his pocket, and we all squealed. This was new! Normally the parents just made a show of pulling the letters out of the closet while a profoundly unhelpful Elmo cheered them on. Fishing! We'd never fished for letters! Ms. Prescott looked amused and concerned; she must have been wondering if there was a hook on that line, and whether she was legally liable if Marlon accidentally snagged somebody's lip or cheek.

"Well. Goodness. Let's go to the closet, then," she said, unwilling to be disagreeable in front of Marlon. We knew the drill, so we remained glued to the carpet while Ms. Prescott walked over to the door. She knocked once, then twice. "Elmo?" she called.

"Is that you, Ms. Prescott?" she answered herself in a decent ventriloquist version of Elmo. This may have been her single most important skill as a teacher.

"Yes! Do you have a letter for us today?"

"Why, yes, yes, I do!"

"I have a friend here to help us get it out. His name is Marlon, and he has a fishing pole!" Normally parents were introduced by their last names, a "Mr." or "Mrs." But my father had easily bypassed those formalities.

"Wow, a fishing pole! That sounds great."

"Are you ready for us to open the door, Elmo?"

"You bet!"

Ms. Prescott theatrically flung the door open and leaned in, scooping up the Elmo puppet in a practiced move.

"He's in the back of the closet, Ms. Prescott," Elmo informed her. "He doesn't want to come out!" (The letters were always masculine.)

"Well, that's why I brought my friend Marlon!" she answered herself, eyes blazing in excitement. We could tell that something about this ritual thrilled her too.

"Okay, Elmo, you ready for me to go fishing?" my father asked Elmo, with a big, slow wink at Ms. Prescott. She blushed again.

"You bet, Marlon!"

"Okay, here I go!" He made an elaborate gesture of casting his line into the closet. For a moment it looked like he hooked something, and he frowned in exaggerated concentration. But then he reeled in the line again. "That's one slippery letter!" he informed us. He cast again. Again, it looked like a sure thing, and he even strained dramatically, pretending to pull on something. But no. "Got away again!" Marlon wiped his brow. "Jeez, maybe I should just give up. What do you guys think—should I call it a day?"

"Nononononono!" we screamed in delight.

"Okay, okay. One more try." He leaned back and cast his reel into the closet another time. For one breathless second, we thought he'd missed again, and the suspense was killing us. But then the line went tight, and Marlon was pulling, and the plushy, oversized letter $Q$ emerged from the closet. Marlon reeled it in and grabbed it firmly. In his hands, the letter looked as though it were squirming, trying to escape. "I got him!" he said. Then the letter lurched away from him, making a break for it, before it careened back around and smashed into his torso. Marlon looked for all the world as though he had stepped on a banana peel as his feet went out from under him, and he fell to the ground in a slapstick parody. We giggled uproariously. Marlon had kept his grip on the rebellious letter, though, and he sprang back upright athletically, putting the letter $Q$ in a headlock. When he smiled over at Ms. Prescott, she looked back at him with an expression of worship.

I laugh to myself now, remembering this episode. No other parent came close to Marlon's performance; he won, hands down. Zelda and I enjoyed a brief moment of celebrity, refracted off our father. It was the sort of performance that so thoroughly demonstrated what a perfect dad he could be, how incandescently enchanting he was with us kids. And he was, I guess. He just couldn't really have relationships with adults or teenagers, and he fled before we fully understood that.

It takes me all of thirty seconds to figure out what Zelda wants me to do next. She has finally tossed me an easy one, one that has all the clues and hints I need. Nadine is staring around wide-eyed, and when I set the laptop down, she again pushes play on the YouTube clip. I can hear the audio as I head for the closet. Zelda couldn't possibly have planned for me to watch it on the big screen in this room, but it is a very nice touch.

I slide open the door to Marlon's walk-in closet, which Nadine has still not really claimed. There's a pair of Marlon's boots in the corner, and an old winter coat of his that he never bothered to take to sunny California. Typical of him to decide that because he didn't immediately need it, he didn't have to do anything about it. It has hung in this closet for more than ten years. Nadine has hung a few of her own coats on the rack, and there are some old boxes filled with photos and other remnants of our family life. This closet is a mausoleum, the Antipovas pre-divorce. I stand on tippy-toe to reach what Zelda has left me.

My father's old fishing box is elegant and timeworn. He found it in an antiques store during one of our autumn vacations as we drove through coppery leaves up in the Adirondacks. It has big buckles and a treasure trove of compartments, which Marlon diligently filled with expensive flies and other fishing accessories that I can't identify. I imagine he can't either. His fascination with fishing was mercifully brief, and he'd barely finished assembling this elaborate collection of accoutrements before abandoning the hobby. Whenever anyone asked why he gave up fishing, he'd answer with a grin and a wink: "Too dry."

I flip open the clasps and stare at the rows of flies, wondering if one of them has been left by Zelda. But in the larger compartment, I find an envelope labeled "P (for Policy)." I pull the folded sheets of paper from the envelope and find myself looking at life insurance documents for Zelda, Nadine, and myself. I scan the opaque language. I don't know what any of these terms mean, and everything is embedded in such bizarre legalese that I can't tell if we owe them money or if it's the other way around. But I'm willing to bet that Zelda has done her homework. I remain crouched in the closet for a few moments longer, inhaling the musty scents of old clothes and papers, before standing up and turning off the light. I take the envelope with me.

Nadine is rewatching the *Sesame Street* clip with a rapt expression, mumbling, "I remember this, I remember this." I give her a kiss on the cheek and push the laptop closer to her. Let her watch *Sesame Street* on YouTube all night. I head downstairs to discover that Marlon has returned from the lake. His eyes look bloodshot, and he seems out of breath. He is standing in the kitchen, drinking lemonade directly from the container.

"Hey, Dad. You know anything about life insurance?" I ask.

He looks startled. "Not really, no. Why?"

"Well, we seem to have some." I slap the envelope down on the kitchen island. "Not sure quite what to make of it."

"Where did you find this?" he asks, flipping through the pages.

"Mom's room."

"Hmm. This is . . . Look, I'll have to look into this. I don't know if this complicates things. The police might want to know about it."

"Why?"

"Well, these policies are pretty new. Just over a year old. And with Zelda's . . . I mean, any time a sizable life insurance policy appears in a murder investigation . . ." He suddenly laughs. "I have no idea what I'm talking about. I watch too much TV. But it seems to me that this is what they're talking about when they go looking for motive."

"Motive? Motive for what?" Opal calls from the living room.

"Nothing, Mom," Marlon responds. Then he lowers his voice: "Let's not tell her about this. She's upset enough."

I nod, agreeing to the conspiracy. "But if the cops think the insurance policy is motive, it will only implicate me and Mom," I point out, suddenly a little nervous. Is that what Zelda has in mind?

"True, though it will look much stranger if you don't disclose it. In any case, I'll call these people in the morning, see if I can make heads or tails of it. You okay, Little A?"

"I don't know why everyone keeps asking me that."

"I just worry, that's all."

I wave him away. "I know, I'm sorry. It's been a long day."

"It has. How about I tuck Nadine in for you?" he offers.

The ungenerous part of me suggests that he knows I've already done it. "She's fine. Gave her the pills, and she's in bed with her night-time baba."

Marlon smiles wryly. "Well, I'm beat," he says, yawning grandly. "I'm going to turn in on the couch. Sleep tight, Little A."

"Night, Dad."

# 18

R appears later that night when Nadine's screams wake me. Her shrill cries make me leap from bed in a terrified fugue state, before I process what is happening. I dash to her room in a panic; in my half-asleep fog, I think that whoever murdered the person in the barn is here to finish off Nadine. In my speed, I fumble with the keys and find my hands shaking violently, in unhappy mimicry of Nadine's tremors. My fingers twitch and dance like spastic insects, and I watch in disembodied dismay as I drop the key to her room again. Marlon has dashed up the stairs by this point, and I can hear Opal hoisting herself up out of bed too. Marlon grabs the keys from me and barges into Nadine's room—his old room.

Nadine is in her bathroom, slamming her head against the mirror. She is screaming her sister's name in a terrified keen, reaching out for her reflection in between head butts to the glass, which has cracked and cut her on her forehead. Blood mats the edge of her once-blond coif. Marlon stands helplessly observing this spectacle, and I stand next to him, looking at Nadine in pure terror.

"Niiiinnnaaaa!" she shrieks.

Opal is the one who musters the presence of mind to stride into the bathroom, fill a glass of water, and splash it in Nadine's face. Nadine immediately stops screaming. She looks around, dazed, unclear about what is going on.

"Marlon? Honey?" she croaks, and Marlon flinches.

"Let's go back to bed, Deeny."

I've never heard this nickname. Nadine cooperates for him, and I happily let him fold her back beneath the blankets and fetch a wash-cloth to wipe the blood from her forehead. There are spots of red on her pristine nightgown. I think about getting her a fresh one, but it all seems so pointless.

"Do either of you know what this is about?" Marlon asks brusquely, as though Opal or I am somehow to blame for this episode. We both look back at him with guilty expressions, because we have no idea.

"I'll go call the doctor," I say. "Can you . . . ?"

Marlon nods in response. He's sitting next to Nadine on the edge of their big bed, and she's clinging to him. He holds her hand. I leave the room, and lead Opal into the library.

Still shaking, I retrieve my phone from my room. I hunt through the contacts and call Dr. Whitcross. It takes a few minutes, but soon I'm listening to his groggy voice on the other line.

"Zelda?"

"What?" After a long, slow moment, I realize that I must have used Zelda's cellphone. Ah, fuck.

"No, I'm sorry, Dr. Whitcross. This is Ava—there's a medical emergency here?" I can hear Stuey sitting up straight, suddenly professional. A woman's voice asks a question in the background.

"No, sweetie, it's work." He seems relieved to not be lying. "What is it?" he asks gruffly. "Normally there's a different line for this."

"I'm sorry to wake you up, but it's my mother. She just woke up in the middle of the night screaming and slamming her head into the mirror. I was just wondering—"

"Has she been taking the right dose of clonazepam?" he interrupts.

"I—I don't know. How can I verify that?"

"Have you been giving her a pink pill that says *clonazepam* on it every day?" Dr. Whitcross answers testily.

"I'll have to check," I respond. "Is there anything else I can do?"

"Give her one and put her back to bed."

I hear a click, and Dr. Whitcross is gone. Annoyed, I go back to Nadine's bedroom and flip open her drug dispenser. I rifle through tomorrow's drugs, but there are no pink pills, or anything with a *C* on it. I open the top drawer of her nightstand, and there's a prescription pill bottle right there, clearly labeled "clonazepam." I unscrew the top and tap out a pill. A piece of paper comes out with it.

*I wasn't sure whether to make this the letter C, but timing-wise, R seemed more appropriate: R, for Rapid Eye Movement behavior disorder, a rather unpleasant condition. REM disorder typically presents in people with Lewy body dementia and can be pretty alarming. You may remember these details from the early diagnostic sessions! A real treat. She's been doing quite a bit better, but she needs her clonazepam like a junkie craving the next fix, and she will turn into a horrific fiend if she doesn't get it promptly. She hasn't taken any since the night before the fire, and based on earlier test runs, it should take her about three days to start in on the really unpleasant dreams. Hopefully this letter is snuggled in right where it's supposed to be, darling A. By the way, how have you been sleeping? You may consider thinking about your own health. May I recommend some light medical reading to keep you up at night? I've got a dossier that you may find alarmingly familiar.*

I glance from Zelda's handwritten note to Marlon, to see if he has noticed. He is too preoccupied with Nadine, who is shaking and staring straight ahead. I hand him the clonazepam, and he barely looks at it.

"Deeny, will you take this, please?" he asks very pleasantly, and she immediately opens her mouth. He pops the pink pill between her pink gums and reaches around for a glass of water. My parents are weirdly intimate, touching each other, and I find it more than a little unsettling. I stand up to leave the room.

Opal is still sitting in the library, staring out across the deck. The sun is just starting to lighten the sky, and I sit down next to her on the couch. For once, she doesn't lean over to be closer or reach out for my skin.

"Getting old is terrible," she says flatly. "A true horror."

"Nadine isn't old. She's just really sick," I answer.

Opal shrugs, more cynical than I've ever seen her. "Does it matter?" she asks softly. We stare out at the fields, which are becoming clearer with every second. "Was she screaming 'Nina'?" Opal finally says, breaking the silence.

"I think so. Her sister," I explain.

"I know, sweetheart." Opal turns her watery green eyes on me suddenly, catching me by surprise.

"She died of some sort of childhood illness, when they were little," I explain. Opal squints closer at me, alert.

"Oh, darling. No, she didn't."

"What do you mean? It was, I don't know, measles or something," I answer.

"It was her parents, and your family curse," she says blankly, and suddenly I have goose bumps. I don't really want to hear more. "Patrick, your mother's father. He was supposed to watch the girls at the beach. Maureen was a teetotaler, but there were days when she couldn't get out of bed. Depression. Patrick drank a quart of whiskey and fell asleep on the beach in front of the house. It was hours before anyone realized what had happened, when they found Nadine shivering in the surf, calling her sister's name."

"What are you saying?"

"Your mother's sister. She drowned. While Nadine watched."

I walk around in the dewy grass, my toes freezing cold. The sun is almost up, casting that weird foreign light I associate with dawn. It's a chilly light, not the warm, burnished sunlight of happy hour. Opal has gone back to bed, and Marlon is still in Nadine's room, both of them presumably asleep. I prowl the front yard, thinking. Zelda is clearly suggesting that I go looking for more information about my mother's disorder, but it's not obvious what she has in mind. The Internet? A medical textbook? I sit down in a damp deck chair and stare out at the property, at the family kingdom. I doze off when the sun is finally up in the sky, drying off the grapevines and my stiff, wet toes.

The jangle of a new message awakens me hours later. I feel confused, thirsty, and too warm. It's fully daylight now. I crack my neck stiffly and check my phone. Nico.

> Ava, please call me. I thought I saw you at the café, but you left before I talk to you. I miss you so much I'm imagine you.

I close the message and stumble back toward the house. I'm vaguely indignant; I should be feeling better, considering how sober I was yesterday. A single glass of wine. Ish. A triumph.

The house is quiet, everyone still sequestered in their rooms. Last night's disruption hangs over us; I can sense the palpable impression of disturbance. Someone has made coffee, though, a hint that routines are still being observed. I pour myself a cup and head upstairs. In my room, I grab my iPad and fluff my downy white comforter over myself. I don't want anything to do with Zelda's game right now. She doesn't control me, not completely. I spend the rest of the day lost in finishing *A Clash of Kings* before plunging into *A Storm of Swords*. For the first time, I feel sorry for Cersei Lannister.

My iPad finally dies, at a fairly crucial moment in the third book, and my charger is nowhere to be found. I howl in frustration at this narrative blue balls. I know that I'm merely forestalling the moment when there will be no more books to read, when I'll reach the end of the fifth book and will have to wait in agony for the sixth. And then the sixth will be finished, and the seventh, and the bottle will be dry forever. But right now, all I want is my next fix. I'm certain there will be a copy somewhere in this house.

I check my bookshelves first, then head immediately to Zelda's, sure that she'll have acquired a copy somewhere. Her bookcases are empty of all George R. R. Martin–related texts, but I wind up sucked into the disarray of her shelves, the buried treasure on every surface. I find an atrocious poem I wrote in fourth grade, folded into an origami crane. I have no idea who could have done this; Zelda didn't have the patience or the dexterity for origami. I turn up Zelda's "ghost series" (an art school project) in a carved wooden box: overexposed Polaroids of outdated technology (typewriters, gas-lit lamps, Marlon's modish cellphone from the nineties). Zelda's labored, handwritten alphabet from kindergarten. Each letter is messy and unfinished. I know my own sheet was obsessively completed, carefully imitated.

Surrounded by all these physical traces, I wonder what it will be like to go to kindergarten fifteen years from now. Whether kids will practice their letters on iPads instead of these lined papers, yellowed and curled and horrifically fragile. Maybe there will be a digital record of every single paper that people produce in their lifetime, a file for each grade. I wonder if this is what so terrifies people about digital technology, the idea that there will be a record of every moment, every mistake, every bad poem or carelessly carved-out letter. These scattered artifacts are just a tiny portion of our lives; what if I could flip through my tablet and find Zelda's history, everything she's ever done? What if the people you met could scan through your drawings from third grade, your U.S. history essays from eleventh grade, your college applications? I realize that this is already reality, that the ancient desktop in our house will have those papers, those applications, in addition to a startling number of our IM conversations from high school onward. I have a primal, irrational desire to destroy that computer. People must be terrified of losing all mystery. No one wants the complete picture, the whole story. It would leave no room for the fictions we need to tell ourselves about ourselves.

Amid this juvenilia, I find a portrait Zelda did of our family in sixth or seventh grade. She was gifted at mimesis, could cleverly capture strange, realist details. Ever the artist. This portrait is elaborate, colored with paint and pencil, the mediums blended together. A different story of our family. One of the four edges is jagged, evidence of having been torn. Marlon has been removed from the picture. Zelda, in an uncharacteristically childish gesture, tore him out shortly after he left. And effectively cut him out of her life. His betrayal was final for her, and while they were always civil, Zelda and Marlon were, in effect, done for when he walked out the door.

In the weeks and maybe months before he decamped, Marlon had barely been home, and every time our parents wound up in a room together, there was a verbal eruption. Nadine would bait him until he cracked, and nothing was more alarming to me than seeing Marlon's other side, his dangerous side. We were so used to Nadine's nastiness that we found her explosions unsurprising—in a way, her behavior reinforced consistency. Nothing to see here. But Marlon's quick rage was unsettling, and whenever I heard the two of them start—usually in the kitchen, where they were both forced to venture regularly in order to refill their glasses—I would try to disappear. Outside, into a book, anything. I hated their catalogue of wrongdoings, the scripted recriminations.

"Jesus, Marl, you're not even a good liar. Your bookie has called three times today. You think I'm an idiot?"

"No, Nadine, I think you're a drunk. And not a nice one. A harping, bitching—"

"You want to throw stones, from behind all that glass?"

"At least I can see straight enough to hit something."

"Oh, please, what are you, twelve?"

"No, I'm a grown-ass man who lives—"

"Just stop! I can't—"

I would turn the dial of my iPod up and stare up at my bedroom ceiling, waiting for the sound of broken glass or a slammed door to signify that one or both of them had stormed off.

Zelda was less affected by these scenes, or at least she seemed less desperate to flee them. She would even lurk at the top of the stairs, eavesdropping.

"What's a bookie?" she whispered to me, trying to piece together the clues of what was driving our parents apart, what exactly they were fighting about. Unfortunately, if she lurked too close, she was likely to be in the way of a hurried egress, usually Marlon's. One time, she stood behind the living room door, her ear pressed to it, so that when Marlon slammed his way out of the room, the door caught her cheek. Even though I was upstairs, reading, I could hear after the smack of the door that terrifying lull before the cry, that silence of someone who has really been hurt. I flung my book aside and raced downstairs to find the three of them, Marlon pink-faced and standing before a screaming Nadine.

"You don't give a fuck who you hurt, not even your own children—"

"Goddamnit, I didn't mean to hurt her! She was just underfoot!" Marlon reached out for Zelda, who flinched from his touch and glared furiously at him, sobbing. "Zaza, I'm sorry, I didn't mean to—"

"I don't care what you meant!" Zelda shrieked. "That is so not the point! What is the matter with you?" She glowered at Nadine with equal fury and ran for the deck, slipping out the screen door in tears. Marlon started to go after her, but I stopped him.

"Leave her alone. She doesn't want to be around you. Either of you." I was shaking; normally I would do anything to avoid this sort of conflict, but the sound of Zelda's wails had pushed me to the edge, and I was furious with both of my parents. Why couldn't they just do this somewhere else and leave us out of it? I followed Zelda outside, heading down the hill, guessing which direction she had gone.

She was sitting in the grass, not so far from the house and staring out at the lake. Her eyes were red and she was still sniffling, but she seemed more angry than hurt, which was a good sign. I so rarely saw her vulnerable. I sat next to her.

"Let me see," I said.

"It's fine," she sniffed, then gave an ironic snort. "At school, they'll think I'm being abused."

"You should tell them you are." I giggled.

"I wouldn't know which of them to blame." Zelda glanced back toward the house.

"Good point." I gently touched her cheekbone; it was already turning a purple-blue color. She flinched but let me carefully poke at it. "You'll be fine. A bruise."

"They can't go on like this."

"I know."

"What will we do?" Zelda asked, and for once, she sounded scared, unsure. She wasn't looking at me. There was no sarcasm, no mockery in her voice. Which meant that it was my job to supply it.

"Let's run away. I'll steal their credit cards, you pack a bag," I said, nudging her.

"They probably won't even notice we're gone."

"They'll notice the money is gone, once they run out of wine."

Zelda snorted again. "Could take a while for that to happen," she said, looking eloquently at our surroundings, at the grid of grapes that stretched across the hill.

"Good—then maybe they won't notice before we're legal adults. Let's do it." I elbowed her again, and she finally turned her head to look at me.

"Where will we go, brainiac?"

"Hollywood! Let's be starlets," I answered.

"Ha. Or we could go to Opal's?"

"And live in a retirement community?" I wrinkled my nose distastefully.

"Yeah. Maybe not. I know: Paris!"

"Not practical. We're minors."

"Okay, let's go live in the woods, then. I'll be the huntress, and you can cook."

"You mean the national forest?" I asked, considering. It was a huge patch of completely empty land. It would take them forever to find us.

"I'm really glad I'm not the only one here with them," she said in a small voice.

"Me too." I leaned my head on her shoulder for a moment, looking out at the water and feeling my sister's fear, anxiety. "If we start now, we can make it to the forest before dark. It's only a few miles."

"Are you serious about this?" Zelda asked, a wicked, excited glint in her eyes. "I mean, I'm totally game if you are."

"It was my idea!" I stood and raced up to the house, Zelda following close at my heels. As ever.

I'll never know how far we were prepared to take it, if we would have escaped from this house, this family. Made our way out to Hollywood and started anew, just us two. But when we got back up to the house, it was Marlon who was packing a suitcase and fleeing west before the sun slipped below the shore across the lake. Leaving the three of us.

I realize it's nearly dinnertime and I haven't eaten all day. The sky is hazy and blank. I stand up and stretch. I'm sliding the incomplete alphabet worksheets back onto the shelf when my hands fumble across a brown folder tucked snugly at an angle between the books. I pull it out and open it up.

# 19

Staring at the scribbled scrap of paper for long minutes, I feel an unhappy click of recognition, a sick sense of foreboding. It's a checklist of sorts, a catalogue of ailments. Memory loss, disorientation, difficulty reading, vocabulary loss, poor judgment, changes in mood or personality, hallucination, changes in blood pressure. I know this checklist well; I've seen it written in the comforting pastel fonts of informational brochures, pressed soothingly into the palms of terrified family members, the smooth, waxy paper wicking away the fearful sweat that dampens the hands of those in the waiting room. I've read through this list on Wikipedia and in doctors' offices, Zelda silently looking over my shoulder, our lips pursed and heads nodding in grim, synchronized recognition. This is an inventory of symptoms for early-onset dementia with Lewy bodies. The disease our mother was diagnosed with two years ago. I remember Zelda carrying this folder around while we were trying to piece together what was happening to Nadine. But now, on its cover, Zelda has printed "SYMPTOMS." The S's at the beginning and the end of the word have been underlined. Unwittingly, unwillingly, I have found the letter S, even as I tried to ignore it. I realize I have unconsciously gone looking in Zelda's paperwork, just as she suggested.

Zelda's handwriting is loopy and discombobulated, and I squint at it. She's circled "poor judgment" and "hallucination." Below, she has scrawled: *consult? Too young!* I flip through the stack of papers, and then I start reading more closely.

Here I find an invoice for a neurologist in Ithaca. I recognize his name, because we dragged Nadine in three years ago, when we were desperately trying to figure out what was going on with her, why she would wake us up in the middle of the night with nightmares, why she couldn't remember who any of our neighbors were. She had gone begrudgingly, muttering profanities the whole way, but we had seen the glimmer of acknowledgment in her eyes, the nearly imperceptible awareness that things were not quite right with her. She had concealed her terror beneath the usual flinty disavowals and biting comments, but Zelda and I had felt the fear radiating off her as we drove into town, sandwiched into the pickup truck. She had stormed out of the appointment when she was presented with a mental acuity test, and we were unable to coax her back in for a consult until weeks later, after she had nearly lost three fingers to frostbite, wandering our driveway in the middle of winter and clueless about how she had gotten there. By that point, her diagnosis had hardly required an expert.

The patient's name on this invoice, however, is not Nadine O'Connor but Zelda Antipova. Three months ago, my sister drove into Ithaca for an appointment with Dr. Felix Laurent, for which she paid four hundred dollars, in cash. The appointment wasn't covered by her health insurance, or she didn't want a paper trail. I realize I likely don't have insurance, here in the States. She hadn't mentioned this appointment in any of the wordy and elaborate emails she'd sent, emails that documented the minutiae of life on Silenus, her every worry and thought, spewed forth in Zeldaesque excessive prose.

The last page in the file finally makes me realize that this is not the folder we compiled for Nadine but a different diagnostic collection. Zelda has obsessively written down a list of times and dates, with accompanying notations.

*Friday, February 19: Woke up in hallway, unsure how I got there. Unable to remember the previous day for nearly an hour.*

*Wednesday, April 20: Jason asked where I got a cut on my hand and I told him from the tractor. He looked at me strangely and said that it had actually come from a broken wineglass and I had instructed him to ask me about it later. Confabulation?*

*Saturday, May 7: Woke Kayla up close to dawn because I was flailing in bed. I had been dreaming that I was tearing every single vine out of Silenus and eating them. REM. Been trying to wash the taste of dirt out of my mouth all day.*

*Sunday, May 8: Woke Stu(pid) up by kicking him and talking in my sleep. I dreamt I was racing Ava, running down to the lakefront. Idiot said it was a nightmare, didn't even mention REM. Started taking low dose of Nadine's clonazepam, which Wikipedia says is a reliable treatment. Don't want him to find out. Though Christ knows he's unlikely to catch on to anything unless I tattoo it on the inside of my thighs. Stole a handful of prescription notes from him, in case I need refills.*

I pace around her bedroom, nearly tripping over a bundle of saris that are knotted into a strange nest on her floor. It seems unlikely that she would have told our mother or father. Or even Opal. I can't imagine Zelda confessing this level of vulnerability to anyone. In fact, I'm not sure I was intended to find this little bundle. There haven't been any clues to lead me here, and the envelope was just crammed onto a bookshelf.

I try to convince myself that Wyatt might know something about Zelda's fears, but I realize I'm considering this because I want to call him, not because I believe that he might have answers. And part of me is hurt that he hasn't called me.

Plus, I would be lying to myself if I denied that one of the loudest, most insistent thoughts careening through my mind as I wade through Zelda's room is: *What about me?* If Zelda suspected that she might have the same disease our mother does, isn't it likely that I do too? As identical twins, we are much more likely to carry the same genetic flaws. If Zelda's brain contains the time bomb that is Lewy body dementia, a gift from our mother, then there's a high probability that mine does. I scan my memory for any indication, any symptom. But, of course, I've experienced nearly all of these sensations and radical failures to perform cognitively simple tasks. I'm a drinker. Waking up from a shitty night's sleep, hallucinating bugs crawling across my eyelids, hunting down words through a hungover haze and lunging clumsily for basic vocabulary: These are all a part of my reality. I've woken up not remembering the past ten hours; I've had violent and unpredictable mood swings. It just goes with the territory of an abused liver. Surely Zelda was able to recognize that too. Of course, that's not how paranoia works, though. We have both lived in fear of becoming our mother for so long that any evidence that it might be chemically taking place would naturally be met with deep pessimism and a sense that the worst has finally happened.

I'm tempted to fling myself into Marlon's rental car and drive to the city, to masquerade as Zelda and try to get my hands on her medical records, see if any kind of diagnosis was made. But surely there's some sort of communication between hospitals; surely if someone's remains, however paltry, pop up at the coroner's, alarm bells go off when they show up for a doctor's appointment twenty miles away. I imagine it working like an airport, where death functions like the ultimate no-fly list. But maybe that's an Orwellian fantasy. Maybe the doctors in Ithaca have no idea that Zelda is (supposedly) dead.

A phone vibrates in my pocket, and I burrow frantically to see which one is ringing. It's my own. I answer in a tizzy, jolted out of a strange numbness by whoever is calling me. It's Wyatt.

"Ava?" He sounds tentative, as though he might be crossing some hard-and-fast line of politeness but feels he must do it anyway. His manners are so much nicer than mine.

"Hi, Wyatt."

"Hi. Listen, I wanted to let you know about something. We discussed it the other night. You were saying you weren't so convinced that Zelda was really dead, and you wanted to know who was, well, found—"

"Who the hell got barbecued in the barn," I finish impatiently. I realize the moment after I've interrupted that he's repeating our conversation for my benefit. He's worried that I won't remember all the details of what we discussed, and he's retracing our conversational footsteps so that I won't be humiliated. Sweet Wyatt. I am so far beyond humiliation. But am I maybe being paranoid? That's another symptom. "Which seems a pertinent question," I add.

"I think so. Zelda's nuts, but I never thought she was homicidally nuts. Well, I did some calling around, and you remember that guy who was screaming his head off? Kyle Richardson?"

"Yeah, I remember."

"Well, I finally got ahold of his mother a little while ago. She said her daughter, Kayla, has been missing for almost six days. She just called it in to the cops a few hours ago. Apparently, she's been keeping irregular hours ever since she started dating your sister."

"What?"

"I said—"

"I heard what you said. Jesus. What does she look like, this girl?"

"Curly blond hair, pretty skinny," Wyatt says. "And, apparently, she just stopped showing up at her job." He takes a beat. "At the funeral home."

"Really?" My mind races. Is that significant? That could be how Zelda is pulling this off. "I want to talk to the brother," I say.

"He's been on a bender for a few days, I guess. You could probably tell, the other night. Maybe not the most stable. He was close to Kayla."

"Where can I find him?"

"Where you can find everybody else this time of the evening: at the brewery. Least that's what his mom says."

I tap my feet on the floor, thoughtfully. Technically, I could probably walk to the brewery, which is just a few miles from here. God knows I've walked home from there, after closing the place out and being either too drunk to drive home or the only person left standing in the parking lot. I don't want to ask Wyatt for favors; it makes me feel needy, incapable. But I'm not sure I trust myself to spend time at the brewery and remain in any state to drive home.

While I'm deliberating, Wyatt makes it simple: "Need a ride? I was just headed out there."

"Oh. Yeah. That'd be good. I was just trying to decide whether or not to take the tractor up there."

Wyatt laughs. "That'd be a sight. I'd like a picture of that, make sure all your cosmopolitan friends in Paris get to see it."

I snort, imagining Nico smiling over a picture of me driving the tractor to the bar. This causes a narrow band to squeeze my rib cage, constricting my breath and making me skitter away from the thought.

"Ten minutes?" Wyatt asks, and I bob my head, even though I'm on the phone and he can't see. When we were teenagers, we played a guessing game, trying to imagine what the other was doing. At some point, this inevitably turned kinky. Talking late into the night, slowly unbuttoning pajamas and feeling the tension build through the phone lines.

"See you in ten." I hang up the phone and skip around the room with light feet, presumably still channeling my former self. With a giggle, I stoop down to change into one of Zelda's costumes, then pause, bent in a half downward dog, about to root through her bazaar of fabric. I don't want to dress like Zelda right now.

I cross the hall, into my white room, and look at my suitcase, neatly stowed at the foot of my bed. I haven't unpacked anything but have refolded each garment and nestled it back into this wheeled caravan, refusing my clothes even temporary accommodations on the racks of my childhood. But I realize I don't want to wear any of my clothes from Paris, either; few things would look more out of place than one of my slinky Zadig & Voltaire tops, all subtle sequins (I didn't think such a thing existed until I moved to Paris) and charcoal grays. I turn to my old closet.

I try on a handful of old, larger dresses, from my old, larger days. Absently, I swish around in the spacious gowns, feeling them hang off my bones. With a sudden flush of shame, I realize what I'm doing and pull the last dress over my head, not bothering to unzip it.

I realize that I will likely be late now, as Wyatt is an on-time kind of guy. But he can wait for me downstairs. I snag a snug dress with a flared skirt, striped with thick swaths of navy blue and white; this dress is not loose, and I have to bend my elbows creatively to get the zipper all the way up my back. That is a skill I didn't have to learn until I moved away from my sister, who always fastened me in. I smooth the dress over my hips and look critically at myself in the mirror. It fits as it did in my senior year of high school. A small miracle. I took something of a gamble in yanking out such a formfitting garment; if I hadn't succeeded in getting the zipper up, I might very well have spent the rest of the night clinging to cold ceramic. I dab on some red lipstick and try to smooth my coarse curls. I wish I had an hour to straighten and tame them, like I used to in high school. I settle for pinning back the frizziest, most uncooperative pieces.

I'm fussing over a gutted tub of eye shadow when I hear the truck pull into the drive.

Wyatt smiles at me when I meet him at the door; he is visibly relieved to see me, Ava, rather than the Zelda apparition I have been dressed as for the last few days. Instead of inviting him inside, I follow him out to his truck and hop in.

"You seem cheerful," Wyatt notes. "Good day?" The question is laced with skepticism and censure, a reminder that I should be mourning, or at least shell-shocked. Oh, but what the hell.

"Actually, yes. I read most of the third book of *Game of Thrones.*" As I say this, I feel a sudden sense of worry about my drastically improved spirits. All through our childhood, Nadine was inclined to moments of intense despair, followed shortly by hyperactive periods of glee. She would spend three days barely opening her eyes and then would lace up her running shoes and disappear for two hours, return-ing sparkle-eyed and exuberant, frenziedly cleaning the house and proposing various plans. This would last for a spell, until she would suddenly return to her miserable brooding. We always thought it was just a personality trait, an inclination toward moodiness, only now I can't help but wonder if it was a symptom all along. If I have that same symptom. I squirm unhappily. "So, this Kayla Richardson girl. Do you know her at all?" I ask.

"I mean, yeah, a bit. She's a few years younger than us, think she graduated in 2012? Kinda flighty, in trouble a lot at school."

"I recognize her name, but I never spent much time with her. And Kyle was a bit notorious, obviously. Fucking twat."

Wyatt snorts in acknowledgment. "Yes, he was. Is." He shakes his head then continues: "Anyway, it seems both Kyle and Mrs. Richard-son are pretty sure Zelda had something to do with Kayla's disappear-ance. I think the fire has them nervous."

After a long pause, reluctant to vocalize it, I ask, "Do you think Kayla is the one in the barn?"

Wyatt bites his lip. "Could be," he finally says. "Christ. Man. If Zelda killed her . . ."

"If Zelda killed her, there's no coming back," I finish. "She can't come back here, unless she wants to get arrested for murder."

"All we know is that somebody died in that barn. We won't know anything more until they get DNA results or dental records or some-thing."

"True," I acknowledge, staring out the window. I reflect, trying to decide whether my sister really could have murdered a twenty-something-year-old girl and burned her body in our barn. When I left for Paris, I would have said no, no fucking way. Zelda might be crazy, unpredictable, and more than a little volatile, but she wouldn't kill someone. She is also impulsive, unswerving, and more or less amoral. Things have been going very wrong for the last two years, and maybe, with her life collapsing around her . . .

"Any other notes? More letters?" Wyatt asks.

"We're up to *S*." I fill him in on the letters of the past two days, enjoying his surprised expression. *P* for *policy*, the letter *Q*, *R* for REM. When I tell him about the doctor Zelda was fucking, he clenches his teeth and squeezes the steering wheel in a restrained show of jealousy, and I feel a corresponding clench of the same emotion. "I guess we can add Kayla to the list. Racking up quite a score card," I can't resist adding. The flicker of anger in his eyes intensifies my own possessiveness and renews my fury at both Zelda and him.

"And *S*?" he prompts.

"I'm pretty sure *S* is for *symptoms*," I say. "Did you happen to notice anything—" I pause, realizing I was about to say "erratic" or "unusual." Those will not be helpful descriptions when dealing with Zelda. The answer is: Of course. "Let me rephrase: Was she more than usually weird these last few months? Forgetful or moody?"

"Well, yes, but I thought that had a lot to do with how much she was drinking. She was blacking out sometimes. But she'd started doing the weirdest thing." He shakes his head. "She was making up these bizarre stories. Like, she would get wasted with me and the next day, when she couldn't remember anything, she would concoct some crazy story of where she'd been. I'd ask her how she bruised her thigh, and she would say that she'd gone for a midnight bike ride through the vines and had banged into a post, even though I knew she'd gotten the bruise from tripping down the steps of her trailer and that she hadn't touched her bike in weeks."

"You were checking to see if she remembered?" I say, mildly hostile.

"Well, she'd started to have a real patchy recollection of what she'd been up to, and I wanted to see how bad it was getting," Wyatt explains reasonably.

I sigh. "That's called confabulation. It's a symptom of Alzheimer's and dementia."

"What? Zelda wasn't— What does that mean? You think she has what your mom does?"

"I think she was worried that she did. She went to see at least one neurologist, got a lot of info on early-onset. Of course, we're a tad paranoid that we're like our mother, so I don't know if it was just . . . fear."

"Was she taking anything for it?" Wyatt asks.

"You're in a better position to answer that than me," I point out.

"I mean, did you find any meds in her trailer?"

"She has a sizable pharmaceutical stash in there. I sincerely hope she wasn't taking all of that shit, but who knows. Moderation isn't one of her strong suits."

"We should check her stash for prescriptions in her name," Wyatt suggests. "See if she got diagnosed with anything or prescribed something. That would at least suggest she's not crazy." He smiles wryly. "Well, clinically."

I nod my head. "Yeah, I guess we can do that on the way home." I pause. "You don't think—I mean, she's only twenty-five. It can't be dementia, right?" I want reassurance.

"It seems unlikely, Ava." Wyatt pats my knee. "Probably just Zelda deflecting, pretending her problem was something other than . . ." He trails off with a cough, and he pinkens delicately.

"Alcoholism," I finish flatly. "You can say it." Wyatt glances over at me anxiously, wanting to see if I'm upset. "It's not exactly a revelation, Wyatt," I say drily. "My entire family—we're all alcoholics. Zelda and I have been drinking pretty heavily since we were fourteen. I know it's . . . I know it's happening. I know it's something of a problem. I'm supposed to say, 'I know it has to stop. I know I need to clean up.' But I don't know that. I very much don't believe that."

"It was something Zelda didn't really want to acknowledge," Wyatt finishes for me. "She felt quite strongly that it wasn't a problem. She pointed out that she didn't have a real job to fuck up, and her personal relationships were already totally damaged. She didn't have any DWIs, had never stolen anything or killed anyone—"

"Well, I guess that means it counts as a problem now," I say sardonically.

"It was a problem before, Ava," he says, his voice flat. I glance away, not meeting his eyes.

We pull into the parking lot of the brewery, and I hop out of the truck, onto the gravel of the steeply inclined driveway. Two Goats is a small operation, a small barn perched on the side of the lake. The beer is decent, they sell a smattering of local wines, and you get as many homemade potato chips as you can eat. But, really, people come for the view. The back deck, filled with picnic tables and bar stools, hangs over a field of grapevines, the lake sparkling below. This is one of the best places to watch summer sunsets on the whole lake. To-night, it's bustling, filled with most of our thirsty neighbors.

I know I shouldn't, but I order a drink. I acknowledge how nice today was, to not have been swimming through an oppressive hang-over. Only it doesn't seem to matter, not to the other me, the one who wants a drink and doesn't really care about tomorrow morning. My other twin. Tonight, I hope a bountiful harvest of fizzy liquid will grace our tankards, foaming exuberantly like profuse Jacuzzis. To avoid bringing it up with Wyatt, I just go ahead and order him a beer, a stout that I know he likes. Wyatt doesn't comment when I hand him his drink. He does take a hefty swallow from the frosty pint glass.

Looking around, I notice a bunch of people from high school, some of my parents' friends; a teacher (geometry?) is standing in the corner.

"Busy," I comment to the bartender, who looks vaguely familiar. I wonder if he was working here two years ago, when Zelda and I spent considerable amounts of time with our elbows marinating on the sticky bar. I hope he doesn't recognize me.

"There's a band playing tonight." He points to the heap of instru-ments on the other side of the room. "They're on break right now."

"Who is it?"

"Richie Stearns," he answers listlessly, wiping down the bar. I nod in recognition; I've heard him play my whole life. Banjos and soulful crooning. I look around, hoping to find Kyle Richardson. If he's here.

At the sound of a raucous whoop from the back deck, Wyatt and I lock eyes, the same expression of exasperation on both our faces. That'll be where our cohorts are. I shoulder my way outside, Wyatt following, and I take a serious slog from my beer, both to avoid spilling it down the front of my dress and to bolster myself for this interaction.

On the back deck, a gaggle of twenty-five-year-old men are engaged in some committed drinking, surrounded by stalagmites of empty glasses growing up from the rustic picnic tables. It's almost dark out, and the fireflies blink languorously in the fields below. There's a big moon hanging low over the lake, orange and strange. I see Kyle, perched on the railing, seeming to hold court over the other men clustered around him, who are staring up at him almost rapturously. His cheeks are flushed a dangerous crimson, and his eyes have the eerie blankness of the sixth or seventh drink. I notice now that he isn't as thin as he was in high school, that his middle has thickened. Although judging from the beefy firmness of his arms, maybe this isn't a result of beer so much as picking heavy things up and putting them down. He catches sight of me and nearly knocks his beer over as he leaps down from the rail.

"What the fuck are you doin' here?" he slurs aggressively.

Wyatt makes a slight movement to get in front of me, but I weave around him.

"Hi again, Kyle."

"I don't want anything to do with your fuckin' family. You're all just a bunch of—psychos!" he spits out triumphantly. He is, of course, one hundred percent correct.

"I just wanted to ask you a couple of questions about your sister," I say evenly. I notice that his cronies have turned toward us. Their testosterone is showing. They can sense imminent conflict, and combined with a significant amount of alcohol, this produces a blurry sort of electricity.

"Shit, is that Ava Antipova?" one of the guys says, and I turn my head, recognizing Josh Wheeler, a perennial stoner and all-around not-nice guy. Of course he and Kyle have stayed friends.

"Hi, Josh," Wyatt says, shouldering closer to me. There was a time when he used to count these guys as "sort of" friends. In a high school like ours, with a graduating class of eighty, you become "sort of" friends with pretty much everyone. I smile pleasantly and wave to the rest of the crew.

"So do you bat the same as your faggoty sister?" Josh leers.

"Are you talking to me or to Kyle?" I ask sweetly, and it takes them a second to see what I'm getting at.

"Fuck you, Ava," Josh says.

"Kyle, you want a cigarette? Talk a second?"

He looks at me very suspiciously but, after a moment, nods blearily. We make our way around the side of the deck to the smoking area, closer to the parking lot.

"Outta beer," he says, almost whining. I hand him a cigarette and light both his and mine, looking over at Wyatt.

"Why don't I go get another round?" he suggests, on cue.

"Thanks. The Belgian one for me," I say lightly. Kyle just holds up his glass mutely, and Wyatt disappears back into the crowd inside.

"Whaddya want, Ava?" Kyle asks, his eyes tiny slits after he inhales a deep lungful of carcinogens. I take a drag on my own stick, feeling deliciously light-headed as tiny pieces of fiberglass shred my lungs, allowing the chemicals to enter my body faster.

"To talk about your sister," I say. "And mine." He says nothing. "Listen," I go on. "I have a better idea of why you were so pissed the other day. I didn't know about Zelda and Kayla, and I had no idea she was missing."

"Yeah, well," Kyle grunts.

"How long has she been gone?"

"Five or six days. She took off with Zelda on Monday, and we haven't heard from her since." There's a note of blame in his voice, as though I'm somehow inculpated in this.

"And they were . . . together?" I'm reluctant to be too blunt. In high school, he was the sort of guy who called people "faggot" for wearing pink.

"Fuck if I know. They were spending a lot of time together, then Kayla got in a fight with our dad and, like, I don't know, 'came out' or whatever homos do. Said she and Zelda were in love." Oh, Christ. Zelda had some young girl mooning around after her, convinced they would be together forever, no doubt. "But Kayla wasn't no queer," Kyle continues, sounding hopeful.

"Maybe," I agree. Wyatt reappears in the doorway, holding two beers instead of three. I'm momentarily concerned that he's decided to cut me off, but he hands me my drink in the curvy beer glass and reaches over to Kyle to give him his. Kyle immediately sloshes some of the liquid down his chin, and a few drops slop onto his shorts, darkening the fabric. He doesn't seem to notice. Wyatt folds his arms across his chest, hands empty.

"How long had Kayla and Zelda been hanging out?" I ask.

"Few months, maybe six? Christmas?" He seems bewildered. "But since it warmed up this spring, Kayla's off with her in her fuckin' trailer more and more. Started using."

"Using what?" Wyatt chimes in.

"Druuugs," Kyle says as though Wyatt is unspeakably slow.

"What kind?"

"Fuck if I know," Kyle repeats. "Expensive, whatever it was."

"Doesn't really narrow it down," I say.

He doesn't hear me. "She stole a whole buncha shit from my mom's jewelry box. Then when my mom chucked her out for a coupla days, she took off to my aunt's and sold her TV. How do you, like, explain that shit without drugs?" He punctuates this query with a rhetorical jab of his finger in my direction. I step back to avoid him knocking my beer into my chest.

"Good point. Did she and Zelda ever hang out with other people? Do you know who their friends were?"

"How the fuck would I know that? Kayla was always off sneaking around—she didn't tell me shit. Mosta what she said the last few months were total lies. That girl is gonna be in so much fuckin' shit when she comes home. . . ." His voice wavers uncertainly.

"Where do you think she might be, Kyle?" Wyatt says. "Why do you think she's laying low?"

"Jesus. You people and your fucking questions. She probably knows there're rumors that somebody killed your crazy-ass sister, and she doesn't want to get picked up. Then she'd have to get clean. Fuck, maybe *she* killed your fucking sister." Kyle chuckles. "Wouldn't that be poetic justice. Irony."

I don't really see how that could be, but I decide not to press it. Wyatt looks dangerously close to starting something, and I put my hand on his forearm. The sudden contact with his warm skin makes me flush, and I realize the beer has just kicked in. My fingers linger for just a second longer than they need to.

"Any proof of that? Theories, maybe?" I ask.

"Fuck! They got in a fight over who got the last squirt of heroin, and Kayla kicked her ass, maybe went too far. You've never seen my little sister when she doesn't get what she wants." Kyle seems to find this idea both plausible and entertaining. He giggles tipsily. "Or maybe she got jealous 'cuz she found out you were fucking her girlfriend," he says to Wyatt, giving him a shove that is not entirely friendly. "Maybe *you* better look out!" He chuckles again and drains down most of the rest of his beer in a gulp.

I sip mine daintily. Somehow it is easier to stay sober when confronted with a convincing reminder of just what being fully toasted looks like. Too bad I'm usually that reminder.

"Have you talked to the cops at all?" I ask Kyle.

"No, why would I?" He seems surprised. "They got their guy, that fucking Jason dude. Why would I rat out my sister? If they catch her with drugs, she'll go to prison. She's got a record, yo."

I look over at Wyatt. I'm distracted by this turn of the conversation with Kyle when my phone starts ringing. Wondering, as always, which phone is vibrating in my bag, I poke around before pulling either phone out. It's my phone, though, and I swipe across the screen to answer it. A local number, not saved to my contacts.

"Hello?"

"Ava Antipova?"

"Yes . . ."

"This is Officer Giles, with the Watkins Glen Police Department. Do you think you could come down to the station?"

"What, now?" I ask. Wyatt raises an eye.

"The coroner was just here," the cop continues. "And he was able to complete his report. We'd like to discuss his findings with you and your family, if possible."

"What do you mean? What did you find?"

"Well, ma'am, I'd really prefer to discuss it in person, with you and your family," the cop says uncertainly.

"Why? I mean, it wasn't Zelda, was it?" I say, the beer making me reckless. Still, I don't need to get dragged down to the station at this time of night just to hear that it wasn't my sister in the fire. They can tell me that on the phone.

"Um, well, see, the coroner was able to find a few pieces of dental evidence, and he says they're a match with your sister's records. He's ruling it a homicide."

# 20

Taped to the windshield of Wyatt's truck is a letter: *T*.

*Dear Tangled, Trusting, Trepidatious Twin,*

*Ta-da! Is the Truth tentatively trying to tell itself? Are there tantaliz-ing tip-offs and traces of what truly transpired? Tell me, tricksy twin, tell. I'm pretty sure I've surprised you, either way. Tell the truth. You weren't expecting: teeth!*

*I know, I know. A little tawdry, right? A bit gruesome, gauche, gory even. But the evidence doesn't lie. Our good friend the coroner might, but dental records are dental records. Tough titty!*

*I'm sure you're scrambling around, looking for elegant solutions and a taut explanation for all this. I'm sure your mind is running at full tilt, tracking down any missing pieces and filling in the blanks where you're just not sure. Much as I have been doing these last few months. When there's a hole, the brain races to plug it, to stop the hemorrhage, stem the tide, close the gap, make up the difference. When you wake up and can't remember where you've been for the last twelve hours, your brain helps you out. Oh, generous synapses! Oh, mysterious neural connections! The brain abhors a vacuum, and it will cram just any old thing in there, to make sure no one notices. But, of course, everyone does. Except you.*

*So. You have some questions for which you need answers. And you will. Answer them. If only because I don't believe in leaving strings loose, untied, untethered. Test those theories! Ask yourself the hard questions. Does Zelda think she can get away with this? What can her long-term plan possibly be? Where is she right now? Who is she? Hilariously enough, these are questions we've been asking all along, our entire lives, right? Can we pull this off? Who are we? What are we doing?*

*Or here's another option: Quit now. Don't keep reading these letters, don't finish the story, don't find out what happens. Settle down with Wyatt. Why not jettison practicality, chuck your qualms aside, and externalize your vast anxiety, go forage in the garden for the biggest zucchini?*

*But here's a tantalizing piece of encouragement. You have all the information you need, right now. You know where I am already, and how I'm doing this. If you use your brain and just THINK, you'll be able to figure it out. Unless, of course, you're concerned. About your brain, I mean. Does your brain work the way it should, Ava dear? Have you noticed any **Symptom**s of your own? (Did you seriously think I skipped S? S has been **there** all along, skittering along the surface, sucking up space, scaring us **shitless**. As I suspect you have suspected before.) How's your clarity these days? Let's find out.*

*You're holding the next letter in your hand. Unearth it, uncover it. Underneath these carefully constructed surfaces we conceal our missing pieces.*

*Your Taunting, Terrifying, Treacherous Twin,*
*Z is for Zelda*

I read the letter aloud to Wyatt in his truck as he drives toward Watkins Glen. He is quiet, staring out the windshield with a blank expression. At one point, I lean over and try to squeeze his thigh, but he shrinks from my hand, and I withdraw, hurt.

"Do you think . . ." he begins after I've read the note. "Do you think she could be dead?"

"I mean . . ." I'm about to say "maybe," but I don't. "No, not really. It just doesn't make sense."

"But then the teeth?"

I shrug. "I'm sure she thought of something. Bribed someone. I don't know."

"But—" he tries again.

"I just don't think so. She's jerking us around, Wy."

"Ava, you need to seriously consider that you're not being entirely logical about this whole thing. I mean, I know you think you know her inside and out—"

"I do, though. That's what she's counting on. And she knows me— that's how she's orchestrating this whole elaborate thing."

"Don't you think it's possible that you're maybe projecting?" he suggests quietly.

"Not really," I snap. I drum my fingers against the panel of the door. I got off the phone with my father a couple of minutes ago; apparently they managed to track him down somewhere in town, and he's going to meet me at the station. He took Opal home to look after Nadine. She said she didn't want to come. I don't blame her.

We pull up outside and I hop out, not waiting for Wyatt to park the truck properly. I run through the glass doors, which seem strangely illuminated on the otherwise darkened street. Marlon is sitting in the waiting room, surrounded by "If You See Something, Say Something" posters and pamphlets on domestic abuse. He looks rough around the edges, his stubble thickening and his eyes raw. I'm glad he didn't get on a plane back to California. I'm more than glad. I'm deeply relieved.

Wyatt walks through the door a moment later, and I expect there to be some sort of bristling, on both of their parts, but instead Marlon looks up at Wyatt with a haggard plea, naked pain etched upon his face, and Wyatt just walks over and sits down next to him. When he gives Marlon a very masculine pat on the shoulder, my heart breaks a tiny bit. The lighting is surreal, and I suddenly feel insanely, absurdly irritable.

"Jesus," I spit out. "Do they need so much fucking fluorescence for the waiting room?"

I pace the floor a bit twitchily. Wyatt eyes me with concern. I feel unhinged and am tempted to get up on a chair and take out the offending bulbs. I'm considering this obviously inadvisable course of action when two cops walk into the room. It's Healy and someone I don't recognize. The new guy has a traditional buzz cut and a slightly puffy look. From the way they're standing, I can tell that Healy is the top and this new fellow is the bottom. I'm relieved that Roberts isn't here. Maybe he had the good sense to get himself excused from this lovely moment of sharing. I have no patience right now for one of Zelda's useful fuck-buddy friends, not when my nerves are so frayed.

"Hi, there. I'm Officer Healy—we spoke earlier—and this is my colleague Officer Giles. We'd like to talk to you about your daughter—and sister—" He acknowledges me with a bob of his head and glances at Wyatt.

"This is Zelda's boyfriend. And mine," I interject. Wyatt turns very pink, and Marlon jerks his head upright. Even from the corner of my eye I can see his jaw tightening and his neck straining in purplish anger. The cops look very uncomfortable. Officer Giles clears his throat.

"Normally when we're notifying next of kin—" he begins, and Officer Healy looks at him in alarm.

"So we're next of kin? Meaning she's definitely dead?" I say with an inappropriate chortle. Wyatt gives me a look very similar to the one Healy is giving Giles. "A comedy of errors! LOL!" I don't seem to be able to stop; I reflect that I've lost any ability to censor myself, if I ever had that skill. But didn't I used to be composed? Isn't there a self, a me, that is articulate and poised? I smooth my striped dress over my hips and rub my lips together, evening my lipstick in an attempt to reassert myself as a reasonable person. Where is my Parisian self, my good self? Evidently, I abandoned her the minute I got off that airplane.

"What my colleague is trying to say," Healy starts to explain, addressing himself to the men, since I've so thoroughly discredited myself, proven myself to be a hysterical female, "is that we've had some bad news from the coroner. I hope this isn't completely unexpected, but we were able to match Zelda's dental records to the remains of the body we recovered in the fire. As of just one hour ago, the coroner issued a death certificate for Zelda Antipova after completing a full autopsy on the remains. I know this must still be difficult and shocking for you, but we wanted to let you know as soon as possible."

He's actually doing a very good job, I think. He sounds professional, practiced. I wouldn't expect that these guys have many opportunities to use their next-of-kin speech. Maybe he did some Wikipedia research to polish his delivery.

"Do we—do you need me to sign anything?" Marlon asks flatly. It is one of the most definitive assumptions of parental responsibility I have seen him take. A signature. I'm impressed by this as well. Damn, everyone is just terrifically impressive in here.

"We have some papers for you. Unfortunately, we are unable to release the remains into your care at the moment. Dr. Whitcross is ruling the death a potential homicide, and we will need to continue the investigation."

"Whitcross?" I say, suddenly alert.

"Dr. Whitcross, the coroner," Giles adds formally, trying to redeem himself.

"The younger or the elder?" I press. Marlon and Wyatt frown at me.

"The son. The younger," Healy answers. Gales of giggles peal out of me. Of course! *Very cute, Zelda.* Everything falls into place with a soothing click, puzzle pieces fitting together. "Shock is very common when hearing this news. What you're experiencing is completely normal," Healy continues, reassuring me. "We have a grief counselor and a nondenominational chaplain who would love to meet with you and help you work through this."

"Do you have a pamphlet?" I ask, cackling. He has already started to reach for one when he realizes that I am joking.

"Ava, maybe I should take you home."

"Are you driving, ma'am? It seems you're under the influence."

"I never understood that phrase," I muse. "Is anyone not under the influence? I mean, of gravity, of their mood, of their basic driving ability?"

"C'mon, Ava. I think it's time for bed." Wyatt reaches a hand out to me, and I take it a bit loopily. Home to bed. Yes. That sounds like a good idea.

We drive back to the house silently; I can tell he doesn't want to ask me what's going on, is concerned for my state of mind. So am I. As he prepares to pull into the driveway, I balk.

"Nononono. I don't want to go in. Opal. And Nadine . . ." My mind recoils at having to face either of them. And I don't want to be in her room.

"Do you want me to take you to the trailer?"

I consider this. It's a better option, for sure. But I don't want to be surrounded by her things, her smells. I want distance. I shake my head.

"Okay," Wyatt says grimly. "The Darling house it is." He swings the truck back onto the road and keeps heading up 414. I settle into the seat. It's been a very long time since I've been to the Darlings'. Strangely, I find the prospect comforting. I pull my phone out and send Nico a text, asking for a favor. I've nearly figured Zelda out; I just need a few more scraps of information.

It's late, but it's not so late that Wyatt's parents are asleep when we get there. The lights are on in their big bungalow, nuzzled back into the woods, up a long driveway. They don't have a lake view from their land, but they do have thick groves of conifers and an impression of abiding coziness, tucked back from the road. A nest. They were the sort of people who put solar panels on their roof in the seventies, who have been growing organic vegetables their whole lives. I glance at Wyatt as we park the truck, to see if he looks apprehensive. Neither of us wants a repeat of the unpleasant scene the last time I was here.

Wyatt's **parents** had disagreed quite strongly with me on whether Wyatt should follow **me to Cornell** or accept a scholarship to Northwestern. His parents wanted him to get away from Watkins Glen, to explore. Subtext: Fuck someone less uptight. Possibly with dreadlocks.

And a penis. Break some rules. They looked at me and they saw my mother, Cape Cod, the pristine world of white conservative Democrats who spent their lives grimly peering out of their floor-to-ceiling windows and suffocating behind their bourgeois pretensions. They could imagine, as I could, Wyatt proposing to me with some moderately expensive conflict diamond, our organized and efficient wedding on the shores of Seneca Lake. We would make our own decorations, and the bridesmaids would wear matching navy blue dresses, tasteful and flattering. We would have two kids, possibly move to Ithaca. I would drink the way my mother did, and Wyatt would be the sort of man who wore khaki pants and drank beer from cans on the weekend while mowing the lawn with a kid on his lap. We would care deeply about how our living room was decorated, and we would invite Dora and Steve over on Sunday afternoons to play with the kids. Dora would occasionally feel the absurd impulse to wear pearls, although she didn't own any real ones, a feeling she would repress and wave off with an amused flutter of the hand, but it would somehow return to her when she was sipping port from Waterford glasses at our big dining room table. Steve would refrain from smoking pot on the days he came over to our house, because it would make him feel wiggy to stand on our white carpet while baked out of his mind.

As Wyatt opens the door for me, I wonder if they have shaken off the ghost of that possible future, as I have. None of that will happen now; they dodged the bullet. I have no doubt they smiled in shocked pleasure when Wyatt mumbled to them that I was moving to Paris. We hadn't been speaking then, but I'm sure he eventually answered their questions about where I had gone. And I'm equally sure that they lit up a celebratory spliff at the news, toasting their son's newly recovered future.

There is music playing in the living room, and a sense of festivity hangs in their warmly lit wooden house. The rustic beams reflect the golden light of candles and domestic content. Whereas Nadine's house is all clean modern angles, hard surfaces, and glittering glass, the Darlings' house is cluttered corners, stacks of paperbacks, mismatched rugs, the mysterious scents of herbs (weed and sage, mostly) wafting through the rafters. I have always treated them coolly, concealing how desperately envious I was of their silly, cheerful home life. I wanted what they had; I had no desire to replicate my parents' life or my mother's fantasy of connubial and familial bliss. I always wanted to say, *I'm not a threat to you! I want to learn how to do this, to leave the pillows scattered on the floor for three days, to drink out of smudged, mismatched glasses. To unclench.* But all they saw was my hostile face, carefully sketched in neat eyeliner, swatches of blush, tidy dresses with reasonable necklines, thin ankles displayed in delicate, impractical flats. Or maybe that's what I wanted them to see.

Dora and Steve are sprawled on the couch, their legs laced together and Janis Joplin crowing on their record player. They glance up in stoned surprise when we enter.

"Wyatt!" Dora says, standing. She looks the same as ever: dark hair flat and volumeless, her face without makeup, a formless dress made out of that ubiquitous yoga material highlighting rather than concealing her squarish, lumpy figure. This is a woman who doesn't, hasn't, will not diet, who does not and never will apply expensive cream to her jawline. She smells of patchouli and tomato sauce. I am bowled over when she gives me a hug, a real genuine snuggle hug. "Ava. Christ. I'm so very sorry about your sister." She pulls back and looks at my face, searching for me in the familiar bone structure of my sister. She has grown accustomed to Zelda, and I am an interloper wearing her body. She squeezes my wrists affectionately, and I try to smile.

"Thanks," I manage. Steve has joined his wife, and he, too, gives me a hug, as well as a peck on the cheek. I smell his sour breath and the scent of primo marijuana that lingers in his bearish beard. His hairline has receded since the last time I was here, and his potbelly is more pronounced beneath his loud Hawaiian shirt. "Hi, Steve."

"Ava. You poor thing. Cosmic injustice." He pats me on the shoulder, with Dora still holding one of my wrists, and I am claustrophobically aware of how close they are. The Darlings are touchers. I take a step backward, unable to help myself.

"Can I just—can I get myself a glass of water?" I say, already moving toward the sink. As I face the cabinets and reach for the cleanest glass in sight, I scan the counters for any open bottles of anything. Wyatt's parents drink, but not the way mine do. They are happy drinkers, the sort of people who can leave a bottle of wine unfinished, out in the open for a day or two. They tend to be high most of the time, so they're not into purely sober living, but they don't spend their days in the dereliction of the addicted, with the relentless anxiety that there will never, in all the world, be enough. I fill a glass from the tap. They don't have a filter installed on the faucet like Nadine does, which means their tap water tastes a little iffy.

"Want something to drink, bunny?" Steve asks me, and I catch both Dora and Wyatt glancing from me to each other. I wonder if Zelda has been especially slushy while she's here, or if I was messier than I remember during that last year at home. I wonder how long it took before Steve was calling Zelda "bunny." He's never called me that before.

"Whatever's easiest," I answer, relieved. "Thanks."

"How about a beer?" Steve asks, heading to the fridge with a bouncy gait. He walks like the steps he takes are too big, as though he's almost hopping from one foot to the other, on the outsides of his feet. He fishes out an unlabeled bottle of beer from the fridge, cracks it open, and presses it into my hand, with another squeeze to my shoulder. I look at it before taking an exploratory sip. "I've been brewing a bit, recently," he tells me. "This batch is pretty good." He nods. "Extra tasty." I smile a thank-you, feeling relief at the cold bottle in my hand.

"Any news?" Steve asks. I look over at Wyatt, unsure what to say.

"They've verified that it was Zelda in the fire," he answers stiffly. Dora and Steve both flinch, and their faces crumple simultaneously in the identical expressions of the long married.

"Oh, God," Steve says. "That is just awful. Shit. I'm so sorry. I mean, I know we were sort of expecting that, but we were definitely holding out hope."

"How is your family doing?" Dora asks.

"Not at all well. But then, that's been the status quo for a while now," I answer.

She snorts, then realizes that the statement may have been intended as a provocation and squints at me with a hint of the old suspicion.

"Well, I think any family that goes through this sort of thing gracefully lacks a soul. You all are enacting your karma, and that's all," she says.

There it is. First pseudospiritual Eastern religious mumbo jumbo of the night. I know what's coming next.

"These are hard lessons, Ava, but they're part of your solar arc. I looked at your chart and your sister's, and I'd be really happy to talk to you sometime about what I intuited there. You might find it useful." She must be stoned, if she's headed straight for the astrology. Or maybe Zelda talked about it with her.

I nod, trying to indicate my lack of interest. "Yeah, okay, Dora. Thanks."

"Is your dad around?" Steve asks, too casually, and I frantically try to remember if they had some sort of unpleasant interaction before Marlon split. Does Marlon owe him money? I can't remember. Seems like he left unpaid debts all over town.

"Yeah, he flew in from California. Brought his mother," I add, with a bitter sip of beer. It's raw and hoppy-tasting, but I actually kind of like it. I sense its great potential for getting one tanked.

"Oh, that must be nice. To have some help with Nadine," Dora says. I nod.

"Listen, guys, it's been a really long day," Wyatt says, clearing his throat. "Ava is gonna crash here tonight, if that's cool. Her house is a bit of a zoo right now."

"Of course, whatever you need. There's leftover spaghetti, if you're hungry," Dora says.

"And plenty more beer in the fridge. Help yourself," Steve adds, obliviously earning himself another nervous squint from Dora.

"'Night, guys," Wyatt says as they bustle toward the stairs, taking their dismissal very graciously. Steve flips off the sound system on his

way out of the room. The Darlings are very serious about energy con-
servation.

"G'night!" I call, flopping down on the couch with my beer. I try
not make eye contact but instead lap the hoppy dregs of beer with my
tongue. I pluck the remnants of a joint from the ashtray and light up,
not waiting to be invited.

"Ava," Wyatt begins softly, coming to sit beside me. I can hear that
it's his serious voice, that he's about to say something Important. I try
to look attentive. "I just. I wanted to say. I'm sorry. About the whole—
thing—with your sister. I shouldn't have."

"She shouldn't have."

"It wasn't—we were both just so angry at you."

"I know," I sigh. It's not that I'm not pissed and hurt about that
still. That it didn't feel catastrophic at the time. It's more that as it was
happening, in almost the same breath that was knocked out of me
when I found out about them, I realized that they had given me an
escape route that I had subconsciously desired. With that betrayal, I
finally had a good reason to go; I could really commit to abandonment. After having done everything I was supposed to do, playing by
the rules all these years, I could just walk off. I'd been an overachiever,
a plays-well-with-others kid, a high school honor society role model, a
star student at an Ivy League college, planning to go into a sensible
and necessary vocation; I'd been take-over-the-family-business
upright-citizen material my whole life. I'd done what I was told, colored impeccably between the lines. This transgression of Zelda's and
Wyatt's should have meant I could go be senseless and frivolous. Go
read books and faff around Europe and be silly, reckless. But, of
course, I didn't leave immediately. I had transgressions of my own to
make.

Their betrayal alone would not have been enough to dislodge me
from Silenus.

"It's what happened afterward, of course," I say casually. "After I
found out about you two." Wyatt looks at me in alarm. We've never
spoken about it, obviously. "I think I knew I was going to leave after

the first glimpse of you together, Zelda squirming away on top of you, your toes curled in ecstasy." He flinches. "That was the end. But it was that night a week later that meant I had to leave. Completed the ritual."

"Look, Ava, we'd all been drinking, we were all upset, it wasn't . . ."

"You think so?" I stare at him, my eyes dark and cruel. "We all had our reasons—the whiskey just helped us along. If it hadn't happened, I never would have had the courage to walk away. Zelda would never have felt like she'd mastered us both. And you . . . you wanted to have both of us, didn't you? To not have to choose, for just one night?"

His silence is the answer.

"Is there more to say about it, Ava?" Wyatt finally asks, his voice full of pain and shame. I sip my beer and lock eyes with him. "Should we—do you want to talk about it?"

"No. I really don't." I set my beer on the coffee table, put the roach back in the ashtray, and raise myself up onto my knees. I reach around and free my zipper, then tug my dress over my head. I can see the outlines of my body in the reflection of the black window, the glare of my white underthings stark in the dim glass. I lean across his body, stretching my whole self out across the planes of his chest and stomach. I can't undo what happened before. Either I can never see him again or I can let it go. "Absolutely no more talking. We're done with that."

# 21

Upstairs, I wake in Wyatt's bed. I'm wearing only my bra and underwear, and, fuzzily, I remember him hoisting me off the couch and carrying me up to bed. I'm grateful not to be on display in the living room, where, after several more beers, I fell asleep tangled up in a scratchy hand-knit blanket and Wyatt's long arms. Usually, when quaffing flask after decanter after pitcher of jammy, noxious booze, I later weep veritable flagons of remorse. But not today. I yawn and stretch out, flopping over onto my back in this strange bed. We didn't spend much time here back when we were together, largely due to his parents' disapproval, as well as to the fact that from the age of about fourteen, my house was a free-for-all. His sheets are clean and smell like they were recently hanging outside on a clothesline, and I inhale the scent of his pillow deeply. I actually feel good. Downstairs, I can hear rustlings and morning conversation, and I imagine the smell of coffee.

I reach for my rumpled dress, which Wyatt has hung over the rail of the bed; I smile at the small, thoughtful gesture. Humming softly, I make the bed, fluff the pillows, open the window to let in some fresh air, and head downstairs.

Dora and Steve are sitting at the kitchen table, and Wyatt is pouring coffee at the kitchen counter. "Muffin?" he says around a mouthful of something, crossing the kitchen to hand me a mug.

"Yes yes yes." I nod. "Morning, Dora, Steve."

Steve smiles at me from behind a newspaper, and Dora waves absently, not looking up from her book. Cool indifference is much better than the scrutiny I'm used to receiving from them, and I smirk at Wyatt. He hands me a blueberry muffin still warm from the oven.

"Come see the new deck. It wasn't here the last time you were." He gestures toward the glass door.

"If you're quiet, maybe you'll see a hummingbird," Steve suggests. "Since I installed the feeder, they come almost every day. Funny little things."

It's a bright day, and the lawn smells clean, freshly mowed. A huge bush of red flowers is in full bloom just off the side of the new deck, scented like expensive cocktails.

"Nice," I say, checking out the new surface in the backyard. Shaded by a big maple and looking out on the pine grove, the deck is indeed very relaxing. I sink into one of the Adirondack chairs and sip my coffee happily. It is nice to pretend that things are normal, that we're just having a lazy breakfast at his parents' house, that the last five or so years haven't actually taken place, that Zelda isn't . . . Zelda.

"So, about yesterday," Wyatt says, as though wishing to dispel the quiet easiness of the day. I stare pointedly at the trees, scanning for hummingbirds, even though I know that you usually hear them before you see them. "What happened at the police station? Was it just shock that made you laugh like that?"

"I'm sure that was a factor. But it was more . . . of a realization. A little epiphany." Wyatt waits patiently for me to go on. "That she's going to go through with this. That she's serious."

"About?"

"She's going whole hog. She's faking her own death, not just playing around, getting everyone riled up. The coroner, Dr. Whitcross? That's the doctor she's been bangin' for the last few months. That's how she's dealing with the dental records and the death certificate."

"You think she bribed him?"

"My guess would be blackmail, frankly. The guy is probably married. She takes a couple pictures of him doing lines off her and her twenty-something-year-old girlfriend, and that takes care of the medical evidence. The life insurance money comes through, the debt mostly goes away, and voilà!" I snap my fingers in illustration. "She gets a clean start."

Wyatt weighs what I've just suggested, staring mutely at the flowers and mulling it over.

"Where is she going to go? She won't have an identity. She'll have to live in the woods or something," he says after a pause, baffled.

"Or I will."

"Wait, what?" Wyatt pauses thoughtfully. "What do you mean?"

"I think Zelda is heading to the City of Light. Paris."

Wyatt's eyebrows shoot up. "Shit. You think she would?"

"Yeah, I kinda do. She could just take my passport and go. I'd be stuck here, unless I reported it stolen, got a new one. And by then she could have already disappeared into Europe, with a head start. I think she might already be there. My boyfriend"—we both flinch at the word—"is convinced he saw me at my favorite café. When he went to go talk to me, I apparently got up and took off before he could say anything. I have a hunch she's already taken my passport and left."

Wyatt looks ashen. "Have you checked?"

"Not yet. That's next."

"Jesus. But why? Because of the debt?"

"That. And maybe health insurance. She's convinced she's got what Mom does, and here in America she's stuck on Medicaid, which will hardly cover a thing. Not ideal for a lengthy, degenerative illness. She figures if she gets to France, or anywhere with socialized medicine, she'll be fine. She can buy a forged passport to replace mine, and she'll be set."

"What about money?"

"That's trickier. She has to wait for the insurance to clear. I think she'll come clean with me then, and she'll ask me for the money. Probably split it with me."

"Why would you give it to her, after she's stolen your identity and fled the country?"

"I'm not sure, but I am a *little* concerned," I say. "She'll want to have leverage, in case she can't just talk me into it. Probably debt in my name, credit cards from a French bank or something. At least that's what I'd do. Though being Zelda, she'll probably think up something even more compelling. A terrifying thought." I shrug. I've been going over it in my mind, trying to get one step ahead of her, thinking of what the rest of the letters might be. I feel pretty sure I'll figure it out only when she wants me to, but I'd be a fool not to try to protect myself.

"And you came up with this hypothesis last night?"

"When I heard that Whitcross was the coroner. It clicked. Up until these dental records, I was sure it was going to be one of her games. That she'd pop up after a week with a 'Surprise!' Laughing at her own cleverness." I shake my head. "But now she's committed. She's legally dead, and if the truth about who's in that fire ever surfaces, she'll probably be wanted for murder too."

"Fuck," Wyatt swears softly, shaking his head. "I thought she was just screwing with us. You, mostly. I'm not sure she ever really cared enough to screw with me." A note of bitterness is audible in his tone. I can't help feeling a similar surge of frustration. How dare he love her, after everything? How could he not?

"I did too. But our little Zelda is growing up."

"What do we do?" he asks helplessly. "Go to the cops?"

"Would *you* believe us? I have a couple of emails and an elaborate theory. They have a body, forensic evidence, a murder suspect already in jail, and a case that's pretty well closed."

"Still, we could check with the airlines, see if anybody using your passport has traveled overseas in the last few days, check the border. That would be proof."

"Proof that someone has my passport, not that Zelda does."

"Seriously? Only someone identical to you could travel with it."

"Or change the picture, sell it to professional forgers. It would be suggestive, not conclusive." I shake my head.

Wyatt is silent for a moment, looking at me. "You don't want her to get caught," he finally says in disbelief. "Holy shit. You're still on her side."

I balk. "It's not that—"

"You're protecting her!"

"She's my twin sister! No, I don't want Interpol to track her down and arrest her for murder and fraud and God knows what else."

"That's what she's counting on! She's counting on you never telling her that this shit is too far, too much! She's fucking manipulating you, Ava. She always has."

"I know that, Wyatt. I'm not an idiot. But what can I do?" I shrug helplessly. I want Wyatt to think that my loyalty to Zelda is what prevents me from turning over everything I've got to the cops. But that's not exactly it. Not entirely. What I want is to get to the end of the alphabet, the end of Zelda's story. I want to know the ending, and I'm willing to suspend sensible decision making to reach it. My narrative desire is greater than my need to see her stopped.

Wyatt stares off the deck, leaning on his knees. He's clearly not happy with me. "Ava. There's something I need to say, and I'm going to just come out with it." He pauses. Looking down. "Your idea of yourself—and of Zelda—I think sometimes you get it wrong. This whole dividing-up-the-world thing that you've always done, I mean, do you think maybe you're sometimes just, well, off?"

"What do you mean?"

"It's like you don't want to compete for space. So Zelda is the bad, wild twin. And you're the good one. And you have these ideas of who you are that fit into those boxes. But do you ever think that maybe it's not that simple?"

I consider what he's said, and I know there might be some truth there. But those boundaries are so important, so necessary, that I can't let them be fictions. Right now, they need to be real.

"I'll think about it," I say. I don't know if he believes me, but he leans forward on his elbows, staring off into the trees. "Wy." He meets my eyes. "Zaza said you loved me because of my vulnerability. Is that—I mean . . ."

Wyatt smiles. "Ava Antipova, are you asking me why I love you?"

I turn pink and glance at him bashfully. "Maybe." What I'm asking might more accurately be: Why do you love me and not my sister?

"Your vulnerability might be part of it, I guess," he admits.

"Really?" I find this disappointing. "I guess I don't think of myself as very vulnerable."

"Well, exactly. You're tough as nails and you take exactly no shit from anyone. But beneath that, you're full of love and affection. You care so deeply about the people you love, and getting a glimpse of that loyalty, that fierceness is . . . well, a privilege. And if you feel even for a second that that love might be directed at you, well . . ."

"I guess I don't really see it that way."

"Because you're so tough and perfect and, like, together, all the time! That's what makes it so powerful to see when you actually, honestly feel something. Like I'm being allowed into a tiny private universe. Most people are an open book, but not you."

"Zelda isn't either."

"No, but she'll always let you know if she's angry, or hurt, or jealous, or pleased. She's just more . . . demonstrative. With you, the first time you told me you loved me was this, like, revelatory experience. I literally felt like I'd won the lottery or something. Struck by lightning." He gives me one of his sweet, slow smiles.

"You remember that day?"

"Ava, it is etched in my memory forever. You wore a blue dress, and I'd never seen you so tongue-tied in my life. It looked like it physically pained you to tell me."

I can't help laughing at the memory. "I was rather uncomfortable, yeah."

"The lilacs were in bloom, it was full spring. . . ."

"Christ, what a romantic," I groan.

"I don't know if I'd ever been so happy."

"Well. It needed to be said." I, too, remembered that day vividly. We were on the back deck, and the long winter had finally loosened its grip. The frozen edges of the lake had thawed; the lawn was green. For months, I had seen Wyatt's skin only in bed, warm and protected beneath the sheets, and out there, as he sat in shorts and a T-shirt, his chalky flesh seemed unprotected, exposed. I felt nearly as naked. I was so young, and scared, and happy. The raw relief of spring made me brave. I don't know if I'm now capable of feeling so limitless. Or so afraid.

We sit quietly, and I'm unsure of what else to say. We are in dangerous territory; we could reminisce, savoring these memories of when it was good. Get lost in what it was like to be young and stupid in love. But that would overwrite how things became, and how we left them.

"Look. A hummingbird," Wyatt finally says, pointing toward the red bush. I squint, looking for the telltale colorful blur. After a moment, I see it, buzzing from one blossom to another.

"There are two." I point to a companion a couple of feet away. "A pair." We watch them quietly.

"Are we making a mistake, Ava?"

"We won't know for a little longer," I say, patting his knee. At the sudden sound, the birds flit away, disappearing into the shadow of the pine trees.

"So what do we do next?"

"Solve the puzzle," I answer, leaning back in my chair. "Her last note said that I was holding the answer in my hand. She must have meant that the answer was in the letter. How did she put it? Something about how underneath something or other we conceal our missing pieces?"

"Underneath. Christ, underneath what?"

"Our careful constructions, duh," I say, smiling, pulling the letter from the pocket of my dress, scanning it, and handing it to him. "Are there any *U* words, aside from that last paragraph?"

Wyatt reads through it quickly. "Just 'untied' and 'untethered.'"

"Okay. That could be . . . a reference to the barn doors?" I suggest. "How they were locked from the outside?"

Wyatt tilts his head skeptically. "Maybe, but that's kind of thin . . ."

"Maybe the most important thing to figure out isn't the next letter, though. We still don't know who was in that barn," I point out.

"How will we figure it out? I mean, we're sort of assuming it was Kayla Richardson, right? If it's not her . . ."

"It could be any number of people. It could be some homeless guy."

"She could have dug up a body and set it on fire first," Wyatt says.

"I think the fact that I find *that* the most comforting hypothesis of the morning is a sign of how generally fucked up this is," I say with a smile.

"Yeah, I prefer that theory too."

"Well, I'm not about to head to the cemetery and check every single fresh grave," I say. "She could have gotten a body from a morgue or a medical school. I mean, maybe if you fuck the right person, bodies are easy enough to procure." I wonder if that's true. Things I never would have asked myself before today. "Come to think of it, maybe she *was* fucking the right person. Kayla? Who works at the funeral home?" Wyatt's eyes widen, and we both contemplate that possibility.

"Okay, so we're left with the letter *U*," he finally says. I sigh in frustration.

"Fuck, Wy. I got nothing. Do we just wait for another clue?"

He grits his teeth. "I don't know."

"Let's go look for my passport. That will at least confirm my theory."

"Before we put the cart in front of the horse."

"Right. Maybe we'll think of something on the way. Or Zelda will send us another hint." I stand up to leave.

"You're the boss," Wyatt says agreeably, and he playfully scoops me up in his arms and spins me. I shriek like a little girl and am momentarily, incandescently happy.

———

In the truck, Nico finally texts me back: I search u at urs. No one there. Y? I tell Wyatt that Zelda isn't at my place, or at least isn't currently at my place. I can see her there, though, flicking through my infinitesimal closet, chuckling over some of my new Parisian clothes. She'll have found the bottle of Cognac on the shelf over my sink and will be sipping it while she tries on my things, playing some of my music. She'll smoke a cigarette out my window, and then she'll scoop up my keys and wander out my door, into the city. All my neighbors will recognize her, and the bartender at my favorite café will offhandedly slide her a *coupe* of Champagne. I wonder if she's bothered to learn any French.

I look at Nico's text unhappily. I haven't called him back, and I've been cagey and secretive in my texts. I haven't even told him that Zelda is technically dead. In fact, if someone were watching me, I might look sort of suspicious. I'm behaving weirdly. If someone had a warrant for my phone, I'd have a hard time explaining my last few messages. Things I should be thinking about. I can smell Wyatt's peculiar blend of scents on my skin and in my hair, and it makes it impossible for me to call Nico, even to formulate what to say to him. He is an abstraction. I look at the abbreviations in the text, all pretty standard messaging. But I find myself reading into things, constructing outlandish scenarios, based on the presence of a solitary *U,* a lonely *Y.* Could Nico be involved, wrapped around Zelda's finger? Paranoid thinking. But isn't that legitimate?

We're at the house before I know it. Marlon's rental is there, and I can see the whole family up on the deck. I sigh inwardly, wishing to spare both myself and Wyatt, but we have to go inside.

We climb the stairs to the second story and join my parents and grandmother on the sunny balcony. Mimosas are half empty on the table. Mom stares glassily out at the vineyard, Opal is flipping through an address book (how quaint), and Marlon is typing on his iPad.

"Morning," I say and receive two unenthusiastic greetings. I suspect they're not impressed by my disappearance last night. But fuck them.

"We've started organizing the memorial service, dear," Opal says, her lips thin.

"How dare you plan my funeral before I'm even dead. You want to kill me!" my mother accuses, trying to stand up from the table. She's too wobbly, though, and aborts halfway through the motion, sinking back into her Adirondack chair and swiping for her mimosa.

"Decided it would be nice to have some closure, even though we might be waiting for the . . . body a little longer," Opal explains, ignoring Nadine.

"And I have to get back to Napa," Marlon says brusquely, not looking up from the email he's typing. "Busy season, and I've got a lot to do."

"Well, we'd hate to tear you away from the important things," I snipe. "Glad you're carving out some time."

He raises his eyes to glare at me with dislike, and I balk. I'm used to his abandonment and his excuses, not his anger. He seems to have hardened overnight. He no longer looks haggard and old, as he has for the last few days, as though Silenus were sapping him of his youth every second he stayed on this soil. His eyes are wide open, his skin looks tighter, and he has shaved. I find it very strange that the official death of his daughter has somehow rejuvenated him. But then, I've never understood my father. I glance at his drink and am surprised to see that it is mostly full. Maybe he figures that Zelda's death puts him one step closer to finishing with this chapter of his life. With Zelda gone, it's just me, Nadine, and Silenus, and the last two won't be around too much longer.

"When will it be? The service?" Wyatt asks.

"Tomorrow," Opal says. "Without any remains, it seems pointless to wait. And she's been dead for days."

"It's not like people will be traveling from all over the world for

Zelda's funeral," I point out. "I'd be surprised if people even come from Ithaca."

"Your sister was loved and treasured," Opal snaps. "I won't hear you jeering at her the day after we learn of her passing." She stands up from the table and gives it a small shove. Her upper arms wobble, the bluish rumpled skin swaying comically with the effort. She strides inside in a huff, thoroughly peeved. I roll my eyes at Wyatt as though we're fifteen, an unvocalized "Jeee-eeez" accompanying my adolescent expression.

"What happened to Ava, sweetheart?" Nadine asks, leaning toward Marlon and squeezing his knee affectionately. He looks trapped, and I almost laugh as he pats her hand in an attempt both to dislodge it and to soothe her.

"Ava's fine, Nadine. Don't worry."

"Oh. Marl. Will you hold me?" She sounds small and timid, and I wonder if she was more like this when they met, with softer edges and some vulnerability. He looks taken aback, but he leans over to give her a squeeze. I retreat from this foreign scene of tenderness. I feel as if I can remember moments like this between them, but they're obscured behind so many years of tension and aggression.

"Do you need help with the organizing?" I ask Marlon.

"I might. I'm trying to let everyone know right now. Is it gauche, do you think, to make a Facebook event?" he asks with a curious frown.

"I've seen it done," Wyatt confirms. "It's efficient."

"Zelda wouldn't mind," I say. "Surely that's what counts."

Marlon grunts and resumes his typing.

"Let me know if you need anything, Mr. Antipova," Wyatt says as we duck back inside. "My parents are happy to help too. With food or any, uh, coordination that needs to happen."

Marlon looks up, surprised, and nods mutely.

Wyatt and I head for my room. I feel my nerves rumble at the prospect of reentering the bedroom, as part of me realizes that last night served to establish at least a partial reinstatement of our relationship.

We're not just old friends and former lovers anymore. There is a currency to our closeness, a now-ness that runs alongside what happened before. The frisson of anxiety that I feel at the sight of clean white sheets spread before us is not because of our past but because of what is happening between us now. I can tell he feels it, in the way he looks at me while trying not to look at me, the way his fingers curl when I stand close to him, as though he is both avoiding and seeking my skin.

I perch on the edge of my bed and open my suitcase, exposing the neat rows of clothes piled inside. Unzipping the liner pouch, I curl my arm inside it up to the elbow, fishing for my zippered folder of indispensable official documents. I tug it out and flip through the pages. There are bank statements proving solvency, a copy of my lease agreement for my apartment in Paris, extra copies of passport photos and photocopies of my passport, a letter documenting my enrollment in grad school. All the accessories of international travel. And there, in the left-hand slot of the folder, the place of privilege, I scoop my finger, expecting to come up empty. I'm meticulously organized, and this is the only place my passport could be.

And lo, no passport. I cock my head toward Wyatt, as though this proves something.

"Does Zelda have a passport? Do you think she would have brought that one too?" Wyatt asks.

"It's in the drawer in her room."

"Can I see it?"

I'm already heading to Zelda's room, and I make my way through her clutter, finding her passport after a quick paw through her top drawer. Wyatt has followed me, and he peers over my shoulder as we look at it. He takes it from my hands and flips through it. "You said she went to France. Why?"

"I have no idea," I say with a shake of my head. "I've tried to puzzle that out. It would have been after she went to the doctor. Maybe she was freaked out about her health and wanted to make up with me? Do it in person?"

"Could be," Wyatt says, sounding unconvinced. I don't blame him. I'm not convinced either. We start to paw through Zelda's papers, deciphering the palimpsest of all the physical documentation she considered important. We become historians of her life, analyzing receipts for dinner and excavating random business cards that have sieved down through to the contact paper that lines the bottom of the drawer. Anything could be important, which renders the stacks illegible, opaque. There are too many letters, too many clues. Too much text. Wyatt picks up the receipt for the hotel she stayed in in Paris, analyzing it.

"Where is this?" he asks.

"Around the corner from my house."

"Is there anything else there? Something she would have to go to Paris for, specifically?"

I think hard. "Other than decent wine and healthcare . . . no, nothing I can think of." I shrug.

"Can you think of something you can do only in France?"

Half a dozen silly quips rise to mind, covering the gamut from the raunchy to the political, but I bite my lip. "I'm sure there must have been something, but . . ." I lift up a stack of papers and fan through what seems to be a pile of bills. The heading on one makes me pause. "Wy? You said she'd been using a burner phone for the last few months?" I ask.

He nods. "Yeah. But she had her iPhone the whole time too. She only used the burner sometimes. I figured it had to do with the drugs or something. Like, she only called her dealer from the TracFone."

"But then why do the cops know about the TracFone and not that she still had her iPhone? Surely it should be the other way around," I muse aloud. "Look at this." I hand him the bill I just found.

"Verizon?"

"Like Healy told me, she canceled her iPhone contract. Here's the thing, though: Ending the service cost a fair bit, and it wasn't due to expire for a few more months. But she canceled it three months ago. When she bought the TracFone."

"And went to Paris," Wyatt adds, looking at the dates on the hotel bill.

"Oh," I say slowly. "Oh."

"What is it?" Wyatt's head jerks up.

"She cancels her iPhone contract, goes to France, and buys a Trac-Fone when she comes home. But we know she keeps using her iPhone." I waggle Zelda's phone in illustration.

"How do you do that, without service?"

"Indeed." Agitatedly, I graze through the papers in the drawer, looking for the receipts that will confirm what I've just suspected. They wouldn't really count as official or important documents in her mind; Zelda kept business cards that she found attractive, postcards she pocketed from interesting places, scraps of napkins and beer coasters, *trouvailles* from her adventures. But I'm pretty sure she will have left these papers for me somewhere in this drawer. I find what I'm looking for on the right-hand side, two pieces of paper stapled together. I skim them and hand them to Wyatt.

"Verizon pay-as-you-go card?" he says, puzzled, waiting for the epiphany to strike. "Is this *V*? Did we skip *U*?"

"It might be *V*. But it's definitely *U*. Read the next page."

"It's in French. *De-ruh-voo* . . ." He looks at me for help.

*"Déverrouiller votre portable,"* I say, enjoying the French words in my mouth. "They passed a law a few years ago in France. You can use any service provider you want, even without a contract, with any phone. It's called 'unlocking.' It's not like here in the States, where Apple ensures that you're stuck with whatever multinational you sell your soul to when you buy your damn phone. I think maybe you can swap out the SIM card with the new iPhones, but Zelda has an ancient 4S."

"So Zelda went to France to get her phone . . . unlocked?"

"Well, partly. I'm sure she had other reasons. But she wanted to use this phone to send me these emails. The cops can subpoena her carrier for access to her messages and conversations, but she hasn't had a contract with them for three months. Verizon will come back and say that as far as they know, she turned that phone off three months ago. She's been using different pay-as-you-go plans for data and cell service for the past few months."

"Don't you have to have an account to do that? Registered, I mean? With your name?"

"Yeah, but it's easy to fake. It's not like signing a contract, where you have to do credit checks and deposits. You just need a name and some ID, and then they give you a phone number. She could have gotten a friend to do it. Lemme guess: Zelda's number changed three months ago?"

"Shit. Yeah. She said some telemarketer was harassing her, so she changed the number. I figured it had something to do with a guy, so I didn't press her too hard on it." Wyatt looks unhappy. I know that he thought he had a piece of Zelda, that she'd opened up to him on some fundamental level while they were together. I've seen other people absolutely convinced that for all Zelda's secrecy and crazy behavior, *they* were the only ones who truly got her, were the only ones Zelda revealed herself to. It's always heartbreaking to watch Zelda's friends and lovers realize for the first time that not only did they never have access to her secret heart but she was actively concealing herself all along. I'm reaching out a hand toward Wyatt in pity when I realize that I'm exactly the same as all of them. I always thought that I was privileged, different, that only I really knew Zelda. Part of me still revolts against the idea that this is not true.

"She's really been planning this," Wyatt finally says. "She's known for a long time that she was going to do this."

"'Fraid so," I respond. I feel bad, I really do. But also a little vindicated. Victorious.

"Would she have had to go all the way to France to do this, though?" Wyatt asks, still skeptical.

"She could probably have found some dodgy tech store in New York who could do it for her, I guess," I admit. "But I think she did it to be elaborate. It gave her a reason to travel to Paris, to insert herself into my new life." The more I think about it, the more I'm certain that I've found *U*.

"Where do you think she is now?" Wyatt muses, rifling through the sheaves of paper. "I mean, she has to be laying low somewhere."

"I still think she's in Paris." It's the only place that makes sense. She planned this whole elaborate game to escape, to get away from Silenus, our parents. And she set it all up for me. Not for Wyatt or for the cop she was fucking. This is about the two of us and always has been. I'm certain that it circles back around to me; she would repeat my escape, to the same place. "Maybe she just wasn't home when Nico went up to my place," I suggest. "I'll ask him to keep checking back, hang out in the café across the street to watch my door for a bit." I open up my phone and text Nico briefly, letting the guilt bubble up for a minute or two while I carefully phrase my request. He'll do it, and he won't ask questions. I wonder if that flexibility is part of what made me fall in love with him to begin with.

But I know she's not at the apartment. Not just because my keys are where I left them, and not just because Nico didn't find her there. Wyatt's hands are plunged into the stack of papers, submerged up to the wrists, and he wiggles his fingers as though they're underwater. He is immersed in Zelda's paper trail. I carefully spread out the papers in Zelda's drawer and slide it firmly shut, forcing Wyatt to remove his hands. I hope he has not memorized the name of Zelda's hotel in Paris. When I find her, I want to do it by myself. This is not a team effort. An ungenerous part of me knows that Wyatt won't suspect me of withholding my hypotheses from him. He couldn't even bring himself to scrutinize Zelda, and he knew what she was like. He thinks I would never lie. Not to him.

"How about a mimosa?" I say brightly, knowing that the prospect of sitting on the deck and getting drunk with me and both of my parents while we plan a funeral will be an adequate deterrent. He grimaces but looks momentarily like he will accept. Shit: He's trying to be supportive. I feel a wave of fondness toward him for his self-sacrifice, but I need him to go home for a spell. "Oh, damn," I say, "I'm a ninny.

Of course you don't want to hang out with Marlon and Nadine. And Opal. You're totally off the hook," I add with a shake of my head.

"No, no, I'd love—"

"Yeah, yeah. Sure you would." I wave him off. "It's okay. I should sit with them and take care of some odds and ends anyway. I'll call you later today?"

Wyatt looks both relieved and distressed. I've managed both to dismiss him and to make him feel guilty for abandoning me during such a traumatic time.

"If you're sure that's okay . . ."

"I think I can manage." I wink, guiding him out of Zelda's room. As we walk by the library, whose sliding doors lead out to the balcony, I hold up one finger, signifying "one minute" to Marlon as he looks over at me, and follow Wyatt down the stairs. I walk him to the front door and pause on the threshold, leaning out onto the steps to plant a kiss firmly on his mouth, taking him by surprise. "Thank you. For last night. For everything."

"Oh, Ava. Of course. You know I—" He cuts himself off. "I'm here for you," he concludes.

"I know." He kisses my forehead and wanders back to his truck, waving to me before hoisting himself up into the cab. I wave back and shut the door.

I bound up the stairs and out onto the balcony, where Marlon is on the phone. It sounds like he's talking to a catering company. We aren't surrounded by the sort of people who will inundate us with casseroles to serve at a memorial service. Just Betsy, and more tuna. He's smart to plan a full table lavishly prepared by strangers. It will make us seem less lonely. I grab his mostly untouched mimosa and bob my head in thanks.

"Ava, we could use help getting in touch with some of Zelda's friends. I've been trying to make a list with this Facebook thing." Opal frowns at the screen of the iPad, which is now in her lap. I see that she has written out by hand a long list of everyone on Zelda's friends list.

"Don't worry about it, Grandma," I suggest flippantly. "Dad's going to make an event."

"Make an event? What does that mean?"

"That Zelda's whole list of people will get invited," I explain. "Dad will make a Facebook event for the service."

"But we don't know their phone numbers. How will we let them know about the event?"

I try not to laugh at the genuine confusion in Opal's voice. "Just don't worry about it, Grandma." I pause. "I wonder how it works with Facebook. Do we contact admin to get Zelda's status changed to dead?" I'll try to remember to research that later. Zelda will get a kick out of it. Opal looks pained.

"Zelda, get me another drink," Nadine snaps. I thought she was napping.

"In a second, Mom," I say, trying to skitter away.

"Don't you think we should call your sister today? Really, it's been a long time since we spoke to her." Nadine sounds fretful, even concerned. I wonder if she's been asking Zelda to call me all this time. I imagine what Zelda would say to end the conversation.

"We already called her, Mom, remember? She was fine, said she was having a great time. She's coming home for a visit soon."

Opal shoots me a judgmental look.

"Oh, of course," Nadine says. "I remember now. She was having a coffee in a Left Bank café, reading up for class. Her French has gotten sublime." Nadine nods, smiling.

I'm taken aback. Is this how she fills in the chinks of her leaky memory? With "remembered" conversations about my charmed life in Paris? Does she spend the day imagining me romping beneath the Eiffel Tower, a baguette under each arm? Or does Zelda spin these yarns for her, imagining me?

"And she's planning to go to the museum at Quai Branly this afternoon," I add softly. "She's writing a paper on it. She met a man named Nico who's a French banker—remember what she said about him?"

"That he has a thick accent and always smells of cigarettes," Nadine responds promptly.

I'm harrowed. "Yeah. And she thinks she loves him, but she's not sure they belong together."

"Nonsense. Ava is a catch, and she knows it." Nadine giggles, more lighthearted than I've seen her for some time. "I'm actually proud of her, you know."

I realize Marlon has stopped talking on the phone and is following this conversation.

"Me too," he says, patting Nadine's hand. "I'm proud of our daughter." He looks over at me, and it's too much. Way too much. I can feel myself shutting down, trying not to experience this poignant family moment. Nadine interrupts, thank God.

"I don't know why you never do anything, Zaza. Rotting away here. If you had any gumption, you'd strike off on your own, do something with your life. You always were content to be second best, though."

I feel two things simultaneously as she says this: a sharp pain in my chest, as though she has slapped me, and a sense of relief at the return to normalcy. Opal flinches and glares furiously at Nadine, prepared to leap to my defense as though I actually were Zelda.

"Ava abandoned you, Mom," I point out. "She's not doing anything noble, or even valuable. She ran away from you and hasn't felt guilty about it for one fucking second since she left," I spit out. "She's a selfish, narcissistic monster. Of course you like her more. She's just like you." I stand up from the table and drain the mimosa in Marlon's glass in one fluid movement. Nadine stares at me stonily, unapologetic. I don't look at either Opal or Marlon as I walk away from the table, leaving behind a fraught silence.

I walk into my room, shutting the door firmly behind myself. My hands are shaking from the scene I just made, and I cluck my tongue in annoyance. You'd think I would be thicker-skinned. I sit down on my bed and stare at my cellphone. *Okay, Zelda. Time to talk.* I dial the number and switch languages in my head, preparing to speak French.

*"Allô, Hôtel Victoires?"* a female voice answers. *V* is for Victoires. Victory.

*"Bonjour,"* I respond, and I continue on in French. "I'm looking for a guest who is staying with you. Do you think you could connect me to her room?"

"The name of the guest?"

"Ava Antipova," I say with satisfaction. I know she picked the hotel nearest my apartment, in my territory but not quite in my space. It is her tentative way of asking me to let her in. She's gone right to my doorstep, but she won't cross it without an invitation. I giggle, thinking that *V* could just as easily be for *vampire*, considering the parasitic nourishment Zelda gets from my life, her need to be invited into my house. She knows she could have had my keys copied, moved into my cozy cupboard. She could probably even have seduced an unsuspecting Nico. But she's not doing any of that, because we're starting over. She's asking me to make space for her in my life. The voice returns to the line.

"I'm sorry, but we don't have any guest registered by that name."

I frown, perplexed. "Zelda Antipova, then?" I offer, though I wonder how she would manage that. As a foreigner, she would need a passport to check into the hotel. The woman on the line barely pauses.

"No, no one by the name of Antipova," she answers, preparing to hang up.

"Wait," I say desperately. "Perhaps she's staying under another name. Dark curly hair, small, beautiful?" I prompt. "She would have checked in recently, a few days ago at most."

"I'm very sorry, but I can't give out information like that," the woman says frostily, and like that she's hung up the phone.

I sit on the edge of my bed, shocked. I was so certain. Just a second ago I knew where Zelda was; it seems unthinkable to suddenly not know, not be able to call my sister. I had already imagined her thrilled and entertained voice on the other end, delighted with the game of hide-and-seek we'd been playing. Bubbling with the pleasure of being discovered, of being found. She would have told me about the bars she'd been drinking in while she waited for me to call, the clever little thoughts that had crossed her mind while I was catching up. I experience a disorienting sense of loss at my false step. I want to talk to her, and I feel as though I might cry in frustration. I begin typing into my phone.

Goddamnit, Zaza. Where the fuck are you hiding?

I send the email in a fury, stabbing at the screen in frustration. Immediately, I receive an email in response:

I'm not where you think I am ☺

"Fucking hell!" I swear to my empty room.

# 22

Very twitchy and anxious, I pace around my room. I've even Googled other hotels near my apartment, looking for any that start with a *V.* Or *W, X, Y,* or *Z,* in case I've gotten ahead of the game with my deduction that Zelda is in France. But I find nothing. I could search all the hotels of Paris, I suppose, call around and see if she's in any of them. I could go to the cops, tell them about my missing passport and my suspicions, and they could check with immigration to see if Zelda flew anywhere. I could call the credit card companies to see if any charges have been made, any flights booked. . . . But Zelda would have booked them on someone else's card, I'm sure of it—stolen one from Jason or Holly or Kayla. Fuck, maybe even Wyatt. I should ask him. The cops knew about her last trip to France, but they hadn't mentioned any others. With a sense of unease, I wonder if I'm being framed. My head is spinning, and I want nothing more than another mimosa.

I text Nico, cryptically asking him if he'll lurk around Hôtel Victoires whenever he has a second and let me know if someone who looks just like me is wandering around in the Second Arrondissement. Moments after I send the text, my phone rings. Nico. I don't answer. I know this is assholic, I know I should pick up and explain, but I don't have it in me. I cover my eyes with my hands and wait for the phone to stop vibrating, too guilty to tap the decline icon. A text arrives shortly after.

I don't know what is going with you, Ava. Is your sister living? Do I look for her? Please call me back. I will go to the hotel when I am finish work. Xoxo

I'm using him. I'm deeply, harrowingly aware of that, but I push it from my mind. I don't respond. It would look strange if I texted back immediately after failing to pick up the phone. Let him think I'm driving. I have just sent him off to squander his evening on what will most likely turn out to be a waste of time.

Irritated, I review my options. Really, I want nothing more than to put Zelda and her shenanigans out of my mind. To do something relaxing, unrelated. But she's the only reason I'm here, and her antics have me thoroughly occupied. It seems unthinkable that I might drive to Ithaca to have a massage, get in touch with old friends, and meet for a drink somewhere in town. I should work on my dissertation, but that seems inconceivable. I'm like a live wire, incapable of quieting the electrical thrum that pulses in me. I feel like screaming. Frantically, I strip off yesterday's clothes and retrieve the bathing suit from the floor. I fling it on, knot a sarong around my midriff, and dash downstairs. Opal and Marlon look up at the noise, but I don't pause to explain.

I snatch up a pristine pair of white Keds, Nadine's. I've seen her wear them only once; they seemed outrageously sporty for her, though they somehow suited her elegant party dress. It was for someone's birthday, though I can't remember whose. Whose birthday? Why can't I remember? After fumbling with the laces, I nearly fall out the glass doors onto the patio.

I run down the grassy slope of the lawn, toward the trail to the water, cinching the sarong tightly around my breasts. Small as they are, they still bounce uncomfortably, unsupported by the slender strings noosed about my neck, and I try to more or less strap them down with the sarong. Limited success. I am moving so fast down the hill that I'm in danger of face-planting, tripping over a stray root and causing serious injury, but I don't care in the slightest. The momentum is the best part, and I feel blissfully out of control as I let my body take over, my feet slamming the dirt one ahead of the other. Heading down.

I make it to the water's edge without tumbling over my own feet. I barely even slow my pace to shuck off the sneakers and fling my sarong aside. I'm still running when I hit the water, and the cold slaps against my thighs and sprays up my belly. My nipples immediately harden. I dive under the water as soon as I am waist-deep and let the chill of Seneca Lake close over my head in relief.


I swim for nearly an hour, doing laps up and down the beach, then swimming out and swimming back, going nowhere. Finally, exhausted and barely able to flail another stroke, I beach myself, crawling up onto the stones, not yet warmed by the sun. I lie on my back just feet from the water, shivering and blue-tinged. My arms are quaking, and I can feel ripples and spasms in my glutes. I'm reminded of how horses look when they've been run hard, the muscles of their hindquarters glistening with sweat and twitching. I drip into the stones.

When the sun has dried me off, I sit up and reach for my sarong, which I tug around my shoulders. Staring out at the water, I have no idea what to do. I rock back and forth on my haunches, mumbling to Zelda. I get up eventually, and walk toward the rickety dock. I step out onto it, and it creaks menacingly below me. I can feel it sway. It used to be a pirate ship, sailing off into the sunset with Zelda at the helm, me the navigator in the back. Sometimes it was an island, and we would hang off it, scooping up rocks and seaweed and tiny fish in a bid for survival. Sometimes it was an Olympic diving board, and we were world-class athletes competing for a double gold. Now it is rotting, unsteady. Unsafe. I bounce, feeling the architecture again shift below me, and spring off it anxiously, back onto solid ground. One big storm and it will float off into the lake.

I prowl up and down the beach, thinking of the lazy days we spent down here. I kick at the rowboat, which lolls on its side. This, too, has seen better days; it now looks fragile and unseaworthy. I'm tempted to hop in it and row to Watkins Glen, but my arms cringe at the thought. It would sink before I got anywhere. I notice that the boards look chewed on. Termites, I imagine. I give the rowboat a parting kick and head uphill, back to the house, which looms oppressively above me. I can just barely see my parents and grandmother on the balcony from here.

The walk uphill is harder than my headlong rush down it, and I'm panting and sweaty by the time I make it to the lawn. The chill of the lake water is gone, and I feel flushed and damp. I flop down onto the lawn in exhaustion, burying my nose in the grass. The scent of smoke seems to have settled on the soft blades. Beneath it, I can smell the ground, the soil that has been my family's livelihood. It doesn't seem to have registered the recent conflagration anywhere in its aromatic makeup.

"Ava!" Marlon calls from the deck. "C'mon up here!" He sounds just like he did when we were little: confident authority tinged with the promise of more fun. Do as I tell you, and we're going to have a ball!

I curl up on the grass and don't look at him. I want to stay here, on the lawn, until it gets dark, until dew turns everything damp and cold. I have a sudden memory of throwing up on this lawn, in right about this spot, after Zelda and I graduated high school. I wonder if my Jäger-soaked vomit fueled an army of drunken worms, which burrowed beneath the opaque lawn and secreted this exact handful of pasteurized soil. I'm part of this lawn! I think giddily. The lining of my stomach is here in this leaf of grass. It is a nice thought. I am comforted. I sit up groggily, my wet hair clinging to my back.

Stumbling inside, I notice that I am famished. The long swim in the cold water has awakened a terrifying hunger; it is not the gently gnawing peckishness of lunchtime but something frantic. I lurch to the fridge and fall upon some potato salad. Opal mainly makes "salads." She is a mayonnaise-based cook. Tuna salad, pasta salad, potato salad, egg salad. I know that in her fridge at home, there is a bulk-sized jar of Hellmann's that will never have the opportunity to go bad. The mayonnaise in our fridge was always tinged with blue mold; Nadine refused to use it on anything, because it was "pure calories." I never really questioned this assessment, though I should have wondered what separated it from other foods.

After having inhaled several cups of gloppy, pale potato salad, I head back upstairs. I feel like a teenager as I pretend not to hear any supplications for me to join the party on the balcony; I stubbornly put my head down and let my hair swing in front of my face as I storm for my bedroom.

Instinctively, once I'm in my room, I check the phones. Nothing. Something is niggling at me, something I forgot to do. I grope for the memory, but it's just out of reach. Like that feeling you get when you're leaving on a long trip and you know that you've forgotten something important—of course, you don't remember what it is until you've already traveled too far to turn around and go back for it. After we talked to Kyle . . . I wanted to go look for . . . But my mind is empty. I can't remember. We're up to *W.* Or, rather, *V. V* wasn't Victoires. I text Wyatt, wondering if he'll remember.

We were going to go check something, after we talked to Kyle. But we got the phone call and ended up at yours etc. and it didn't happen. What were we going to do?

I strip off my bathing suit as I wait for a response, reaching over to hang it on the hooks I installed when I was thirteen. One set on the back of my door, for towels, and one near the closet, for my bathrobe. I was very precise about never swapping their function. I liked everything to go where it belonged. I pause momentarily, wondering which hook my bathing suit should go on: Is it more towel or more bathrobe? Then I remember my sarong, which complicates things further. It's a garment, sure, but it's shaped like a towel. . . . I hang it on a towel hook, my bathing suit on the bathrobe hook. Then I realize what a preposterous amount of time I've spent on that gripping internal debate and toss them both onto the floor, as Zelda would. But I almost immediately pick them back up and rehang them, this time on the opposite hooks. I feel better.

Her medications? You wanted to see if she'd been prescribed anything.

Ah, yes. I wanted to see if Zelda was really sick or if she was just flipping out over nothing. I suppose the best place to start would be the trailer. I wish I'd looked more thoroughly when I was hunting for her stash. But I gave up after finding the Valium and heroin. I know there will be more.

Clothed in a lightweight shift dress and sandals, I scuttle out of the house again. The day is heating up, and I consider taking the truck to Zelda's trailer, but that seems absurd, so I walk, dust coating my feet and ankles. My hair is drying into a strange frizzy creature with a life of its own. The door of the trailer sticks briefly, and I nudge it open with my shoulder. Heat gusts out. It is stuffy inside and smells overly ripe, stale. I open a few windows and light a stick of incense before settling onto Zelda's bed and hunting through her usual hiding places, the dark crannies of her home.

Thirty minutes later, I'm left with a few wads of cash and a dildo but no more drugs. I'm baffled. Zelda typically hoarded a pharmacy: uppers, downers, hallucinogens. So far, I've not even been able to find a joint squirreled away in any of her usual spots. Something niggles at me, something I've ignored or overlooked. Would she have hidden something in her bedroom? I doubt it—there aren't enough hollow places, not enough surfaces to be pulled back in order to reveal what's underneath.

With a jolt, I remember the letter we found on Wyatt's truck. I fish it out from my bag and look at the cryptic final sentence: *Underneath these carefully constructed surfaces we conceal our missing pieces.* The letter *U,* for something concealed *underneath* a constructed surface. Not *unlocked,* after all.

I walk outside to the deck, Zelda's long-ago summer project, jump off the edge, and peer below. There's a tiny crawl space beneath it, and I'm just able to cram myself in. I inch along, scanning. In the corner, I see a zip-lock bag taped where two pieces of wood meet, lurking like a spider's tight ball of eggs. I tug it down and edge back out from beneath the deck.

A playful hand has labeled the bag with permanent ink: *U found U!*

Inside, I find Zelda's variety show of mind-altering substances. A bag with some pot (it smells like the terrifically strong stuff they grow locally), a depleted eight ball of coke. Mom's name is on a few prescription bottles: codeine for the rheumatism in her hands, some more clonazepam. The only prescription in Zelda's name is for Ritalin, and the bottle is mostly untouched. I wonder if she was selling the tablets; Zelda certainly doesn't need any more energy. There's no sign of any pills like the others my mother takes, nothing that indicates Zelda was ever diagnosed. Then I remember that she mentioned stealing prescription pads from Whitcross—she wouldn't have needed a diagnosis for the medications.

But there's nothing in her name. No SSRIs, no meds to help neurological symptoms like tremors and shakes. Maybe she wasn't certain enough of her self-diagnosis to forge a prescription. She was paranoid, for sure, but probably very aware of the fact that paranoia and delusions are symptoms of dementia.

As I pull out one of the last bottles, a piece of paper tumbles from the bag. Zelda's handwriting.

*What's missing, sweet sister mine?*

I frown. Well, the rest of the alphabet, obviously. What can she mean? How on earth would I know what isn't here? I crumple up the paper and sit back on the deck. She sent me snooping around her stash. And she wants me to look for something that's supposed to be here. She has every pharmaceutical under the sun, except for the ones I came looking for. Does she know I came hunting for proof of her illness? Or does she want me to look for something else?

In irritation, I take the bags back out and sift through the semi-translucent orange vials again. I read where each prescription was filled, look at every name. I check for generic as well as brand name. I have no idea what she wants from me. I uncrumple the note and read it again. This time, I flip it over and see that she has written on the back too.

*You'll find it in Mom's room, where it ultimately belongs.*

Still doesn't mean anything to me, but at least I know where to go looking. I pack all the pills into the grubby bag again and slap it back into the corner of the crawl space. I leave the Airstream and mosey on toward the house, thinking.

I pad inside, where it is cooler, and take a long drink of water from the tap, not bothering to fetch a glass. The sort of thing that Nadine hates. Usually, I do too. I head upstairs, prepared to dodge everybody again, but Marlon is asleep on the balcony in a patio chair, and I don't see Opal. Mom is sitting in her chair, staring blankly down at the water with a flaccid expression. She doesn't even blink. For a second, I am certain that she's dead, but then she tilts her head slightly at the sound of my footsteps, and I let out a breath that is maybe not quite as relieved as it should be.

"Mom, come inside," I whisper, trying not to wake Marlon. Nadine purses her lips and continues staring. "Mom. You'll get sunburned."

She doesn't even bother shaking her head, just looks off into the distance, at the vines she grew. Or, rather, paid other people to grow. I'm about to fight with her when I realize I just don't care. I'll bring her a hat later.

Her room is cool and dark, and the fan has been left on. I realize with a jolt what a terrible caretaker I've been during the last few days, how I've relied on Marlon and Opal to deal with her. All the while carrying a chip on my shoulder because I've been saddled with her. If my father and grandmother hadn't been here, Nadine would still be in her dirty nightgown, rolling around in her musty sheets without having eaten breakfast or taken her medications. Zelda has been doing this every day for two years. Jesus.

My phone vibrates. I tear at my pocket, trying to reach it, assuming it's Zelda, that she's somehow intuited my presence here in this room. But there's nothing—no message, no email. I realize that it was actually my own phone buzzing at me and see a text from Nico.

I am at the bar across Hotel Victoires. Looking for your twin I assume. I will call if I will see her. Please call me.

I slide the phone back into my pocket. I will. I will. But first I need to find whatever Zelda has squirreled away up here. Maybe she meant that she was taking Mom's dementia drugs? When Nadine was first diagnosed and we were just getting used to the daily regimen of fistfuls of meds with unpronounceable names, we called them her Forget-Me-Nots. I prowl around the room, checking in the twin nightstands next to the bed first. Everything in the room has a double: one for Nadine and one for Marlon. Two nightstands, one on either side of the bed, two tasteful laundry hampers next to each other near the bathroom, two reading chairs in opposite corners, with matching throws draped artistically over their winged backs. Nadine never redecorated, but she had at least begun to occupy the dresser and closet that had once been Marlon's. She kept some of her own books on his nightstand. Still, there was lopsidedness to the room, like a limb that's been in a cast displayed next to its healthy partner. Nadine fully occupied only one half of the room.

I check the bathroom, where the bizarre array of prescription bottles is lined up along the edge of the medicine cabinet. I don't recognize all of them; Nadine has fresh infantry in the battle against her own rotting brain. I scan the names. Next I go over to the bed and look at her pill dispenser—or, rather, her massive pill dispenser, divided into the seven days of the week, then further divided into the three meals of the day. I've been disbursing her meds from this container, which someone (presumably Zelda) stocked before the fire. Twenty-one compartments, all crammed with medications that she chokes down in tiny increments. The dispenser is nearly empty. I shake it, and there are only five compartments still filled with pills—through tomorrow. Fuck. Did I get that list of meds from Dr. Whitcross? What did I do with it? I sigh as I start to contemplate the task of hunting down all the pills, refilling prescriptions. It could take all afternoon. I drop to my hands and knees, hoping to find a list written out in the nightstand, but instead I come upon another dispenser, nearly full. I pick it up in surprise. It's another week's worth of medication. Has it been here all along?

I flip open the lid, expecting to see the rainbow jumble of pills that look too big for any human being to force down their throat, but that's not what I find. In the first compartment, there are only eight familiar-looking pills, all with a distinctive *V* printed on them. The missing letter *V.* I take one out and hold it up. I know these pills. Zelda and I discovered them as college freshmen, when I had my wisdom teeth removed. It had been hellishly painful, and I walked out of the pharmacy clutching a slender tube of Vicodin. Zelda took half of them, and we spent a couple of days in a blissful state of painlessness, dreamily watching movies on the couch and occasionally giggling over my appearance, with my swollen chipmunk cheeks and dilated pupils. We managed to finagle two refills from the dentist before he cut us off, and

Zelda promptly resolved to get her teeth out too. I imagine the dental records from that surgery were the ones she had bribed the coroner to use in order to falsely identify her body. I wonder if there is a way to tell Kayla Richardson's mother not to wait up for her daughter without incriminating myself. Maybe Kayla is still out there, though. I remember that she works for the funeral home—maybe she's helping? Maybe she and Zelda are hiding in someone's off-grid yurt less than ten miles from here. Maybe someone else is dead in the barn, someone whose mother hasn't missed them.

I toss a Vicodin into my mouth and crack open the next compartment in the drug dispenser. These are not Vicodin. They are the missing Xanax, of course, the ones I'd been looking for the second time I went to Zelda's trailer. It had surprised me then that she didn't have any. This must be what she meant. These were the missing drugs from her hidey-hole. It should have been painfully obvious, like looking into my mother's fridge and finding only salads and fresh-cooked meals and not a single bottle of white wine or vodka stuffed deep into the freezer behind the ice-bitten peas. How could I not think of it? Of course, I did think of it, that second day in the trailer. My brain is sluggish. I am forgetful.

I cradle the dispenser in my lap, staring at the Vicodin and Xanax nestled next to each other, a cozy cocktail that could easily dispatch someone's worldly concerns. This was obviously not supposed to be Nadine's medication for tomorrow and the next few days. I flip open all twenty-one compartments and find only Vicodin and Xanax, alternating for the entire week. Something about this makes me very nervous, and I'm not quite sure why.

I open all the drawers of the nightstand, rummaging through them. Maybe there's another dispenser and this is just the recreational one that helps keep Nadine and Zelda even-keeled. Instead, I find a bag of empty prescription bottles. I dump it out onto the floor. All prescribed to Zelda Antipova. Vicodin and Xanax, probably ten bottles altogether, dating back months. Different doctors have prescribed them, from as far away as Geneva. The last few are from Whitcross—

the missing prescription pad. Why would she keep them all? And here, out in the open? Part of me knows, but I can't quite let that thought gain traction. It's something we've talked about before, but something I can't really contemplate.

Only Zelda never did care for subtlety, and she's not about to embrace it now. She refuses to run the risk of being misunderstood.

# 23

Well, sister mine,

Part of you knew this is where we would end up, that this was the whole point. We talked about it once, do you remember, when Mom first got sick? We even tried to bring it up with her, though that conversation went appallingly wrong. Ultimately, I think, she might have agreed to it, but around that time she was re-entrenching every time we suggested a bloody thing and was violently dismissive of anything either of us could think up. Gentle hints that she might want to eat some solid food or put on pants were met with full-on hysterics. She said I probably couldn't be re- lied on to follow anything through, and she barely trusted me to do her laundry, let alone see her off gently into that good night. But you're the good sister! Angelic, Accountable Ava! Always available to do the Right Thing. Until you weren't. Until a lifetime of enacting your dutiful dharma collapsed beneath your overwhelming desire to just get the fuck outta Dodge and live your life. Which I understood. I did, Little A. I was pissed and hurt and felt abandoned, but boy oh boy did I get it. Who wouldn't want to flee this moribund place? I give it back to you now. Waltz, you dark and jaded nymph, through these quiet gardens of excessive, balmy peace! Snort.

But what you have in front of you is your penance. Just because the *choice you made was utterly understandable doesn't mean that you're off the hook for it. You have some making up to do, missy. And, honestly, I kind of feel like I got the long end of the stick on this one. SO. Without further ado, Ava my dear, here is what your future holds (though I think you have a pretty good inkling):*

*a) You have in front of you a veritable pharmakon. These puppies offer you salvation, dearest sister, and all you have to do is . . .*

*b) Administer them. Nadine will hold out her shaky gnarled hands, those gigantic, expensive rings rattling around on her skeletal digits, and she'll toss back her head and swallow it down. (Do you remember that Alanis Morissette CD? God, I just thought of that.)*

*c) You'll hand out these little ingestibles in the proper order—that is, alphabetically. (Of course!) A fistful of Vicodin, followed by a fistful of Xanax. (You're getting two letters at once! Twins!) Wait a bit, lather, rinse, repeat, until blessed unconsciousness ensues. My feeling, based on some very flimsy research, is that this combo is more likely to prove lethal than, say, an overdose of heroin. I think. At least Wikipedia says so. And Mom's squeamish about needles. And I'm low on smack. So.*

*d) Even if it is no more effective than some other pharmaceuticals, it's at least much easier to explain to the authorities, who will come sniffing around eventually.*

*e) When they do (come sniffing), they'll learn that I've been collecting Vicodin and Xanax for months, stockpiling it and storing it (perhaps foolishly) in Our Demented Mother's bedroom. It would seem that I kept many of them in a pill dispenser by the bed, which certainly calls my judgment into (further) question. A halfway decent psychiatrist will suggest that this is a classic unconscious Electra complex, and that I was subconsciously laying the groundwork for my mother's death (Damn that Clytemnestra!).*

*f) You will cry and look grief-stricken and shocked. You will blame yourself for not being more attentive, not monitoring her closely enough at night, not making sure everything in her bedroom was safe, for getting too drunk. But you're still so shaken up by the death (murder!) of your twin sister, and—and—*

*g) And they'll write it up as an accidental death, eventually. The in-surance people will fork out. Then you'll be free, darling sister! Free of Mom, free of debt, free to do as you please! For a moment or two, at least.*

*I wish I'd had the guts to do it myself, and I'm still wondering why I couldn't go through with it. The night of the fire, I sat there on the edge of the bed, the pills in my lap, planning to finish everything up after all. Thinking back to that evening, one of the last few with the three of us, all semilucid, talking about this. But I always knew that it couldn't be me. You're the right one for the job, Little A! You can do it!*

*I suggest you burn this note. Obvs.*

*Love,*
*Who else,*
*Zelda*

I fold up the handwritten letter that lined the bottom of the bag and lean back against the bed. I pop another Vicodin into my mouth and close my eyes. I should have known that Zelda wouldn't be able to walk away without punishing me. I snap the compartments of the pill dispenser firmly shut and tuck the whole thing into the nightstand, nestled behind a book. One of the twinned Afghan rugs that flank both sides of the bed scratches me through the thin fabric of my dress. I sit there, waiting to feel the first cozy swoop of the Vicodin before standing up.

Of course I have a clear memory of that night, not long after Nadine was diagnosed, when we sat around the kitchen table, glasses in hand. Trying to be as pragmatic as possible. I have tried not to think about it.

"What would you want, Zaza?"

"I'd want you to off me the minute my hands were too shaky for me to drink out of a fucking martini glass," she had snorted. "But that's me. I tread this world lightly!"

"What about Mom? What would she want?"

"I don't know, Ava. I just don't."

Now I go over to Nadine's closet, which is crammed full of clothes while Marlon's stands empty, in anticipation. From the top shelf above the dress rack I pull down a hatbox and remove a beautiful, wide-brimmed straw hat in pale cream, with a black silk band. I have always loved this hat. I remember visiting Opal in Florida, for one of our last family vacations together, and watching my mother walk barefoot on the beach in this hat. There was a violent pink sunset dying behind her, and she wore a buttoned cover-up that would have looked too formal for the beach on anyone else but suited her perfectly. She didn't have a glass in her hand, for once. She didn't need one; she was alone, without Marlon or Opal or Zelda or me. She looked serene, and I crouched near a sand dune to watch her burrow her toes into the low tide and dislodge a sand dollar. She squatted on the beach to pick it up and stayed poised on her haunches in a surprisingly athletic pose, holding her prize and looking out over the water. Maybe nostalgia and my desperate need for a perfect memory add this last detail in, but I remember a school of dolphins bursting out of the waves nearby, skating through the rosy water.

I sniff my mother's hat, smelling for a trace of her hair before she was taking so many medications, before she stank of age. But I smell only the box it has been stored in. I project the fragrance of sand and salt water onto it, such vivid scents that they are easy to imagine, and I think briefly that I should take my mother to the ocean, to Cape Cod, where she grew up. I could put her in a chair by the water and let her dig her toes into the sand there, bring her a glass of wine and a plate of baked clams, remind her of where we are when she looks puzzled and angry. Maybe we could talk about her sister, Nina, help her heal after a lifetime of refusing to acknowledge her death. Maybe we could sit there, cathecting together.

I think about sitting with Zelda at the kitchen table, after Mom's diagnosis, talking over our options. They were limited. Lewy body dementia is degenerative, incurable. We could let our mother descend deeper, lose more of herself until she basically forgot how to breathe. Or we could do something. Choose the ending now. Go to Oregon? Switzerland? We promised to keep it as an option, a possibility as Mom's condition worsened. And it has worsened. Zelda has sweetened the pot, with the insurance policies, but we talked about it long before. Even Nadine had hinted at it, though she couldn't ask us. She couldn't admit to needing us, to being so vulnerable. And, of course, I did go to Oregon, though I think I never fully admitted that this could have been one of my reasons for fleeing to the West Coast and following Jordan home.

On the balcony, Marlon is now snoring mildly. I creep quietly around him and put the hat on Nadine's head, looking at the skin on her neck and décolletage, to see if she's sunburned yet. She seems okay. As I tug the hat over her disheveled hair, she reaches up and grabs my wrist, surprising me with the texture of her rippled fingertips, so wrinkled they feel waterlogged.

"What is it, Mom?"

"What? Oh, nothing. I just—thank you."

"You're welcome."

"It's nice of you. To look after me, these past few years. I know it's not how you want to spend your life. But you're so sweet, Ava. A good girl."

I swallow hard, feeling around for the Vicodin in my neurochemicals. Not nearly stoned enough. Blindly, I make my way downstairs, homing instinctively on the wine cellar.

It is cool and musty below the house, and I feel a familiar frisson of pleasure at the way it smells down here, full of moisture and secrets and age. I walk along the wine racks, fondling the cool necks of the bottles. Something deeply interior flushes with pleasure at the sight of this abundance, and I contentedly stroke each glass curve, sensuously moving along the racks. I stop at a fifteen-year-old bottle of Meursault that Zelda and I stowed away in the cellar when we graduated high school, seven years ago; our father had mailed it as a gift, along with a bottle of Champagne that was meant to be drunk immediately. Zaza and I occasionally mused over when we would open the wine; what occasion would warrant it? When will it be most wonderful? I look at the label.

"I don't care what your *W* is, Zaza. *W* is for *wine*," I announce to the dusty flagons. I walk upstairs with the bottle cradled in my arms. It is covered with accumulated silt, and I know it will leave a trace on my dress. In the kitchen I pull down four wineglasses and hold their stems delicately between my fingers, dangling upside down, clinking together.

On the balcony, I nudge Marlon's shoulder, and his eyes flutter open uncertainly.

"What is it?"

"Meursault," I answer with a smile. "I thought it was time." He stares blankly at me, then at the bottle, trying to place it. I can see the moment when he remembers on his face, which twitches, pained. "Zelda and I were never quite sure when to uncork it," I explain. "I don't think we should wait any longer." I set down the glasses and methodically open the wine with the corkscrew that has been sitting on the deck railing since my evening of excess with Wyatt. I sniff the cork and pass it to Marlon. He shuts his eyes and breathes in the scents, then hands it to Nadine, who fondles it absently before breathing in its mysterious complexity. She looks like she might try to eat it, though, so I take it back.

"Is it cold enough?" Marlon asks in concern.

"I hope so. It was in the cellar. Should be around fifty degrees, if the cellar's doing its job."

Marlon grunts in response and reaches out to touch the bottle. We are like a trio of acolytes, all suddenly alert and respectful in the presence of this sacred liquid. I pour the wine evenly into the four glasses, the ochre substance sloshing toward the rim. We wordlessly claim our glasses; Nadine looks perkier and more coherent. We sit and sip, saying nothing, the fourth glass perched on the little table to warm in the sun.

# 24

**E**X**pecting** sunshine when I awake the next morning, I'm dismayed to see gray skies greet me instead. I look out at the ashes of the barn, which have long since cooled. Even the smell of burnt wood has dissipated, and I'm almost sad; it reminded me of bonfires, nights clustered around a flame while Zelda and I initiated mischief. I wonder if the whole heap will turn into a soggy mess if it rains. When it rains. I suppose we should do something about it. Clean it up, rake it over. Will we be able to grow grass on it ever again? How? I speculate briefly about the way one goes about such a thing and eventually realize that it is yet another task that will fall to the people who actually run this place, who grow the few grapes we manage to produce.

Zelda's memorial is scheduled for this morning. Marlon needs to get back to California, and after very little discussion, it was determined that no one would be coming from far away; we don't have any real family, and Zelda never left here. It's nicer to think about prosaic details than to wonder where Zelda is, what havoc she is currently wreaking. The last pair of letters briefly flash through my mind. I'm perfectly happy to dwell on what to dress Mom in and who will bring food. Marlon and I had a forty-minute conversation over what wine to serve. I lobbied for the sparkling, which I'm certain is what Zelda wants, but Marlon has opted for a lavish reserve Chardonnay and one of our older red blends. I wonder if he suspects that Silenus is on its last legs and he wants everyone's final taste of the fruits of his long-ago labor to be the best we have. If the best is what he wants, however, I feel we should drink someone else's wine.

I realize I've been staring out at the barn for twenty minutes before my head snaps up alertly. The Vicodin makes me very spacey, apparently. I've been swallowing them down at quite a pace since I discovered Zelda's stash yesterday. I have resolutely not thought about the penance she has imposed.

In a little while, I peek in on Nadine, who is still asleep, and I climb listlessly back into bed. I can hear Opal muttering wearily to herself in the kitchen, raving quietly about Jesus, extolling his virtues in song; she's probably organizing glasses and eliminating imaginary dust bunnies. We're having the memorial at the tasting room, and it's unlikely anyone will even come to the house, yet Opal is determinedly preparing the living room for exacting visitors who will presumably check behind the couch to see if dirt has accumulated there.

I heard Marlon pull out of the driveway early this morning. I wonder where he's been going these last few days. A bar? To see his former mistress? Gambling? Part of me doesn't expect him to come back. I'll get a text from the airport right before he's supposed to kick off the service, saying he's really sorry, he just couldn't bear it, he's going to Montana to clear his mind for a while. Opal will shake her head in disappointment, but she will defend him, citing his wild, untamable nature. She will tell the story of how he sought out solitude as a young boy, the story we've all heard before, of when his father ran over the dog with the truck and shot the poor thing in the head in the backyard. Grandpa Will offered Marlon the gun, since it was his dog, but Marlon just shook his head and hopped on his bicycle. He was gone for nearly two days, and Opal has never been able to oblige him to say where he went. Opal always relates this story proudly, insistently, as though Marlon's inability to face unpleasantness as a boy somehow excuses him for leaving us. If he doesn't come back today, I will tell everyone that he was supposed to lead the service, apologize for his desertion, and uncork the wine. I will have nothing else to say.

I stare at my phone. All morning, I've been waiting for a message or phone call from Nico, but he hasn't uttered a digital peep since he texted yesterday to say that he sat at the bar of Hôtel Victoires for four hours with nothing to report. He sounded grumpy and interrogatory, and he didn't respond to my last text. I assumed he'd gone home to bed, but then I can't help thinking he normally would have sent me a message once he was up. It's already afternoon in Paris, and I've heard nothing.

Part of me suspects that he'll leave, too, that he'll just never text me back. He'll count himself lucky to have dodged a bullet—that crazy American—and he'll marry one of the girls he went to university with, someone with two names, like Marie-Claire or Anne-Sophie. They'll move closer to her parents in Lyon, and his kids will finish at the top of their lycée; one will go to the university Nico himself wanted to attend but didn't quite have the grades for, and the other will move to the United States, maybe even to attend Cornell. He will have a strange memory of me then, though he won't have thought about me in years, and he will wonder if I still live on the vineyard here. On impulse, he will fly in to visit his daughter and will track me down (on Facebook, if it still exists; on some other sort of uncanny digital avatar if not) and will appear, unannounced, on my doorstep, hoping to have a brief affair. He will have gone slightly soft in his middle, and he will have less hair. We will have fond, illicit sex, possibly in this very room, though more likely in my mother's, where I will have been sleeping since I finally transitioned into her bedroom ten years before.

I shake off this elaborate yarn, telling myself I'm being absurd. He probably met up with some friends to drink at Le Tambour for the rest of the night and is lying in my bed, playing hooky, sleeping off a terrific hangover, and will call as soon as his head stops throbbing, maybe sometime later this afternoon. I realize that I'm again filling in the chinks with fantasies, stuffing the cracks of absence with stories. I have no idea where he is, or where my father is, or where Zelda is. Where the person who was my mother has vanished to. They are gone, and anything I can think up about them is a fiction.

I look through both Zelda's closet and mine, trying to decide whether to be shocking (Zelda) or sedate (Ava). There's some sort of South American gown in Zelda's wardrobe that I find very tempting, but as I look at myself in the mirror, I realize I don't want to be high-profile, dramatic. I want to blend in, disappear into everyone else. I'm too exhausted to be the missing half of our usual equation. I don't know how to be without her. I am not me without her in contrast.

Eventually, I yank a terrifically boring black sheath with cap sleeves off the hanger in my room and pull it over my head. I straighten my hair and flick a mascara brush across my eyelashes a few times. For the last touch, I creep into my mother's bedroom and borrow a string of pearls from her jewelry box.

"Momma." I nudge Nadine. "Time to get up." She rolls over onto her stomach, resolutely uninterested in cooperating. I think about all those years of waking up at six A.M. to go to school, about Nadine's absolute impatience with any dithering. I don't remember her ever asking us twice to get up and get dressed. "Nadine, I'm going to ask you exactly once to get up. The rest is up to you," I say in a quiet, firm voice, mimicking her. I wonder if her own parents said that to her on slow mornings.

It works. She squints at me, clearly unhappy, but she does sit up-right and toss off one of her blankets.

"Thank you," I respond evenly. "It's time to get dressed for the service. It's at noon, and we have to bring a lot of stuff over to the tasting room." Not that Nadine will be participating much, but at least she'll be ready to go. I lead her to the bathroom, holding on to one of her thin, quivering wrists. I help her into the shower and sit her down on the chair there, realizing that this is the first time I have showered her since I've been home. Opal must have done it at some stage. At least, I hope it was Opal, rather than Marlon. Nadine would be morti-fied to have him see her naked this way.

She wants to wear a floral tea dress. The colors are relatively muted, and I realize I don't give a shit which dress she ends up in. Let the woman wear whatever she wants to wear to her daughter's memorial service. We'll all be grateful if she has no idea what's going on.

I lead Nadine downstairs, where Opal is still clanging around.

"Oh, good! I was worried I'd have to come up and snuggle you both out of bed!" she says cheerily. "Do you remember how I used to do that, A?" I do. I never cared for it. I can only assume that she wouldn't think of trying it with Nadine.

"What can I do to help?"

"Well, you're already in your nice dress, I don't want you to muss it. . . ." She clucks, looking me up and down. "You look very nice, Ava. Exactly . . . right." She bobs her head in approval. She is clearly relieved not to have to contend with the Zelda specter of the last few days.

"Thanks."

"You too, Nadine." Nadine doesn't answer, just shuffles toward the couch. "Have you taken your meds yet, Nadine?" Opal asks.

"Shit. I forgot to give them to her. Let me just . . ." I dash up the stairs before Opal can offer. The pill dispenser is sitting on her dresser. This is the last day of her real meds; after tonight, I will have to figure out what her medication regimen is. Or.

Downstairs, I hand Nadine her pills, and she looks at me expectantly, almost puppylike. I'm torn; I want to keep her quiet and encourage her to take her pills without a fuss, but it's going to be a long day, and once she starts drinking, it will be tough to slow her down. I bring her a glass of tonic water with lime, hoping she won't notice the absence of gin.

"Right. So, we have to get these casseroles and things over to the tasting room. I don't know whether to heat them up and then bring them, because they'll be cold. . . . Or maybe we should heat them during the service and bring them over right after?" Opal is staring helplessly at the countertops covered in Pyrex dishes wrapped in tinfoil, literally wringing her hands. I have a grim suspicion that our neighbor Betsy is responsible for most of these. Casseroles. Jesus. What happened to the catering? I discuss the minutiae with my grandmother, letting her micromanage.

Twenty minutes later, I find myself feeling thoroughly ridiculous, driving the tractor in my mother's pearls and Zelda's farm boots. I'm panting and sweaty by the time I've unloaded several armfuls of our neighbor's goodwill and dragged them up the steps to the tasting room's kitchen. It's going to be a hot day, and I can already smell my own sweat. My hair has probably turned frizzy and disheveled, and I imagine my makeup has collapsed as well. People will be arriving in an hour, and I still haven't brought over the tablecloths, candles, photos of Zelda. . . . The wine hasn't been brought up from the cellar, the dishes need to be unracked from the dishwasher. I wonder if the tasting room is supposed to open today—indeed, whether the tasting room is ever open. Did Zelda pour sips for tipsy tourists?

Taking a deep breath, I head back down to the tractor, making a list of everything that needs to be done in order of importance. Where the fuck is Marlon? Just one other person would make all the difference, and I'm stuck with an eighty-year-old busybody and a senile sixty-year-old who is likely to wander into the lake and drown. I add this to the list of things for which to upbraid Zelda when she finally reappears. I wouldn't put it past her to make an entrance during her funeral, the unforgivable maniac. It would rather undermine her devious scheme, though. Fuming at her silently, I realize how on edge I've felt all day—I'm nervous but also excited. We're nearing the end of the alphabet. Maybe today I will get to see my sister. The commingling of joy and relief I will feel at the sight of her, the smell of her.

As I drive the tractor back toward the big house, a battered station wagon pulls into our driveway, and I feel a surge of panic. That can't be guests, can it? But as the car crunches to a halt, Wyatt steps out of the backseat, and I almost leap off the tractor to run to him. His parents emerge from their ancient Volvo and wave to me.

"Hi, guys," I call, dismounting from the tractor and sprinting up the hill toward them. My cheeks are flushed, and sweat is trickling down the small of my back.

"Ava! We came early to help," Wyatt says.

"Put us to work!" Dora says.

I almost cry with relief. "Christ, thank you. I thought this whole fucking thing was going to fall apart."

Steve laughs uproariously at my tone, and I realize they've probably never heard me swear before. With a wild upwelling of hope, I wonder if I can change, if they could learn to like me.

"How about the wine?" Wyatt prompts. "Have you already brought it up from the cellar?"

"Nope. I'll come over with you and show you which cases we want. Um, Dora . . ." I pause, uncomfortable at the thought of ordering her around, but she looks capable and keen to help out. "There are some tablecloths and decorations for the tasting room inside. Maybe you and Steve can load them in your car and bring them over? My grandmother is inside, and she can show you what needs to come."

"Got it." Dora salutes me semiseriously and disappears inside. I gesture to Wyatt, and we head back over to the tasting room.

"Things under control here?" he asks, looking closely at me in concern. "You doing okay?"

"Oh, you know," I breathe shakily. "I'll be fine. Nervous that Zelda is going to pop up at some point." Wyatt says nothing. "Or that someone will show up to arrest me." This possibility has had me more than a little concerned.

Wyatt grunts. "Any more notes?" he asks gruffly.

"Not yet. That has me on edge too," I add. "Oh, by the way: I got *U* wrong. The letter, I mean," I correct myself swiftly. "It wasn't *unlocked*. It was *underneath*. The deck."

"Carefully constructed," Wyatt says. I nod and recount how I found *V* and *X*, Vicodin and Xanax. I don't tell him what Zelda wants me to do with them, what I've been mulling over.

"What do you think *W* is?" he asks.

"Maybe it's for Wyatt," I answer, stopping at the entrance to the tasting room and draping my arms around his neck to give him a kiss. I don't want to talk about Zelda's game anymore; I suspect that if I allow myself to feel anything at all, I will collapse into a weepy hot mess.

"I don't know how you can live with all this, Ava," Wyatt says. He strokes my hair. "You're incredible."

"I've had a lifetime of practice." I untangle myself from him and open the door to the tasting room cellar with my key, inhaling the pleasant scent of our *cave:* grapy and woody and musty all at once. I point out the wine that Marlon wants to use, and Wyatt dutifully lifts two cases of the Chardonnay while I struggle with one box of the red blend. I have no idea how many people we're expecting, but three cases seems bountiful, at least for now.

By the time we make it up the stairs into the tasting room, I'm panting, and a vein in my head is throbbing. My sweat has an unhealthy smell, and I wonder if I should change my dress. Wyatt and I unpack the bottles of white and plunge them into an ice bath. My mouth waters as I handle the cool glass, and I'm extremely tempted to open a bottle right now.

"Is it too early for a glass?" Wyatt asks, half-kidding, and I chuckle.

"Was just thinking exactly that. I still have to set up and herd people over here, so I suppose it's too early for me. But help yourself."

"I'll wait for a civilized moment," Wyatt says. I hear footsteps on the deck; Dora and Steve bustle in with armfuls of fabric spilling out of boxes.

"God, it's been so long since we were here!" Dora exclaims. "It's so effing pretty."

"Totally," Steve agrees, sounding happily stoned.

"Yeah, shame my family is crawling all over it," I reply. "Otherwise it would be lovely."

Tactfully ignoring what I've just said, the Darlings begin unpacking tablecloths and vases. It seems outrageous to make the space appear festive, but once we've arranged everything, it does look like we're going to have a party. Zelda would appreciate it. I dispatch Dora back to the big house for the speakers and send Steve to pick some wildflower posies for the empty vases. Wyatt opens bottles for a few minutes, and I fuss distractedly, though I can't stop staring at the road, waiting for Marlon's rented convertible to swing into the drive. Wyatt comes over and grabs my hands; I've been shredding a stray doily into little paper snowflakes.

"I know this is awful," he says soothingly. "You, having to enact this . . . whatever it is. Pretend this game is real. Zelda's put you in a shitty situation."

"Yes, yes, she has." I shake my hands, trying to dispel my physical tension. "Is it crazy that I feel something like stage fright? I'm really fucking anxious," I admit.

"No. You're performing, after all."

I nod. "I think Marlon booked," I say weakly.

"Really? He's not here?" Wyatt stiffens and looks toward the window, as though Marlon will be in sight.

"Left this morning. I think he bailed."

"Shit. That asshole!" Wyatt looks murderous. I could kiss him. I do.

*"C'est la vie,"* I say lightly. "We'll just get through this afternoon."

"I'm here, Ava. I'm not going anywhere," he murmurs.

Dora and Steve come back with both sound equipment and floral arrangements moments later, and we bustle around, adding our finishing touches. A car pulls into the driveway as we're testing out the music, and I swallow hard. Here we go.

"I'll be right back. I've gotta go collect Nadine and Opal. And change my dress," I add with a delicate sniff.

Wyatt nods. "I'll hold down the fort."

I pour myself a serious slug of wine and toss it back medicinally. Then I dash over toward the house to usher Nadine and Opal over, only to find that Opal is already tugging Nadine across the lawn. They look like two frail old ladies, not women from two different generations. Nadine has a contemptuous and stubborn expression on her face, but Opal won't be deterred. She refuses to slow down as they make their way along the dirt path. I catch up to them and seize my mother's other arm. She doesn't acknowledge me.

"No wheelchair?" I ask, miffed.

"She wouldn't get in, and I saw the car pull up. So we made a deal," Opal says stiffly.

I don't inquire about the details; I can guess that it involved bribery and threats. That is, after all, the method Nadine is most familiar with, whether she's doling out or receiving. Opal is surprisingly spry as they trek along the trail. Another car pulls into the tasting room parking lot, and I dash for my room.

I start tearing off my dress as I climb the stairs, struggling with the zipper and finally just yanking the garment over my head in frustration. Then I crouch in front of my suitcase in my underwear, rifling through it for something quick and easy. There's a pretty green dress that isn't quite right for a funeral, but at least it doesn't reek of wine-soaked sweat. As I pull it free, something blue falls to the floor.

I reach over and pick up my passport.

I freeze, staring down at it. Slowly, I open it and look at my own name inside. My passport, not Zelda's. I toss it onto my bed and tug the dress on. I feel spinny, and it's not because of the pills. Only I can't think about this new development right now. Later. If I think about it right now, I won't make it through this charade. I run back over to the tasting room as more cars turn into the driveway. Country people are punctual.

Inside, Nadine has been installed in a chair near the corner of the room. Wyatt is handing her a glass of wine. She sips it, pacified, though she doesn't acknowledge Wyatt. Opal has settled in by the door, where she can play the matriarch and personally greet everyone who enters. I cross the room and grab Wyatt firmly by the arm, wondering at the impropriety of this gesture; many of the people who come today will know about his relationship with Zelda, and there's something indecorous, if not downright trashy, about me reclaiming him, here and now. But I'm not sure I give a shit.

"I found my passport," I hiss.

He looks at me in guppy-faced surprise. "But then . . . ?" he says.

I shake my head cluelessly. *I don't know.* Something feels wrong, and I have started trembling. People are filtering into the room, and soon there's a small crowd milling awkwardly around, everyone speaking in hushed tones. A few people step out onto the deck, then immediately retreat inside, and I realize that the barn is fully visible from outside. I refill my glass and top Nadine's off before greeting a few people I knew in high school. One of our high school teachers arrives, and when I overhear what she's saying, I realize she's confused me with Zelda; that is, she thinks that Zelda was the good student who submitted insightful papers on time, and she's under the impression that I am the frequently stoned wild card who once gave a presentation on the invention of the dental dam. She looks at me nervously, as though I'm about to attempt a similar feat today. I don't have the heart to interrupt her rhapsodies and inform her that I am, in fact, the model student who wrote such a comprehensive report on the more or less local treasure *The Last of the Mohicans* and that she has been defaming the dead with her offhand comments about "my" unseemly behavior.

I see Mr. Bartoletti across the room and scuttle away from him, a knot of dread forming in my stomach. Whatever else happens, we still owe him a large check.

A handful of people try to talk to my mother, either out of respect or because they don't realize how demented she really is these days. While she was never the most gracious of socializers, it's apparent that Nadine has achieved new levels of disregard, and even those who were used to her former bitchiness are taken aback by her lack of any response whatsoever. I should probably intercede, but I don't want to. It occurs to me again that if Zelda's not in France, she could show up here at any moment, and my hands shake, sloshing my wine.

As twelve-fifteen approaches, my nervousness starts to escalate into panic. Marlon has flown the coop, and he was the only one who prepared anything to say at this shindig. He had a poem or two, a few nice words, a picture that he was supposed to display somewhere. He's our emcee. I could chuck Opal under the bus and ask her to speak a few words. Maybe I should cue up our Zelda playlist now, to buy time.

Instead, I open my mouth and welcome everyone. I feel detached. It's like I'm in one of those dreams where you're giving a presentation, or reciting lines or speaking in public, and you realize you have no idea what you've been saying and even less idea what you're going to say next: the sensation that words are nonsense but you are expected to keep producing them in front of your audience. I mumble my way through a thank-you and an invitation to drink wine—

"—as much as you like, really, who knows how long we'll all be here, ha ha, today we're serving our very special reserve Chardonnay from 2012, very oaky, and our Silenus red blend from 2008, cracking out the good stuff—" I take a gulp from my own glass and suck in a deep breath, trying to rein it in. I'm a terrible performer. As I'm speaking, the door swings open and in steps a skinny girl with tight, springy curls and a strong resemblance to Kyle Richardson. Kayla.

My silence stretches on, extending beyond a short pause and into dead quiet as our guests shift nervously from foot to foot. I blink a few times, gulp some more wine, and wrap it up: "So, we're going to be really informal today, just like Zelda would have wanted. I have a, um, playlist of some tunes, and we'll just . . . take it from there." I bob my head and dart toward the bar, which Kayla has sidled up to. I reach for her arm, squeezing her just above the elbow more firmly than I should. She squeaks, and her eyes widen when she sees my face.

"Where the fuck have you been?" I demand.

"Zelda?" she says, her mouth unattractively agape.

"No, you ninny. I have no idea where Zelda is. But I think you do." I angle her toward the stairs to the cellar. "Go down that staircase and wait for me at the bottom," I hiss. "I'll be there in a second. Don't you dare fucking go anywhere." People are starting to look at us and murmur. I paste on a smile and head to the speaker setup, where I cue the playlist that I lifted from Zelda's phone. It occurs to me in a moment of horror that I should have listened all the way through it, in case

Zelda has embedded a surprise for all of us near the end. Too late now. I dart down the stairs into the wine cellar before anyone can offer me more condolences. Wyatt is watching me in concern.

Kayla is standing at the foot of the stairs, looking around uncertainly. She seems nervous; she's scratching her arms and rocking back and forth.

"What the fuck is going on, Kayla?" I ask.

"Look, I really don't know. Your sister is nuts. I mean, fabulously nuts. I was totally in love with her, but she's gotten pretty . . . weird these last few months." Kayla fidgets with her bag. "Listen, do you think I could have some of that?" She points to my wineglass. "I'm trying to get clean, but I feel like I'm crawling out of my skin."

I hand her the last swallow in my glass and reach for another bottle. We don't have a corkscrew handy, so I grab one of the sparkling wines; it's what we were supposed to be drinking anyway. It fizzes spectacularly when I crack it open, too warm to gently burble as it's meant to. Or we fucked up the fermentation process. I can't remember if this is one of the naturally fermented French-style bottles or the variety where the carbonation gets added post-ferment. Of course, it genuinely does not matter. *Stop chattering, Ava. Pull it together.* Once Kayla takes a sip, she seems to calm down.

"Okay. So what's the story?" I prod.

"I—okay, look, don't get mad, I only did what Zelda asked. She said you'd understand."

"Okay." I grit my teeth.

"You know she and I were, like, together?" she asks. I nod. "Not, like, *together* together, just sometimes, on and off. She was just so strange and mysterious, and then we were hanging with Jason a lot, and the drugs. It was sort of, like, a mini Bohemia or whatever. Totally wild, but, like, good." Kayla takes a deep breath. "But for, like, six months, she's been totally bonkers. She'll be crazy busy and excited about something, then she won't even speak to me for two weeks. The drugs were getting kind of bad, for all of us. . . ."

"And?"

"Listen, you have to promise you're not going to turn me in or anything. Zelda promised you were cool."

"I promise, Kayla."

"We were selling a bit. Not a lot, just to, like, friends. But we were into Jason for some money, and he was getting all pushy about it. Zelda always acted like she didn't have to worry about money, and when she showed me this place, I realized why. I mean, shit, look at it!" Kayla whistles. "But then she told me she was in debt like crazy, not just Jason, you know, and she told me everything about your mom. Anyway, she said she had to disappear for a while, and she had a plan to fix it." Kayla accepts the bottle from me and tips a significant portion of its contents into her mouth, choking on the bubbles. Here at Silenus, we'd never quite managed to achieve the soft carbonation of a Prosecco or Champagne. Shame. Another failure. "She said I should keep quiet for a week, just to stay out of trouble, you know. Made me promise. And then she said that if everything went okay, there would be a funeral and I should come."

"Great. And?" I press.

"Well, she gave me this, like, list? Of stuff to do, in a certain order? She said it would work best because of my job at the funeral home—I could grease the way. That's the word she used. *Grease*." She giggles. A few things fall into place with her revelation.

"The dental records? Was that you?"

"Well, not exactly. Zee said I should show you this, 'cuz you'd want to know the details. It's a schedule that she wanted me to follow." She pulls a rumpled piece of paper from her bag.

*NOTES FOR SWEET KAY:*

*June 22, afternoon: Send in eulogy to newspaper using funeral home email address.*

*June 24, 9:15 AM: Send a text to Holly with a reminder to post the photo we talked about, and make sure she tags me in it!*

*June 24, afternoon, evening: Watch Ava (wear wig). When she heads to the strip club, send the text to Trent Roberts with Jason Reynolds's whereabouts and a gentle poke, so that he's riled.*

*June 25, 8:30 AM: Ring the doorbell at the house and leave the envelope labeled "Open me" on the doorstep. Watch to confirm Ava gets it, but DO NOT GET SEEN!*

*June 26, 8 AM: Dr. Whitcross does autopsies on Sundays, when he's not at the practice. Be sure to deliver the dental records to the morgue before then, on Sunday morning. He may already have a copy, but we have to be sure! Be very vague if he asks why you have them, but make sure he has them when he starts the autopsy.*

*June 26, 9:30 PM: Drive to Two Goats and leave the letter labeled "T" taped to the windshield of Wyatt's truck while Ava is inside—she'll leave at 10, when the bar closes.*

*June 27 or 28: Watch Facebook for details about my memorial service. Show up about half an hour after it starts, go straight to Ava, and ask to speak to her alone. Give her the last letter, and leave her be while she reads it.*

*Make sure not to answer any phone calls or texts, and stay in the yurt on the other side of the national forest. Don't go into town, don't get seen, and definitely don't talk to your brother, the loudmouthed twat. Thanks a mil, sweet Kay! See you on the flip side.*

"So I did what she told me," Kayla sighs as I finish skimming the precise document. "I guess I don't know how to do anything else. That's just how she is. When Zee says jump . . ."

"You're not the only one up in the air. Don't worry."

"Wanna know what's weird? I'm not. Worrying. Like, I still think it's going to be fine. I trust that girl. Crazy, right?" Kayla smiles helplessly.

"It might be."

"This is the last one," she says, holding an envelope out to me. "I'm gonna go upstairs. She said to leave you be. She said you'd know where to find her, after you read it. And then you'd tell me what to do, where to meet her."

I nod blankly, the feeling of wrongness intensifying. Kayla snakes around me to climb the staircase, leaving the letter in my hand. A simple white envelope, addressed with the letter *Y* and a single line in Latin: *Nihil sapientiae odiosius acumine nimio.*

# 25

Young, yoked, and yearning Ava,

You yield yet? Are you tired of my yammering? Have you figured out yet what I have done? And, most pertinently: Why, why, why? Y is for (wh)y. Here you are, at the end, ready to know. Maybe you've begun to suspect what really happened out there in our yard. You realize that you've been overthinking this from the get-go. Too clever, sweet Ava, too willing to ascribe double meaning where there is none. Tell me (and be truthful): What was your first thought when you heard about the barn and my tragic immolation? Darling sister mine, I'm certain that it went something along the lines of "That's exactly what Zelda would want." And that's where you should have stopped thinking. Because it is. Was.

Do you remember when Momma started to get sick? The problem is that we don't really know when that happened. We know when we started to really notice. When she would take hours to drive home from town and look shiftily away when we asked where she had been, because she had no idea and had been driving lost around the lake. When she would start screaming that we had stolen all of her things, that we had locked them up somewhere in secret storage and were going to sell them off. When we would find her passed out somewhere utterly bizarre and she would have no idea how she got there.

*But. She'd been passing out in unpredictable places since our child-hood. How many times did we find her with a gin and tonic still propped upright in her floppy fingers? The absolute preoccupation of the drunk with protecting their next drink, even while unconscious. All those times she took the car and was gone for half a day, off drinking somewhere, or up to fuck knows what. Her deranged meltdowns that would end with accusations, paranoid ravings, sheer fury. Mom was never well, has never been well. We just started to notice it in her fifties.*

*Do you think about that a lot, Ava? I know I have, these last two years, without you here. While I watch her get worse, while she rots slowly in this house she has come to loathe, surrounded by people she barely rec-ognizes, clinging to the one thing that has always comforted her. Her sole port in the storm of her brain chemistry. I think about whether she has transmitted it, whether those same chemicals are lurking, nascent, in my brain, in our brains. I've been thinking maybe they've already kicked in. Maybe they've been there all along, just like with Nadine. The disease is degenerative, eroding more and more essential brain function with every month, every year. But who's to say it only starts with diagnosis? Presumably it's been there, waiting and chewing away at your good bits for years, if not decades, before you haul yourself in to some beleaguered medical professional, who looks at you with pity and hands you a bro-chure. It's manageable, they say. Treatable. We can make you comfortable. Of course, that's assuming you have money, health insurance, resources. A family that will take care of you and sit with you in your slow, unseemly decline.*

*Which brings us here. I can only imagine where you are now. Did you hold the service in the big house or the tasting room? Maybe you rented a tent, outside on the lawn (though I can only assume that if you did this, it would have to be out of sight of the wreckage of the barn, for decency's sake). My best guess is that as a family, you elected to hold the little cer-emony as close to the alcohol as possible, so I'd bet on the tasting room. I'm right, aren't I?*

*I've been gambling all along. Or, rather, when I arranged all of this, I* made a giant leap, put it all on black, or however that saying goes. (Maybe if I'd lived longer, gambling would be one of my vices—like it is for our father—but my short life was only able to truly embrace the small handful of depravities for which I'm best known.) I had to guess what you would do, and when. The what was easier than the when, naturally. But I have a feeling I got it right. Because I know you, twin mine, deep down in the places you barely know yourself. I've got you pegged.

So here we are. The DNA testing will come back eventually, even though the dental records are conclusive. (Did you call my dentist? Were you trying to figure out if he had something to do with it? I hope you did, and found all the fun detours there. But perhaps learning about Whitcross provided you with enough explanation to satisfy your wish fulfillment, your projection.) You've looked everywhere to avoid recognizing the truth, my little sister, second-born but first-named. In that, you are like our mother. And our father. Escape is what you seek, by any means available. Maybe you drink until you're unconscious, maybe you run away from the people you love, to the opposite coast or to Paris. Maybe you look for any truth other than the one you've got, filling in the holes with any fiction that's at hand. I know that of all of us Antipovas, I have uncovered the most long-term solution to our desire for escape. It's hard not to feel like I've won, though I'll spare you any posthumous gloating.

Oh, Ava. It's so bizarre to write this, knowing that I'll be gone when you finally read it. Thinking of you holding these eerie sheaves in your shaky palms gives me pause, and I almost want to go through with the disappearing act that you've been so cleverly uncovering these past few days. This whole adventure has been quite exciting—so zany, in fact, that I pretty quickly forgot that its conclusion is just fucking morbid. Part of me wants to be waiting in your apartment in Paris when you read this. But Paris was never going to be far enough to escape. You know that.

The pills weren't just another piece of the game, you know. I'll be taking a few fistfuls after I finish writing this. Jason is coming over soon; I texted him on phone number two, which I left lying around in plain sight *at the Airstream. Phone number one is tucked safely away for you to find, with Gmail Delay Send all set up, ready to go, with timed emails for you to receive over the next few days. Jason is a shithead, and I'm partly hoping he'll go down for my "murder." Kayla's got her instructional packet, and she'll nudge things along as you get to the bottom of my little puzzle, keep things from going off the rails too thoroughly. She's a sweet kid, and I think she won't fuck it up. I told her to kick the drugs. It's a terrible habit. The truth is really going to bum her out—guess you're holding the bag for that one too!*

*After Jason leaves, I'll lock the barn doors with the chain and padlock from the outside. Then I'll crawl around to the big window out back, where I've left the rope ladder dangling, and I'll climb up into the hayloft. I'll swallow down a bunch of pills with Champagne. (Not the shit we make—something nice, for my last bottle. Is it ridiculous that that thought, the notion of a Last Bottle of Wine, gives me more pause than anything else?) I'm hoping to be completely unconscious, if not dead, by the time the candle burns all the way down and ignites the hay, which is pretty thoroughly soaked in gasoline, as are the very timbers. And then I'm hoping to be dead of overdose or smoke inhalation by the time the fire spreads to my chair by the window, looking out onto the lake and the stars. If not, hopefully the Vicodin/Xanax/Champagne cocktail will take the edge off being burned alive. It certainly takes the edge off being alive. Saint Joan once again.*

*I knew you wouldn't believe it. I knew you would need to turn it into a complex game, a competition that you could somehow win by puzzling it out. So I made you a little story. Sister darling, the stories we tell ourselves! Maybe because we were twins, we sought a way to differentiate, to oh so rigorously sketch out our borders. You needed to say, to speak the ways you were different. I'm Ava, I'm the ambitious one; that's Zelda, she's the messy one. As though you could determine your own story, secure the ending you wanted through obsessive narration. Do you remember smoking pot on the deck, before shit went so wrong? We lay there, on the gigantic Pendleton blanket that our mother loved and that I unapologetically stole from the house. She flipped her shit so thoroughly when she couldn't find it, but we convinced her she was having one of her paranoid episodes. (See, see how even a simple object has a story in our family?) We lay there, looking at the sky and smoking some of that lovely lovely weed, and you insisted on talking, telling me the way you were, summarizing your selfness with amazement. You said: "I've always known what I've wanted, I've had a desire, Zaza, to get somewhere. I've been jealous of you, with your waywardness and your directionality-lessness"—here you giggled at yourself, your words, your lack of words—"but when it comes down to it, that's how I have to be, and you have to be how you have to be. It's like together we make up all of a whole person." And I asked you about Wyatt, if you knew what you wanted from him. And you paused, and you nodded, and you said: "I want him to believe in the story of myself."*

*And he does, dear sister! That's the loveliest bit. Wyatt lacks the imagination that would permit him to conjure up a conflicting tale about you. He swallows the myth whole, happily.*

*But for me. For me, I won't be happy with the story until I know what the ending is. Till I know how the sentence ends. The ending has been torturing me, and I can't live with that uncertainty. I can write the ending myself, dab the finishing touches on. I've gotten here, to the last letter. I could go on, keep writing. I would prefer not to.*

*I thought of including the whole alphabet here, with descriptions of the nitty-gritty, how I chose each letter and how I made it happen. But in the end, I want you to sculpt that story yourself. I want there to be mystery, letters you wonder about and never find. You don't get to have perfect resolution. Not all letters arrive at their destination.*

*I hope it's been easier for you, because I don't want you to suffer inordinately. A little, perhaps. That's why I've left you Mom. Think of it as a punishment, a penance, a performance of propitiation. Atone for your sins and help ease her out of the shell she's been living in. Maybe join her. I've stockpiled enough for both of you. Or not. Crawl into Wyatt's arms. Turn over my cellphone to the police. Tell everyone what really happened.*

*Maybe you'll hate me for doing this, for this merry little chase. I accept*

*that. But I didn't want to just leave you. I wanted to give you back a piece*
*of yourself. Maybe the piece that I always had. That I was. Now it's just*
*you, and what you want. I entered the world before you, and now I've left*
*it first. You've never had the chance to see the world without me. You're free*
*now, Ava. All the decisions you make from here on out are yours. I love*
*you.*

> *Here we are, at the end.*
> *Z is for Zelda*

I sit on the bottom step for long minutes, reading and rereading
Zelda's last letter. I realize I should get up, but I can't move. The only
thing I can feel is a loud, resounding NO. No. Not this. This is not the
end. I hear someone speaking loudly upstairs, and I realize that Marlon has arrived. Muted laughter greets something witty he has said. I
pull out Zelda's phone and flick through the emails of the past few
days, inspecting the dates and times of each one. Abruptly, I stand up
and collapse over one of the barrels near the staircase, emptying my
stomach of fizzy liquid that tastes of creamy Chardonnay. I keep gag-
ging well after there's nothing left to retch up. The sensation feels
good, as though by reversing digestion I am reversing time, moving
backward. Maybe if I crouch here vomiting long enough, I can go
back to before the fire. Back to before I left Silenus. Back before Nadine got sick. Before Wyatt and Zelda, before college, before high
school. Before Marlon left. How far back would I have to go, though,
to right things? To that moment when Marlon gave us the wrong
names, marking each of us as the person we would be for the rest of
our lives? Maybe then.

I finally stand and wipe my mouth with the back of my hand. With
my other hand, I wipe beneath my eyes, where my mascara has surely
ended up. I smooth my dress, perform all the rote gestures of compos-
ing myself. Following the rules, making sure I don't create a scene. I
head upstairs and quietly let myself into the room. Only a few heads

turn to look at me; everyone else is watching Marlon. He is standing at the front of the room, telling the story of the first time he held Zelda in his arms, how she blustered and kicked, his feisty first-born child, though he thought she was second. I notice that he has a large picture of Zelda on an easel next to him; it's a photograph from just over two years ago, one that I took. Zelda is standing down by the lake, half turned toward me, grinning mischievously. She's wearing a loose caftan, and with the sunlight shining through it, you can clearly see the contours of her body, nymphlike and disconcertingly sexual. It's a strange photo for Marlon to have chosen, but somehow it's exactly right. We can see Zelda as she really was beneath the flimsy fabric, feral and wild, refusing to be tamed. I know that offscreen, I am holding the camera, clad in civilized trousers and a shirt with a bow, trying to capture her and failing.

Late that afternoon, people eventually trickle away. Marlon helps Nadine back to the house, and I am touched, watching them walk along the path between the house and the tasting room they built together, Nadine hobbling unsteadily and Marlon holding her up. Everything they made together is collapsing. I feel a deep pang of pity for them, these flawed human beings who made me, and who have created nothing but unhappiness for all of us. Of course, this is never what they wanted.

Kayla waits for me, but I dismiss her abruptly. The poor thing has no idea what she was in love with, or what she's about to feel.

Wyatt touches my arm, and I flinch. I don't want to talk to him now. I can't look at him. If I do, I will break.

"Ava? You okay?" I don't say anything, just continue staring out at the barn. The letter is still folded in my hand. I can't seem to put it into my pocket. "Ava?" he repeats. I don't look over at him. He waits for a few moments, but when I don't respond, he sighs and turns around. I hear his steps across the wooden deck, and then I'm alone.

I stand on the deck for most of the afternoon's remainder, thinking, staring. When the sun starts to fall into the lake, I shake off my inertia and walk to the big house. I head upstairs to my mother's bedroom, where Zelda has left the pills. My mother is downstairs on the couch, watching a movie. Marlon is outside reading. I get what I need and come back down.

"Mom." She doesn't look up at first. "Mom. There's something I want to show you." She stares up at me blankly, uncomprehendingly. "Take a walk with me." Precariously, she stands. Her eyes are unfocused and seem to twitch back and forth. I've seen them do this before.

"Zelda, I've had it with your performances. I'm tired. Go ask your father to watch."

"This is a surprise just for you, Mom. You and me. You'll see."

She shakes her head reluctantly, but I hold on to her arm and guide her out the door. She's still wearing her espadrilles from earlier. Good. That's good. Painstakingly, we make our way down the hill to the lakefront. Moving at Nadine's pace, it takes us a long time, and the sun is dipping faster than I thought it would. When we finally reach the water, Nadine is irritable and tired, and she keeps trying to turn around and head back to the house. But I nudge her farther.

At the lakefront, I let go of her arm and fetch the rowboat beached on the stones at the edge. I shove it toward the water, carving furrows into the pebbles. When the hull is in the water, I gesture to Nadine, who hesitates but then steps forward, almost eagerly. She is so light that I almost lift her into the boat, and she sits down on the bench, rocking. I hop in and shove off from the shore with a paddle. I feel a splinter dig into the pad of one finger as I awkwardly try to angle the boat toward the center of the lake.

"Sunset cruise, Momma. It's the perfect night for it."

"Zelda, are you sure this is a good idea? This boat seems rather . . ." Nadine trails off uncertainly, looking back at the shore with concern.

The sun is halfway behind the hills that line the lake, and the temperature on the surface of the water is dropping quickly. Though I'm sweaty from the exertion, I shiver. "Zelda?" Nadine says again, querulously.

"No, Mom. I'm not Zelda. I'm Ava."

# 26

Zelda's words ricochet through my head as I tug inexpertly at the oars. She fills me entirely and she is all I feel, in the emptiness of this lake, of myself. The boat is unwieldy, and I am in desperately bad physical condition. I'm barely even thinking about what I'm doing. I *can't* think about what I'm doing, or about what has happened, has been happening. Nadine is hunkered down on the bench opposite me, staring wide-eyed at the surface of the water. It's a dark complex magenta, catching the sunset in its final moments. My breath comes harder and starts to hitch in my throat as I strain, pulling the boat deeper and deeper into Seneca Lake. I haven't had a fully conscious thought since I opened Zelda's letter, and I feel as though I'm not even making choices any longer. Instinctively, I want to put distance between myself and the vineyard, to have a body of water between us. Fleeing across the water, again. The rickety rowboat is proving to be more shipshape than I thought. Zelda. *Zelda.*

"Mom," I say softly. I stop rowing, letting the boat coast. My mother turns her wobbly head toward me. "Mommy. What happened to your sister?" At first she doesn't answer. When she does, her words drag.

"It was an accident. There was nothing I could do."

"What happened on the beach that day?"

"I don't remember," she says, her voice so small that it's almost as though she has transformed into the eight-year-old she was. I sit silently, watching the angry sun drop swiftly behind the black hills that rim the lake. I can see the fireflies winking from the trees along the shore that we have left behind. In the dark, it's almost hard to tell which is our dock, which sloping hill has consumed so much of our family. Down the lake, close to Watkins Glen, a large boat cruises north, furiously lit up with fairy lights. It looks like a steamboat from the glory days of boat travel, resplendently anachronistic. Tourists on a booze cruise, eating overcooked crab legs that have been flown in frozen from Alaska.

"Dad was drunk, as usual," Nadine continues with a shrug, and she trails a finger in the water. "That day, he was just raving. Drinking out of the bottle. He passed out in the sun. Snoring. And Nina said we should sneak off and swim out farther than we were usually allowed."

"You didn't go in with her?" I ask, trying not to blame.

"No. I was scared," my mother says bitterly. "The waves were big that day. I watched Nina's head bob up and down, and she turned back to wave every now and again. She was too far out. She disappeared into the water, while I watched. And I couldn't. I couldn't follow her in. I watched." She leans over the edge of the boat and smacks the water with her palm, making a violent slapping noise. I'm worried that her movement might sink the boat, but I say nothing, afraid to interrupt her story. Did Zelda know?

"Jesus." I breathe deeply. Something is happening far back in my throat.

"I would have been a different person, you know. If she had lived. I would have been different. A different mother. Zelda—she reminded me so much of Nina." We're silent in the boat, listening to the faint slap of water along the hull.

"You know, you can start all kinds of relationships in your life," Nadine continues. "But you only start life once. And you start it with a limited number of people. Those people, they do something to you."

Whatever is in my throat loosens, and I start to cry. At first, tears ooze from my eyes, and I whimper, my back hunched. I sob. *Oh God, Zelda.* But soon I'm not crying, I'm not weeping. Something is trying to claw its way out of me. I cling to the oars and scream, letting myself lurch between hysteria and rage. I kick the bottom of the boat. My arms fold across my belly, which aches from the muscular exertion of my tears. I cry like a toddler, inconsolable, thrashing, for solid minutes. *Zelda, no. Please don't.* Some irrational, wordless part of my brain begs. Begs something nameless for something I can easily name. *Please don't let her be dead. Pleasepleasepleaseplease.* I am perfectly fixed on one thought, more precisely concentrated on one thing than I have ever been in my life: a denial of her death. *She cannot be dead.* Cannot. And, quite simply, she is.

Nadine sits impassively across from me, watching the festive cruise boat come closer and closer to us. I flail and scream until my body finally seems unable to continue its spastic convulsions. I speak to her, to my other self, mumbling to her between screams. After a while, the sheer physical effort of this grief makes me go limp. I feel dead. Maybe I am the dead twin. It is fully dark now, eerie out here on the water by ourselves. The pills still sit in the hull, rattling whenever I shuffle my feet. The boat is still afloat, but I can feel water pooling near my curled toes. I know the horror of loss. It's unspeakable; I have learned something that can't be said. Another secret gift from my sister. Nadine leans over dreamily and pats my knee. She is almost smiling. I wipe fluids from my face, my abused eyelids inflated to hood my vision.

"Mom," I say to her.

"Yes?" she asks.

"What do you want to do, Mom?"

"This is nice, just like this." She tilts her head back and looks at the stars, grinning. It's been a long time since I saw her smile like that. "This is just fine."

"Mom, do you know what I'm asking?" I insist. "I need to know what you want to do. I need you to decide."

"I'm through with decisions."

"I need you to make one more. Please." I don't want to beg her, but I will. She leans toward me, and I see that her eyes are twitching crazily, her head bobbing. I wait for her to speak. But instead of answering me, she suddenly goes taut, and she makes a strange choking noise that is not part of her usual repertoire.

"Mom? Are you okay?" I reach over for her, but her body is suddenly rigid and flailing. Her convulsive movements nearly fling her from the rowboat, and I grab her arms in terror, rolling her to the leaky boards. In a blind panic, I start rowing for shore. As we reach the shallows, the cruise boat skates by us barely thirty feet away, and the wake splashes over the side of our vessel. In three feet of water, the rowboat is swamped, and the bow goes under the black water. I reach for Nadine, who is still seizing, and I tug her to shore before her head goes under. Her body is light, and I haul her up the beach; it seems like I barely even have to exert myself to get her up onto the cooling rocks. My cellphone is with the bag of pills, nestling into the smooth pebbles three feet below the dark water.

Zelda didn't know the truth of the family curse, and in a twist of true irony, her terror of it is what killed her. Nadine's autopsy saved my life, and maybe could have saved Zelda's. Our mother's official cause of death wasn't overdose. I never disbursed Zelda's cocktail; maybe I never would have. I didn't let her sink into the waters of our lake. But my choices killed Nadine just the same. By the time I made it up to the house, I was wheezing and scarcely able to breathe. I expected to find my father, but Marlon had left without saying goodbye, caught his flight back to the West Coast and brought his mother with him. He had left us after all, again. The house was dark and lonely, and I dialed 911 with shaking fingers before running back down to where my mother lay, flopping about like a fish. The seizure, likely brought on by the stress of the memorial service, left her in a coma. She was unconscious for two days before she died of pancreatitis and congestive heart failure. Cause of death: Wernicke-Korsakoff syndrome. An uncommon form of dementia caused by a thiamine deficiency, usually brought on by alcoholism and malnutrition. Most likely genetic, written out in the letters of our DNA. Not dementia with Lewy bodies or early-onset Alzheimer's. Nadine had been misdiagnosed, and maybe she would have survived if she'd been treated with intravenous thiamine. The doctors had gotten the story wrong.

As had I, so certain had I been that Zelda was alive, that I would metaphysically intuit it if she was truly dead. Wrong again, Ava.

Zelda's terror of inheriting our mother's disease was certainly legitimate, but the disease that scared her so much was the wrong one. Our disease was treatable. All we had to do was quit drinking and eat properly. Take our thiamine. All those fabulous letters too. *W, S, K, G.*

I sat in the hospital for two days, staring catatonically at the fluorescent lamps, knowing that I could have prevented this. If I hadn't left, I might have taken Nadine to a doctor who could have caught it. Later, I even found a brochure on Wernicke-Korsakoff in the pile of glossy sheets we had accumulated over the years. I could have noticed the ataxia, which might have alerted us to the erroneous diagnosis. If I hadn't been so taken in by Zelda's abecedarian story, her construct. But when I got that last letter, in a quick instant, in a jiffy, all my bitterly maintained hopes were vaporized, incinerated on the smoldering pyre of my sister's enduring and exceptional cruelty. I took her at her word, saw her as the architect of the story and not as one of its flawed players.

I'm convinced that Zelda had Wernicke's encephalopathy, the precursor to the full-blown syndrome. The doctors told me it was possible but unlikely, due to her age. But Zelda was always precocious. A common symptom is impaired decision making.

I never called Nico back. Frankly, though, I simply wasn't able to explain it to him, to think of anything other than my own pain. I hope he forgives me, but I wouldn't blame him if he didn't. Another pawn in Zelda's game. Though I was the one to use him, not Zelda. I'm trying to learn to take responsibility. Another fiction, perhaps.

Wyatt arrived at the hospital within an hour of Nadine's admission, and he waited for me—"Whether you want me or not," as he said. He was stubborn, and I was feeling a lot less so; I allowed myself to curl up in his arms in the harsh fluorescence of the hospital's family area. He held me while I went thoroughly to pieces again and again, each time with an intensity that felt terminal. He fed me M&M's from the vending machine. He even called Marlon, the ever-absent M, and succeeded in conveying his disappointment at my father's hasty departure with an uncharacteristic display of snark. We talked, mostly about Zelda, and he managed, in his naïve way, to help me see what she had tried so hard to give me.

"Ava, she was trying to show you that you can live without her, that you can be as many versions of yourself as you need to be. She gave you yourself, and herself too."

"Maybe."

"I was thinking. Do you think she meant for you to know that she went to Paris?" he asked me.

"I'm pretty sure she wanted me to think that's where she'd disappeared to," I said, puzzled.

"But the first time—did she mean for you to know she had already been?"

"I don't know," I said, my voice gruff. The waiting room was stark and empty, and the M&M's had made me queasy.

"I think she went to say goodbye to you without really saying goodbye to you," Wyatt said, stroking my dirty hair and kissing my forehead. Another thing left unsaid. I let him rock me while I wept brokenly, again.

Zelda and I had been cannibalizing each other for such a long time that it's still difficult not to gnaw hungrily on my own portion, but maybe I will get used to the bounty. Certainly my newly augmented dimensions gesture to a healthier appetite.

Nadine's body was wheeled off to be sliced open and then rendered into ash. I put her bottle-shaped urn straight into the wine rack in the kitchen, where it sat (I like to think contentedly) for several months. Eventually, Wyatt convinced me how pathological this seemed, and was, and I saw his point. There are enough ghosts here. Not the least of which is my own face, staring at me with Zelda's. Wyatt helped me scatter Nadine with Zelda, in the black skeleton of the barn, the dead letters of their DNA spiraling together. Waiting. After we finished, he put his hands over my belly, kissed it, and promised both of us that we did not have to repeat the past.

Wyatt is a generous human, and he believes that Zelda's final game was a kindness to me. Over the last few months, I've come to agree, though I'm still so furious with her that it wakes me in the night. I think that while I can nearly understand what she was trying to say to me, I will never fully comprehend it. There are still missing pieces. It's maddeningly painful not to be able to speak with the dead. But maybe what Zelda was trying to tell me is that it's nearly as difficult to speak with the living.

# Acknowledgments

Thanks to Molly Atlas, who has believed in this book from the first read; to my editor, Kara Cesare, for her enthusiasm, insight, and patience; to everyone at Random House who helped usher the manuscript from Word doc into an actual printed book—Bonnie Thompson, Loren Noveck, and all the other folks who toiled on behalf of the novel; to everyone at ICM and Curtis Brown—Felicity Blunt, Roxane Edouard; and everyone who read the book and offered up suggestions along the way.

Thanks to my sister, Emily, for believing me when I said that Ava and Zelda have nothing to do with us; to my mom, Peggy, and my dad, Mike, for encouraging my lifelong literary obsession; to my mother- and father-in-law, Elbert and Marinda, who caught some foolish medical errors in the manuscript and have been keen readers since the early days; to the folks at Brooklyn Winery and to Katy Koken at Bloomer Creek Vineyard, for answering wine questions. Thanks be to early readers: Geoff Gilbert, Dan Gunn, Lauren Steyn, Chris Honey, Seamus Vasey, Katy Schoedel, Joanna Cerro.

And the last thanks go to Jan Steyn, without whom I wouldn't have been able to write this book—my first reader, my favorite reader.

## ABOUT THE AUTHOR

CAITE DOLAN-LEACH is a writer and literary translator. She was born in the Finger Lakes and is a graduate of Trinity College Dublin and the American University in Paris. *Dead Letters* is her first novel.

## ABOUT THE TYPE

This book was set in Baskerville, a typeface designed by John Baskerville (1706–75), an amateur printer and typefounder, and cut for him by John Handy in 1750. The type became popular again when the Lanston Monotype Corporation of London revived the classic roman face in 1923. The Mergenthaler Linotype Company in England and the United States cut a version of Baskerville in 1931, making it one of the most widely used typefaces today.